# Mulligan

R. A. Boudreau

This is a work of fiction. Names, characters, incidents, and places are products of the author's imagination or are used fictitiously. Any resemblance to actual events or locales or persons, living or dead, is entirely coincidental.

Cover photo © 2011 Shirley Hendrix Boudreau

Copyright © 2012 R.A. Boudreau

All rights reserved.

ISBN - 13: 978-0615572659
ISBN-10: 0615572650

# ACKNOWLEDGEMENTS

This novel is dedicated to three fabulous, special people who inspired me, nudged me to this point in my life, showed me possibilities I never considered for myself, and helped me become a better human being:

My late wife, Mary (McCann) Boudreau, who had more faith in my talents and abilities than I ever did and who taught me by example how to be a caring and giving person. Her life, ended by damned breast cancer in 2003, was far, far too brief.

Shirley Hendrix Boudreau, the amazing woman who found me in 2008 after I had decided the best I could hope for was a life alone. She won my heart and brought immeasurable fullness and joy to my existence. Her enthusiastic encouragement as I wrote *Mulligan* is the reason this book finally came to be (although I'm sure my late wife Mary had a hand in it as well).

Ted Bird, a friend who meant far more to me than he ever knew. A great songwriter and musician whose accomplishments as a composer and performer truly inspired me to explore my own creative potential. His was another life cut far too short by cancer. His albums *Made in America* and *To Absent Friends* will keep his voice, his talent, and his spirit alive for many years to come. He was one of the best human beings I have ever known. I thank his wife, Jane, and his daughter Allyson, for allowing me to honor him by bringing his heart and soul into this story.

And a very special thanks to Lucille Mota-Costa and Shirley Hendrix Boudreau, both wonderfully accomplished artists, who collaborated to design *Mulligan's* cover.

"How about it, Sean?" he whispers to himself, half hoping. "One more try?"

Sean Francis Xavier O'Connor stares at his computer from the doorway on the far side of a windowless room within his eclectic, cramped apartment fifty yards from Wickford's serene picture-postcard harbor. The third-floor quarters are far enough from Providence to escape urban tensions, which make him uncomfortable, yet close enough to the real world to make him feel adequately connected with life. He leans against a five-shelf bookcase he has fashioned from bricks and boards, not sure if he is ready to write, yet feeling the urge burbling inside him.

A solitary table lamp lights the keyboard and little else. His computer screen challenges him.

Microsoft Word is open, the way he left it an hour ago, a blank new document with the cursor flashing lazily. Again, his mind wriggles "one last time" into his consciousness. The need has bedeviled him for months, yet he has resisted, sensing that trying to write once more would do him no good.

Has he ever come up with anything he could call satisfying or, at the least, having at least a modicum of potential for publication?

He understands his reluctance but has a gnawing inner notion that he needs to overcome it. His gut feeling is that "one more time" really means "one last chance." And he knows that it all boils down to one simple point: he simply needs to try once more to write or else risk forever regretting that he'd failed to follow this urge.

It's not a matter of writing a blockbuster; Sean knows it's not within his ability or his fortune to do so. He simply wants to leave something, however little noted, that someone perhaps a generation hence might notice and read.

After a while, he crosses the room in slow steps and sits down in front of the computer, his hands resting on either side of the keyboard. He is unsure, uncomfortable, and for a long time he fidgets about how to begin, having no particular idea what his story will be about – although a notion of what kind of story he wants to write has begun taking the vaguest shape in the backwater recesses of his mind.

He's written often before, mostly short stories with a beginning and an end, but never to a degree where he thought he really could succeed. Some are still filed away in a cardboard box in one of his closets; many more simply, and without regret, erased with the click of mouse button or an unceremonious dumping into his wastebasket.

He knows he has a turn of phrase now and then, a way with words, a zest for interesting characters that could – might – win him praise were he not afraid to follow through. After all, he's spent his professional life as a journalist, and competent writing has always been one of his strong points. There was a time, not too many years ago, when he believed that — if he could pull himself together and focus and ignore the distractions that have foiled him thus far – he could write the story of a lifetime. For the moment, though, staring at the screen, he feels helpless – yet the insistent craving to write that has been goading him won't quit.

He sighs and shakes his head.

He's on his second beer. He sips and swallows then lights another cigarette, even though he no longer inhales. The mentholated tobacco taste feels good on his tongue. It's been a victory for him: ten years without inhaling. His lungs have for all these years felt much better. He should take the final step and throw the cigarettes away.

Not yet, though.

Time passes and he checks his watch. He's been in the room nearly an hour and feels rooted here, the computer screen daring him. He considers that it may be best if he simply left his apartment to do other things, to mingle in the world until he no longer wants to write. Yet, he lingers.

What the hell will he write about? He puffs again on his cigarette. Blows a slow stream of smoke toward the ceiling. Watches the smoke dissipate. Sighs again. He knows the kind of story he hopes to write, but he has no idea of what it will be about. It's like wanting to deliver a rousing speech that will bring an audience to its feet, but having little clue as to what he should talk about.

Maybe he should simply let go and allow it to happen. He knows – a deep, instinctual knowing – that it may work this time. But he knows he needs to free up his mind. More than that, he needs to cross the intimidating threshold that has always seemed to impede him.

Can he do it? He leans back in his swivel chair and closes his eyes. After a long moment, he sits up and stares at the keyboard.

One last time.

This is it, he tells himself, sitting straighter in his chair.

The decision to move ahead rouses him. Perhaps now he'll be able to burn onto paper all he has learned, all he has ever wanted to weave into a story that will define him, letting him make at last his mark on life before his life is over.

He takes a deep breath and sips beer again from his bottle. Puffs more on his cigarette and blows the smoke out in a wispy cloud that floats lazily upward. Then more beer.

He needs a beginning. But how to put it in words? First person or third person? Present or past tense? Story line?

He wants to be drunk, but he cannot write if he's "under the influence", as his mother sometimes referred to his father. He drains the bottle and tosses it into the battered brown plastic wastebasket in the corner. It clinks as it hits other dead soldiers.

Sucking deeply on his cigarette, he slouches in his chair until he is relatively comfortable and puts his fingers on the keyboard.

What the fuck, he says to himself.

He should have more than just a general hunch about what kind of book he'd love to write, more than a vague sense of the topic, but nevertheless he begins typing:

## *CHAPTER 1*

*The music again.*

*Since Mary died, I leave the music on around the clock. No matter if I am awake or asleep, the music plays. Turning it off will only let her absence drill itself more deeply into my mind, disrupting everything I am trying to do to make my life normal again – if it ever can be normal again. Listening seems to soothe me, and I crave the soothing. I can't live without it.*

*Amy's in the driveway, unloading from her car the few things I asked her to buy at the supermarket. As always, she has complied, taking care of her father-in-law in a pleasant, patient and cheerful and uncomplaining way. My son is a lucky man.*

*The music is playing in the background as I let Amy in the door.*

*You shouldn't listen to that, she says as she enters, two plastic shopping bags in her hands. You're always playing her favorite music and it always upsets you. Why do you listen?*

*I can't help it, I tell her. Now and then I just need to hear it. Mary loved those songs. They ground me. They help me remember her.*

*Your son worries about you more than you know, she tells me. You should get out more, she says, meaning with all her heart to be helpful, caring about me, perhaps only because I am her husband's father. But I appreciate her words while I almost resent her attempts to save me.*

*No, I tell her. Sometimes we have to face our needs, whether they be for music or food or love or work or travel or ice cream – or simply salvation. The music makes me stronger, I say authoritatively. I have to do this. I'll be fine soon.*

*She looks at me with deep concern in her eyes and tells me she understands. Then she puts the groceries away and kisses me on the cheek and leaves. I close the door behind her and lock it – Mary always wanted the doors locked – then I sit by the window and listen some more to the music. It reminds me so very much of Mary. Sometimes it stirs me to tears.*

With irritation, Sean reads what he has just written, glides the cursor over the text and deletes it without regret. The "stirs me to tears" bit is over the top. Pitifully melodramatic. It's not what he envisioned, nor what he wants to write. And why write in the first person? It makes no sense to him.

He knows he needs a direction. Hell, even just a starting point would be something.

There is more than a tiny hint of frustration needling him. This time he fights it, trying to energize his withering wisps of belief that some day, given the right circumstances, he could write a story he could be proud of.

How many attempts has he made in the past? Perhaps as many as three dozen, he's sure, the majority tossed away the way one would flip a cigarette into the gutter. Most of them short stories, two of them half-baked novels. None memorable, he admits to himself, and he's embarrassed by the thought.

He pushes the beer aside, stubs out his half-smoked cigarette in the saucer he uses as an ashtray and braces himself to write again, sorely aware that he may very well lack the hope and faith and drive he sorely needs to inspire his words. Yet, on this night, for some ill-defined reason, he is determined to plod forward even though he has no idea where he is going or how he will get there.

It may be his only way of bringing a story to life. And it may well be the one last chance he has to succeed. Or not.

He slips off his store-bought glasses and wipes them with his shirt, props them back on his nose, and stares some more at his computer screen.

For a long while, in the smothering silence of the room, he allows his mind to wander, to roam into corners he never knew were there. He sips beer and lights another cigarette.

Finally, as he rummages for something that just might work, something that might kick-start him, a nub of an idea begins to swirl. Sean considers it for more long minutes, then whispers a small prayer and starts anew, this time with a blunt and practical beginning.

He types slowly, and chooses his words with care:

***Aidan's Story***

*On September 28, his forty-third birthday, certainly without wishing so, Aidan McCann finally and quite unwillingly began to become an adult, a development that had taken place years and even decades after his friends and others had crossed their thresholds to maturity.*

*The unexpected change had shaken him. How on earth could he ever have anticipated such a thing to happen, particularly at this stage of his earthly existence?*

*Life, he had always religiously believed, was far too short to take as seriously as his parents and his brothers and his cousins and his friends had always insisted on taking it, all the while lecturing him – with sharply decreasing subtlety as he grew older – on the endless things he would certainly regret should he continue to live his whimsical ways with his cavalier disregard for the consequences the road he'd chosen would inevitably bring him.*

*And always, with comfortably smug certainty, Aidan managed to brush off their cautions and pressed onward, heeding his insistent personal drummer, living as if sure that tomorrow would never happen and as if the most important thing was to fall asleep each night knowing he'd tucked another enviably enjoyable day under his belt.*

*On that fateful birthday morning, a Sunday, the fun and freedom to which he had always aspired had been for nearly six years personified primarily by Ashling McManus, an auburn-haired beauty who'd actually emigrated from Ireland with her parents when she was eighteen and who spoke still in the sweet and lilting Irish accent Aidan had always found so attractive.*

*He himself was a first-generation Irish-American who'd always wished he had grown up in the north of Ireland from where his parents had come. He might have even become part of the Irish Republican Army, fighting the fookin' Brits, as his dad always referred to the occupiers. Instead, he'd had a conventional upbringing on the top floor of a three-story tenement off Quincy Street in the Dorchester section of Boston, among many other Irish-Americans there and in South Boston whose fate was to be lost in the crowd of others just like them.*

*Tired of Boston, but far more tired of being in the direct line of fire from his family and friends, Aidan opted to move to Rhode Island in his mid-twenties. He'd never regretted the move, yet soon learned that his life options had become far more limited in the small state tucked snugly under the armpit of Massachusetts. Hell, the state was barely bigger than metropolitan Boston itself. Yet for him it was a new beginning he could hardly afford to pass up. It was a gateway to a new life, and he figured it would likely cost him one way or another. But he was willing to pay whatever it cost.*

*Shortly after moving into two low-rent rooms which offered nothing to boast about, he left his barely adequate quarters near the village of Wickford one morning and was walking along a sidewalk when he suddenly recalled Reverend Martin Luther King's words: "Free at last. Free at last. Thank God almighty, I'm free at last." The thought brought a smile to his face, and he walked on.*

*But freedom didn't grace him with the kinds of blessings he'd hoped for.*

*Two weeks of job-hunting, several dozen turn-downs, and being reduced to rationing his last twenty-four dollars and the quarter-tank of fuel in his car finally funneled into a cash-register job at a liquor store less than two miles from where he lived. The pay wasn't great, the future was cloudy, but the owner was good enough to offer him a cash advance so he could pay his rent and buy some food. Even nine dollars an hour to start was better than sleeping on a bench by the harbor. And he knew he'd starve before he'd ever go back to Dorchester to ask for food and a place to sleep.*

*The job was relatively decent. Yet Aidan continued to hope that something better would come up over the coming weeks and months. Nothing ever did, of course. After all, he had only a high school education and a half-year of college. With luck, that should be worth at least twelve or fifteen dollars an hour. But the economy was not especially rosy and his continued feelers produced nothing. So he accepted his fate and worked his schedule and made friends and lived his free-spirited ways, happy he was not in Boston being slammed by his family and not pressured to live up to anyone's preconceived notions of who and what he should be when he grew up.*

*The liquor store was where he was working when he met Ashling, not that she ever visited his liquor store or any other. He'd bumped into her – literally, and surprisingly without injury – as he was rushing out of the local bank and ten minutes late for his job.*

*She, fortunately or unfortunately, had ended up in his way and he, and she, wound up on the sidewalk outside the bank's entrance, she cussing liberally at him -- and he taken immediately by her accent and her beauty.*

*Even now, he was astounded that he'd had the presence of mind, as they struggled to their feet and assessed any possible injuries, to ask her to dinner in recompense for his utter stupidity in running her down. He was even more astounded then when she accepted his invitation.*

*So began the years they shared together.*

*Ashling and he made a great couple, Aidan knew. She was more than pretty enough to get admiring looks wherever he took her, and he loved it that he could bask in her aura. She enjoyed his company and tolerated his ways for the most part. She was most definitely interested in marriage, having hinted at it more than a few times over the past year or two, and Aidan had yet to steer her away from her thoughts on the subject because he didn't want to end it just yet. She was delightful company, good for time-passing conversation over a few drinks, great for dancing now and then, and wonderful, of course, for being an utterly free spirit in bed. Soon, he knew, he'd have to ease her out of the picture and find someone who was not really interested in the whole marriage thing. But was not freedom what life was truly about?*

*Still, for the time being, Ashling complemented him nicely. Aidan thought he was a fairly handsome man – at least he hoped so. Put a suit on him, trim his hair, and make sure his goatee was neatly clipped, he'd look as professional and as serious as any executive. His lively blue eyes and his naturally effervescent Irish charm captivated anyone he met. At just about six-two and still relatively slim despite the beers and the whiskey and the vodka and the cheap food he favored, he drew eyes toward him by simply entering a room.*

*Aidan never once envied his brother's pudgy figure or his sister's prim looks. Aidan had got the best of the family's genes. And it would surely do him poorly if he were ever seen with a less-than-pretty woman.*

Sean tosses his empty beer bottle into the wastebasket next to his makeshift desk – a piece of plywood perched on a pair of cheap two-drawer file cabinets -- and gives great consideration to tossing his first paragraphs into the trash also. Instead, he pushes his chair back and heads to the kitchen for another beer and more cigarettes. In a few moments he returns and reads what he's just written.

His gut tells him that there's something taking shape in what he's typed so far, but he can't yet get a clear handle on it, and he seriously thinks of going off to bed. It's late and he needs to be showering by seven to get to work on time.

Somehow, work is the last thing on his mind. He's thinking about the story, but he's also thinking about how life could have been had he tried harder, had he had better breaks, had he tried much earlier to get the most out of his talents — whatever they might be. As he muses, he realizes he is feeling nothing more than regret.

He wonders if this is what's driving him now — the hope of washing away that regret.

Whatever, he's sensing in Aidan the kernel of an interesting character, someone with potential, so he forces his fingers to the keyboard one more time:

***Unnerved***

*Aidan's unsettling transition to adulthood – at least his first awareness of it — happened like this:*

*He awoke before dawn on his birthday morning, mulling his new milestone – forty-three, for Christ's sake – and feeling for the first time ever the implications of his aging weighing on him, finding himself indulging in an unanticipated self-examination, and becoming aware of the first wonderings about why he had wasted so much of his allotted time on earth shirking anything resembling responsibility and maturity.*

*The thoughts unnerved him and he lay uncomfortably in his bed trying to shake them, wondering where in hell they'd come from. The thoughts seemed to be assailing him from many directions, and he tried to kill them by focusing his mind on other things.*

*But the effort failed. The more he fought the thoughts, the more insistent they became. The turmoil surging in his mind roiled him and made him increasingly uneasy and confused.*

*He needed to get up, as if doing so would help him escape what was besetting him.*

*Afraid of waking Ashling, and hoping a stiff cup of coffee could erase the questions that had cropped up so unexpectedly – so unexplainably – Aidan slipped quietly out of bed.*

*In the kitchen of his apartment, a larger one than the cramped quarters he occupied when he moved to Wickford, Aidan filled the innards of his second-hand coffee maker and flipped the switch. Then, still clad only in his wrinkled black boxers, he sat at the kitchen table, lit a cigarette, inhaled deeply and tried to tune out his thoughts as the coffee aroma began to waft toward him.*

*A flash of memory:*

*"Christ, Aidan, when the hell are you going to grow the fuck up?" his brother had yelled at him when Aidan had asked him for another*

*loan to cover an overdue and overly serious bar tab from the Irish pub within walking distance of the tiny apartment he'd rented in Dorchester a year after he dropped out of college.*

*The chastisement happened when Aidan was twenty-five and already between his sixth and seventh jobs. Aidan thought his brother, a successful lawyer, was an establishment asshole who had condemned himself to a conventional existence wearing a necktie and stodgy suits for the rest of his years.*

*Aidan had always held that you took a job when you really needed money, and for no other reason. He had never seen any sense in actually pursuing a career that might turn out to be decades long. If you stayed too long in a job it sucked the life from you, he believed. He'd seen its consequences in his parents and their friends who had aged poorly during forty years or more on the job, and had often died – as had the fathers of some of his friends – too ungodly soon after retirement.*

*Still, he'd been at the liquor store for close to twenty years, never having found any incentive to move on to something better.*

*Back then, after the chastisement, his brother had grudgingly once again given him the money he needed, but promised on his life he would never again help Aidan.*

*Aidan, as every time before, brushed away his brother's stern words, ever sure Ian would never keep his promise. His brother's attitude made Aidan want a shot or two of Jameson. Which is what he did after his brother walked away. Four months later, Aidan escaped to Rhode Island.*

Not bad, Sean thinks as he reads what he's written. He lights yet another cigarette but forgoes another beer until he figures where his story is taking him.

A bit of his life may be creeping into it, and he considers to what extent. After some thought, he decides that the best stories are those that contain the meat of real experiences and real lives. And he has one heck of a story to tell if he can only bring to the keyboard all he has learned and experienced. And he can't tell the story without weaving parts of himself into it.

It's growing later and he is almost too tired to write and is beginning to crave the comfort of his bed.

There are some things about Aidan that Sean imagines are part of his own essence, but he's trying to create someone who is far removed from himself and his life. He was Aidan's age three years ago, but he's not as tall or as handsome as he is imagining Aidan to be. Sean's father did in fact die less than a year after retiring, but Sean has never had a woman in his life like the one he is creating for Aidan. Unlike Aidan, he was married once and the marriage lasted fourteen years before she took up with a fellow at work and decided that life with Sean was no longer good enough for her. He has been single ever since and dates rarely. And he can never imagine himself working a cash register in any store.

He is reasonably content with his job as a feature reporter for the local weekly newspaper. He's always seen his work as giving him a chance to keep up his writing skills while providing him ample time to write on his own and giving him fodder for developing perhaps unique and memorable characters, if he ever chose to follow through. His only problem has been that he's spent far less time writing than he should have, always postponing his story creation for one flimsy excuse or another. For a long time he's been regretting not being more serious about the fiction he's always dreamed of producing.

He leans back in his chair and contemplates the text on his

computer screen. Another puff on his cigarette, another cloud of smoke swirling upward. The room is getting stuffy and Sean begins to come up with reasons why he should leave the story and go off to sleep. His bedroom gets a bit of a breeze from Narragansett Bay sometimes and it would be a relief from the stale and too-warm air of his office. But he is feeling something and knows he must add some more to the story while his brain seems to be on some kind of track. He'll regret his lack of sleep in the morning.

Once more, his fingers, so tired now, begin tapping the keys…

### *Happy birthday, luv*

*The unfettered thoughts tumbling through Aidan's mind were as close as he'd ever got to an examination of conscience. He recalled the black-clad, white-bibbed nuns explaining in grade school how one should conduct an examination of conscience before going to confession on Saturday mornings, to sort out one's sins before whispering to the priest through the confessional's semi-transparent screen. But even in the second grade he thought it was stupid.*

*This, everything that was whirling through his mind, was far more important than Saturday confessions, he sensed, though he was not sure why. He poured his first mug of very black coffee and sat sullenly at the kitchen table – brooding and thinking.*

*Halfway to eighty-six, Aidan's brain mentioned for no apparent reason. Here I am, forty-three, and that makes me halfway to eighty-friggin'-six. What for Christ's sake do I have to show for it, he asked himself. A nothing-special apartment, a woman who fuckin' wants to marry me, an old Ford Taurus that needs new tires, an overdue electric bill, maybe two days' food in the place, and not enough cash for much else. Tonight would be a night he and Ashling would go for pizza and she would pay, happily, because she thought it would further cement their inexorable path to marriage. And he didn't really give a shit. But now he wondered what the hell she saw in him. Women!*

*Aidan's brother had been right. Grow the fuck up. Aidan had always fought to avoid the topic, to avoid this very confrontation with himself. He had wanted to say to his brother Ian: how the hell does one grow up when one does not want to grow up? Aidan had never wanted to grow up. There was nothing better, in Aidan's mind, than running out to the local liquor store, buying a case of cheap beer or a pint of Karkov vodka, and hanging with some friends to watch the Patriots or the Bruins or the Red Sox or the Celtics. Even with Ashling in his life, he managed to see his friends at least a couple of nights a week. That's the way life ought to be. No goddam need to grow up.*

*Yet, suddenly, here he was, now about six hours into his forty-third birthday, aggravatingly and fearfully aware that he probably had already squandered the best years of his life. He felt an uncomfortable chill, and cupped the steaming mug even more tightly in his hands.*

*"There you are, birthday boy," Ashling sang as she slipped into the kitchen on bare feet, her short nightie barely covering her butt, her hair a tortured yet attractive case of bed-head, her eyes in a sleepy squint even in the dim light of the kitchen. "You're out of bed unusually early."*

*Aidan continued to stare down into his mug and wished she had stayed in bed longer.*

*She spoke again. "Happy birthday, luv." Still, he didn't respond.*

*After a moment, she said, "Am I to take it that this is not a particularly happy birthday?"*

*When he continued to ignore her, she brushed away his moody silence with a gesture of her hand and got busy in the kitchen. Several times, as she worked, she looked over at him, trying to diagnose what was going on this morning. Aidan was not one to speak much about what was inside him, although Ashling had learned to read him fairly well, under most circumstances. This, however, did not seem to her to be one of those circumstances.*

*She had also learned to leave him alone in his moody times.*

*Aidan didn't hear her when she asked if he wanted some bacon and eggs, and grunted only because her voice had prompted the automatic response he gave when he wasn't interested in anything else.*

*As she pulled the cast-iron fry pan from the drawer beneath the oven, Aidan was largely unaware. All that simmered through his mind was a tangle of thoughts and emotions – and fears – that had seized his undivided attention.*

*Is this what it's all about?*

*He finished his coffee quickly, needing the security of another full cup, knowing a few throat-burning shots of whiskey would suit him far better now. He wished pretty Ashling, with her tight butt and beautifully firm boobs, was not here. Not now. Not ever.*

*What the fuck was happening to him?*

*He rose up from the table and slouched to the counter where the coffee maker sat. At the last instant, he put his mug down and opened the kitchen cabinet above the refrigerator and grabbed his nearly empty bottle of Jameson.*

*Ashling clamped onto his arm.*

*"What in heaven's name are you doing, Aidan?" Ashling asked. "Are you really wanting liquor so early in the morning? Put that away and sit down, for the love of the Blessed Mother. I'll have breakfast for you in a matter of minutes."*

*She drew close to him and caressed his cheek. "What on earth's the matter, dear luv? Did you have an awful night?"*

*Aidan, stubborn as ever, kept it all to himself. If it hadn't been for the sweet comforting caress of her Irish accent, he would have thrown her out of the apartment before she could object.*

Sean has to pee. He's become an accomplished beer recycler. He stands at the toilet, aware now that he hasn't given the bathroom a real cleaning in maybe two months. Tomorrow, he promises himself. As he urinates, he thinks about how he should handle Aidan. He's beginning to sense what Aidan's about, and he's not sure he likes him. Still, he seems interesting – so far.

He zips up, flushes the toilet, and grabs a box of Wheat Thins on the way back to his computer. He should sleep, but he can't. So he munches one of the small crackers, and contemplates the text on the screen, wondering what might be to come.

He's often wondered how successful authors feel as they bring their imaginations to life in typed words. He can't imagine that they feel as uncertain as he's been in filling the few pages he's manage to turn out so far. He knows that many authors plot out their books before beginning the writing. But he also knows that his mind doesn't work that way. Perhaps it's because he's spent so much time as a journalist; you root around for the facts and the article just seems to flow onto the page — or, these days, the word processor.

Writing about Aidan has felt, so far, like producing a feature article, but with no research notes to prop him up. Looking at what he's written so far, he hopes he can come up with a plot outline to guide him forward. Otherwise, he fears, the story might chug ahead only to fizzle into nothing because has no idea of where it should be going.

He considers leaving his story and heading off to bed. He has a gut feeling, though, that if he does so without giving more life to Aidan, he might well lose whatever tenuous spark is moving him now.

So he types some more:

***Solution?***

*It was early afternoon.*

*Ashling, annoyed by Aidan's distant and surly mood, had gone to visit one of her girlfriends who was nearly nine months pregnant with someone's baby. Aidan had run out of Jameson and now sipped away at the second of two hefty vodkas on the rocks, barely aware that she had gone. He had not yet showered or shaved or left the kitchen. His thoughts and fears had transfixed him. The drinking had so far done nothing to help him focus.*

*If Ian were here now, Aidan knew with solid certainty, his pompous brother would be blathering that Aidan's life sucked because he had utterly nothing to be proud of, no accomplishments to speak of, and nothing he could point to that made him worthwhile person.*

*"When was the last time you did anything but sleep, eat, party and fuck," Aidan imagined his brother telling him. "Sure you have a job, but any half-brain could do what you do and still be a better man."*

*Aidan felt empty, aimless – precisely as his brother would have described him. He took in a mouthful of vodka and surveyed the kitchen. A dump, Aidan thought. The gas stove had to be maybe thirty years old, the paint-chipped white metal cabinets depressing, the linoleum floor -- an odd mix of greens and grays -- beginning to wear into shabbiness. All this for over nine hundred a month. Heat extra.*

*For the first time, he wondered how Ashling had managed to put up with it for so long. Christ!*

*He rose from the table and got the notepad Ashling kept in the drawer next to the sink and managed to find a pencil tucked away in another drawer. Returning to the table, he pushed the vodka aside and hung his head in thought. After a while, he picked up the pencil and wrote:*

*"Problem: everything is fucked up. Solution: who the hell knows?"*

*Then he got up from his chair, tucked the note carefully into his shirt pocket, poured the remaining vodka back into its bottle, and placed it where he'd remember to grab it as he left. Then he went to try to shower away the feelings that were dragging him down. He wanted to be out of the apartment before Ashling returned.*

*Aidan's favorite place for letting go of everything was on the rocks surrounding the Beavertail lighthouse at the southern tip of Jamestown, the upscale island tucked in the middle of Narragansett Bay between Aidan's town and Newport.*

*From the rocks, he could look out at endless miles of ocean, dotted usually on fine summer days with scores of boats, mostly sloops heeling over with their sails full of wind. On this day, there were a dozen boats making their way out of the Bay's East Passage. To Aidan, it was a picture postcard – and probably the only place he truly loved. But then he'd never really been anywhere. He'd never even been on a sailboat.*

*He found his favorite spot, an isolated nook in the rocks where he could relax unbothered by the scores of others who came almost daily to the place when the weather was good. He pulled the half-empty pint of Karkov from his back pocket and leaned back on the stone, nicely warmed by the brilliant late-September sun, toasting the welcome isolation with a throat-burning swig from his bottle. He shook his head and stared out at the water.*

*What the fuck, he thought to himself.*

*Aidan knew he was not stupid. He figured he was at least as smart as Ian, maybe even smarter, but in a different way. He had more street smarts, no doubt about it. If he'd chosen to complete college, he was sure he would have been markedly more successful than his smug brother. But college – then, at least – offered him no satisfaction.*

*His sister was another matter: seven years older and no longer on speaking terms with him because, as she'd told him the last time she'd actually addressed him directly, he was a shameful blot on the family and a major disappointment that surely flew in the face of all the sacrifices their parents had made to afford the three of them a good life.*

*She was the smartest one in the family, a neurosurgeon at one of the big hospitals in Boston. Aidan didn't even know if Margaret still lived in her plush ten-room colonial thirty minutes from where they'd grown up. After all, it had been nearly twelve years since they'd spoken. Even when Aidan returned to Dorchester for Christmas and*

*Thanksgiving, she conveniently stayed away until he left. She probably never thought of him at all anymore*

*It was a shock, really, to find himself suddenly and shockingly adrift, his wasted years finally mocking him, and having absolutely no idea where to turn.*

*It's funny, he thought as he sipped more vodka: while he was burning through his twenty-something and thirty-something years, he never had the least inkling at all that he was wasting his time. Life was good then; more fun than life ought to be. Now, out of the blue, he wanted to blame someone for not grabbing him by the collar and whipping him around, saying, "This is where you've got to go, Aidan. This is the path to a good, fulfilling life. So get your irresponsible ass in motion and do what you've got to do to make your family proud of you."*

*Jesus, he muttered. That's what his brother and sister had tried to do for him time after time. And he had always dismissed them.*

*Again he brought the bottle to his lips and took another swig. The alcohol took longer to affect him after all these years. He truly enjoyed drinking — beer, whiskey, vodka, rum, wine — even though maybe he drank too much and too often.*

*The thought brought Lenny to mind, one of the downsliding regulars at the liquor store – a veteran alcoholic who showed up there nearly every day waiting for the doors to open for business, was there again around mid-afternoon, and usually was one of the last customers at night.*

*Aidan and a couple of other store employees had once figured out that Lenny had to drink at least two six-packs of beer and a liter of cheap gin every day, sometimes punctuated with a pint of one of the disgustingly fruity brandies that he could buy pretty much at half-price. Yet Lenny rarely gave any sign that his blood-alcohol level was chronically perhaps at least three times the legal limit. For all his faults, the man could hold his booze.*

*Lenny would get under Aidan's skin on occasion. He didn't like the man, detested him actually. Lenny was fat and unkempt and sometimes made disparaging remarks about other customers – within earshot, of course. Perhaps the one thing that made Aidan dislike Lenny the most was Lenny's insistence on shooting the shit with Aidan when things were slow at the checkout register. After consuming half his daily ration of booze, Lenny inevitably envisioned himself as a philosopher with an unwaveringly correct handle on life.*

*"I've been around for fifty-seven years," he told Aidan once, "and I've seen everything there is to see. You better believe it. And I'll tell you this, my friend: no matter what you do, life is gonna fuck you up. You don't get anywhere unless life gives you the breaks, but life's stingy that way. You know what I mean? Doesn't matter how hard you try. Sooner or later life is gonna smack you down and you're gonna find it fuckin' hard to get back up. Put that in your fuckin' pipe and smoke it!"*

*Last week, mostly because he was bored, Aidan asked Lenny why life had turned out so that Lenny worshiped the liquor store in the way other people worshiped their God. The man was mellowed out enough that he took no offense at the question, even asking Aidan to repeat it so that he was sure he understood.*

*"I don't mean to bust your balls, Lenny, but how the hell did you wind up like this?" Aidan asked. "I mean, you drink and eat and shit and sleep..."*

*"And collect my disability checks," Lenny answered with a crooked grin. His teeth showed serious neglect.*

*"But how did you...?"*

*"It's what I keep telling you about how life fucks you," Lenny said earnestly, as if begging Aidan to believe him. "I had a good life until sixteen years ago, my friend, then everything kicked me in the balls. Nothing's been right ever since. And now my doctor wants me to have some fuckin' operation — something in my stomach. I got a deep down feeling that life's gonna get much worse for me."*

*"What happened sixteen years ago?" Aidan asked.*

*"I got fucked big time," Lenny said, his jaw clenching, and tears welling in his rheumy eyes. "Big time."*

*"How?" Aidan asked.*

*But Lenny said no more and left the store.*

Sean wants desperately to keep writing. But it's beyond late and fatigue is overwhelming every part of his being. There's something happening here, he senses, and he's feeling some movement, as if he's finding the ground under his feet and heading in the kind of productive direction he wants.

Lenny can be a turning point for Aidan, albeit an odd one. If there was anything about Lenny that was instructive, it was the fact that he seemed to have surrendered totally to whatever vagaries of life assaulted him. The man Sean is creating wasn't a quitter; in fact, Sean had considered giving Lenny a background that included two tours in Vietnam, where he earned two Purple Hearts. Sean isn't sure if he needs to elaborate in any detail about Lenny's past. Still, Sean's vision of Lenny – the images that swirled in his mind as he wrote about the man – is that of a man who hides, not only from himself, but also from what he really is.

The fact is that Lenny is based on a man Sean knows well, who often sat at the bar where Sean often had his meals alone. They'd begun talking years before, not long after Sean first arrived in Wickford. His name was Gregory – he disliked being called Greg – and he was a drunk, a fact he readily admitted on many occasions.

Gregory was a Vietnam veteran, although he rarely opened up about what happened during his two tours of duty there. The scars were quite obvious to Sean: the psychic ones as well as the blatant indentation on the left side of Gregory's head where he had been hit by a bullet that fortunately – or not – had failed to kill him.

What Sean liked about Gregory is that he could talk to him about anything at all, and by the next encounter at the bar, the man would have forgotten every bit of the conversation, at least the most critical points. Sean had first noticed this probably after a year or so of the rather sporadic relationship he had with the man; Sean was lucky to run into Gregory perhaps twice a week. Part of it had to do with Sean's budget. While his salary was good, it would be spendthrift to lay out fifty or sixty dollars a week satisfying his yen for seafood. The other part of it was that he could take Gregory only in small doses.

Gregory was everything that Sean was happy he himself was not. Gregory was obese, messy for the most part, had clearly neglected teeth, limped from one of his war injuries, had lost his driver's license, had no friends Sean was aware of, and lived in a sinfully dilapidated two-room apartment in a house that should have been condemned years ago (Sean had driven him home once — but only once). Yet he and Gregory shared something that Sean was not proud of and had never told anyone until he felt he could safely mention to Gregory – but only after the man had downed perhaps his fifth vodka.

When he told Gregory, the man had stared at him for some time, his eyes working to focus, then he let his head slump forward and he then stared into his vodka. Initially, Sean thought Gregory had not heard a word he said, or had completely misunderstood Sean's words. But Sean was not about to repeat himself; it had been more than difficult to divulge the secret in the first place, and he was afraid repeating it might increase the chances that someone else sitting at the bar might overhear.

After a long time, well after Sean decided that Gregory has simply not been able to grasp what Sean had said, Gregory turned his head and stared into Sean's eyes.

"What the fuck are you ashamed of?" he said. "Shit, if I was you, I'd be fuckin' proud of it. Look what you did, for Christ's sake! You didn't play by the goddamned rules and you won. Jesus! Celebrate!"

Gregory looked at his glass and asked the bartender for another vodka on the rocks. The bartender asked him, "Are you okay? I mean, are you okay to walk home?"

Gregory gave him crooked smile. "I could have six more of these and still walk home without falling down." Then he laughed a gurgling laugh that brought up some phlegm that he spit into a soiled handkerchief. With a deft motion, he tucked it back in his pocket and said to Sean, "Now let's get back to your deep, dark secret."

Sean waited for him to continue, but all Gregory said was, "I have deep, dark secrets, too." Then, with a wink, he told Sean, "But there is no way in hell that I'm ever going to tell them to you." Again the hoarse and phlegm-producing laugh.

Sean had already finished his meal, and was nearly done with his second and last draught beer. He decided that Gregory had nothing more to add, and he felt confident that the conversation would be deleted from Gregory's mind before his head hit the pillow that night. He chugged the rest of his beer and bade a goodnight to Gregory, wishing him well on his walk home.

Gregory reached out and clamped a hand on Sean's arm, just as the bartender slid another vodka on the rocks in from of him. Gregory kept his hand on Sean's arm while he lifted the glass and drank half of it down in a single swallow.

"I gotta tell you something," Gregory said, his words more slurred. "You are now my hero, Mr. Sean. You did something I never could've done. You bluffed your way into something really good. Now that's a talent, and I gotta congratulate you on that. But tell me something."

"What's that?" Sean asked, wishing Gregory would let go of his arm.

"Why in hell would you tell people you graduated from college when you didn't? I mean, I got no problem lying about things, but – shit – no one is gonna nail me for it because I'm not worth their time of day. But you…."

"I wanted to write. I wasn't good enough to get a scholarship, and my mother couldn't afford the tuition. When my father died, he didn't have much to leave her."

Gregory sipped again. Amazingly, despite the alcohol he had imbibed, his mind seemed to be working clearly. "So how the fuck did you ever get to write for a goddam newspaper?" He laughed again, "Maybe I can use the same trick to get myself a job at the paper!" Again the disconcerting laugh, and again Gregory had to bring out the handkerchief.

Sean chose not to watch.

When Gregory was finished with his handkerchief business, Sean swiveled his stool to face him. "I went to my home town paper, up in Massachusetts, and I asked if there were any jobs there. I needed a job and I figured they might need a custodian or someone to work in the pressroom. The lady I asked told me to go up to the second floor and talk with the managing editor – Mr. Gallagher. After I got to his office and he invited me in, he asked me only four questions. The first one was, 'Can you write?' I told him that I wrote for my high school newspaper, which was true. The next question was, 'Can you type?" I told him I could and would be happy to show him. He said it would not be necessary to show him. The third question was, "Would you like to be a reporter?" Now that question floored me because, like I said, I was just hoping for a basic job, although I would have killed to become a reporter. Naturally, I told him yes – emphatically. His last question, which almost knocked me off my chair, was, "Can you start Monday morning at seven?" I stood up and said, "Yes!" He stood, shook my hand, and said, "Welcome aboard."

"So, on Monday morning, I showed up at seven, was introduced to the city editor who assigned me to one of the other reporters for orientation and to get me started. By the end of the day, after the first edition was printed, I was a reporter. After that, I never told anyone I never went to college. I just pretended I had, and no one ever asked."

"Is that why you're working at the Wickford paper?"

Sean nodded, almost ruefully. "Yup,' he admitted. "That first paper never checked my background. The bigger dailies almost always check up on who they're hiring."

"So you're stuck here, eh?"

"It's not a bad place to be stuck in."

With that, Gregory let go of his arm. "You better get goin'. I figure you gotta get up early tomorrow."

"I do," Sean said, feeling lighter than he had when he had come in. "Thanks for listening." He gave Gregory a pat on the shoulder, stood up, and headed home.

Sean leans back in his chair. Remembering the liberating admission he'd made to Gregory has made him forget about sleep for the moment. He looks at the computer screen for a moment, then straightens up in his chair and writes some more:

***I'm gonna fart myself to death***

*Aidan was upset that Lenny had told him about the surgery, about his fear that his life would get worse. Was this part of the reason why Aidan was so suddenly fretting about his life? Did Lenny's steep and self-pitying downslide awaken something fearful deep inside himself? Sitting on the rocks above the waves, he tried to sort through it all.*

*A day after he had the first unnerving conversation with Lenny, the rumpled, unshaven man was back at the store as usual, choosing Aidan's register again.*

*"I'm not gonna make it through the surgery," he told Aidan, unbidden. "They gotta open my belly and I know it's gonna to kill me. I'm scared."*

*"Doctors today are really good," Aidan said, not knowing what he was talking about. "I wouldn't worry about any surgery on me."*

*"You been operated on?" Lenny asked.*

*"Yeah, once," Aidan fibbed. Lenny looked away.*

*"So tell me," Aidan said. "How did you get fucked big time way back when?"*

*"It doesn't matter," Lenny answered. "Not any more. I'm gonna die on the operating table. I had a dream about it." Lenny's chin was quivering, his hands shaking.*

*"Like I said, doctors are really good these days," Aidan said, wanting to get off the subject of death. "Thousands of people are operated on every day, Lenny."*

*"And how many of them die?"*

*"Let's talk more the next time you're in," Aidan told the man. "I've got customers behind you."*

*He turned quickly to the next customer in line and said, "May I help you?"*

*Lenny shuffled out of the store without another word. Flustered by*

*Lenny's fears, Aidan wiped his hands on his jeans as if trying to brush Lenny off of him and began punching keys on the register.*

*Lenny had bothered him that day. Lenny bothered him still, and Aidan could not fathom why.*

*Four days before Aidan's birthday threw him for a loop, one of the guys at the liquor store — Angie — told him offhandedly that Lenny had died. Aidan, who would have been happy to be able to shrug it off, felt real pity for the man and felt his own stomach churn over what life could do to people.*

*On the rocks above the waves, Aidan lifted his bottle in a toast to Lenny and drank the last of the vodka, then got to his feet and began climbing up to where his car was parked. He no longer heard the surf crashing behind him, no longer felt the sun. There was still too much on his mind.*

*He didn't want to go home, and his shift at the store wouldn't start for another two hours. He decided to stop in at Dugan's Ale House on the way back. He'd put up with Ashling after he got home from the store.*

*Even his car was a testament to his lack of any success in his life. The old Ford Taurus was about the only thing he could afford when he bought it used -- pre-owned, the dealer said – the year before he met Ashling. It was still running, so that was something. But it was a piece of shit. He rolled down all the windows – the air conditioning had quit the summer before last – started the engine, and headed back toward town.*

*The place that was Aidan's home away from home was Dugan's. He stopped in at least two or three times a week, unless Ashling bugged him too much about it. Lately, she'd been pretty quiet. You never knew when women were going to start nagging you about something.*

*He had friends at Dugan's – friends in the sense that they all got along fine as long as the drinks kept flowing and none of them was in some foul mood because life had messed something up. Aidan's preferred seat was at one corner of the rectangular bar, and most of the regulars knew to keep it empty in case he showed up. They might be drinking friends but, Aidan knew, they were quite capable of diagnosing what was happening in life, ably analyzing every curve ball life threw their way. Friends somehow managed to help you navigate through life.*

*If anyone had pressed him, Aidan would have admitted he didn't recall anything about his ride from Beavertail's rocks to the parking lot at the pub. His half-drunk mind was in overdrive and it was driving him nuts. The only moment it all seemed to ease up was when he entered Dugan's and bee-lined to his bar stool.*

*At this hour of the day, Ernie was the only customer he recognized. The old man had to be pushing eighty but he had a wild sense of humor and didn't give a shit about anything anymore. In Aidan's mind, Ernie had freed himself from all the trials and tribulations of life and was now happily coasting toward the finish line. Lucky bastard.*

*"Jameson, Mike," Aidan told the bartender.*

*"What's up, Aidan?" Mike asked while pulling a glass from the shelf.*

*"Nothing a miracle can't cure," Aidan said. Then he turned to Ernie. "What's happening, my friend?"*

*"Same as you," Ernie said. "A miracle would do me fine. Viagra costs too fucking much." The old man laughed then choked on his laugh. Too many years working in fiberglass dust at one of the local marinas. He wiped his mouth with his napkin. "When's life been any goddamn different?"*

*Aidan shrugged as Mike pushed the Jameson in front of him. "Never, I guess," he replied.*

*"Havin' trouble with your honey?" Ernie asked. "You look like somebody's kicked you around the school yard."*

*"Nah. One of my customers died. I found out yesterday," Aidan said, not choosing to bring Ashling into the conversation. "You know Lenny, the fat guy with the limp, lived up in those apartments just off Post Road?"*

*"Oh, him. Hell, he used to come here every damn day until he figured buying at the liquor store would let him drink a lot more for the same amount of dough he spent at the bar."*

*Ernie shrugged. "We all gotta die sometime. With my luck, I'm gonna fart myself to death."*

*"I don't wanna be anywhere near you when that happens," Aidan said with a little "hah" as a laugh. He sipped his whiskey and grew pensive again. "Lenny knew he was gonna die. He said he dreamed it. And it happened. Shit, he was only in his fifties or sixties, I guess."*

*Mike the bartender, not to be left out, tossed in a "fuckin' right everybody's gotta die sooner or later. My uncle dropped dead when he was only forty-two."*

*Aidan and Ernie ignored him, and the place was silent save the televisions that were turned up louder than they needed to be.*

*An hour later, Aidan reported for work, earlier than he needed to be there, striding to the restroom at the back of the store to pee one more time before getting behind the register. Drinking hadn't helped much, so he was hoping a solid stream of customers would quell the jumble that was trampling his brain.*

*The first customer he rang up took a minute to rattle off a new joke that made him nearly choke with laughter, and Aidan was grateful.*

*It might be a tolerable shift after all. In the back of his mind, he looked forward to holding Ashling close after he got home.*

*If she wasn't pissed off at him.*

Jesus, I'm so damned tired, Sean thinks, staring at the computer screen, barely able to focus. On a jury-rigged shelf above his computer, the cheap digital clock with red numerals taunts him with 02:47 AM.

Am I going to sleep or not, he asks himself. He knows that work in the morning will not go well unless he's awake enough to get it done. He needs at least four hours' sleep – he can function with just that — otherwise he'll mess up his day for sure.

He scans the page on the computer screen, then regretfully gives up and goes to his bed. Morning will not be fun.

At seven, with clouds making the morning darker than he prefers, his alarm pushes him out of bed. Grousing, he shuffles into wakefulness, pees, showers, shaves, and otherwise makes himself presentable.

He leaves his apartment, drives up to the local Burger King for a breakfast sandwich and a cup of coffee then heads back to Wickford Village to begin being a journalist again. On the way, he wonders what he would have chosen to become had he been able to go to college. It is a question he's always avoided before, but it's an interesting one that he might actually ponder one day.

Minutes later, he walks into the newsroom, already itching for the day to be over so he can write some more. He would like to think that he already knows what the next chapter will be about. The truth is that he won't know until he actually sits down and begins writing again.

Over the next few hours, stuck in the newsroom, Sean tries to build the first draft of his feature article, his tired mind vacillating between the task at hand and the story he's creating from nothing. Every effort to focus on his job fails. He finds himself having to reread his notes two or three times before he can produce a few more meager sentences. Even the simple task of typing, complicated by his fatigue, brings him flashbacks of the paragraphs he wrote last night, and he finds himself thinking of Aidan and wondering about what will happen to Aidan as the story moves forward.

***That's life for you***

*It was after ten-thirty on a dismally cloudy morning when Aidan awoke, the day following his bummer of a birthday. The evening before, Ashling had left a small chocolate birthday cake on the kitchen table for him, candles ready to be lighted. But he'd left work feeling stressed and opted for another round or two at Dugan's before going home two hours later. Ashling had been asleep, and he passed out next to her. He never noticed the cake until he slouched into the kitchen that morning to make himself some coffee. When he finally saw it there, next to an envelope with his name on it, along with two dessert plates and neatly folded birthday napkins, he knew he could be reasonably sure that he had hurt her feelings by failing to notice what she'd done to try to make his birthday a good one.*

*If he'd been aware of Ashling's departure for work that morning, he couldn't recall. He himself was scheduled to work from noon to nine. He liked the shift; it gave him time to sleep in and got him out of work early enough so he could meet friends for a few drinks. Tonight, though, his gut told him that he'd be wiser to forego the bar time and spend the evening instead with Ashling. She most likely would be asleep by the time he got home from work, probably dozing on the couch as she liked to do when he was not home. But he knew – after his failure to be there for the cake – that life would be less threatening if he went home to her.*

*He showered, shaved around his goatee, and dressed for the day. Finding nothing in the refrigerator, he drove to the M&N's breakfast place a mile away to fill himself with eggs and sausage and home fries and some much-needed coffee. The waitress, Karen, smiled when she saw him enter. Aidan smiled back. She was young, blond and attractive, and Aidan had for a time considered trying to bed her. But it would have spoiled the light-as-air relationship he and she had come to find comfortable over the years, and would have destroyed whatever he had with Ashling. As he made himself at home at the counter, Karen brought him his first steaming cup of coffee. There was no need to ask what he wanted for breakfast; he had the same damn thing every time.*

*Aidan pulled the morning newspaper from a stack at the end of the counter and scanned the sports section, pissed that the Red Sox had blown a three-run lead in the ninth inning. No World Series this year. He pushed the sports section aside and moved on to the comics.*

*When his food came, he ate slowly to pass the time and had two more cups of coffee – black and strong. When he was finished, he left Karen a two-dollar tip, complimented her on her new hairstyle – actually just a change from a ponytail to a French braid -- and headed back out to his car. She had a great butt. Her face, though, has lost some of the freshness that had once made her so appealing. That's life for you.*

*By the time he drove the four miles to the liquor store, it would be close enough to his starting time to suit him.*

*The store was the largest one in town, with more of everything than any other place within a fifteen-mile radius. Aidan, of course, got a nice employee discount, which enabled him to keep a decent stash at home, which he often needed to replenish.*

*On a good day, he'd process as many as thirty or more customers an hour through his checkout lane, scanning the booze quickly, collecting the payment, making change and packing the stuff in bags or boxes – customer's choice – all the while keep up a patter that kept most customers amused. Of course, some customers didn't want to talk and didn't want anyone to talk to them. Aidan had learned over time to spot the unfriendly ones – the assholes, as he called them privately – and he let them have their way when they came to his register. He disliked it when they chose his register, and loved it when they left.*

*Aidan guessed he knew better than five hundred customers by name and maybe another five hundred or more by their face.*

*"Angie!" Aidan yelled as he entered the store. Angie was, a bald and marvelously rotund Italian guy whose schedule at the register overlapped Aidan's two or three times a week. Angie actually believed America would be far better off if everyone was Italian and loved only Italian cooking. He'd been working at the store since he retired from his construction job ten years earlier.*

*"Hey, Mr. Irish," Angie replied while scanning a customer's six-pack of Bud. "You're early. Brown-nosing the boss?"*

*Aidan mouthed the words "fuck you" and Angie laughed. "You are such a class act for a Mick," Angie said, with more than a hint of sarcasm. Angie considered the Irish in America descendants of illegal immigrants. But Aidan knew Angie liked him.*

*Aidan moved toward the back of the store, to the office where Lou, the storeowner, held court. "Hey. Lou," Aidan said as he knocked once on the office door. "Can I get out early on Saturday?"*

*"Christ, Aidan, I already made up the schedule," Lou said, sourly. Lou liked everything to happen flawlessly, but in the liquor store business they seldom did. Consequently, Lou was usually in a dour mood that made most customers avoid him. Somehow Lou liked it that way and stayed in his office most of the time, keeping tabs on the goings-on via the twelve surveillance cameras that played into the three monitors on the wall above his desk. Aidan had always thought Lou would have had a happier life in some other job.*

*Aidan asked again. Lou made a hissing sound, like a snake would when threatened. "Does it have to be Saturday, for God's sake?"*

*"I'm just busting you," Aidan said, laughing. He enjoyed getting Lou revved up about something. "I don't need the time off."*

*"You bastard,' Lou said. "Get out of my office."*

*"Yes, sir," Aidan said, still chuckling.*

*He left the office, high-fived one of the stock boys who was putting top-shelf wines on the top shelf in the imported wines section, then slipped behind his register.*

*Another day, another dollar.*

# Mulligan

By late morning, Sean still has been unable to build enthusiasm for the feature he's been assigned: a two-part story about the restoration of one the stately colonial homes that line Wickford's historic Main Street. He's done the research, obtained the interviews, and made notes on the additional information he needs to make the story a good one. Yet he has written barely enough to get the article started. Aidan keeps wiggling into his mind and Sean keeps trying to push him away. Unsuccessfully, for the most part.

When lunchtime comes, Sean heads out for his fifty-yard walk to the café near the harbor for a sandwich and some time away from the office. On his way, he flips open his cell phone and calls his friend Ted.

Ted Cooper has been a musician for longer than the twenty years Sean has known him, playing clubs to a loyal following from Providence to Matunuck Beach on Rhode Island's south coast. Ted writes his own music, an eclectic collection from rock to blues to ballads that most people can't help liking.

"I probably couldn't have done it if I knew how to read music," Ted told Sean once.

"But how can you write songs unless you can read?" Sean asked, somewhat astounded at what Ted had told him.

"I hear the songs in my head and pick them out on my guitar and scratch out the lyrics in a notebook. It's hard to explain. You've just gotta hear the music." Ted fingered an air guitar. "I know a guy. I bring him a tape of what I play and he puts the music down on paper. Then we do the arrangements together."

Sean doesn't often hear the music when he churns out his features for the newspaper. And he knows the reason he's being distracted by Aidan is that he's pretty sure he is finally hearing the music this time.

The phone rings a fourth time before Ted answers. "Sean!" Ted is one of those guys whose smile comes through clearly on the phone. "Where have you been, man? What's happening?"

"Mostly nothing much. But I'm writing – again," Sean says, emphasizing the "again" because Ted knows Sean has been trying for a long time to write something publishable. Sean gives a small laugh. "I think I need some of your inspiration. You playing tonight?"

"My regular at Shoreside," Ted said, mentioning the club he's played three nights a week for at least the past dozen years. "I'll be finishing around midnight."

"Good enough. How about I meet you there?"

"You got it, man. It'll be nice to see you again."

Sean flips his phone shut and walks back to work, smiling. Ted has always had a knack of inspiring him. He is hoping the magic works again tonight.

Three hours later, though, his smile is long gone and he pushes back from his desk in exasperation. The feature article is not going the way he wants. More than a few times as he labors to craft compelling sentences and paragraphs, he finds himself at an utter loss. The right words won't come, and he's having a frustrating time linking all the pithy bits of information he's labored so hard to dig up on the ten-room home. Aidan keeps intruding, and Sean can't keep his mind focused on work. So he tells his editor he needs to get some more information and leaves work early, heading home instead. He promises himself that he'll finish the article by Monday, come hell or high water.

In the quiet comfort of his apartment, he sheds his sport coat and tie, opens a cold beer and fires up his computer. His mind is tossing over a half-dozen plot lines to which he could assign Aidan's future. Yet none seem to have much substance. Everything is too vague, nebulous, and Sean worries that without serious forward progress, he might have to get rid of Aidan and start all over again – if ever he were again as inspired.

He needs to persist, he knows. He needs to pump out words until he finds the way. He recalls a college professor who told him that the easiest way to start writing a term paper was to begin writing about the first thing that came to mind on the topic, and to continue writing until he found the beginning. Sean knows he's already found the beginning; he just needs to begin finding the rest of the story.

So he chooses to force himself, and writes some more. He wants to show Ted some substance.

***The difference between a chat and a conversation***

*Aidan slipped behind his counter and checked to make sure the cash register rolls didn't need to be changed, opened the drawer to makes sure he had enough bills and coins, and scanned the cigarette rack above him to see if he needed to open a few more cartons. Finally, he took a look at the shelves of pints and half-pints and nips behind him, making quick mental notes about which needed to be restocked.*

*"What time are you outa here, Angie?" Aidan asked. Angie said "thanks" to a customer then answered, "Four. You here until closing?"*

*"As usual. Busy today?"*

*Angie gave a snort/laugh. "Not bad. Busy enough so that time doesn't drag too much." He cocked a thumb toward the back of the store. "I gotta pee."*

*"Go for it," Aidan told him as Angie waddled down the middle aisle toward the men's room in back.*

*Three customers were browsing the wine racks and four more entered while Angie was in the back. Aidan recognized five of them. He replenished his stock of Marlboros and waited until someone came to lay their selections on his counter.*

*The transactions were almost always the same, unless Aidan knew the customer fairly well: "Will that be all? ...That'll be eighteen-ninety-five out of twenty... Let me get you a bag... Thank you...Have a nice day or evening or weekend." In the tick of the clock, he'd turn his attention the next customer. At least he enjoyed most of the people who passed through his register. Some were jerks, but you found jerks pretty much everywhere. You just had to know how to stop them from getting to you. The rest were pretty good people.*

*But not Carl.*

*Carl was the quintessential jerk, in Aidan's view. The lanky guy with the shaved head and phony-diamond studs in his ears had the interpersonal skills of a hermit and, in Aidan's humble opinion, the mind of a severely disturbed ten-year-old. Without exception, Carl brought a foul, often fart-oriented or sex-oriented joke to the counter along with his six-pack of whatever beer suited his wallet at the time. Carl would roll out the joke, laugh or snicker too much, and promise Aidan – or whoever had waited on him – that he'd have more great jokes next time. And Aidan – or whoever had waited on him – would stifle a groan as Carl left the store to do whatever perverse things he did in his private life.*

*Thankfully, Carl was busy comparing prices on some of the store's cheap-beer specials, and Aidan hoped Angie would finish peeing in time to maybe take the honor of serving him.*

*Irv Anderson was there, browsing the more expensive wines. Irv owned an auto dealership not far from the store and now and then would suggest that Aidan could have a good future as a car salesman. To Aidan, selling cars for a living would be three steps down from where he was now. Every car salesman he'd ever dealt with had tried to screw him somehow or other. And Aidan didn't think he could muster the aura of sleaze that he assigned to most car salesmen. Still, Irv was a nice guy and seemed genuinely to be interested in giving Aidan a boost. Aidan always said thanks but no thanks, and always with a smile.*

*Cappy Reardon had his nose in the bins of discount wines, looking for the bargains he thrived on. He'd been retired for about ten years and came to find wines that fit his fixed income. And he always set aside two dollars a week for PowerBall tickets, dreaming of one day giving a lot of money to his children and grandchildren. The stocky, stooped, bald man looked a lot older than he was, but that was probably all the years Cappy had spent working in ship repair over at Quonset Point, most of the work outdoors pretty much regardless of the weather.*

*As Aidan surveyed the customers, Angie returned from the men's room and slipped in behind his register. "Thanks," he told Aidan."*

*"No prob," Aidan said. "When you gotta pee, you gotta pee."*

*"Felt damn good," Angie chuckled.*

*Keith, one of Aidan's favorite regulars, was the first to get to Aidan's register, dropping a case of Budweiser Light on top of the counter. Keith worked at Electric Boat, where they made nuclear submarine components, and he'd been coming to the store as long as Aidan had been working there. About a year after Aidan started in the job, as Keith paid for whatever it was that he'd bought that day, Aidan asked him what he thought of the New England Patriots' chances in the game against the Jets coming up on Sunday. Keith turned out to be a fervent Patriots fan.*

*Thus, a conversation was born.*

*Aidan had always enjoyed people and once he got the liquor store job he quickly got in the habit of either chatting with his customers, when he could, or carrying on a conversation with them. The conversations could last weeks or months or years, depending on how Aidan felt about a particular customer. The difference between a chat and a conversation, in Aidan's mind, was simple: a chat lasted the duration of one visit to his counter; a conversation was always to be continued the next time the customer showed up. Remarkably, he and the customers he conversed with almost always recalled where they'd left off two days ago or two weeks ago, and they kept it alive.*

*With Keith, Aidan had been having a long conversation. And the conversation was sure to continue.*

The warm summer evening has guaranteed that the outside decks at Shoreside are filled with talk and laughter and drinking and dancing and an infinite supply of pick-up lines. Fridays are always busy at the place, busy with people escaping from whatever kind of week they've had.

Sean had to park his car two hundred yards away from the beachside club and now makes his way though the pulsating crowd to the entrance. The bouncer eyes him and waves him in.

Ted is still playing and singing, blues at the moment, his music driving a shared empathy for hard times or lost love or tragic fates that everyone thought they shared. Some are dancing slowly to the pulsing rhythm of his music. Behind him, Herb coaxes heart-hurt sounds on his saxophone while the bass player, Dan, fingers the strings of an old bass fiddle that wears the kind of scars that seem to fit the music perfectly.

Ted usually wrapped up each performance with a bit of blues – to settle people down, he said – followed by one of his signature neo-country-rock numbers that always left his audiences wanting more. With a simple "Thank you all so much. Have a great night and safe drive home," he'd give a wave and step off the stage, heading out to the deck to have a cigarette, one of six he allowed himself every day.

Sean works his way closer to the stage and Ted spots him and nods in his direction. A minute later the number is over, the crowd applauds, and Ted bids them all goodnight. He aims a finger at the deck, and Sean gives him a thumbs up and heads out, taking time to check out the young women who have obviously dressed to catch a man's eye – more than enough cleavage, tight tops, tight jeans hung so low that a sneeze would reveal pubic hair if it hadn't been trimmed down to a neat little patch. One young woman's camisole had slipped enough so that her left nipple was advertising its presence – or her availability for more than flirtatious conversation. She's pretty and Sean knows in his gut that it would be an impossible dream that he might convince her to go home with him tonight. He's too old; she's too young. He tells himself that young women don't have enough experience to be truly great lovers. He takes a final wistful look at her nipple and goes out into the balmy night air.

Surf sounds reach the deck and Sean can barely make out the wave foam as it slides ashore twenty yards from the club. He leans against the rail and waits for Ted. From inside the club, Ted's final number is rocking the house. From the vibrations pulsing through the deck, Sean guesses that just about everyone is dancing. He looks through the window. Only a few are bellied up to the bar, mostly guys who haven't hooked up yet, he guesses.

Here on the deck, everyone seems connected. Almost all of them are smoking; smoking is illegal inside the club. Every few seconds some wafting smoke slips around his head, filling his nostrils with the odor of tobacco.

Sean has heard Ted's number more than a few times. His friend should be coming out on the deck in about two minutes.

He is anxious to tell Ted about the story, about Aidan.

***Go for it***

*"You've been drinking the same stuff forever," Aidan told Keith as he rang up Keith's purchase "Don't you ever think of trying Sam Adams or Bass Ale or Shipyard sometime?"*

*"Not really," Keith said. "I mean, I've had some before and it's okay. I'm just used to having my Budweiser."*

*Keith handed cash to Aidan. "How are things going for you these days?" Keith asked.*

*"Same old, same old, as they say. I've got a job, I wake up every morning, I've got a woman, and I eat okay. What else is there?" Aidan laughed.*

*He counted out Keith's change and handed it to him.*

*"Those things matter for sure," Keith said. "Remember what we talked about last time? Electric Boat's hiring again, in case you're interested."*

*"Me? I haven't got a thing that would qualify me to work building submarines." Aidan laughed. "If they need a bartender to set up shop during lunch hour, I could probably do that."*

*"Hey, I'm serious," Keith said. "They got good training programs. Right now they want welders – and they got a welding school. A couple of months of training and you'll be in. They even pay you while you train."*

*"How much?"*

*"Sure as hell more than you get here." Keith said. "And you'd fit right in."*

*"Is that what you do there? Welding?"*

*"That's how I started out. About eight years ago, I decided I wanted to do something different, so I got training for the sheet metal shop. Now I'm a foreman."*

*Two other customers were lined up behind Keith.*

*"I'd better move," he said to Aidan. He grabbed a pencil from the lottery ticket rack and flipped over one of the tickets. Seconds later, he handed his phone number to Aidan. "Give me a call whenever you got some free time during the day. I'll get you in for an interview."*

*Aidan began scanning the bottles the next customer was placing on the counter.*

*"I'll think about it," Aidan said, not sure if he would consider it or not.*

*"Go for it," Keith said as he turned away and headed for the exit. "You got nothing to lose."*

"What's up, man?" Ted says as he comes up behind Sean. "Here, I got you a cold one," he says, extending a bottle of Sam Adams to his friend.

Ted himself doesn't drink, although he did when he was in college. He's never exactly explained to Sean why he had given up alcohol, and Sean figures that it probably has to do with the creative process. For Ted, Sean guesses, alcohol makes writing music more difficult. For Sean, alcohol unlocks him.

"Thanks," Sean says, giving his friend a one-armed hug. "Great to see you."

"Same here, man." Ted pulls out a cigarette and lights it carefully, savoring the first inhalation of smoke and letting it out slowly so it drifts upward in a long and meandering stream in the minimal breeze of the evening.

"Christ, that always tastes so damn good."

"We're an odd pair, "Sean says. "I drink and you eschew drinking. I smoke but don't inhale, and you inhale. I think we both have some kind of defects."

"Hell, I have no problem admitting that I'm flawed." Ted laughs. "Let's head over to the back side of the deck. It's quieter there. Good place to talk."

"Lead the way, your eminence," Sean says before tilting the bottle of beer for another refreshing swallow.

Oddly, despite the dense crowd at the beach club, the back corner of the deck is virtually empty and quiet enough so both of them can hear themselves think.

"So you're writing again," Ted says as he leans his elbows on the railing. "You're a damn good writer, Sean. It's about time you tackled fiction again. Tell me all about it."

Ted has a way of making Sean – or anyone, for that matter – feel that he truly wants to know their thoughts and views and ideas and hopes and aspirations. He has that kind of knack with people. Sean wishes he could be that way too, but he doesn't think he knows how.

Sean takes a moment to organize his thoughts. He wants to explain his story clearly. If he can impart to Ted the nature of Aidan and the others in the story, Ted may give him the push he needs to keep going with the project. Somehow, over the years of their friendship, Ted has become the single person who's been able to literally press Sean to believe in his own potential. At the same time, Sean feels somehow inadequate because he has to turn to his friend in order to shed his own timidity about finding his voice and believing in his own abilities. Tonight, he pushes such thoughts aside, thankful that he can trust Ted's opinions to help him find his way.

"The main character is Aidan," Sean begins, holding out the manila folder containing the pages he has already written. For the next ten minutes, he explains Aidan McCann and Ashling and the other characters he's already created. All the while, he's watching Ted closely for any reactions, hoping Ted will find that this story — unlike the others he's shown to Ted in the past — has the kind of potential that will make it worthwhile finishing.

"After you get home, read what I've done so far," Sean says. "Let me know tomorrow if it's worth continuing."

***Isn't that up to you, though?***

*Ashling wanted to go out for the evening.*

*It was Wednesday, three days after Aidan's birthday and Aidan, for a change, had worked a day shift and got home just about five-thirty. She was waiting for him when he walked in the door.*

*She had deftly made a non-issue of the birthday cake that Aidan had missed; she and he had devoured half of it when he got back from work the next evening. He had read the birthday card slowly, probably noticing for the first time the depth of the sentiment she had chosen. They had hugged, and he'd made a point of holding her close for a long time.*

*On this evening, she had come up behind him and wrapped her arms around his waist.*

*"I believe it would be a good idea for us to go out to dinner tonight," she said, resting the side of her face against his back.*

*"You do?" Aidan said, in a teasing voice.*

*"We haven't been out at all for nearly three weeks, luv," she said, turning him around so she could face him, her caressing Irish lilt again tilting him in whatever way she wanted him to be. "It's not like us to be like this, my sweet. Your work schedule has been more than awful and we need to celebrate your birthday properly." She hugged him again and pushed her hips into his. She knew he liked it when she did that.*

*Ashling had taken him by surprise tonight. Most of the time, especially in the middle of the week, she preferred to sit home reading or watching television. Her job left her tired with its often-long hours. If they ever did anything together, it was usually on weekends. More often than not, during the week, Aidan would plan something with one of his friends and Ashling would stay home.*

*Aidan considered how to answer her. The last thing he wanted to do was extend the celebration — or non-celebration of his birthday.*

*Besides, he already had an informal commitment from his friend Keenan to get together for a few cold ones and some pool at the pub. But Keenan hadn't called yet to make the plans final.*

*Still, Aidan knew from experience that playing along with Ashling was often the best way to avoid the little bits of strife that sometimes cropped up between them.*

*"Where would you like to go?" Aidan asked her, returning her hug. "A burger joint?"*

*Ashling laughed and kissed him on the cheek. "Well, my dark and sometimes brooding boy, you'll have to do far better than that if you'd like to enjoy the pleasures this Irish princess is fully capable of providing." She scrunched closer to him, her pelvis continuing to press into his. "Sharing birthday cake was not enough; you need a special birthday evening, my sweet."*

*God, she could make him want her when she really tried. Sometimes he could resist, but tonight his gut told him he should let her have her way. She did, after all, have a bit of an Irish temper that had on more than a few occasions burned him quite considerably.*

*"That new place by the Shell gas station," she told him. "Eileen at work says she and her husband dined there last Friday evening and she says it's the best restaurant that has opened in this town in at least twenty years."*

*"Expensive?" Aidan asked, not without cause.*

*"We can afford it," she said. "We both got paid on Friday. And you had nearly five hours of overtime, did you not?"*

*"Three," he said, not admitting to another three. Aidan had no interest in keeping track of income and expenses – in fact he'd never expressed any interest in what her salary was. Ashling, though, liked to keep track of their combined income, having promised him she'd get him on a budget that would make his life - their lives - easier if not the slightest bit more luxurious. Aidan had learned soon to fib about the hours he worked and what he earned. He preferred to have the extra, unaccounted cash in his pocket. What man didn't?*

*"We have to dress up for this?" Aidan asked.*

*"Wear your good jeans, if you like, and that nice blue-striped button-down shirt you have. That should be fine enough." She gave him a brief yet intense kiss on the lips. "Let me freshen my makeup before I appear in public. Royalty has to appear well-tended at all times, you see." She slipped out his arms and headed into the bathroom.*

*Aidan went to the bedroom and changed into something moderately presentable. He was almost glad Keenan hadn't called. It had been a while since he and Ashling had had an upscale date. Usually they visited either the pub or the Italian place a couple of miles away. Good food, good drinks, and low prices.*

*Outside, The Porthole Grille looked unassuming, though the new owners had given the exterior a look that was far more inviting that the various facades on the several different family style restaurants that had occupied the corner over the past few decades. Inside, the restaurant had a comfortably urbane ambiance, like some of the better restaurants in Providence, and it made Aidan wish he'd at least worn a good pair of khakis instead of his jeans. Looking good was important to him, especially if he was in a nice place.*

*The petite hostess greeted them with a smile. "Two?" she asked.*

*"We have a reservation," Ashling said. "McCann." She turned and grinned at Aidan. He was surprised that she'd planned ahead.*

*"You're pretty sure of yourself all the time, aren't you," he said, returning her smile, though without as much enthusiasm. He liked being in control and it sometimes flustered him when she showed she could be as much in control as he."*

*"You love it," she said, still grinning.*

*The hostess picked up two menus and a wine list and said, "This way, please," and led them to a cozy table for two in the corner of a back dining room. For the moment they were the only ones in that part of the restaurant.*

*"I suppose you arranged for this table, too?" Aidan said.*

*"Would you expect me to leave anything to chance?" she said, her smile brilliant. Before he could respond, she said, "It's far nicer inside than Eileen described to me. Don't you think?*

*As he was about to agree with her, a waitress appeared and introduced herself.*

*"My name is Laura, and I'm happy to serve you tonight. Would you care to start with a drink?"*

*Ashling, as always whenever they dined out, asked for a glass of pinot grigio.*

*Aidan, because one of the guys at work had long ago convinced him that the only drink to order at a fine restaurant was a martini made to exacting specifications, said "A Tangueray martini, please, straight up, one olive, and very, very dry."*

*He didn't really care for them that much, but they had the wonderful ability of loosening him up.*

*The waitress finished writing the drink order, said she'd be back in a few minutes with some fresh-baked bread, and gave them her best "I'll take great care of you" smile.*

*After she was gone, Aidan looked around. "Not bad. This place used to be a friggin' dump."*

*"Watch your tongue," Ashling said, only half in jest. She had learned a long time ago that Aidan was sometimes less careful with his words than most men – and not always to the benefit of their image as a couple. She wondered sometimes if he was simply and incurably roguish, something that certainly had always aroused a lively interest in her.*

*"The last place here was Conte's Family Festival Restaurant." Aidan said in response "I'll eat most anything, as you know, but Conte's food sucked big time."*

*"Not all restaurants are wonderful," she said.*

*"In Rhode Island, they almost have to be great to survive."*

*"And — point made — Conte's is no longer here."*

*"That's what I'm telling you."*

*"Hasn't it become very nice now?" she said, eyeing the room's décor, her fingers sampling the smooth texture of the napkin in front of her. "I'll wager that you and I will both love this place by the time our meal is over." In her Irish way, she pronounced "you" as yew, rather than yoo. Again, she made Aidan melt a bit.*

*Aidan looked around. In the few minutes since they'd arrived, other customers had been seated in the front dining room. He and Ashling, though, remained the only customers in this back part of the restaurant. If Ashling had in fact asked for a table alone in the back room, Aidan was impressed. For a moment, he was content that they were alone.*

*He flipped open his menu and began examining the listings.*

*"I would like you to have the prime rib," Ashling told him.*

*Aidan located the entrée on the menu. "Twenty-two dollars? Are you crazy? This meal will cost us about seventy bucks?"*

*"So?" she said, again flashing him with her beguiling grin.*

*"You found a hundred dollar bill in the parking lot?"*

*"No," she said, still smiling. "I can afford it. And you love prime rib, so tonight you shall have it."*

*"And what if I prefer macaroni and cheese?"*

"It's not on the menu, my silly man."

Laura the waitress returned to the table, bearing the drinks of choice on a well-balanced tray.

"Pinot grigio for you," she said, placing the graceful wine glass in front of Ashling. To Aidan she said, "And here is your martini. Are you ready to order, or would you like more time?"

"We are most certainly ready," Ashling said, her exuberance showing. Aidan stared at her. She was up to something, and he could not for the life of him figure what it was.

"My sweet man will have the prime rib," she told the waitress. "Medium, my love. Right?"

"Right," he said, after a brief hesitation. It seemed as if she was directing the meal. Thankfully, she allowed him to choose between mashed or baked potato, and order his preferred vegetable.

"And you?" the waitress asked Ashling.

"I'll have your baked stuffed shrimp, please. With rice and asparagus." Ashling looked at Aidan. "And for me another glass of wine when the meal is served. If his martini looks low, please bring him another one as well."

The waitress thanked them and glided out of the room, leaving them alone again.

"You never do anything without a reason," Aidan told Ashling. "What's up? Are you pregnant?"

"And would you like me to be?"

Aidan stared at her and then looked away. "I don't know."

Ashling gave a small laugh. "So you need to know "what's up', is that it?"

"It would help."

Ashling leaned over the table and locked her eyes on Aidan's. "Do you want it straight, or shall I cushion it for you?"

'Cut the crap, Ashling. Don't play games with me. Let's not make this a bad night." He immediately regretted his tone of voice.

"Isn't that up to you, though?" Ashling looked around. The room was still empty save her and the man she loved.

She leaned back in her chair, holding her wine glass a few inches above the table.

"We've been together a good long time," she told him. "We get along fabulously together. I am happy to tolerate your foibles; after all, you are a man." The irresistible grin again. "But you are the man of my dreams, Aidan McCann. For all your faults, and for all that is *good about you, I have been for a long time utterly in love with you, as if you haven't noticed."*

*Aidan swallowed hard. Shit, she was going to pull the "I-love-you-to-pieces-and-can't live-without-you" bit. He took a long sip of his martini and let it burn into his throat.*

*"Ashling..."*

*"Shush, luv. For the moment you need to listen to me." She reached across and took his hand. He didn't yield easily, but she grasped it and held on. Talk of love, in whatever relationship he'd become involved in, had always made him less than comfortable. And Ashling's opening words tonight made him even more so. He cared about her – deeply, if he were honest with himself – but since the beginning he had tried assiduously to maintain the fine balance between commitment and casual cohabitation.*

*Ashling picked up her glass of wine, swirled it, sniffed, and sipped. After letting the silence build between them, she said, "Yes, I love you, Aidan. If I am completely wrong about what there has been between us, perhaps my feelings mean little to you. But, my sweet man, I could love no man more. And I want us to be married. I don't want us to be living together in this limbo between total happiness and nothing to look forward to. I would like us to be married so we can have the life we both deserve. So we can fulfill each other and grow old together." Her eyes would not let go of his, and he could not help fidgeting his seat.*

*After another long sip of his martini, Aidan leaned back in his chair, as if surrendering. There was a long silence before he spoke, and Ashling knew well enough to give him all the time he needed.*

*"Married," he said, then fell silent, staring down at the tabletop.*

"Aidan's an asshole," Ted tells Sean after listening to his friend's outline of the story, "but I can see a lot of potential in him."

Sean is trying to formulate a response to Ted's reaction when Ted holds up a hand. "Look," Ted says. "Let me compare it to what I do."

"Go for it," Sean says, anticipating a negative review from his friend

"What I'm trying to say is this: music doesn't do much for anyone unless it invades their emotions, their heart, their soul. If my music reinforces what people believe about themselves, they like me. If not, they don't pay any attention at all. I write music that I believe in. I can't write any other way."

"So?" Sean asks.

"Write what you believe in, Sean. Don't worry about readers who won't like you; there are a lot of others who will. With Aidan and the others in the story, it sounds like you're beginning to build compelling characters. But you have to go beyond just 'beginning to build them.' Make Aidan so real that people swear they've met him somewhere along the line. And Ashling, and Ian, and Margaret, and even that drunk you mentioned. Make them breathe."

"Lenny – he's the drunk I mentioned," Sean says, for no good reason. He sips from his beer and nods. "I know I need to make all of them as real as I can. It's not that. I guess I'm having a crisis of confidence."

"You're always having a crisis of confidence. You're a damn good writer, Sean. I've read your stuff."

"Maybe in the context of a reporter for a small-town weekly."

"No," Ted says. "In the context of all the reporters I read in a bunch of other newspapers. You're good."

"Then why don't I feel that way?"

Ted lights another cigarette, his last for the day. "The honest truth? Because I think you don't let yourself feel that way."

"Come on, Ted. No pop psychology."

“I’m not into that stuff, Sean. I just know you, maybe better than you know yourself.”

“So tell me my future, great oracle.”

“It’s not about that,” Ted says. “Believe in yourself, man. Do you think I’d be writing songs and playing here if I didn’t think I was reasonably good at it?”

“But you’re an accomplished musician. You’ve got an album in the music stores.”

“Sean, it all comes back to believing in yourself. I’ve wondered all along how someone with your gift for writing could still be on the outer edges of becoming a successful writer.” Ted tosses the cigarette into the sand-filled bucket on the deck. “Believe in yourself and there’s nothing you can’t accomplish. Unless, in your case, it involves the most esoteric aspects of astrophysics. You, like me, have some built-in limitations.”

Sean gives his friend a one-armed hug around the shoulder and leaves to go back to his writing. Ted shouts after him: “Give me a call on Monday. I want to read your what you’ve written so far.”

***Why in hell would I stay away?***

*There was a message on the answering machine when Aidan and Ashling returned home. Ashling checked it while Aidan headed into the bathroom. When he came out, Ashling was standing in the living room doorway waiting for him.*

*"It's your mother, luv," She told him. "You're brother called..."*

*Aidan saw it in Ashling's eyes. "Jesus Christ!"*

*"He called about ten minutes before we got home. She passed on earlier this evening."*

*Aidan dropped onto the couch. "Jesus Christ," he said again, feeling suddenly deeply guilty that he had not seen his mother in nearly a month. The Alzheimer's had left her disconnected from everyone, so what was the point? But now he wished he'd visited her one more time, talked with her about the old days, about the memories he shared with her. Maybe, God willing, she would have remembered him for a brief and lucid moment or two.*

*"Your brother wants you to call," Ashling said, sitting next to him and putting a comforting arm around his shoulders. She brushed away a tear that grew from the sadness she felt about his loss. He'd always told her how much his mother meant to him. And Ashling herself had grown wonderfully close to her over the years she'd been with Aidan.*

*Aidan sat quietly for a long time, slouched and deflated, saying nothing, only staring at the far wall of the room. Ashling knew enough to let him have his silence. After a while, he got up, filled a small glass with ice and vodka and dialed his brother.*

*Aidan ached for his mother but also dreaded having to deal with his brother and sister. He took a deep swallow as the phone began to ring.*

*"Hello," the female voice said. It was Ian's wife Anne who had always held Aidan in low regard. Aidan had always considered her a leech on his brother's success.*

*"This is Aidan. Is my brother there?"*

*"Hold on," she said in her far-too-serious voice, without acknowledging him by name. He suspected she despised him as much as he despised her – and he didn't give a shit.*

*It was at least thirty long seconds before Ian picked up the phone. "Aidan," his brother said, nothing in his voice indicating any emotion at all. It was simply a statement of fact, as if Aidan were someone – or something – to be tolerated under the circumstances.*

*What a close-knit family, Aidan thought, with a hefty dash of bitterness.*

*"So she's gone," Aidan said.*

*"They found her yesterday afternoon when they were bringing her some refreshments to drink. Dad and I and Margaret have already made arrangements. Will you be coming to the funeral?" Ian asked.*

*Aidan wanted to punch his brother. Instead he took another long sip of vodka and stayed calm. "What kind of question is that? Why in hell would I stay away? She's my mother. And what the hell do you mean that you and dad and Margaret made arrangements? Why the fuck didn't you call me yesterday?"*

*"Frankly, I was simply trying to save you a needless round trip to Boston," Ian said, not succeeding in projecting a conciliatory tone. Instead, he came across as smug. "Dad agreed."*

*"I had a right to be part of the arrangements!"*

*"You also had an obligation to visit your mother far more than you ever did," Ian said. "You've stayed away a lot in the past. You could have visited more."*

*"I did, you jerk. I saw her at least two or three times a month. Dad knows; Ashling knows. It's nearly seventy miles from here, for God's sake. How often did you see her?"*

*"It's not the issue here," Ian said.*

*"But it is the issue," Aidan shot back. "The staff told me last fall that you only came to see her once a month at most."*

*"I have a busy schedule."*

*"Fuck you." Aidan wanted to slam the phone down on his brother. Instead he said, "Where's the wake?"*

*" McGinn Funeral Home on Dorchester Avenue. Tomorrow, starting at four."*

*Aidan was fuming. "We'll be there."*

*"Good" Ian said. Then, abruptly, "I've got to go." With a click, he was gone.*

*Aidan hung up the phone and drained much of the vodka that remained in his glass. Ashling stayed close to him, moving her fingers through his hair, hoping he would know how much she cared, how much she wanted to comfort him.*

*"I could hear him," she said. "He surely has no respect for you."*

*"The bastard. He and Margaret made the arrangements without me. They didn't even see fit to let me know on the day she died."*

*"The wake is tomorrow, then?" She asked.*

*"At four," he said. Then he drained the rest of the vodka and went to get some more. An hour later, he gradually passed into unconsciousness where he sat.*

Sean feels odd about what he has written. His mother, now in her late seventies, is still alive – and here he is, killing off Aidan's mom. Surprisingly, he feels somewhat guilty and almost has to remind himself that Aidan's mother is a snippet of the fiction he is trying to write. He makes a mental note to call his mother tomorrow.

He scrolls back a half dozen pages and reads what he's written.

Is it good?

Sean honestly doesn't know. He recalls Ted's remarks about his confidence, but still can't let himself feel that he's doing good writing here. The words sometimes pour from him – usually in short bursts – but he can't stand far back enough to get the perspective he needs to see if he's doing it right. All he knows is that Aidan and Ashling and Lenny and Ian and the others are starting to come to life in his head and that he is beginning to know who they truly are. But, he asks himself, when does a writer finally know that everything is moving in the right direction?

He knows how it is when he writes a feature for the newspaper: he cobbles together the facts and the background bits and weaves them in a way he hopes will lure the reader along. More often than not, he's no more than a dozen paragraphs into the story when he senses that all is falling into place as it should.

Why isn't it as easy now?

Again, he scrolls back through the pages he's written – over three dozen. When can he expect that "falling into place" feeling? All he knows is that he'll probably have to keep writing until he finds out.

He pushes back from his computer and stands. Another beer and he will get to work once more. He heads off to the kitchen, doubt worming into his hopes. When he returns and sits again at his keyboard, he takes a deep breath and types.

Soon, the bottle of beer begins to grow warm.

***Aidan squirmed***

*At two-fifteen, Ashling urged Aidan out the door of the apartment and down to where her car was parked in the small lot at the rear of the building. Hers is a Honda Civic, newer and far more reliable than his old Taurus, which she would dare not trust on the round trip.*

*Aidan, still swimming in the shock that his mother was no longer alive, tacitly accepted Ashling's offer to drive. He would have preferred staying home, as if that would offer him some protection from the sickening reality of her death. With Ashling in charge of getting to the funeral home, he could drift mindlessly into what was to come, and so he slid into the passenger seat without comment.*

*As much as he would have begged to avoid dealing with her passing, and as much as he feared any distasteful interaction with his brother and sister, he would fail his mother if he stayed away.*

*Eight minutes later, Ashling merged onto Route 4 heading to I-95 toward Boston. Aidan was pale and taciturn and staring out the window.*

*In little more than an hour, if traffic were not bad, they would be at the funeral home.*

*The prospect of attending his mother's wake, as inevitable as it was, churned Aidan's stomach and made him long for a Jameson's bottle worth of oblivion. For all his bluster and failings, he loved his mother deeply and always felt guilty for never living up to her aspirations for him. And he always sensed that, without any reasons he could discern, she loved him more than she loved either his brother or sister.*

*He was terrified of seeing her dead in her coffin, and wondered if he could withstand the grief of her loss. In the stressed edges of his mind, he prayed that the death of his mother wouldn't kill his father with grief.*

*"Everything will be all right, luv," Ashling said, as if reading him.*

*"It was awful when my grandfather died. I was fourteen and I loved him dearly. I know it's unimaginably painful that your mother has passed on. But you will be stronger because of it, just as I grew stronger because my beloved grandfather died."*

*Aidan heard her from the periphery where he floated. He knew she meant well, yet he didn't know how to tell her he wanted only to be let alone. If the truth be told, he was afraid of hurting her feelings. She loved him deeply and cared for him deeply, yet he could not fathom what reasons she might have for doing so. Who the hell was he to deserve her? In this way, she always puzzled him. She was one of the people in his life and he had feelings for her, just as he had feelings for his other friends — male or female. How could she not see that was the limit of it?*

*At that moment, as the car coursed along the Interstate through Providence, Aidan recalled her at the restaurant, broaching the subject of marriage. Jesus! He didn't need that thorny issue to deal with just now. He was hoping she'd have the decency to stay away from the topic now that his mother had just died.*

*Ashling wouldn't, it turned out.*

*The "Welcome to Massachusetts" sign was barely five minutes behind them when Ashling seemed about to raise the topic again.*

*"We have been together for over six years now, Aidan, and we've been living together for nearly five."*

*"Sounds about right," Aidan said, too lost in his pain of loss to say more.*

*"My sweet man. Just know that I honestly love you and that I am always here for you – especially now. Fair enough, luv?"*

*Aidan squirmed and looked out his window. That's all she was going to say? He'd almost expected her to elaborate more on what she'd said at the restaurant. Now, unexpectedly, her words somehow soothed him when he sorely needed soothing. How on earth did she always manage to handle things just right? He had to admit he much admired her for it. Once again, as in so many times past, he had no choice but to agree with her. "Fair enough," he mumbled.*

*Ashling reached over and put her hand warmly on his arm. "Thank you, sweet Aidan."*

*It wasn't until they were closing in on greater Boston that she spoke again. They'd be at the funeral home in less than fifteen minutes, traffic permitting. Ashling was not one to abide speed limits. Aidan had been sitting pretty much in silence, absorbed in thoughts and memories and chewing absently on a fingernail.*

*"I loved your mother very much," Ashling said. She'd visited Aidan's mother perhaps two dozen times since she and he had moved in together, though she'd always hoped for more visits. She and Ellen had bonded quickly and were close.*

*Despite the relatively rare personal visits, Ashling and Aidan's mother managed to speak on the phone several times a month, the kinds of conversations that seemed so natural between two Irish women. Ellen McCann was wise, kindly, and tolerant – much like Ashling hoped she herself could become one day. As to why she saw Aidan's mother only rarely, Ashling believed it was simply a matter of Aidan's not wanting to lead his mother into believing that Ashling may eventually become his wife. He'd made many trips on his own to Dorchester. Only now and then would he take Ashling with him.*

*"She must have been a marvelous mother for you and your brother and sister. Such a loving woman."*

*"She did her best, under the circumstances," Aidan said, beginning to feel the first little sparks of guilt over the many things he should have said to his mother but never did.*

*"I know she was proud of you."*

*"Bullshit." Aidan turned his head further away so Ashling could not see his face. "It was always Ian and Margaret who lived up to her expectations, and to my father's. I was the black sheep. Always was, always will be."*

*"She told me different," Ashling said. "When we came to see her at Christmas three years ago."*

*Aidan kept his silence. Why in hell did Ashling insist on prattling on? He wanted to be left alone to his thoughts and his expanding grief.*

*"We were in the kitchen, she and I. You were in the parlor with the others. We were talking about many things and I listened more than I spoke, because the wise woman she was always illuminated so much about life for me."*

*"You always stayed in the kitchen with her," Aidan said.*

*"Well, I have to admit that your brother and sister were never very much my cup of tea. Not after I saw the way they treated you."*

*"So what else is new?"*

*"She and I were talking over tea," Ashling continued. "Do you realize she never once made tea from a teabag? Always she did it with loose tea, the way my mum did when we lived in Ireland. Anyway, we were talking. Or rather, she was talking."*

*Aidan grunted. He could hear his mother's voice.*

*Ashling kept speaking, her Irish accent seeming to deepen. "And she said this to me: 'Aidan is my special one. He is as free as anyone could hope to be, certainly more so than poor Ian and Margaret. They've become trapped in their lives and they call it success. No – it's Aidan that has the Irish spirit. My unruly son simply has to find himself, but I think that journey may take quite a while yet. I have faith, though. God knows I've tried to teach him over the years, and I pray that some of my teachings have sunk in on him. It's just that he has to move at his own pace, Ashling. I'm sure you know that by now. And I'm sure you know that the best thing for him is you.'"*

*Aidan could not say anything. He didn't want Ashling to hear the mourning in his voice or see the tears that threatened to roll out of his eyes. He wished she would simply shut up.*

*"I knew precisely what she was talking about," Ashling said. "She and I had had similar conversations before, but never to the depth she went during that visit. In retrospect, I think she was aware that the conversations she and I shared now and then were not long from coming to an end."*

*Ashling looked over. "Are you listening, Aidan? This is important."*

*After a moment, Aidan answered. "I'm listening."*

*"I recall you came into the kitchen to get another beer for yourself and gave her a peck on the cheek before going to rejoin whatever battle you were having with your brother and sister – and maybe even your father. I wish you could have seen the glow on her face after you did that. She looked at me and said, 'God forgive me, but he is the son who, I know, will be the best of my children. Some just take longer to reach what God has in mind for them. Don't ask me how I know. It's a mother's certainty. He is far stronger than he knows, far smarter than he admits, and far more capable of achieving his dreams than he believes. His father, so stubborn about everything, has always doubted him. But I? Never. Guide him, Ashling, but do so subtly and quietly as you would motivate an obstinate but promising man so he can finally see his true worth. Time is passing, far too quickly. Who knows where we'll all be tomorrow.'"*

*Ashling's words – his mother's words – were uncomfortable for Aidan to hear. It was difficult to believe his mother had actually said such things about him. The deep hunch that he'd long had — that she liked him more than the other two — had always been mostly wishful thinking on his part. God knows, he had never given his parents any reason to be proud of him*

*Ashling was about to speak again when Aidan raised hand. "Get off here where it says Columbia Avenue," he told her. "Go left at the bottom of the ramp. Dorchester Avenue is a couple of hundred yards ahead. Turn left there."*

*Ashling slipped off the Southeast Expressway and followed the directions Aidan had given. Once they were on Dorchester Avenue, Aidan told her the funeral home was about a half mile on the right, if his memory served him right. "Just look for the McGinn sign," he said.*

*"There's one more thing," Ashling said. "About your mother."*

*Aidan hesitated, then said, "What's that?"*

*"She always wished you had finished college."*

*"I'm sure," was all that Aidan said.*

*Ashling looked at him and shook her head. A long moment later she was turning into the funeral home's parking lot, wondering how Aidan would do now that the harsh side of life was staring him in the face.*

Ted answers Sean's call on the fourth ring. Sean wastes no time. "When do you want to read it?"

"Your story?" Ted asks.

"My story," Sean confirms. He is not sure he should be letting anyone read it just now. The story is too young, and too raw for his tastes. Maybe he should wait until it is finished. But he can't. He needs his friend's guidance.

"When?"

"Whenever," Sean replies.

"Let's get together at Duffy's," Ted suggests. I could use some chowder and clam cakes."

Tonight?"

"Seven's good for me."

"I'll be there," Sean says.

After Ted hangs up, Sean grabs himself another beer and sits in front of his keyboard. He feels as if he needs to add a bit more before he sits with his friend. He has five hours left to flesh out the story. He sips from his beer, swallows, exhales, and writes some more.

***I can't stand this…***

*Funeral homes, studiously designed to bring comfort to the bereaved, were – in Aidan's opinion – places of aching discomfort.*

*He recalled the first wake he'd ever attended, for the father of one of the members of his Cub Scout troop, dead of a heart attack (which Aidan's young mind heard as a hard attack) at the age of forty-two. The waxy-faced and unnatural-looking body in the coffin scared him to death, and he averted his eyes as much as possible, even as his own father pushed him forward to kneel before the coffin and pray. His sharpest memory of that difficult evening was of his friend Carl sitting off to the side, weeping, his red-eyed mother's arm around his shoulders.*

*And Aidan had no idea of how to comfort him.*

*The second funeral he'd attended was eleven years ago – that of an acquaintance who'd been killed in an automobile accident. Even then, Aidan had gone most unwillingly. A friend, uncomfortable paying his respects alone, had pressed him, and Aidan had finally and reluctantly relented. The wake, thank God, was around a closed casket. Even so, Aidan dreaded the visit, wished he were elsewhere, and ended up getting blessedly drunk later that day.*

*This time though, as desperately as he wished to be somewhere else with life predictable and unchanged, he could not beg his way out of the obligation to be here. From inside the car, he stared at the building, which was long ago perhaps a fine mansion for a local well-to-do banker or merchant. In one of the first-floor rooms, he knew, his mother's body was on display. He pictured his father, perhaps teary-eyed, or maybe far too shocked by her loss to cry at all, sitting by the coffin, thanking those who came for their kind expressions of sympathy. He could not bring himself to picture his mother in her coffin.*

*He shivered.*

*"Let's go in, luv," Ashling said. "There's no sense at all in sitting here in the car."*

*"Oh God," Aidan muttered, so softly that Ashling barely heard him.*

*She reached over and put her hand on his, a tender gesture she meant to reassure him of her love. "We'll go in together," she said in her soft and comforting voice. "It's hard for me to fathom that she's gone from us, and I know it must be so utterly anguishing to you, luv. But we need to honor her and thank her for raising you and loving you as she did."*

*Aidan rubbed his hands over his face then looked at her. After a moment, he whispered: "Let's go, goddammit."*

*Ashling made sure to take his hand as they walked across the parking lot, and she noticed how tightly he clasped her hand in his. Even though the wake would not begin for another ten minutes, there were already at least twenty cars there, likely more. She recognized Ian's black sedan – an ostentatious Mercedes, of course – with Margaret's slightly more modest white Lexus a short distance away.*

*She understood why Aidan was so afraid of entering the funeral home. He, unlike her, had never before lost anyone so close to him. Even his grandparents, she knew, had died before he was aware that they had ever existed, passing away and buried somewhere in Ireland. He'd never been touched by their deaths.*

*Aidan seemed to be holding back, so Ashling walked slowly, letting him approach this ordeal in his own time, in his own way. She wondered, for a brief moment, if part of his reluctance was the guilt she sensed he'd always felt for moving away to Rhode Island. Ellen had told her once that Aidan had apologized to her for leaving Dorchester. And although Ashling knew that his mother had long ago forgiven him, she knew that Aidan's guilt about his long ago departure would never leave him.*

*Ashling led him up the four steps to the imposing front door of the funeral home and pulled him ever so gently into the foyer.*

*A greeter was there, an elderly and appropriately somber white-haired man in a dark suit, white shirt, and mournful gray tie, and he directed them to the viewing room. Ashling thanked him and moved on, Aidan in tow and silent.*

*"It will be okay, luv," Ashling told him as they approached the entrance to the room. Low voices drifted out into the corridor. A sign on the outside of the room showed Aidan's mother's name.*

*"Oh, God," Aidan whispered again as he read the words. It was finally beginning to drill into the deepest part of his heart that his mother was gone forever. He didn't want to see her dead. Still, he let Ashling lead him. And he followed, his mouth dry and cold fear in his core.*

*The room was loosely filled with people. Many he recognized, but more than a few were strangers to him. Perhaps a dozen or so sat in sprinkled knots on the cushioned folding chairs facing the coffin. The rest stood in loose groups, talking in soft tones, looking around now and then to see who might have come and who was not there.*

*Those he recognized were mostly friends of his parents – at least two dozen Irish from their Dorchester neighborhood: old widow women most likely from St. Mark's Church his mother and father attended every Sunday and holy day and assorted days in between; and a smattering of old men with whom his father likely shared a pint or three with now and then at McGee's Pub or Murtaugh's who had been coworkers in years past.*

*To one side of the room, standing in front of a row of chairs against the wall, Aidan's father was being kept company by Ian and his wife and Margaret and her husband, and of course Margaret's often insufferable children. And just to his father's left, mostly obscured by people chatting together, was his mother's coffin, surrounded – no, nearly overwhelmed – by too many flowers.*

*Again he shivered and looked away, not dealing very well at all with the pain and the fear. Again Ashling pulled him forward.*

*Suddenly, he could see the coffin clearly, his mother reposed in her favorite green dress, bought years ago at Filene's Basement, looking peaceful, serene, and dead. It was nothing he'd ever wanted to see. It made him wish he had been the first to die.*

*"I can't stand this," he whispered to Ashling. "Jesus…"*

*She put her arm around his waist.*

*"I wish I could have been with her. Dying alone…"*

*Ashling pulled him close. "She wouldn't have known you were there, luv. But you can say goodbye now," she told him. "She can see you, she can hear you. She's here, whether you believe it or not. Talk to her in your heart. She'll hear you. I promise."*

*"Bullshit," Aidan whispered sharply.*

*"Believe me, luv, I know. Just have faith. Talk to her."*

*On the opposite side of the room, Aidan's father lifted his head and saw her and his son. He extended a hand, as if gesturing them to come to him.*

*Ashling pulled Aidan forward again. "Your dad is needing you, Aidan," she said. "Come with me."*

*Before they had moved five feet, though, a red-faced and obese man in a poorly fitted gray suit stepped in front of them and grabbed Aidan by the shoulders.*

*"My God, you've grown the hell up," he said, in a voice too loud for the room. "Aidan, right? By Jesus, you've really grown up, haven't you."*

*"I'm sorry?" Aidan said, not knowing who the hell had confronted him.*

*"Peter Kelleher," the man said, in a way that was far too jovial for Aidan's mother's wake. "Your parents and I have known each other for fifty years. My late wife and I would visit now and then to play cribbage with your parents."*

*Aidan looked lost.*

*Ashling stepped in. "Thank you, Mr. Kelleher. I'm sure Aidan would love to speak with you a bit later, but he needs to speak with his father now." She smiled at the man and led Aidan away.*

*Kelleher gave her a blank look. A second later, he backed away, letting her and Aidan continue on their path. She led Aidan through at least five small minglings of people, some of who recognized Aidan and called subdued greetings to him, but she didn't let him stop for anyone.*

*It took thirty seconds for Ashling to nudge Aidan within a foot of his father. She didn't fail to notice the expression on Ian's face, or the way Margaret lifted her chin and turned away as a way of saying her youngest brother was somewhat less worthy of her attention than anyone else in the room.*

*It was Aidan's father who set the tone, reaching out for his son's hand and pulling him close and wrapping him in his arms.*

*"She's gone," his father said in a soft wail that was agony to Aidan's ears. "I can't believe she's gone, your mother. She's gone...." His voice trailed off, yet he kept Aidan in his embrace, and Aidan had no idea what to do. His father had never been emotional, always somewhat distant, always stoic. And his father had never before hugged him.*

*"I know, dad," Aidan said, awkwardly returning his father's sad embrace. "I can't believe it either."*

*His father continued to hold him near. "Remember this, son." He spoke into Aidan's ear, softly enough to make Aidan wonder if he deliberately didn't want Ian or Margaret to hear. "She loved you, more than you know. Had she not had that withering of her mind, she would have wanted to say goodbye herself. I am so happy that you've come."*

*One final hug and Aidan's father let Aidan slip away. "So you've brought Ashling," he said, a slight glimmer of a smile on his teary-eyed face.*

*"Ellen loved you as well, my dear," he told Ashling, taking her hand and pulling her close for an embrace. "She always said to me that you would be the one to help Aidan build a good life. Thank you for coming to say goodbye to my Ellen."*

*"I will always miss her," Ashling told him, her heart hurting for him, for his loss. "She has for all this time been like a mother to me, and an extraordinarily dear friend. How could I ever forget how wonderful she was? I will miss her deeply and always."*

*Ashling wrapped her arms around the old man, holding him tightly. "You were blessed to have her all these years. And I know your loss must be utterly unbearable. Neither Aidan and I have the words to comfort you, but just know that we love you and will do all we can to help you in these tortured days."*

*When she released her hug and stepped back, Aidan's father looked her straight in the eye and said. "You are already, in my heart and soul, not just my future daughter-in-law, but my true and forever daughter."*

*Ashling stared at him, wiping away the tears that had already been building in her eyes. "Thank you, Mr. McCann, from the depths of my heart. It's been quite a while since I decided that you, sweet man, were a wonderful father to me as well. I could not be more blessed."*

*Aidan's father took her hand one last time. "You will stay this evening?"*

*"Of course," she told him. "We'll be getting a room at the Quincy Bay Motel down the street. And we'll be here for you."*

*"No," Aidan's father said. "Stay with me. I have Aidan's old room that he shared with Ian. Or you can stay in Margaret's old room. Both are neat and comfortable – and I would love to not be alone tonight."*

*Ashling looked at him and saw hopefulness in his eyes. "How could we refuse?" she said.*

*"It's done, then?" he said.*

*"It's done, indeed," Ashling replied, letting go of his hand.*

*When she turned, Aidan was already in deep discussion with his brother, and their expressions told of nothing good going on.*

Duffy's Tavern long ago became a Wickford icon, tucked at the side of Tower Hill Road, a short walk from Wickford Village. If you want great seafood anywhere in town, Duffy's is the only place to go. Sean, when he could afford it, would go to the tavern at least twice a month for baked stuffed lobster, or steamers, or as much of the raw bar that he could pay for.

As usual, Sean arrives early and settles into a corner booth where he and Ted can talk in relative privacy. He sits and orders a beer, then places the manila folder on the table. In it are the forty or so pages he has already written. Will Ted think they're worth the effort he's put into them so far?

The thing about Ted that has always impressed Sean is Ted's enviable ability to cut through life's bullshit. To no one else would Sean entrust judgment of whether or not he was wasting his time typing away in the isolation of his cramped writing room.

Sean resists the pull to take the manuscript out to read it one more time before Ted arrives; he's almost tempted to try to pencil in some last-minute improvements. He feels itchy; Ted's verdict may well dictate whether Sean continues writing or whether he dumps the story, as he has so many others.

The beer arrives and Sean downs half of it in three large swallows. He needs insulation in case Ted tells him an awful truth about his story. He looks at his watch. Ted, always punctual, will be here in a couple of minutes.

The waitress approaches. "Would you like an appetizer?"

Sean shakes his head. "Not now, thanks. I'm waiting for a friend."

"No problem," she says. "Just let me know when you want something." She turns and walks away. She's wearing tight shorts and an equally tight nautical t-shirt, and Sean can't help noticing her delightfully slender butt. Just as she disappears through the kitchen doors, Ted enters into Sean's line of sight.

"Ted!" Sean calls, loud enough to be heard over the ambient noise of six television sets and a loud cacophony of two-dozen intertwined voices at the bar talking about who-knows-what.

Ted smiles and points a finger at Sean, as if saying, “Gotcha.” Four paces later, he slips into the booth and reaches across to shake Sean’s hand.

“What’s up, man?” Ted asks. As long as Sean has known him, Ted has always used the same greeting when they’ve gotten together.

“Nada,” Sean says. “Want some buffalo wings? I’m hungry.”

“Why not,” Ted replies. He gestures toward the manila envelope. “The story?”

Sean nods, then looks for the waitress.

***No longer prodigal?***

*"So what did dad say to you?" Ian was asking when Ashling came to Aidan's side and took his hand.*

*"Nothing much." Aidan wanted to keep the conversation as brief as possible. As long as he could remember, Ian always churned his stomach. "He's pretty devastated by this. He's going to miss mom – a lot."*

*"He'll be all right," Ian said, without excessive conviction. "We'll all miss her. But she had a long life and she had a lot to be proud of – a lawyer, a neurosurgeon..."*

*"And me," Aidan said.*

*Ian paused briefly. "She was always disappointed in you," Ian said finally, with a certain smugness that made Aidan want to plant a fist in his face.*

*"She definitely was," Margaret offered, without invitation. "I always could tell."*

*"Neither of you understands, do you?" Ashling interjected quietly, trying to keep her voice low in respect for the occasion. She had a proverbial Irish temper and would never back down whenever she knew she was right.*

*"Your mother always favored Aidan," she said with unexpected fierceness, "always had faith in him, and always regretted that the both of you were so full of yourselves that you lost the true and dear connections to your family that good people treasure."*

*Ian glared at her, his face reddening, his fists clenched by his side. "What business do you have criticizing our family? You have no idea what Margaret and I have gone through to achieve the success we've been blessed with. What have you done with your life that sets you apart? What, for that matter, has Aidan done. Nothing!"*

*Ashling began to stick a finger in front of Ian's face when Aidan's father reached out and grabbed Ian's arm, nearly pulling him off balance. "This wake, as you should well know, is to honor your dead mother. If you and your sister cannot control yourselves, I will ask you to leave. I may be grieving, but I will not let anyone turn this evening away from the woman we are here to honor. Am I understood?"*

*Ian stared at his father as if the old man had has slapped him. Margaret stepped back clumsily, as if trying to avoid her father's sharp words. Neither of them said a word.*

*"This is your brother, your flesh and blood, and this is the lovely woman who will, I pray, one day be his wife," Cornelius said. "I expect – and will always expect – you two to treat him and Ashling with the same respect that you gave your mother or that you give me. Your mother and I did not come here from Ireland to raise children who had no respect for others. Do you hear me?"*

*Ian looked first at his sister, then at Aidan and Ashling. The disdain was not as well hidden as he hoped. "Yes, dad. We understand."*

*To Aidan and Ashling, the old man said gently, "The two of you should move on. Mrs. McElroy and Mrs. McCarthy are over there, and they would love to see you again. Go visit with them for a bit."*

*"Thanks, dad," Aidan said, not quite understanding how his family's dynamics had changed so fast and hoping that Ashling might be able to enlighten him later. For now, he felt a warmth he had not felt in years. Maybe he was no longer the prodigal son.*

*Over the course of the wake, Aidan and Ashling managed to spend a few minutes with almost everyone Aidan remembered from his growing-up years. It had always been a close Irish-American community, the neighborhood where he'd lived until leaving for Rhode Island. Over the years, though, he'd always had a nagging and not-so-subtle feeling that he'd let all of them down – nearly as much as he believed he'd disappointed his parents – by not achieving the kind of success they'd all come to America to provide for their children, born and unborn. He could recite a lengthy litany of those of his generation in the neighborhood who had made a mark in business and politics and education and whatever else there was to succeed in, and that included those that worked in factories or repairing city streets.*

*Aidan couldn't find a place for himself on that list. And now he was beginning to wonder why he hadn't tried harder or sooner.*

*At seven o'clock, Father James McGovern, who was a young curate in the parish when Aidan went away and now showed white hair and a creased face, walked respectfully to the small lectern to the right of the coffin. With calm deliberation, he pulled notes from inside his jacket, placed a prayer book in front of him, and said, "Please be seated."*

# Mulligan

The buffalo wings are spicy and Sean drinks again from the mug of beer, trying to ease the burning on his tongue. Ted, a lover of all foods spicy in the extreme, laughs as Sean takes great mouthfuls of the cold liquid.

"Easy, easy," he tells Sean. "We can't talk about your story if you're sloshed."

"I'm fine," Sean says. "I like the wings. It's the after-effects that bother me."

"I'm going to have to toughen you up."

"You've tried for years. It hasn't worked."

"One of the great disappointments in my life," Ted says. "Let me see the story."

Sean pauses and puts a hand on the manila envelope. After a moment, he says, "It's not very polished. I mean, it needs some more editing, certainly some more detail. I think I need to flesh it out some more."

Ted nods patiently, then smiles. "No excuses. Let me see."

Sean hesitates briefly then slides it across the table. "Be kind," he says, with a weak laugh. "I'm very sensitive."

Ted takes possession of the envelope and opens it, sliding the contents out in front of him. He looks at the stack of pages. "You've got quite a bit here."

"It hasn't been easy."

"You think writing songs is easy? Writing's never easy, man."

Sean signals the waitress for another beer for him, and another Coke for Ted.

"Go ahead, read it," Sean says, anxious about Ted's verdict. "I'll be quiet. You be kind."

"I'll be honest," Ted replies. "That's what you want, right?"

Sean pauses. "I want encouragement."

"I'll be honest," Ted says again.

Sean nods. That's all he expects from Ted. And it will make him or break him, he thinks.

He wants the other beer to be here.

Ted leans over the manuscript, elbows on the table. He is focused and reads slowly, sometimes returning to a previous page for a moment or two, then moving on.

Ted's head is down, and Sean can't clearly see any of Ted's facial expressions and it leaves him fretful.

The waitress brings the drinks. Sean swallows a third of his beer, wanting to feel a bit of numbness before hearing what Ted has to say.

It takes Ted over a half hour to read and sometimes re-read sections of – the manuscript. Finally, he leans back in the booth and pushes the story to the side. In the meantime, Sean has finished his third beer and is on his fourth. He's almost to the point where he might not give a shit about Ted's evaluation. Ted looks across the table at him.

"I want to read more," is all he says.

"What do you mean?"

"You've got me hooked. I want to read more."

"Don't mess with me," Sean says.

"Mess with you? No way, man. You've got me hooked." Ted leans across the table. "Sure, it needs polishing. Yes, it needs to be fleshed out. But you've definitely got me hooked."

Sean slumps in his seat. "You mean that?"

"Shit, man. How much reassurance do you need?"

"A lot," Sean replies.

"So, I'm giving it to you." Ted sips from his Coke. "Where does the story go from here?"

"I'll find out tonight when I write some more." Sean says, almost smiling.

**Whiskey, Aidan… please**

*Aidan's father returned to the apartment after one o'clock in the morning, drunk. His friend Daniel had rung the doorbell and Aidan, worried sick about where his father was, swooped down three flights of stairs at full speed.*

*"Connie needed this," Daniel said, embarrassment in his face. "Don't judge him – or me. Dying makes all of us seek to be numbed against the bitter parts of life."*

*Aidan's dad leaned against Daniel and looked up at his son. "She's gone, Aidan. Just like that, she's gone. I was supposed to die first. I was fookin' supposed to die first. The men are always the ones who are supposed to die first."*

*Aidan took his father's hand. "Come, dad." He guided his father gently through the doorway. "Thank you for looking out for him, Daniel"*

*"That's how we Irish stick together," the white-haired, red-faced man said. "I can see myself home." He turned away and went – too carefully – down the steps to the street.*

*It struck Aidan at that moment how many of his father's generation had strong Irish accents still. As always, it made him wish he had one.*

*"Come, dad," Aidan said, leading his father up the stairs. "You need some sleep. We all do. The funeral is at nine."*

*"I can't believe she's gone, Aidan. Why in heaven's name am I still alive?" His voice approached a wail.*

*Aidan paused. "Maybe because I need you now."*

*"I need some whiskey," his father said. "One more drink so I can sleep the sleep of the dead tonight."*

*"We'll see," Aidan said, guiding his father up the staircase one slow step at a time.*

*Ashling was waiting at the top of the stairs and she took Aidan's father's hand. "Come with me, Mr. McCann," she said. "Let me fix you a cup of tea and then you can sleep as long as you like."*

*"Ellen's gone," he wailed again, his eyes wet. "I was supposed to die first."*

*"That's not always how things happen," Ashling said calmly. "We take what God gives us."*

*"I hate God," Cornelius said.*

*"No, Mr. McCann," she told him gently. "God has allowed you and us to share wonderful times with Mrs. McCann. That is a priceless blessing."*

*"Fook you," the old man said.*

*She ignored him. "Sit in the living room with your son. I'll make us some tea."*

*Aidan guided his father into the living room, as full of memories as any room could be. The corner where the Christmas tree always stood. The sofa and easy chairs where his mother and father had had lively conversations and headstrong debates about everything under the sun. The coffee table where Aidan himself had fallen and earned a four-stitches cut above his left eye. He pushed his father gently onto the sofa.*

*"Ashling makes wonderful tea," he told his father. "Are you all right?"*

*"Whiskey, Aidan. Please."*

*"No. Tonight, it's tea." Aidan peered toward the kitchen where Ashling hovered over the stove.*

*"Oh, Aidan, I loved your mother more than I could ever tell."*

*"I know, dad," Aidan said, even though the truth was that his mother and father had had uncounted arguments about uncounted things where voices were raised and faces became red, and huffing and puffing were put on impressive display.*

*"Yes, we fought," Cornelius said, as if reading Aidan's mind. "Yet we loved and respected each other. Love is not whether you fight or not; it's whether you respect each other – and whether or not you are each other's best friend."*

*The old man slumped against the sofa cushions. "Whiskey, Aidan."*

*"We'll have some for breakfast," Aidan replied, trying for some relief in levity. A few moments later, he said, "Here's Ashling with our tea."*

*She placed a tray on the old coffee table that was scarred with memories, then sat on the sofa next to Cornelius.*

*"Your mother always made wonderful tea," Cornelius said, wistfully, as Ashling began pouring into the cups. "Every evening after dinner she'd make tea and milk and we'd drink it at the table with you and your brother and sister while you did your homework. Never would she make tea with teabags; it was not the way it was done back home in Armagh, and was not proper to do here."*

*"I remember," Aidan said, suddenly recalling now how much time his parents had spent with him night after academic night to make sure he did his homework well and learned his lessons. After all, it would be to the family's great shame if their sons and daughter did not do better than any of the ordinary children in the school.*

*"I was not an easy child, was I?"*

*His father took the cup Ashling offered him and leaned forward on the couch, holding the saucer in one hand and steadying the cup with the other. "You were the worst," Cornelius said to Aidan. "You always fought us every step of the way, no matter what we tried to do to help you. We couldn't fathom what was wrong with you. For a long time we thought you just didn't want to learn anything. And your mother was afraid you might have to become a trash collector – or worse."*

*The old man was slurring his words, but Aidan knew he still had his wits about him.*

*Aidan's dad sipped from his cup, savored the tea, then placed the cup and saucer on the coffee table. He looked at Ashling, then at Aidan, and slumped back against the sofa.*

*"You managed to be a great disappointment," he said to his son.*

*Ashling saw dismay and confusion in Aidan's eyes and took Cornelius's hand. "Aidan turned out fine," she said. "You and Ellen did a remarkable job raising him. If it hadn't been for you, he'd most surely be worthless."*

*Aidan cast a shocked look at her and mouthed, "What!?" She merely smiled a smug smile back at him.*

*"I want some Jameson," Cornelius said. "This is not a time for tea."*

*"It's late. The tea is better for you," Aidan said.*

*Cornelius looked deeply into his son's eyes. "When you are my age," he said with great deliberation, "you will be able to tell me what is better for me. For now, I know more about life than you, and I want some Jameson."*

*He turned to Ashling. "It's in the kitchen, the second cabinet to the right of the sink."*

*Ashling looked at Aidan, shrugged, and got up from the sofa and headed for the kitchen.*

*Aidan looked at his watch. It was already nearly two in the morning, and he'd been awake since well before the crack of dawn. He craved for sleep. Still, he knew, despite what his father had said just now, that his father needed him – needed him – not his brother or his sister. Despite his fatigue, he could not let his father down, nor could he lose this opportunity to gain at last his father's approval.*

*He waited until Ashling brought a small glass and the bottle of Jameson to the coffee table. Then he asked:*

*"If I was such an awful son, and I'm sure I was, why then are you taking me back now?"*

*"Because you loved your mother so much," Cornelius answered. "And for one other very important reason."*

*"And what reason is that?"*

*"Pour me some of my whiskey and I'll tell you."*

Between nine in the evening when he and Ted parted ways at Duffy's, and three-forty-five in the morning when he finally surrendered to fatigue, Sean completed one brief but difficult chapter. It is stuck in his mind as he drifts into sleep with his face buried in his pillow.

He wakes up at seven, his alarm clock chirping him into an irritating degree of wakefulness, his body too tired even to get up to pee, and his mind too sleep-muddled to want anything more than a return to soothing oblivion. But Sean knows better: his mind, once stirred, will never let him sleep when it has things to do.

He groans beneath his blanket, all too painfully aware that more sleep is clearly out of the question. Once his mind begins clicking away, no matter what the hour, further sleep is suddenly no more than an outlandish wish.

Sean moans a string of curses, silences the alarm clock, and leaves his bed. If this were a weekend morning, he could deal with the disappointment of waking up too soon. But this is Monday, and he is due at work in an hour. He curses again as he enters the shower, and curses more as he shaves, and continues to curse as he dresses and prepares to head out the door.

He's focused only on his story, and the prospect of working his Monday away at the newspaper is a distraction he would like to be rid of. He wants, more than anything, to spend the day crawling more deeply into Aidan's mind and moving Aidan forward in the things that will determine the ultimate course of his life. Sean knows that going to work each day in the newsroom will never accrue to his success with his story. He also knows he cannot survive without his biweekly paycheck.

When he arrives at the office, Sean says nothing to anyone and simply walks through the tiny newsroom to his corner desk and falls into his chair.

Candace, the classified advertising rep, calls out from across the room: "Hangover, Sean?"

"Just disappointment I didn't win the lottery Saturday night," he calls back.

"Right," she answers, laughing. "Want some aspirin?"

"Nah – I'm fine. Didn't sleep well. That's all."

She gives a doubtful look and begins to say something else, but Sean waves her off. "I need to work," he tells her as he swivels his chair so his back is to her. She respects him enough to keep her mouth shut.

He rubs his eyes and digs his notes out of the top right-hand drawer of his desk then fires up his computer. While it goes through its ritual of coming alive, he gets up, goes to the back of the five-desk newsroom, and pours a mug full of coffee, hoping it's stronger than it looks.

The computer is up and running by the time he returns. He takes a careful sip of coffee, swallows the magically hot liquid, sips again, then puts the mug on the desk. He'd very much prefer to be sleeping.

He scans his notes without really seeing the words. There's far too much on his mind to concentrate on the article he's been working on. Ted's comments about his story have encouraged him, and he wishes he could have spent hours more writing during the night. For nearly fifteen minutes he sits at his desk, unable to focus on what he's supposed to be doing, growing frustrated that he has to be here.

He drinks the last of the coffee and makes a decision.

"Candy," Sean says.

The woman looks up, her fifty-year old face somehow looking older than it had at the end of last week.

"Tell Phil I've got to take a sick day. I really feel crappy," he tells her as he rises slowly from his chair. "I can't work on hardly any sleep. My brain feels dead."

"What about deadline?" she asks. "Want me to…"

"Tell him I'll have everything to him on time." Sean picks up his notes and shows her. "I'll get some sleep and then work on this stuff at home."

"If that's what you want," she says, again giving him that look. She can't recall Sean's ever leaving work because he didn't feel especially well.

"That's what I want," he says, making his way toward the door with exaggeratedly fatigued steps.

Candace shrugs her shoulders and tells him to take care of himself as he closes the door behind him.

Sean feels he's done the right thing and is anxious to get back to his apartment. He has no intention of sleeping. The urge to write is too overwhelming, too insistent. Ted's words have ignited him.

As he crosses the street, he feels much better.

***You have become the good son***

*Aidan poured two fingers of Jameson into the small glass Ashling brought from the kitchen and handed it to his father.*

*"Go easy with that," he told his father. "You've already had plenty tonight."*

*"That was mostly beer," Cornelius said in protest. "Doesn't count that much, really."*

*Aidan looked at Ashling and rolled his eyes.*

*"Indeed, the beer counts, Mr. McCann," she said in a gentle voice. "We just want you to be all right."*

*Cornelius sipped from the glass and rolled the whiskey around on his tongue, closing his eyes as he finally swallowed with a soft grunt of pleasure. Then he looked at Ashling with puzzlement in his eyes.*

*"Why have you always called me Mr. McCann — and Ellen Mrs. McCann?"*

*"My parents raised me to address my elders with respect," she told him. "It's as simple as all that."*

*"You should call me Connie," he said. "That's what all my friends call me, and that's respectful enough." He gave a small laugh then turned his attention again to his Jameson. "Respectful enough," he repeated.*

*Ashling put her hand on his arm. "Thank you. I shall do that from now on."*

*The old man remained silent for a long moment.*

*Then, without looking up from his glass, he said. "You, Aidan, despite the heartaches you gave your mother – and me – you were the only of our children who showed the sort of spirit that has always made the Irish great.*

*"I've told you the stories of our family in the old country, about your uncles and some of your cousins there. They always made their*

*own way in life, pushing hard to be what they believed they were meant to be. And it was without any airs or pretensions. That sort of thing never becomes a good Irishman. A man can't find his way until he finds himself.*

*"I doubt you ever really knew it, but you have been always trying to find yourself, from the time you were a small boy. Your mother and I knew it all along. But it's something your brother and sister never did, and I still don't understand why. Ian and Margaret — they pushed themselves into being oh-so-successful and oh-so-fancy, and they lost the Irish they'd been born with.*

*"Your mother and I wondered if they didn't want to be part of us anymore because we lived in a tenement and had jobs and friends that were not fancy at all. They'd visit, but we always felt they came only because they felt an obligation to do so – not because they wanted to be here at all. It always seemed that they wished to live in another world.*

*"But you were always different, in the kind of good way I and your mother understood. And we always had faith that you would find yourself, sooner or later. And indeed you almost have, whether you know it yet or not. You have become the good son, and God help me for feeling the way I do about Ian and Margaret. But they have abandoned their hearts so that they could live lives with riches they thought were worth chasing. I'm sad that they chose the wrong road."*

*Cornelius looked up at Aidan. "Do you understand?"*

*Aidan was looking at his father, trying to absorb what he was hearing, straining to understand what his father meant. Then he looked at Ashling, as if hoping she could illuminate what was going on. She simply nodded at him and gave an encouraging smile, as if to say, "This is what is meant to be."*

*"I'm not sure I do, dad," Aidan answered truthfully. "You and mom have always been proud of Ian and Margaret; you both said so many more times than I can count."*

*Aidan turned to Ashling. "Could you get me a glass please? This is likely to be a long conversation."*

*"Of course, luv," she said. "And it seems I might as well get one for myself, too."*

*As she left, Aidan repeated what he'd said to his father. "From where I sat, it always seemed that it was Ian and Margaret filled you with pride. Not me."*

*Cornelius lifted his glass to his nose and sniffed the whiskey's aroma, as if savoring the bouquet of a fine wine, then looked away.*

*Ashling returned with a glass for Aidan and one for herself. Aidan picked up the bottle and poured some Jameson for her and then a bit more of a helping for himself. He didn't bother sniffing the whiskey; he just took a substantial mouthful and swallowed.*

*"What were we supposed to do, Aidan?" his father said at last. "Were we supposed to praise you for leaving college, for working menial jobs, for acting irresponsibly, for ignoring your potential? What were we supposed to do?"*

*Cornelius looked directly at Aidan, then turned to Ashling. "If we had praised him for making a mess of his life as he so capably did for so long," he told her as if explaining it all to a child, "he would have surely taken it that we approved his chosen path, and God knows he would have continued to stumble along until the day he died. The fact is that he nearly became worthless and we were deeply worried for him."*

*The old man was speaking remarkably clearly for someone who'd obviously had a great deal too much to drink. Ashling wondered if he'd be able to get up from where he sat.*

*"But Ian and Margaret?" Aidan asked, still not sure where his father was going with all this talk.*

*"How could we not praise them for their hard work and all the things they accomplished. They are bright and they achieved the goals they set," Cornelius said. "But it didn't mean that they had earned our respect."*

*His father drank again, and again let the whiskey roll around on his tongue for a long while before swallowing. "You can't live your life without doing what you need to do to earn and keep the respect that makes a man a real man, and a woman a real woman. Your mother was a real woman. She stayed bound to her roots without giving into any temptations to be someone she was not meant to be."*

*"But how can you say that Ian was not meant to be a lawyer, or Margaret not meant to be a surgeon?"*

*"There's the rub," Cornelius said, pointing an emphatic finger in Aidan's direction. Then he turned to Ashling and held out his nearly empty glass. "May I have a bit more whiskey, dear?"*

*Ashling looked at Aidan, and Aidan sighed. "What the hell, give him more."*

*"Perhaps they were meant to be the lawyer and the surgeon," Cornelius said, holding his glass steady as Ashling poured. When she*

*finished, he said, "Thank you, dear."*

*"But," Cornelius continued, "They didn't have to do it in a way that weakened their ties with their family, their heritage, and all that keeps us Irish. And yet they did. It was like they needed to move far from all of us, even though the real distance was only a matter of miles.*

*"Your mother was painfully disappointed, though she never showed it to anyone but me. She spoke about it rarely, but there was always pain in her voice when she did."*

*"Aidan has maintained his ties, and proudly so," Ashling said. "I've never had any doubt that he loves his Irish roots."*

*"It's been even more clear since he met you," Cornelius told her. "You've been a great and good influence on him."*

*"But I've turned into nothing," Aidan said, still not getting what his father was saying. "Look at me. I'm nobody."*

*Cornelius sipped his whiskey. "You were nobody. For a long time, you were certainly a nobody. But your mother and I believed you were trying to find yourself, to find your own worth. Of course, stubborn as you always were, you had to do it your damned own way, for God's sake. I have a feeling that you are finally ready to become the Aidan who is meant to be." His father's words were slurred, but Aidan absorbed each one carefully.*

*Cornelius turned to Ashling. "Do you understand what I'm trying to tell him?" he asked Ashling.*

*Ashling nodded. "He has changed, slowly, over the past several years," she told him. "But it hasn't been me who's helped him change. As you said, he's always been too stubborn. He has paid scant attention to what I've tried to bring to his life. But he is surely the kind of son any good Irish family would love to have. He's strong. He cares deeply about his family and his heritage. He remembers all the stories you and Ellen told him about the Irish who came before him. And he has the deepest respect for all those who came to this country to make their way, no matter what hardships they had to face."*

*She looked at Aidan. Then, to Cornelius, she said, "I've often wondered if your son has always tried to create hardships for himself so he could prove himself to you and Mrs. McCann, and to the other Irish he grew up with. Maybe even to his brother and sister as well. You know: an Irishman who can overcome the worst of life's challenges becomes someone esteemed by all."*

*Cornelius reached over and took her hand. "So you can see into his heart, can you?"*

*She smiled and then gave a rather impish look at Aidan. "I believe so."*

*Aidan tried to respond to his father, but before he could put together the words, his father said, "It's off to bed for me, before I can't walk between here and there."*

*Then, he downed the rest of his Jameson and, with great and shaky effort, rose to his feet, steadied himself carefully and walked away to his room while mumbling, "Goodnight to both of you. Pray for your dear mother, Aidan. Pray for her."*

*Aidan could say only, "I will, dad."*

*Ashling picked up the glasses from the coffee table. "We need sleep, too, luv. Your bedroom?*

*"My old bedroom," he replied.*

*She brought the glasses to the kitchen counter then returned and took his hand. He led her to the room he'd slept in as a child. It was an odd but comforting feeling to be there again.*

As soon as he returns to his apartment, Sean tosses his work-notes file folder onto his couch and moves quickly into his makeshift office. He'd left the computer running all night and all day, as if it were a way of preserving his train of thought, and now calls up the manuscript.

As always, once the story shows up on the screen, he stares at it, his mind drifting as he reviews what he's done and considers what he may want to do this time. After a while, he scrolls down to where he left off in the early hours of the morning.

Sean never really knows whether what he's written is good or not; he depends on Ted to make those assessments for him. He simply keeps pressing ahead, writing what he hopes will tell the kind of story he truly wants to tell. If this is indeed "one last time" in his quest to write one great story, he wants to dig into himself as deeply as he can and give his readers – if ever there are any – a tale that draws them into the world and the characters he feels compelled to fashion out of fragments of ideas that puff into existence in his mind.

This is a crucial point, Sean knows. He knows he must push Aidan forward, into what is for now an uncertain future. He sighs and wonders again if he is capable of carrying it off.

Even though it's still morning, he already has a cold beer sitting to the right of his computer. He feels less guilty about drinking so early in the day than he does about leaving work on a lie. But the beer frees him, and he hopes the one beer will unlock him enough so he can write well.

He takes a long swig from the bottle then puts his fingers on the keyboard and waits while his mind reflects on what he's written thus far, and on what he should add to the story.

An instant later, he pushes himself away from his desk, leans back, and covers his eyes with his hands. A wisp of a thought – of memory – has come to mind, almost too ephemeral to grasp, yet Sean senses he must seize it and flesh it out. His instinct tells him it will strengthen story – if only he can pin it down and explore it.

He rubs his eyes and concentrates, trying to keep the thought from turning into mist. He can't afford to loose the fragile grip his mind has on the memory. In a less serious time, he would have called it a senior moment.

He stays still in his chair, covers his face with his hands and concentrates intently. How many minutes he does this eludes him. After a time, though, he uncovers his eyes, allows himself a subtle smile, and slowly slides his chair back to his desk.

The memory, finally secured in the front of his mind, is about the man with the narrowed eyes he'd become acquainted with early in his journalistic career. Back then, Sean had worked for a small-city daily north of Boston – his first job as a reporter – and was responsible for covering just about anything that took place in his district.

The man whose face had cropped up in Sean's mind so many years later was the self-styled head of an ad hoc neighborhood association in an area where even the best three-decker tenements needed a lot of exterior cosmetics to make them look even passably habitable.

His name was Louis something-or-other – Sean can't dredge up his last name at the moment – and the thing about him that always made Sean uncomfortable was the look of deep and unwavering suspicion on the guy's face. It was the perpetual squint that did it. Louis Whoever gave the impression that no matter what you said or did, he did not for one second believe he could trust you.

Because the neighborhood was in Sean's district, he had to cover the association's meetings. And so he did, but never with any enjoyment or satisfaction. Most of the time he tried to fathom what the sour-faced and squinty man was thinking or planning, or what his words and actions really meant. And Sean was always amazed at the number of neighbors who turned out for the monthly meetings the man chaired.

Sean recalls having had dozens of conversations with the man over the four years he worked at the daily, none of which were remarkable or worthy of remembering. Except for one:

"I'm not stupid, you know," Louis said to him as Sean stood in the shade of an old oak in the squinty man's well-worn back yard. About thirty people were standing there in twos or threes, talking and laughing and relaxing now that they'd had their fill of grilled burgers and hot dogs. It was the annual cookout that Louis had held each of the twelve years since he'd started the association.

"I never thought you were," Sean answered, somewhat blindsided by Louis's out-of-the-blue statement. He almost said more, but let the forming words fade because he honestly didn't know what to say.

"It's the way you look at me," Louis said, obviously intent on pursuing the matter. "You always look at me in the same way."

Sean looked at Louis, but was made uncomfortable as always because all he could see of the man's eyes were slits. It was as if Louis had no eyeballs behind his nearly closed lids. How in hell do you read someone if you can't see their goddamned eyes? Was Louis angry, or was he just venting a bit about something that got under his skin?

"And how's that?" Sean asked, realizing instantly that his question sounded more like a challenge than an honest inquiry into what Louis meant. "I mean, how do I look at you," he added, hoping it made his initial question seem less defensive.

"Like you don't trust me," Louis said flatly. "When you cover the meetings or even when you come to the cookout, every time I talk you have this look on your face that tells me you just don't trust me."

Sean had to struggle not to laugh out loud. He looked down and pressed his lips together until the urge to laugh had passed. Louis thought he looked like he didn't trust the man? Did Louis have any idea at all that he himself always looked as if absolutely everything was worthy of his intense and perpetual suspicion? Christ!

Sean finally looked up. Louis was regarding him with the same sour look that always decorated his face.

"Well?" Louis asked.

Sean took a deep breath. He had no answer, so he simply turned and walked away. The man told him to come back but Sean shook his head and kept walking.

***Aidan, is that you?***

*Aidan woke before dawn. Ashling, as usual, was curled up against him as if craving his presence even as she slept. He liked it that she stayed close to him during the night.*

*In the dim light of the room, he looked at her and was glad she had stayed in his life. He often wondered why she'd put up with him for so long. A lesser woman would have cut her losses and gone; he had spent years trying to be someone who was not easy to live with. To him, a good life was a life of freedom, and being tied down was its antithesis. It was beginning to seem as if he'd been wrong all this time.*

*Aidan was not particularly good at self-examination. But after hearing all his father had to say through his whiskey in the late-night hours they'd shared in the living room, in the shadow of his mother's death, Aidan found himself – much as he had on his forty-third birthday – trying to stand back and look at himself.*

*If his father was right, Aidan thought, perhaps he still had time for some sort of salvation; forty-three was not a point of no return. If his father was right, he had enough intelligence, strength, and determination to become someone his father and Ashling and he himself could be proud of – and he began to taste a hope that perhaps his father was right. In the early morning darkness and in the quiet of the room, though, he had no idea of how to go about becoming someone better.*

*For much of an hour, he lay in bed next to the woman who clearly loved him, and tried to envision what he could do – should do – to turn himself around. In his musings, it struck him that maybe something was being handed to him on a platter, and suddenly he was afraid he might not be able to know what it was. He was forty-three – and halfway to damn-near ninety. He began to wonder if this was the beginning of the end of his life, or perhaps the beginning of the best of his life.*

*Again, he had no way of knowing.*

*Ashling stirred next to him, resting her head near his shoulder, her right arm lying across his stomach. He liked it that she was with him in the old double bed he'd shared with his brother as a child. As he lay there, memories began to flow back to him, remembrances of life here in the third-floor tenement he'd shared with his parents and his brother and his sister. Some of the times were very good times, he had to admit.*

*As he became more restless, Aidan decided to leave the bed before he woke Ashling. She'd been exhausted by the time they'd gone to bed, and he knew she sorely needed several more hours of sleep.*

*Easing out of bed as gently and quietly as he could, Aidan found his clothes and dressed and as silently as possible left the room.*

*Even now, after all these years, he could navigate the tenement in the dark. Nothing had been rearranged since he'd moved to Rhode Island. There was, for him now, great comfort in the sameness.*

*The bedrooms were on one side of the tenement, sharing a small hallway that opened into the dining room which had long ago been turned into the room where everyone sat to watch television. The built-in china cabinet's glass doors displayed crammed papers and many small boxes and carelessly stowed bits of memorabilia. Aidan guessed the family's entire history could be written in detail using the cabinet's contents as source material.*

*As he came out of the hallway, Aidan noticed that they must have forgotten to turn off a kitchen light before going to bed. Judging from the faint glow, the small lamp on the kitchen table must have been the one left on. It was a welcoming light and he moved toward it.*

*Before he reached the kitchen door, he heard his father calling softly, "Aidan, is that you?"*

*"It's me," Aidan answered as he rounded the corner, somewhat but not especially surprised that his dad was awake so early. His father was standing in front of the coffee maker, filling it with water, still dressed as he had been when they'd been talking – and drinking – in the living room.*

*"Do you like coffee, Aidan?" Cornelius asked. "I don't recall. Your mother always made the coffee, and I was always off to work before you came to breakfast."*

*"I didn't then, but I do now. Black will be fine," Aidan said. "How come you're up so early? I thought for sure that you'd be dead to the world until at least noon."*

*His father added scoops of coffee to the filter he'd placed in the machine. "I never sleep later than six o'clock. Besides, your mother has been on my mind. Sleep is hardly possible even though I'd welcome escaping to it now."*

*"Sit at the table," he told Aidan as he reached into the cabinet and retrieved two mugs. Aidan recognized one as the mug his mother had*

*always used for her daily cups of tea. The other was his father's, whether for tea or coffee.*

*The old man placed the mugs on the table, giving Aidan Ellen's mug, then sat across from his son to await the coffee's brewing.*

*"It's so hard to believe she's gone," Aidan's father said. He gazed away for a long moment. He knew his father would not allow himself to shed a tear if anyone was present. "I suppose I'll just have to accept the fact that God wanted to take her."*

*Aidan wasn't sure what to say that might comfort him. "We'll all miss her," is all he could say at the moment. "We'll all miss her," he repeated, his voice fading*

*"Her death teaches us something," Cornelius said. "Do you know what that is?"*

*On little sleep, Aidan was not prepared to answer questions of any depth, so he just shook his head.*

*"It's that we always have to treasure who we have in our lives," Cornelius said flatly. Then, with a quick upturn of his head, the old man looked directly into Aidan's eyes. "Do you love Ashling?"*

*Aidan absorbed the question and hesitated.*

*"It's a simple yes or no, my boy. Do you love her?"*

*Aidan turned his head, as if looking toward the bedroom where Ashling was sleeping.*

*"I suppose," he answered.*

*His father waved the back of his hand at him. "You can't simply suppose you are in love with someone. You love or you don't; it's that simple."*

*Aidan took a deep breath and let the air out slowly. "In that case, I do."*

*"You should tell her. Your mother told me at least four years ago that Ashling said you never told her if you loved her or not. Yet you know that she loves you dearly and has for a long time." Cornelius saw that the coffee machine was finishing its brewing cycle and rose from the table to fetch the pot.*

*"I'm not a stupid old man. I saw how she was looking at you last night," he said over his shoulder. "There is more love in her eyes that you can appreciate, and you seem never to notice." He picked up the pot and turned back to the table.*

*"She's right for you, you know." he asked as he poured coffee into Aidan's mug. "What is it that's holding you back?"*

*"I don't know, dad," Aidan said finally. "I guess I never thought I could be a husband or whatever. She wants to get married, you know."*

*"As if that hasn't been obvious for a long time – at least to the rest of us." His father filled his own mug and returned the pot to the counter. "Don't tell me you couldn't see it."*

*"Mom saw it too?"*

*"How could she not? Ashling and your mother had many long conversations."*

*Aidan looked deeply into his coffee mug, unsure about how to deal with the topic his father seemed intent on pursuing. The kitchen was silent, solemnly silent, for several long moments. Cornelius kept looking at his youngest son and waited for him to speak.*

*"I don't trust myself," Aidan said, finally.*

*His father seemed surprised by Aidan's statement and shifted in his chair, sipping from his mug and buying time to figure out what his son meant.*

*Aidan, to his father's chagrin, didn't add anything to his terse statement. Finally, Cornelius asked: "And why do you not trust yourself?"*

*"This is quite an interrogation," Aidan said. He tried to hide his annoyance, but it was too friggin' early in the morning for this kind or any kind of serious discussion, especially with his mind still saturated with fatigue and whiskey.*

*Cornelius paused for a long moment. "Before she could no longer speak, your mother made me promise that you and I would talk about these things one day. She knew from early on that Ashling was the right one for you."*

*Aidan looked away.*

*"So," his father asked, "what is all this stuff about not trusting yourself?"*

*Aidan slouched in his chair and stared into the table. "Because I never felt anyone could trust me."*

*His father looked at him, puzzled. He began to say something then shut his mouth looked away.*

*Aidan looked away too. Then, in little more than a whisper, he said, "Just look at me."*

At four-thirty, Sean dials Ted's cell phone. His shift at Electric Boat ended at an hour earlier and he was normally home by four.
Ted answers on the second ring.

"Mister Sean!" he says with his typical enthusiasm. "What's up, man?"

"Same old shit, truth be known. Are you playing tonight?"

"A night off, for a change." Ted sounds relieved. "Actually, two nights off. Two big private parties at Shoreside. Jane's happy about it. So's Allyson. I don't get a lot of time off when the summer's in full swing."

"Cool," Sean says. "I won't bother you, then. You need family time."

"Sounds like you need to talk."

"Nothing important. It can wait."

Ted chuckles. "My sixth sense tells me otherwise."

"I mean it," Sean says, "it can wait. I just need to bounce a few things off of you – about the story, I mean."

"You need my wisdom and advice. You'll fidget yourself into a frenzy otherwise." Ted laughs out loud. "Hell, I know you better than you know yourself."

Sean exhales audibly. "You're being a smart-ass."

"Let's get together. Jane and Allyson are off shopping. Knowing them, they'll be gone for at least another two or three hours, maybe more. Duffy's?"

"Dugan's," Sean says, feeling a sudden urge for at least an ersatz Irish environment. "Twenty minutes?"

"A half hour. See you there."

"Fine by me," Sean says.

Sean places the phone back in its cradle. Two minutes later he's at his desk, printing out the last few chapters of his story.

He still doesn't understand why he needs Ted's approval, but somehow every good word from Ted has always helped him move forward. It's been that way a long time. On reflection, Sean accepts that he has always sought Ted's judgments. He supposes it has to do with his own inability to see his work objectively. He's a decent writer – the thousands of news and feature stories he's written over the years, and the half-dozen awards he's won, are proof of the breadth of his ability. Yet, he can't convince himself that he can translate his life experience into a compelling story. Sometimes, his doubts keep him dithering about details and words and plot lines — and the story only inches along. Ted is the only person he knows who can kill his needless unconfident perseverations.

But this story – he knows in his heart – is truly his last chance. Should he not succeed this time, he'll likely spend his latter years sitting glumly in a rocking chair, ruing his failure to live up to the potential he hoped he had.

Ted's guidance counts. It's almost as if Ted has become, over time, his mentor. Ted, after all, had already proven himself to be a creative success. Forty-eight songs written and performed, thirty-six of them on three albums, two nominated for Grammy Awards.

As for himself, Sean has always been stuck believing he has done only prosaic things that in retrospect seem mundane, to say the least, in comparison to his friend's successes. If there were to be a saving grace in his otherwise ordinary life, this one story – if it turns out to be what he is beginning to envision – is his only salvation. Of this, he is utterly certain. And it's scary.

Dugan's Ale House did not quite suit Sean's idea of what a true Irish pub would be. Ten flat-screen televisions lined the walls around the large rectangular bar, most of them tuned to sports channels. There were tables filling one end of the large room, most of them high-tops, for those more interested in eating than drinking. And there was an obligatory dartboard that showed few signs of any heavy use. In an adjacent room, the main attractions were a couple of pool tables.

Still, the décor had a respectable Irish theme — signs and posters covering the walls in exuberant fashion — and it was possible to get a fair variety of Irish beers and ales and stouts, as well as some fine Irish whiskeys. For this town, it was quite passable, although Sean sometimes found it too noisy for his taste.

Ted and he had met here for conversation perhaps fifty times over the past five years, the last get-together here about two months ago.

A corner booth by the front window is available and Sean slips into it. He can see the entrance from where he sits. One of the two waitresses idling by the bar heads his way. She's slender and auburn-haired, a ponytail swaying as she walks. She and Sean have been on a first-name basis for the past three years.

"Waiting for a friend, Stephanie," he tells her. "I'll order when he gets here."

"No prob," she replies, then quickly pirouettes and heads back to her spot by the bar. Seeing her always makes him wish he were fifteen years younger.

Ted arrives a few minutes later and spots Sean right away.

"You caught me at the right time," Ted says as he slips into the booth. "Jane called right after I spoke with you. She and Allyson are going to have dinner together so they can extend their shopping at least until seven or so."

Ted looks over at the pages stacked to Sean's right. "You didn't bring much."

"It's all I've done since we met last."

Stephanie returns. "Ready for some drinks?" She looks at Ted and a smile grows on her face. "Hey, I know you! You're Ted Cooper! I've got one of your albums!" She's almost breathless. "I love your music! I've seen you at Shoreside about twenty times."

Ted smiles. "If I had a million fans like you, I'd be famous." He laughs. "Next time you're there, come and see me. I'll treat you to a drink.

Stephanie beams. Then, catching herself, she spurts, "I'm so sorry! I meant to take your drink order.

"Don't worry about it," Ted smiles. "We're in no rush. I'll have a ginger ale, please."

Sean horns his way into the dialogue from which he'd ben briefly excluded. "Jameson on the rocks for me."

She jots down the order and smiles at Ted again. "My name's Stephanie – if you need anything."

"Gotcha," Ted says. "Thanks."

Her smile broadens as she spins and hurries back to the bar. Seconds later she's huddled together with the other waitress and the bartender.

"Maybe some day someone will recognize me that way," Sean says, somewhat jokingly.

Ted looks across at him. "You'll get there. It's just a matter of time."

"No – it's a matter of finally getting it right this time."

Ted nods then reaches across the table to pick up the chapters. "Mind if I start reading now?"

"I need to explain a few things before you…"

Ted holds up his hand. "Come on, man. No excuses, no explanations. Let me dig into these chapters without any preconceived notions."

Sean nods, then leans back in the booth. "Go to it," he says. "I've got enough TV screens here to keep me busy for now."

Ted sets the manuscript on the table in front of him and begins to read. He takes his time, absorbing every word.

Sean waits, hoping for the best, his mind scouring his memory of the pages, trying to figure where he may have screwed up the story. Was this chapter too convoluted, or was that chapter superfluous? Or was the other chapter a bit too intense or corny or unclear? Are the characters genuine? Is the dialogue helping the story to unfold?

He hates the pressure he is putting on himself.

Stephanie returns with their drinks and smiles at Ted even though he doesn't notice.

With his Jameson in front of him, Sean watches Ted closely, seeking clues as to his friend's reaction to the newest chapters. Sean is unable to convince himself that Ted will like these new pages better than the earlier ones. But Ted, as always, reads carefully and without expression.

After a bit, Sean looks down and lifts his glass, and lets the Jameson caress his tongue.

As he waits for Ted to finish with the new chapters, it strikes Sean that Ted is his only real friend. Sean knows a lot of other men and sometimes gets together with them for a drink or to catch a basketball game or hockey game in Providence. He has known more people for much longer than he's known Ted, but in the seventeen years since they met – when Sean had been assigned to write an in-depth article about Ted's music – the bond between them had grown. It was Ted to whom Sean turned most often for company, conversation, and advice.

He is more than thankful for their friendship. But he hopes that the friendship won't tempt Ted to give more glowing opinions than he might otherwise. This story is far too important, and Sean's hopes for it are far too great.

***We are human…***

*Cornelius was not sure what to say to Aidan. He didn't quite understand what to make of what his son had just told him. The lad didn't trust himself. What kind of statement was that, for the love of God?*

*Needing a moment to think, he rose from the table and walked slowly to the coffee maker. "Would you like more coffee, Aidan" he asked his son.*

*Aidan would have preferred a stiff drink. The conversation was stressing him, but he couldn't bring himself to leave the table despite his deep desire to escape his father's probing.*

*"Sure," he replied, limply.*

*Cornelius brought the pot to the table and refilled Aidan's mug, then his own. Then he placed the pot on the table and, with a sigh, sat back down.*

*For a while, Cornelius just stared at his son, confused.*

*"Tell me what you mean about trust, Aidan," Cornelius said finally in a kindly, coaxing voice. "You know, I've had a lot of experience with trust. I trusted that I could leave Ireland and build a life here in this new country. I trusted I could find a good job and support my family. I trusted that your dear mother and I could raise good children. I trusted that you and your brother and your sister could make good lives for yourself. And I have trusted in God and in the Blessed Virgin and the Church. I have experience with trust."*

*Cornelius paused. Then he leaned across the table toward Aidan. "Trust me to understand what you're trying to say," he said, earnestly.*

*Aidan felt uncomfortable, yet – oddly – his father's tone was tempting him to open up.*

*Aidan had never opened up; it was his nature, he believed, to keep everything to himself. Letting others peek inside your soul, your mind, your feelings – it never led to much good. Keep things to yourself and no one can screw with you. As the conversation with his father, in the pre-dawn intimacy of their kitchen table talk, he wasn't sure he could do as his father asked.*

*Cornelius, for his part, was ready to give his son all the time in the world. He'd learned patience a long time ago.*

*After a long while in silence, Cornelius said softly. "Your mother…."*

*Aidan waited for his father to finish, but Cornelius let the words waft away. Looking down into his mug, Aidan said, "I disappointed her – and you. I'm sorry."*

*"She trusted you to find yourself," was all his father said.*

*Aidan took a deep breath and slouched in his chair. Pushing his mug to the side and laying both hands flat on the table, he looked away and – hesitantly – began to speak:*

*"You can't trust yourself if you've never done anything right. You can't trust yourself if the important things you try to do just get totally messed up. You can't trust yourself when everybody thinks you're a loser."*

*"A loser? You are no such thing," his father said. "You are a…"*

*"Name one thing I've ever succeeded at, dad," Aidan said, interrupting him. "Name one single thing. You and mom were disappointed that I dropped out of college. I didn't drop out because I wanted to. I dropped out because I couldn't cut it. I couldn't get A or B on anything I did. Compared to Ian and Margaret, I sucked. Christ, I was lucky to get a C in anything." Aidan lowered his head and fell silent.*

*Cornelius leaned back in his chair and pondered his son. Here in the kitchen, he wished he had had this conversation with his son a long time ago, but he never really knew what to ask, what to say. How do you talk with someone when you don't understand what they're about? It was Ellen who had enlightened him, maybe ten years ago now. But he had kept away from a conversation – or, what he really feared, a confrontation with the son who had become prodigal in his own fashion. Why hadn't Ellen spoken with the boy? Cornelius soon guessed the answer: she knew her husband had to arrive at this point on his own, otherwise the conversation would be without the substance and passion that father had to impart to son.*

*"Ian told me once," Aidan said, finally speaking again, mostly to fill the sound vacuum that weighed on him. "Ian told me once that I'd be wasting time if I stayed in college. He said I wasn't meant to follow in his footsteps – good grades, important honors, praise from professors. He told me I was either dumb or a slacker. In either case, I'd be wasting your money and my time."*

*"And you believed him, of course."*

*"Because you and mom were always praising him and urging on to higher things. And you did the same with Margaret; she was the prima donna of our family's academic world. Even Ian was jealous."*

*Aidan did not allow himself to look at his father. "You boasted about them to family and neighbors. I don't ever remember you boasting about me. You never gave me much praise. And when you praised me a bit for doing something right, you watered it down by criticizing me for not doing it as right as it should have been done. 'It's good you got a B on that test, Aidan. But if you had only tried harder, you could have had an A.'"*

*"Parents can't always do the right thing. We are human..."*

*"So are children. So am I."*

*Soft footsteps behind him made Aidan turn. Ashling shuffled sleepily into the kitchen, wrapped in a blanket, her eyes not yet completely open.*

*"Good morning," Cornelius said to her, doing his best to smile. "I don't suppose you would like a cup of coffee."*

*"Good morning," she said, her voice croaky from sleep. "Have the both of you slept at all?"*

*Neither man answered her.*

*She looked at Aidan's father. "Yes, please, coffee would be most welcome." She made her way to the table and sat.*

*Aidan reached out and put his hand on hers. "I managed a couple of hours of sleep. Dad was here when I woke up," he said to her. "I have no idea if he slept at all."*

*"Not a wink," his father called back as he fussed to make a fresh pot of coffee. "I can't imagine how a man can sleep while his wife is laid out in her coffin." He came back to the table and sat. "But I'll be fine. And coffee will be ready in a bit."*

*"We need to get ready soon for the funeral," she reminded them. "I asked, and the funeral home told me we should be there no later than a quarter to nine. The funeral Mass is at ten."*

*Cornelius nodded somberly. "I'll get ready as soon as I have a bit more coffee." Then he looked fondly at Ashling. "You didn't sleep much yourself, my dear."*

*"Enough to get me through the day," she said. "Are you doing okay?"*

*"No," Cornelius said. "But there's no need to concern yourself about me. I'll survive until my time comes."*

*Ashling put her hand on the old man's arm. For a long moment, the three of them sat in silence, the coffee maker burbling on the counter.*

*Finally, Ashling asked, "Is anyone interested in breakfast?"*

*"I may have some of the eggs and ham in the fridge," Cornelius said, pushing away from the table. "Let me look to see if we have enough."*

*"You stay seated there, Mr. McCa... — I mean, Connie," Ashling as she moved toward the refrigerator. "I shall do the cooking this morning. We can surely do with whatever is in the house."*

*Cornelius smiled and thanked her. In this moment, he sorely missed the comfort of his wife's presence in the kitchen.*

*Aidan leaned back in his chair, looking at his father as his father watched over Ashling as she browsed through the refrigerator. Why was it that he and his father had never had such a conversation before?*

*All during Aidan's growing-up years, his father had been the strong, mostly silent presence in the family. It was he who meted out the discipline, usually only after Aidan's mother pointed out the need for a heavy hand.*

*True, his father often worked two jobs or took on as much overtime as he could manage whenever the opportunity arose. He recalled his father coming home and slumping at the kitchen table to await his cup of tea. Perhaps his father had been just too tired to talk with him.*

*Yet Aidan had memory snippets, from years ago, of conversations his father had had with Ian and with Margaret – brief but pithy exchanges about their academic successes or the extracurricular activities they excelled in. Ian, who played rugby and shone as a member of the debate team and who, to Aidan, seemed to be his father's favorite son. And Margaret who won science prizes and did amazingly well on the women's track team, turning in superlative performances in cross-country, hurdles, and once setting a school record in the mile.*

*Sitting now in the kitchen, Aidan could not remember a single serious conversation his father had had with him, except for scoldings and complaints about how he fared in school – and -- the last one – the lecture he received when he decided to drop out of college.*

*Aidan was still pissed off about that.*

*There were at least forty people at Ellen's funeral, most of them friends and neighbors, all of them old. Ellen's only relatives were her daughter, her two sons, her husband, and her sister, Alice, who still lived near where she and Ellen were born. Ellen, in her final years of her disease, would react blankly at the mention of Alice's name. The Alzheimer's had left nothing.*

*Aidan thought his mother would have approved of how the funeral went along: simple, with a quiet elegance and an incense-laced atmosphere of prayers being wafted to heaven on her behalf.*

*A woman parishioner sang softly from the church's choir loft, her soprano voice surprisingly soothing.*

*Aidan and Ashling sat with Cornelius in the first pew. Ian and his wife and Margaret and her husband and two children sat behind them.*

*Aidan and his father, in a quiet conspiracy, had each managed to imbibe a hefty shot of whiskey before leaving for the funeral. Aidan, sitting and waiting for the mass to start, was thankful he had done so. A sidelong look at his father told him his father was better off for it as well.*

*It was not until the mourners had gathered in the cemetery, around the hole in the ground that would contain Ellen's coffin, that Cornelius began weeping softly. Ashling put her arm around him. Aidan stayed close. Ian and Margaret simply watched.*

# Mulligan

Early on Friday afternoon, Sean is taken in a wheelchair from his room to the hospital exit where a cab will be waiting to take him home.

He feels drained, weak. The gastroenterologist assigned to him estimated he had lost as much as three pints of blood, but Sean feels as if he'd lost maybe twice that much, given how shaky he is. He wishes the hospital would have kept him another day or two; he'd probably feel stronger by then. But he knows about the demands of health insurers. He's done news stories about how they push sick people out of hospitals to keep costs down. Being the one now pushed, not quite forty-eight hours after a panicked twelve-mile ambulance ride to South County Hospital and an overnight stay in the intensive care unit, he resents being forced to go home before he feels he's well enough.

The young man wheeling the chair along the corridors toward the exit pushes him in silence. Sean is thankful because he is in no mood for talk anyway. He's anxious to get home and crawl into bed and sleep for as long as he can. Perhaps he will wake up feeling more alive than he feels now. In his hand, he carries his discharge papers and prescriptions the doctor gave him. One to help him sleep, the other to help his unexpected ulcer to heal. He'll have to ask the cab driver to stop at the pharmacy around the corner from his apartment.

The day before yesterday, as Ted sat across from him at Dugan's Ale House reading more of his manuscript, Sean suddenly felt a rapidly growing discomfort in his belly, the pressure building with startling quickness. Within less than a minute or so, he felt as if he was about to pass out, felt his skin growing sweaty and cold and clammy. He pushed his chair back abruptly, ready to dash to the men's room. Ted looked up, startled by Sean's sudden move and shocked by his sudden extreme pallor. Before Sean could say anything, before he could even jump to his feet…blood, a thick gush of blackish blood gushed from his mouth and he began slumping to the floor, the black fluid spreading over the worn hardwood, his panicked mind telling him he was dying.

He woke up in the ambulance, however long later, his shirt open, cardiac leads stuck to his chest, nasal cannulas feeding him oxygen, the siren whooping and screaming. He was propped up on the gurney, not sure how much alive he was, fighting not to vomit again. Through the rear windows, he could see cars moving back onto the road after having yielded for the flashing lights and the howling electronics.

The EMT working on him began asking questions about how he felt, about when he'd first noticed symptoms, about pains he might be feeling, about allergies, about his age and medical history – all questions that Sean felt too weak to deal with.

In the emergency room, a handful of calmly hurried nurses and doctors converged on him. Blood pressure cuffs, temperature, abdominal palpations, and more questions – what had he eaten, what medications was he taking regularly, had anything like this happened before, how much does he drink, when did he eat last, and other questions and comments now lost in the fog of the emergency.

In the meantime, a phlebotomist started an IV drip in his right arm while the doctor told him he'd be receiving an anesthetic so they could do an endoscopy.

"It seems likely that you have a bleeding ulcer," he said to Sean. "We need to get a good look to see what we're dealing with. You'll be asleep for about half-hour or so."

Sean welcomed the respite from his anxiety.

The doctor had been right about the ulcer and he had found two additional ones. To the doctor's question about whether he experienced heartburn or other stomach related symptoms, Sean told him that he had on occasion, but not enough for him to become concerned.

"I'm prescribing some Nexium," he was told, for his gastric reflux.

"You've had reflux for many years, judging by the condition of your stomach and your esophagus," the doctor said.

The doctor added that abstention from alcohol, blood thinners, aspirin – and a few other things on a list the doctor gave him – would let the ulcer heal so he could return to a normal life within a couple of months.

Sean agreed to the doctor's advice, then closed his eyes and gave silent and prayerful thanks that he didn't have some kind of terminal condition.

The cab is waiting and the young man behind the wheelchair pushes him to the cab's rear door and opens it. Sean stands up slowly, his legs not as strong as they had been only two days ago, and slides into the back seat. The young man mutters, "Take care" then turns away to head back into the building.

Sean gives the driver his address and asks him to stop at the pharmacy in Wickford before dropping him off at home.

"You got it," the driver says. As he pulls away from the building, he asks, "You been in there long?"

"Almost two whole days," Sean replies. "I swear they'd push you out tomorrow if you have a heart attack tonight."

"I hear ya," the driver says, launching into a rambling story about one of his aunts who'd been admitted and discharged umpteen times from different hospitals for different ailments. Sean is content to let him talk. All he wants now is to be home again.

The driver stops his continuing narration only when he pulls up in front of the drug store twenty minutes after leaving the hospital.

Fifteen minutes later, Sean is back in his apartment. Before he can sit, Ted phones.

"Hey, man, I thought you were going to call me when you were being discharged," he says, clearly upset.

"I didn't want to bother you at work. I took a cab."

"I called the hospital and they said you'd left already. Are you doing okay?"

"So the doctor says. I feel like I've been sucked on by a vampire gang."

"Look, I'll be over in a little while. I got out of work early and I'm getting some stuff at the supermarket – prepared foods, some stuff you can fix for yourself. The doctor didn't say you can't have pizza, did he?"

"I can eat just about anything, he said."

"I'll bring some pizza and some beer for you."

"No beer."

"No beer?"

"No alcohol. Period."

"Never again?"

"I'm tired. I'll tell you when you get here."

Sean lies down on his sofa, the only spot in his house that lets him get a partial view of Wickford Harbor. He wishes he could sleep, but the idea of letting himself slip into unconsciousness makes him nervous. There shouldn't be any more bleeding, the doctor said. But Sean had his doubts. Anyway, Ted will be along soon, and Sean is thankful for his friend's caring.

The bleeding ulcer had been a shock. Sure, Sean had had occasional heartburn – but who didn't? Sean begins to dig into his memory, trying to figure if there was anything he could finger as the cause. His natural instinct was to get into some serious research on the causes and outcomes of bleeding ulcers, but he had no strength for such an effort. Anyway, he's too worn to do much thinking. When he drops off to sleep, he is unaware of his transition away from wakefulness.

A hand on his shoulder wakes him after whatever amount of time had passed.

"Good thing you left the door unlocked," Ted is saying as Sean focuses his eyes and tries to orient himself. Ted is crouching next to the sofa. "I'll bet they shipped you out of the hospital without feeding you. Right?"

"Hey," Sean says, a groggy greeting for his friend. "Got some toast and tea this morning around seven before they evicted me."

Ted stands. "I've got some chicken soup and some nice, crusty Italian bread. You up for that yet?"

Sean manages to pull himself up to a sitting position. The effort tires him. "In a few. Thanks for coming."

"Friends take care of friends."

Sean tries to stand but thinks better of it – at least for the time being.

"Besides," Ted adds, "I never got a chance to tell you what I thought of the chapters you showed me when you decided to take a side trip to the hospital."

"You still have the pages?"

"At home. I'll bring them the next time we get together."

Ted puts the chicken soup container on the kitchen counter and sets the Italian bread on the table. After a quick look into Sean's refrigerator, he says, "There's nothing edible here."

"I usually do take-out."

"That could give you an ulcer."

"You going to stay a while?" Sean asks.

"I told Jane I'd be home for dinner, so that gives me a couple of hours."

Ted pulls a kitchen chair into the living room and sits across from Sean. "You really freaked everyone out at Dugan's," he says, chuckling

"Hell, I freaked myself out." Sean gives a weak laugh.

"Some guy ran over from the bar saying he knew how to do CPR and mouth-to-mouth and lots of other stuff. He took one look at you – believe me, you looked friggin' gory with all that blood on your clothes and on the floor and on your face – and he changed his mind. He did manage to take your pulse though."

"I take it I had a pulse."

"Apparently so." Ted chuckled. "And you were breathing."

"Who called the ambulance?"

"The bartender yelled that she was going to make the call, but some guy was quicker on his cell phone."

“I think I remember you being there in the ER.”

“I was there. They let me see you once they had things under control, but you were kind of wavering about passing out again. Then they gave you a sedative or something so they could put an endoscope down your throat. After that, there wasn’t much I could do, so I headed home.”

“Please thank Jane for visiting me yesterday afternoon. The nurses were very nice, but having Jane stop by really brightened my day.”

“She promised me she’d check in on you after her shift in the neonatal unit.”

“I’m glad she’s a nurse,” Sean says. “She stopped by the nurses’ station and got an update on me. She reassured me that I was almost certainly going to live.” Sean laughs. Then, with effort, he stands up slowly and stretches. “I’m tired of lying down and tired of sitting. And I’d give anything for a beer.”

“You’re out of luck for a while, I guess.”

Sean walks in small steps to the kitchen, breaks off a chunk of Italian bread, and makes his way back to the sofa. He hates feeling so weak.

“So tell me what you thought about the stuff I showed you,” he says to Ted as he sits.

Ted stares at Sean for a moment. “You might actually turn out to be a decent writer one day.”

“So you didn’t like it that much?”

“Au contraire, or whatever the French say. It was great. But just a tip, though: Push Aidan a bit. He’s got to evolve more.”

“He’s evolving,” Sean says. “I need to evolve with him. That’s the only way it’s going to work.”

“Knock yourself out,” Ted says. “I think you’re on the right track.”

Sean leans back on the sofa and closes his eyes briefly. “If I have enough energy tomorrow, I’m going to write some more. Doctor told me to take at least three days out of work because I lost so much blood. I might as well spend my time writing.”

“Soup now?” Ted asks.

“As long as you serve it. That little walk to the kitchen wore me out.”

“You’re getting old and decrepit, my friend.”

Later, Ted leaves and Sean sleeps. When tomorrow comes, Sean manages to spend a bit of time writing…

***It's got your name on it***

*Seven months after his mother's casket was lowered into the ground on a brilliantly sunny day she would have savored, Aidan was still speaking with his father as he never had before. Twice a week, at least, in the early evening, Aidan would telephone him to see how he was doing, if he was eating well, and if he needed anything.*

*While Ashling called Cornelius occasionally as well, it was clear that the aging and widowed man was especially appreciative of his youngest son's reaching out. And the conversations were good. In Cornelius's mind, they were cause for hope that his Aidan would be all right as life moved along. In Aidan's mind they were an increasing sign that his father truly cared about what Aidan could do with his life. "If you put your mind to it," his father would say.*

*Much to Aidan's surprise, his conversations with his dad ranged over a score of topics he never knew his father had any interest in. To him, during the many years of his life in Dorchester, his father – rather, his father's life – was as mysterious as the rituals of the church in which he was raised. Only more mundane. Cornelius never revealed much of himself to his children except when discipline was needed, or a serious talking-to warranted. His dad always rose early, always left the tenement in time to punch in for first shift, and always returned home tired and expecting the steaming cup of tea his mother always had ready for him. Sometimes, when circumstances forced him into a second job – as when Ian and Margaret needed help financing their college educations – it seemed he was almost always gone from the apartment, and sometimes Aidan saw him briefly only once or twice a week.*

*The stories were coming out now, in their conversations, things his father or his mother had never told him. His mother's frightened joy that she had become pregnant again – with Aidan – while she still mourned the daughter she had lost two days after the child's delivery a mere year before. His father's love of card-playing, especially bridge – and his father's unwavering belief that his mother cheated when they played with friends and she was paired against him. The fact that Ian had been nearly expelled from high school for plagiarizing six consecutive paragraphs from a text written by St. Thomas Aquinas. And his father's deep insights into politics and religion and people.*

*How had his dad become so astute, Aidan wondered. His father, as he had learned long ago from his mother, had only completed grade school in Ireland, needing to leave learning behind to work his family's less-than-prosperous farm in Silverbridge. At eighteen, funded by contributions from a half-dozen relatives and his parents, he bought a steamer ticket to America where he was to meet with an Irish couple, friends of his parents, who would help him find a job and a place to live. There was no choice because there was nothing for him in Ireland. He was, after all, Catholic – and Catholics were not exactly embraced in his home country and opportunities were scarce. Besides, his older brother was getting married, and there would otherwise be no room for his bride in the traditional two-room thatched-roof farm cottage that the family had lived in for two generations. So Cornelius had to leave.*

*Aidan's mother – who, in Ireland, lived only eight miles from Cornelius's family – had arrived in Boston a month later, and ended up in a rooming house but two blocks from where Cornelius was staying. Still, it took two years before they met, a week for Cornelius to fall in love with her, and eight months more before Ellen decided she was in love with the handsome young Irishman with the delightfully dry sense of humor.*

*The phone calls with his father usually were on Sundays and Wednesdays, though sometimes more frequently if Aidan sensed his father was lonesome or otherwise not doing well. At least four times a month, Aidan drove to Dorchester to take his dad out for lunch, or for the two of them to go to one of his dad's favorite hangouts to talk for a while over beers and snacks.*

*On this particular Sunday, while Aidan and Ashling were watching the New England Patriots on television, it was Cornelius who dialed his son. It was usual for Ashling to answer when the phone rang; Aidan, long ago trained to avoid the phone after years of unwelcome calls from the phone company, the gas company, the electric company and many others who insisted on reminding him of debts for which he was in serious arrears, was still shy about picking up the receiver.*

*Aidan was mostly focused on the game – the Patriots were in position to make a game-winning field goal – and waited as Ashling took the call. While in Aidan's foreground, with two seconds left in the game, Aidan watched the Pats kicker put the ball dead center between the goal posts, in his background he vaguely heard Ashling say, "Oh, hello, Connie. What a pleasant surprise to get your call. I hope all is well."*

*With the pleasure of the Patriot's too-close win still surging in Aidan's blood, he fell back in relief against the couch and waited for Ashling to pass him the phone.*

*For several minutes, Ashling spoke with Cornelius quietly. She was standing by the kitchen counter, her back to Aidan. Now and then, he'd notice her head nodding and he'd catch snippets of her voice, but nothing he could understand, so he kept his attention on the post-game wrap-up. He was surprised his dad had called during the last seconds of the game.*

*Finally, Ashling turned and signaled Aidan.*

*'It's your dad, luv." Her face was neutral, unlit by the pleased expression she usually showed when Cornelius called.*

*Aidan stood. "Is everything okay?"*

*"He needs to talk with you."*

*Aidan asked again. "Is everything okay?"*

*She held out the phone. "Come here. He'll tell you himself."*

*Aidan stood and headed into the kitchen. Ashling spun to unwind herself from the overstretched phone cord and passed the receiver to him. She gave him a quick kiss on the cheek as he put the phone to his ear and went to sit on the couch.*

*"Dad?" Aidan said. "What's up? Everything okay there?" He tried to sound casual, surprised that he felt suddenly anxious.*

*"I'm doing as well as can be expected," Cornelius said. "There's no need to be worrying about me. In fact, I'm meeting Jimmy – you remember Jimmy Sheehan, don't you? – I'm meeting him in a bit. We'll be sharing some Jameson and some conversation for the rest of the afternoon. It's hard staying here in the tenement without your mother."*

*Aidan paused, getting just a taste of his father's loneliness. "Just don't drink too much," he said a second later. "Did you catch the Patriots' game? How was that for a heart-attack finish?"*

*"They won?"*

*"Field goal with second left to play."*

*"Damn them. I turned off the foolish television halfway through the last quarter because they were giving me indigestion. Three interceptions and two missed field goals."*

*"Well, they turned it around." Aidan paused. "So, what's up? I didn't expect you to call today."*

*He could hear his father take a deep breath. "Last night, I couldn't sleep. Sleep's hard to come by now that your mother is gone. So I wanted to keep busy, and I started going through some of her things. You know, it's been all these months since we buried her, and I still haven't been able to bring myself to give her clothes away or do anything with her shoes or anything. It's all just sitting there. But she's not coming back, is she?"*

*There was silence on the end of the line. Aidan waited. A moment later, he heard his father blowing his nose.*

*"So, I began going through her things," his father said at last. "You know, just trying to figure what I might do with them. She had favorite things, I know, and I want to give them out to you and your brother and sister – and some to Ashling, too."*

*Another pause. "For the life of me, I never thought I'd ever be up in the middle of the night trying to figure what to do with your mother's things. Husbands are supposed to die first, you know. That's what I used to tell her. But here's what I want to tell you: she left an envelope for you. It's got your name on it. It feels like a letter. Or some kind of paper inside."*

*"A letter for me?" Aidan said. Memories came back to him of his mother at the kitchen table, writing long letters to her family in Ireland. Six or seven times a month, she'd write to them. In return she got letters in the mail that made her smile – and sometimes, like when her parents or her aunts and uncles died – made her cry.*

*"Open it." Aidan said to his father.*

*"It's for you to open," his father told him. "She addressed it to you, so it's up to you to open it."*

*Aidan knew his father was right. A moment passed before he asked: "Did she leave envelopes for Ian and Margaret?"*

*"I haven't found any. If she did, she put them some other place." His father blew his nose again. "Maybe if you come up next Sunday..."*

*"I can come up today." Aidan looked at his watch. "It's not quite four-thirty. I can be there by six at the latest. Tell Jimmy Sheehan you'll go out with him another time."*

*His father hesitated.*

*"We can have dinner together – you and me," Aidan added.*

*"I don't have much in the house, but I could..."*

*"We'll go out. Murtaugh's has good food, if I remember."*

*"Jimmy'll be disappointed." Again a long hesitation. "Maybe it would be best if you came to get the letter tonight. Can Ashling come?"*

*"She's got to work in the morning. There's no telling what time I'll get back if you and I have a few with our meal."*

*"All right," his father said. "I'll be waiting for you."*

*"Thanks, dad. See you in a bit."*

*Ashling had been waiting on the couch, the television volume turned low so she could make sure Aidan was all right with what his father was telling him. She didn't know whether Cornelius had read the letter and she was concerned he might pass along some upsetting information to Aidan.*

*As Aidan returned to the living room, she reached out a hand to him, and he took it.*

*"I'll be fine here, luv," she told him. "Did he tell you what's in the letter?"*

*"He said it was up to me to open it, since mom addressed it to me." He squeezed her hand. "I've got to go."*

*"I understand. Just be sure to drive safely. I want you back in as good a shape as you are now."*

*Aidan looked at her, a lingering look that was unlike him. "I love you, you know. You make my life so much better."*

*His words took her somewhat by surprise. It was not often he told her of his feelings for her, although he'd slowly begun speaking more about love during the past few months. But she had long ago learned to tell by his actions how much he really loved her. That's what had kept her with him all these years.*

*She stood and hugged him, holding him for a long time. "Go, luv. I'll wait up for you."*

*Aidan returned her hug and gave her a quick kiss before grabbing his keys and heading for the door.*

*Ashling watched him go, letting it sink in that he had been coming into himself very nicely since his mother had died. She watched him close the door and said a quick prayer that the letter he was about to open would help him grow some more.*

Sean has surprised himself. Despite how weak he's felt since leaving the hospital, he's managed to spend nearly four hours today working on the story. Until now, despite having written a bit yesterday, mostly typing what he'd already composed in his mind during his idling, he has spent most of his time on the couch, sometimes watching television, sometimes dozing, not having enough energy to do much else. Today he felt the need to press ahead while he had enough time on his hands.

He has, so far, tried not to dwell on the ramifications of his stay in the intensive care unit. Still, the whole ulcer incident has left him feeling less certain about many things that have always lingered in the undercurrents of his mind, left him uncomfortable about the future, and left him – what? – hoping life would not cut him off at the knees too soon.

Ted has come by every day after his shift at Electric Boat, usually spending an hour or so in Sean's apartment, and always bringing something for Sean to eat. Last evening, it had been a large pizza along with a nut bread Jane had baked for him. Sean's been nibbling at the last remaining slice of pizza as he's worked on his story. The nut bread will wait until morning and a hot cup of coffee.

It's barely eight o'clock in the evening, but he's ready for bed now. He'll return to his job in the morning.

Sean leans back in his chair, taking the last few bites of the pizza, and reads what he has written – amazed that he was able to produce so much despite his fatigue.

He wishes sometimes that he could be one of those writers who pounds out two dozen or more pages a day. With him, it's a plodding affair. He has to let his mind work through everything before he types. Even then, he questions what he's writing and what he's thinking about writing.

Sean considers himself his own worst critic.

He and Ted had talked about the story while they ate pizza. Ted, encouraging as always, asked Sean if he had a particular goal with the story. Sean had answered, lamely he thought, that he was letting the story unfold itself.

"It's as if it's writing itself in some back corner of my mind while I work or sleep or watch television or drive to the store," Sean told Ted. "Then it could be when I'm typing a feature article or listening to a radio talk show or when I get up at night to pee – it pops up, waiting to be typed. So I type. I'm amazed the story still makes sense."

Ted laughed. "It makes a lot of sense. I think you're working it really well. I'm not a literary critic, but I read a lot of books. This one is good."

Sean finished his pizza and put down his can of soda. "So you think I can get somewhere with it?"

"First, you've got to be a bit more confident about it."

"It's not in my nature."

"So – you still didn't answer my question," Ted said. "Where are you going with your story?"

"I answered your question."

"No – you just told me that the story writes itself. What happens if it stops writing itself?"

Sean laughed. "Believe me – that's happened before. More than a few times."

"I'll tell you what I think," Ted said, a more serious look on his face. "I don't think you'll ever know where the story is going until you know why you chose to create someone like Aidan."

"He just popped up in my mind. It was that simple."

"But why Aidan? Why that kind of person? Why not write about a businessman, or a journalist – you have a lot of experience with that – or why not write a crime novel, a mystery, a ghost story? But you chose Aidan. Why?"

Now, having just written more about Aidan – and second-guessing himself yet again on whether he's produced anything worthwhile – he finds himself saddled by his friend's out-of-left-field question and his lack of any viable answer.

Why in hell did he decide to create someone like Aidan? He has no idea how to answer the question. He figures he'll simply have to keep writing, hoping the answer will arise on its own in its own due time.

Did Updike go through this sort of thing? Hemingway? Faulkner? Fitzgerald?

Sean snorts a small laugh then gets up from his chair to head off to bed. He needs more sleep than he knows he's going to get.

In the morning, somewhat before dawn, pressuring himself, he rises, brews a cup of coffee, and begins writing again, hoping, in part, that more writing will help him understand where Aidan came from.

***It won't burn you***

*After Aidan left the apartment, Ashling poured herself a glass of Merlot and dialed Cornelius. She wasn't sure if Aidan's dad had caller ID on his telephone, but doubted that he'd ever pay attention to it if he did.*

*As always, Cornelius picked up the phone as if wondering who it might be on the other end of the line and, as always, was pleasantly surprised that it was Ashling who was calling. It was one of her secrets that she called Aidan's father once or twice a week to make sure he was doing well after losing Ellen and to bring him up to date on how his youngest and sometimes errant son was doing.*

*"It's you," Cornelius said, the smile on his face coming through the phone as clear as can be. "Aidan is on his way, is he?"*

*"He left about ten minutes ago," she told him. "You know him – I expect he's not broken a speed limit in the past twenty-five years. He'll be there soon enough."*

*"He takes after his mother that way," Cornelius said. "She never had a driving license – though she tried to learn a long time ago. Yet she always insisted that I watch my speed when I was driving. Aidan must have learned from her."*

*"He'll likely be there in an hour or so," Ashling said. "I figure he'll be having something to drink when you and he go to dinner tonight. If he has too much, make sure he stays with you tonight. I don't want him weaving all the way home."*

*"I'll make sure," Cornelius said.*

*Then, after a pause, he asked. "Is Aidan still doing all right? He doesn't tell me much about how he's doing."*

*Ashling had to laugh. Aidan was famously closed-mouth about most everything, but she had long ago figured how to read him and how to coax information from him. To her, it was almost as if he wanted – needed – her to wring everything from him, as if he had no idea how to bring himself up in conversation. She recalled that she had once told him that it seemed he didn't exist in his own mind, that he never looked at himself from within.*

*She'd asked how he could do that. He'd answered that it made life easier to deal with*

*"Aidan is Aidan," she told Cornelius. "But I believe he's certainly changing – in good ways. He's been different over the last many months, ever since his birthday. He seems more serious and certainly more introspective. And he may get a new job."*

*"He's still at that liquor store, is he?"*

*"For now," she replied, her voice hopeful. "One of his customers – a fellow who Aidan says works at Electric Boat, where they make the nuclear submarines – has urged Aidan to consider applying for a job there. It seems they have a training program for welding or some such thing."*

*"A skilled trade," Cornelius said. "That would surely give him better pay than working at that liquor store. Better benefits too, I would think."*

*"Aidan hasn't said too much about it. But I know it's been on his mind. I have a feeling that such an opportunity might be one he can't resist.*

*"He can't stay at the liquor store forever," Cornelius said. That kind of job is for people who can't do anything else, or for retired people like me. Doesn't he realize he's already – what – forty-three?"*

*"He thinks he hasn't yet hit thirty." She laughed out loud.*

*"By God," his father said. "He's yet to grow up, then?"*

*"Oh, be assured he is growing up," Ashling said. "He's told he me he might very well consider the opportunity. Sometimes it seems he's tired of working at the store, so that's what may push him along".*

*"Have you tried kicking him in the rear?" Cornelius said, a laugh creeping in to his voice.*

*"Very subtly," Ashling replied.*

*As Ashling and Cornelius talked on the phone, Aidan drove in the center lane of I-95 north, wishing that Ashling had come with him to visit his dad. Since his mother's death, his father always seemed brighter when Ashling was there, less morose than Aidan thought he'd be otherwise. But maybe tonight, Aidan told himself, it was better that she stayed home. Even after seven months, he often teetered on a fine emotional edge as far as his mother's death was concerned, and he had no idea how the envelope she'd addressed to him would affect him. He never wanted Ashling to see in him any state of weakness. His father, long ago, had become an example of how a strong man ought to behave. And Aidan, better son than he thought he had been, had often found himself emulating his father while usually, at the same time, trying to deny such tendencies because he wanted to show himself to be so much different.*

*The ride to Dorchester seemed long, even though the Sunday afternoon traffic was lighter than usual.*

*Aidan was not one to obsess on anything. What happened in life was either worth taking seriously or not. And Aidan was picky about what he took seriously.*

*But this envelope thing...*

*What could it contain? Perhaps it was, as his father had suggested, a letter. But if that's what it was, what on earth would his mother have written to him about. She'd never had any problems talking with him directly about anything she considered important. So why a letter? How long ago had she written it? Had she ever meant to give it to him personally? She'd never before written a letter to him, not counting the brief notes she jotted in birthday cards, Christmas cards, and the like.*

*More confusing was why there was an envelope for him and none – at least none his father had yet found – for his sister and brother. Did the envelope contain some family secret? Did it contain a confession? Did it contain her disappointment that he had done so little with his life?*

*Aidan had always hated the unknown, avoided the uncertain; such things wobbled his world. Despite his pleas, his father had declined to open the envelope. Now, the long ride from Wickford was giving Aidan more than enough time to stew – and fret – about what his mother had written.*

*Jesus, how he detested anxiety.*

*Had Ashling come with him, she could have calmed him and helped him put this thing in perspective. However she managed it, she had a knack for bringing him down to earth when, left to himself, he would otherwise twirl and twist ever more rapidly upward until he would nearly burst.*

*He felt himself spiraling now, yet he drove on, wanting – but unable – to return home to Ashling.*

*As much as this turn of events discomfited him, he knew he had to go through with it, if only to please his dad. And in the midst of his fretting, he had a flashback to his father, standing in the kitchen, telling a fourteen-year-old Aidan that difficult things were all a part of growing up.*

*"How timely," Aidan said aloud as he drove. He almost had to laugh. "How timely," he said again.*

*Less than fifteen minutes after getting onto the Southeast Expressway, Aidan parked across the street from the brown-shingled triple-decker where his father lived. He looked up as he left his car, almost as if he expected his dad to be leaning on the third-floor porch railing to greet him. But the porch was empty, and the only light came from a table lamp in the living room.*

*He rang the doorbell and waited for his father to buzz him in. One day, he reminded himself, he needed to get a copy of his father's apartment key in case of an emergency.*

*He hoped his dad was not expecting to spend time chatting in the apartment before they went out to eat. Aidan was anxious to get his dad over to Murtaugh's. Aidan not only needed more than a bit of whiskey to ground him as he and his dad dealt with the letter, he needed to be away from where his mother had lived and where she'd sat to write the letter to him. The possible contents of the envelope were looming over him, and he disliked the stress he was feeling.*

*When the buzzer finally came, Aidan pushed the door open and began the climb up the stairs. Was the wallpaper always the same faded floral pattern? Aidan couldn't remember. The smells, though, had always been the same. Irish smells. Different than the smells in the Jewish homes he had been to, or the Greek home one of his best friends in high school, or those that permeate Italian tenements. Four or five times over the years his parents had lived here, new first- and second-floor tenants had come and gone. But they had always been Irish, and they had brought their smells with them. It was comfort.*

*His dad was standing in the doorway as Aidan climbed the last half-dozen steps. He was smiling, gesturing Aidan to come in.*

*"I need to get my jacket," his father said. "In case it gets chilly later."*

*"The radio said it's going to go down to the low fifties," Aidan said as he came to the top landing and shook his dad's outstretched hand.*

*"You've got no jacket?"*

*"I'm rugged, dad. Go get yours."*

*As his father headed toward wherever his jacket was hung, Aidan asked, "Are you sure that Murtaugh's is okay with you?"*

*"It's quite all right," his father called back over his shoulder, "I go there now and then with some friends. It was the last place I took your mother before she had the Alzheimer's come upon her. She always liked the food."*

*A moment later he came back to the living room, carrying his jacket over his arm. "I remember that she had the mixed grill – you know, with the Irish sausage, the Irish bacon, and the pork chop. It was always one of your mother's favorites."*

*"One of mine too," Aidan said. "Are you ready to go?"*

*"I am, indeed."*

*Aidan paused and took in a long breath. "Do you have the letter with you?"*

*Cornelius reached into his pants pocket and drew out a white envelope he had neatly folded in half. "I do."*

*Aidan looked at the envelope, feeling another wave of tension.*

*As if sensing his son's discomfort, Cornelius held it out to him. "It won't burn you. Your mother would never do anything to hurt you or your brother and sister. She had a heart of gold, that woman. Take it."*

*Aidan slipped the envelope from his father's hand, as if taking a speeding ticket from a cop, and quickly slipped it into the pocket of his jeans. "Let's go," he said. "I'm really hungry."*

*"As am I," his father said. "Mrs. Donoghue next door cooked a ham for Sunday dinner and brought me a couple of slices this afternoon. I'll save them until tomorrow. She does that now and then, you know. I don't cook as much as I should."*

*Cornelius closed the door behind him and made sure the deadbolt had locked properly. As they descended the stairs together, Aidan leading the way, his father put a hand on his shoulder. "You're a good boy, Aidan. I'm glad you came tonight."*

*"Thanks, dad." In his heart, he was hoping he'd be later thanking his father for passing along the envelope his mother had left for him. What she had written remained to be seen. He could find no way to insulate himself from might be to come.*

*Murtaugh's had never made any pretense of being a true Irish pub, even though it had been on the edge of this Irish neighborhood for perhaps sixty years or more. It had always looked much like any Boston bar and grille for those who had not a lot to spend, but who appreciated good beer, Irish whiskey, and a few Irish menu items that – for such a place – were quite good. It was the place where Aidan had his first legal drink on turning twenty-one – actually his first four legal drinks – and had staggered home where his parents' disapproval had ambushed him. Had they only known that he'd been enjoying alcohol ever since he was thirteen, courtesy of a local drunk who had often taken his money to purchase a bottle of pre-mixed Screwdriver for him and his friends, he would have been undoubtedly dead in short order.*

*Aidan held the door for his father as they walked in. The bar, along the wall to the left, had barely a single unoccupied stool. The tables and booths on the other side of the room were only sparsely occupied. The appearance of Cornelius prompted perhaps a dozen greetings from silver-haired men who – at least some of them – had escaped from their wives to spend drinking and talking time with cronies they had spent time with over many years.*

*Two or three recognized Aidan from the funeral and called him over for handshakes and energetic pats on the shoulder and, naturally, offers to buy him a drink. The inquiries were all the same: how are you doing in Rhode Island? Are you moving back now that your dad is alone? Are you married yet?*

*He answered each question patiently, even those repeated by others, and let each of them know he was happy to run into them and appreciated their interest in how life was treating him.*

*"I figured it was about time that my dad and I had a serious drinking session," he told them. "Besides, if I don't feed him...."*

*"He has a tough time boiling oatmeal," cracked a fellow Aidan remembered as James. "It's a wonder he's not starved to death by now. He always said your mother was a wonderful cook." The others checked their laughter at the chuckle level in respect to Ellen's passing.*

*With a wave and a smile, Aidan ended the conversation at the bar and led his father to a booth at a far corner of the room.*

*"Jimmy Sheehan doesn't come here?" Aidan remarked as they sat.*

*"He doesn't come here often. He says the atmosphere is not right."*

*As they made themselves comfortable, the lone waitress appeared and laid menus on the table.*

*"Good evening, gentlemen," she said, as if using the term loosely. "Something to drink."*

*"Food and drink," said Aidan. "Dad?"*

*Cornelius paused, then asked his son, "What are you planning on having?"*

*"Jameson – on the rocks."*

*"Then I'll have one as well, if it's all the same to you." His dad turned looked up at the waitress. "Two Jamesons on the rocks, please."*

*"I'll be right back," she said, and headed back toward the bar. She looked as if she'd been working there for the past half-century.*

*Aidan flipped open his menu then reached across the table and opened his dad's. "If you're hungry, pick something that'll fill you up until tomorrow noon. It's on me."*

*He knew his father's retirement income was not enough for the drinking and eating they'd be doing tonight. Aidan could afford it – this time.*

*Cornelius accepted the offer and thanked Aidan. "They have a steak here that's supposed to be pretty good," he said. "I haven't had a steak in a long time."*

*"It's on me," Aidan repeated. "Go for it."*

*"Here it is," Cornelius said, running a finger down the menu in the dim light. "Sirloin steak with a baked potato and vegetable and a salad."*

*"Then that's what you'll have," Aidan told him. "Ashling would be*

*upset with me if I got you anything less."*

*The waitress returned with the drinks, placing them on coasters and asking if they were ready to order. A minute later, she'd written everything down then, on obviously tired feet, made her way back toward the bar and through the kitchen door just to the right.*

*Aidan lifted his glass and waited for his father to do the same. "To a better day tomorrow, and the next day, and the next," he said. Together they sipped and put the glasses down.*

*"The days haven't been much better since we lost your mother," his dad said. "Still, I'm doing better than I ever expected. You never know when you're going to lose someone close to you."*

*Aidan took another swallow of his Jameson and let it play on his tongue before swallowing. He waited for a bit for his father to bring up the letter, but his father was lost in thought – likely about Aidan's mother – and sat there taking frequent small sips of his whiskey.*

*"So," Aidan said, finally, "Where did you find the letter?"*

*Cornelius looked befuddled for an instant. "Ah, the one your mother left for you." He mused for a moment, then said, "It was in her dresser, the bottom drawer where she kept things that meant something to her – you know, like souvenirs and pictures and little gifts you children had made for her or gave her over the years." His dad gave a small and quiet laugh. "Never did I imagine how much stuff she had in there. There was a lot, let me tell you."*

*"It was just laying there? The letter?"*

*"It was," his dad said. "Near the front of the drawer, under a Christmas ornament you had made for her in fourth grade."*

*Aidan recalled the ornament – glitter and glue on pieces of red and green construction paper fashioned, not quite artistically, in the shape of a Christmas tree. The nuns in the lower grades seemed smitten by the unlimited creative possibilities of glitter and glue.*

*Aidan sipped his whiskey again. "And nothing for Ian or Margaret?" It was a serious question, for Aidan had always known his mother to treat each of them equally, and couldn't understand why she had left something addressed to him, yet nothing for his successful siblings.*

*"There's nothing I've found yet. At least not in her dresser." Cornelius again fell into musing.*

*Aidan pulled the envelope from his pocket and laid it on the table. He was not quite ready to open it, but he knew he had to do so before the evening was out. He felt it would not be right to open it when his father was not around. He sipped again at his whiskey and pushed the envelope more to the side.*

*Cornelius caught Aidan's motion and brought himself into the present. "You should open it," he said.*

*"Now?"*

*"Why not now? She left it for you. You should open it for her sake."*

*Aidan looked down at the envelope.*

*"For her sake," Aidan repeated. Once more he brought the Jameson to his lips, this time taking a long sip that drained nearly the rest of the glass. Then he pulled the envelope toward him.*

Ted's question about Aidan reared up again in Sean's consciousness as he was giving in to sleep last night. After Ted challenged him about why he'd chosen to create a man like Aidan, Sean wrote with more focus, trying to give Aidan more much more definition, as if doing so would give him a way of answering Ted's question. At the same time, he was trying to give more depth to Ashling and to Aidan's dad. Yet, he couldn't be sure he was really bringing Aidan to life.

Sean has returned to work. Today was his first day on the job, and it left him tired. He'll be back on his full schedule on Monday. Now, at home, he unwraps the sandwich he bought as takeout from the little shop near the corner bookstore after leaving the paper. His job is not on his mind. His story is. Sean bites into his sandwich and tries to figure what he must do.

He's astute enough to know that Ted's question is probably the key to whether Sean's story will be good rather than just another failed attempt at writing fiction.

So who the hell is Aidan, and why did he come up with him as the central character?

During some desultory musing, he toys with the possibility that in some odd way it was Aidan who had picked him. After all, Aidan had come to him spontaneously as he made a last-ditch effort to put something worthwhile on paper.

Sometimes, while he typed, it almost felt as if Aidan was constructing himself.

After a while, Sean decides that Aidan is likely no more than a blending of people he himself has known over the years. It takes almost no effort for him to identify elements within Aidan's character that mirror bits and pieces of people he's known over the span of his life. But then there are aspects of Aidan that came from who-the-heck-knows-where, almost as if he was allowing Aidan to build himself.

Sean isn't sure he can buy the idea that a character can create himself; it seems more logical that Sean's mind and memories and experiences had combined outside of Sean's consciousness to come up with Aidan and all his flaws.

Would Ted accept such a rationalization? Would it make any sense to him?

It would have to do.

Sean grabs a soda from the refrigerator – disappointed that alcohol in any form is off-limits as long as his ulcer remains unhealed. He takes the can to his living room and leans back on his couch. He's not sure whether Ted will drop by tonight after work – it's Thursday, and Ted sometimes plays a gig at Matunuck on alternating Thursdays. But whenever he and Ted reconnect, Sean will give him the only answer he can come up with. He gazes out the window and thinks.

Two cans of soda have not worked for him. He misses beer. The past half hour has produced nothing. Sean moves to his makeshift desk and lights a cigarette. At least, that has not been banned from his daily routine. He sucks in the smoke and blows it out slowly – still not inhaling. It feels good.

His mind continues to probe Aidan's character, hoping the issue will work itself out eventually. For the present, though, he is reasonably satisfied with who Aidan is and how he is moving forward.

Sean needs to write some more. For some reason, he is optimistic he may complete the story by the end of September, three months from now.

He brings the story up on his computer screen and begins reading the last several pages, considering how to move it along. He closes his eyes and allows his mind to weave its way to wherever it will take him this time. After a while, as always, he sets his hands above the keyboard and, one halting word at a time, he types.

***To Alice…***

*For a minute or two, Aidan toyed with the envelope, turning it over in his hand, looking again at his mother's handwriting and the way she underlined his name. "For Aidan," it said.*

*"No idea when she wrote it, huh?" he asked his father.*

*"None," Cornelius answered. "But it had to have been before she had to go into the nursing home. So that would have been…"*

*"Three years ago, at least," Aidan said.*

*"Yes," his father said. "It seems such a long time past, doesn't it." He looked across the table at his son. "Do you miss her?"*

*"More than I thought I would," Aidan said.*

*"Good," was all his father said in reply. Aidan thought he saw his father's eyes become a bit watery.*

*Cornelius picked up his glass and held it out to Aidan. "To your sweet mother."*

*Aidan clinked his glass against his dad's. "To mom."*

*They sipped, and for a moment were swept up in memories.*

*Cornelius put down his glass and pointed at the envelope in Aidan's hand. "Open it."*

*Aidan looked again at the envelope.*

*"It's time."*

*Aidan pulled a small Swiss Army knife from his pocket and slit through to top of the envelope. After folding the blade and putting the knife away, he pulled the envelope's contents out as his father watched intently.*

*There were three pages, folded together neatly, done in his mother's flowing handwriting. He remembered the times his mother had told him that when she attended school in Northern Ireland her teacher had often praised her penmanship. Little memories like that had been popping up in Aidan's head ever since his mother died.*

*Aidan flattened the letter on the table without looking at it. His father gave him a hand gesture that meant "get on with it." So Aidan finished what was left of his Jameson and began to read in silence.*

*"Dear Aidan," his mother had begun. He could almost hear her speak his name.*

*"My brother in Ireland was much like you, full of spirit and determined that he would live his life his own way. I have always known that is how you are. You may think I have not been aware of what you have been going through, or the things that have caused you distress. But I have been quite aware.*

*"Your father, dear man, has been less able to see you as I see you. But he has tried to understand you. In some ways, you and he are alike, although it may take him a while longer, if ever, to understand how it is so.*

*"Of course, I am sure you may be wondering why I am writing this letter to you. I will make sure to put it where your father will not find it unless I die before he does. And if not, then you will find it. He always thought that my bottom drawer full of souvenirs and small gifts was a waste of space. But if you are reading this, then I am surely gone and he has bravely gone through my belongings, though it may take him a long time to come to terms with disposing of them. Please remind him that my clothing and other things may do a lot of good if he donates them to the St. Vincent de Paul Society or to the parish.*

*"I am writing this letter because I've been feeling lately as if my mind is becoming far less aware than I would like. I forget things and sometimes forget where I am or what I was doing. I pray to the Virgin Mary that it is not Allzymers or whatever way they spell it. But if that is so, then I need write to you now.*

*"Just so you know, I am not writing to Ian or Margaret. They do not need my counsel. They have made their lives the way they want them, and I expect that they are happy in their own way, although I wish Margaret and Ian would come down off their high horses one day. I think they still need to grow up a bit, but do not ever tell them what I am saying here. I don't know what it will be like in heaven, but if it is possible, I will strike you down if you ever mention a word of this to them."*

*Aidan felt his father's hand on his wrist. "You have a bit of a smile on your face," his dad said. "Is it a good letter?"*

*Aidan answered: "Two more pages to go. I'll let you know then. But mom's personality sure shines through."*

*"I thought it might," Cornelius said. He looked toward the kitchen. "Here comes that waitress with our food."*

*"About time," Aidan said, refolding the letter and pushing it to the side. "Another drink for you."*

*"I think we both need one," his dad said.*

*The waitress put the plates in front of them, said "Enjoy, gentlemen."*

*As she began to turn away, in too much of a hurry, Cornelius thought, he raised his voice a bit. "Two more Jamesons, please."*

*"Right away," she tossed back as she returned to the bar.*

*Aidan ignored his food and continued to read.*

*"It'll get cold," his father said, pointing at Aidan's plate. "Eat."*

*"In a minute," Aidan replied. "Let me read a bit more."*

*His father cut a piece of steak and pushed it into his mouth. Chewing, he asked, "So what is your mother saying now?" as if she were sitting there with them.*

*"Let me finish it first," Aidan said. He picked up his knife and fork, but kept reading instead of eating.*

*"You," Aidan's mother continued, "were always the stubborn one, the one your father often felt needed a taste of his belt, although only did that once when you were eleven. After he and I had a talk, he never did that again, although there were times I perhaps should have let him. But you were bright and curious and wanting to understand everything around you. I think what I love most about you is that you always craved adventure of any kind and want to taste everything, unlike Ian and Margaret who decided too soon in life what they wanted to be when they grew up.*

*"You took your time growing up, as if you knew somehow that such growing would come in its own good time. Honestly, Aidan, I thought you would have grown up by the time you were thirty at the latest. I cannot help thinking that you lost your way somehow. As I write this, you are almost thirty-nine. Your birthday is in four weeks. But, except for that sweet young woman who seems to see something in you – it is Ashling of whom I am speaking – you have not moved as far forward in your life as I had hoped. I have prayed in church on Sunday and at night before falling asleep that you would wake up and become who you are meant to be."*

*The waitress returned with their fresh glasses of whiskey. Aidan pushed the letter aside and sliced into his steak. He had to stop reading; his mother too accurately knew what was inside him. He recalled that when he was a boy at home, she had him completely convinced that truly had eyes in the back of her head. He'd even gone so far as to pick through her hair to see the eyes of which she boasted, but she stopped him – laughing heartily – before he could verify what had been worrying him so much.*

*"Have you finished the letter?" his father asked, taking a sip of his Jameson while chewing on a piece of beef.*

*"Not yet," Aidan replied.*

*"She wrote quite a bit, your mother."*

*"Uh-huh."*

*"Anything important?" Cornelius was itchingly curious about what Ellen had put in the letter to her younger son.*

*"Honestly, I don't know," Aidan said. "I'm a little more than halfway through. I think she's starting to get to the important stuff."*

*"Let me know what she says," Cornelius said before pushing another piece of steak into his mouth.*

*The two of them ate in silence for a while, Aidan hungrier than he'd expected to be. His father, with his intense focus on what was on his plate, had obviously been at least equally hungry.*

*It wasn't until Aidan finished his meal and pushed his plate aside that he broke the silence of their meal.*

*"Tell me something, dad," he said, readying to sip from his Jameson. "How was mom with Ian and Margaret? They always did so well in school and just about everything else, she must have been really proud of them."*

*Cornelius downed the last bit of baked potato on his plate and leaned back, contemplating his youngest son. "There's nothing in what she thought about them that would be worth talking about. If she had anything at all to say about them, I would imagine she would be saying them in the letter there."*

*Aidan nodded. "She mentions them both," he said. "But I would like to know what you know about how she regarded them."*

*His father leaned back in his seat and toyed with his napkin. "Do you remember when the ambulance came one evening for Mr. O'Connor next door – they lived on the second floor? You were about nine or ten at the time."*

*Aidan grinned. "I remember."*

*"And do you remember what happened to you?"*

*Aidan laughed. "I could never forget. You and mom grounded me for about a month."*

*"It was for a week," Cornelius said, shaking his head. "And do you remember why?"*

*Aidan sat up straight as his mind resurrected the memory. "I climbed up to the second floor back porch and then sneaked into their apartment to see what was going on. They had an oxygen mask on Mr. O'Connor, and Mrs. O'Connor – I remember she was very fat – was crying hysterically. Another neighbor was trying to stop her from rushing over to the stretcher."*

*Cornelius nodded. "Yes. You remember. But do you remember asking one of the men from the ambulance what he was doing to help Mr. O'Connor?"*

*Aidan had the vague feeling that his father was almost castigating him again for what he did all those years ago.*

*"I was a kid, dad. Kids do dumb things."*

*"That's not the point I was about to make."*

*Aidan gave his dad a "what-are-you-talking-about" look. "And your point is?" he asked.*

*"When your brother Ian was but four years old, he told your mother that he wanted to be important and wear a suit every day." A slight smile crossed Cornelius's face. "Where he got that notion we never knew. It was as if it had come out of thin air. Perhaps it was from television or some such thing."*

*Another sip of the Jameson before him, then a close look at the glass as if to check how much was left for him to enjoy.*

*"When he went to school each day, he insisted on dressing well, which meant your mother had to press his pants and starch his shirt. It never bothered him that other children sometimes mocked him for his dress, or for the fastidious and thorough way he did everything. He could take care of himself, but even at a young age, he was seen as a little old man with little humor and much focus."*

*"Your sister," Cornelius continued, " was very different yet very much the same. She, too, had made up her mind at a young age as to what she wanted to be when she grew up. For her, it was medicine. At first, it was to become a great doctor who would help poor people in distant countries. But later, for whatever her reasons, she decided that it would be better to make a lot of money. She told your mother one day that she wanted to have more millions than Ian. Where that came from, I could never guess. They were both strange children."*

*Aidan was leaning on his elbows, studying his father as the old man spoke. He was not sure whether his father was endorsing Ian's and Margaret's approach to life. When his father paused, Aidan asked, "So what did mom think of their plans for themselves?"*

*"Your mother, as you know, had high hopes for the three of you. But she was afraid that Ian – and later, Margaret – was too serious. She always believed that coming to America would give her children – our children – the chance to enjoy being children. Not like us; your mother was working cleaning other people's houses when she was nine, and I worked at farm chores from the time before I started school. She believed that children should have time to enjoy life before they finally had to grow up."*

*Cornelius sipped the last of his Jameson. Quietly, Aidan signaled toward the bar for two more.*

*His father fell quiet for a moment, his eyes staring at some place far away beyond Aidan's left shoulder, almost as if his memories were beginning to crowd him.*

*"The fact is," Cornelius said, his voice suddenly loud, "the fact is that your mother felt that Ian and Margaret…"*

*"Never took time to enjoy their childhood?" Aidan offered.*

*His father looked at him. "It was not that exactly, although I'm sure it was part of it. But your mother felt most strongly about the fact that your brother and your sister, the two of them, decided to be what they wanted to be for the wrong reasons."*

*"For money," Aidan said.*

*"For money, and to be big shots each in their own way. We always believed that people are best who are the salt of the earth, who care about their families and friends and neighbors. It's the way your mother and I were raised. We tried to raise the three of you in the same way."*

*The bartender himself brought the drinks to the table. Aidan thanked him. A silence settled over father and son as Aidan watched his father study the glass filled with warmly amber liquid.*

*"It's not often I have Jameson," his father said before taking a sip and savoring it. After he swallowed, he said, "In Ireland, a favorite was Jameson and lemonade. The women in particular liked it. But your mother was not a partaker and she was always after her sister to leave the liquor alone. But Alice has always loved her Jameson and lemonade. Now your mother's gone and Alice is still alive at eighty-six."*

*Cornelius shook his head and stared down into his glass again. "It doesn't seem fair that your mother, who led her life in a good and healthy way, God bless her… it's just not fair that she's the one who's gone while Alice continues to drink."*

*Aidan had to suppress a smile. Alice had flown from Ireland to visit his mother on at least four occasions over the years, and Aidan had immediately taken to her. She was feisty, irreverent, wonderfully humorous, and committed to having at least two Jamesons and lemonade each day – which, of course, led to frequent whispered arguments between his mother and Alice. And Alice always won her way.*

*Cornelius lifted his glass. "To Alice," he said, solemnly.*

*After he and Aidan had dutifully consumed enough whiskey to honor Alice, Cornelius laid his hands flat on the table and looked his son directly into the eyes.*

*"You are like Alice," he said. Quickly, he swept his hand back and forth in front of him as is to sweep away his words. "What I mean is that you are like your mother, in your kindness and consideration and your loyalty and your wish for a serene life. But you are also like Alice in that you are adventurous, curious, lively, and more than willing to have a good*

*time if the opportunity arises."*

*Aidan detected a slight slur beginning to creep into his dad's speech. The drinks in front of them would be the last tonight. Besides Aidan still had to return to Rhode Island where Ashling was undoubtedly waiting, and not without a wee bit or worry, for his safe arrival.*

*"So tell me," Aidan said. "How did mom regard my brother and sister? I can tell you now that I never saw a great deal of warmth between them."*

*"Read the rest of her letter," his dad said. "If she says too little about the things you are interested in learning, I will do my best to tell you what I know."*

*Aidan picked up the letter. "Fair enough," he said.*

Sean worked four-hour days at the paper on Thursday and Friday, trying to wrap up material he had been working on before his ulcer exploded, and working to lay the groundwork for a couple of other features his editor had assigned to him. He still felt drained, and working tired him quickly. At no time did he sense that his editor was pressing him. One of Sean's comforts was that his editor prized his skills at uncovering information and the adeptness of his writing, so unless he really screwed up he'd remain employed. He promises himself that he'll put in a full week as soon as Monday rolls around.

While changing from his khakis and oxford shirt, his work costume, into something more relaxing – in this case, a polo shirt and a pair of jeans – Sean considers his options for a Friday evening alone. Sean has never had many close friends, but his life has always been filled with acquaintances – people he's met in the course of his work, mostly. Ted is his closest friend, but Ted is married and has family obligations. Friends Sean had when he was married had all been lost over time. Only one or two, who believed his ex had given him a raw deal, contacted him now and then each year.

Considering what he might do this evening is an empty exercise, he knows. He goes through the same ritual every weekend evening. If past is prologue — and, for Sean, it often is — he'll most likely head to some restaurant or other, then maybe spend time browsing one of the bookstores on Warwick's miles-long shopping strip. If he takes things slowly, it will be after ten when he gets home – a good time to get to bed and read himself to sleep with whatever book he chooses to buy.

He could stay home, of course, continuing his recuperation.

But staying at home this evening is not an option. The aftermath of the bleeding ulcer has left him with a bad case of cabin fever – and cabin fever can itself be debilitating.

He's already agreed with himself that he'll leave Aidan alone for the evening; Sean needs to separate himself from the story, he thinks, in order to get it moving ahead more energetically. Besides, he doesn't have enough energy to sit and think and write for hours.

So, his mind made up, he checks to see that he has enough cash in his wallet, turns on the one lamp that will stay lighted until he gets home, grabs a sweater in case it gets chilly later in the evening, and heads for the door.

***Ignorant of life***

*"There's nothing I can do," Aidan's mother wrote, "that can change your brother or sister. I always wished they would remain a closer part of our family, but it suited them to keep their distance somewhat. But I am going to behave as your mother here and tell you that you must change your own life before you regret everything. It's odd, but I always believed that you had what it took to become successful – and I am not saying that you would be a millionaire or some fancy person who had little reason to truly care about others. Success is none of those things. Success is becoming a man who has room in his heart for good deeds and room in his mind to grow always better. You have always had the potential. Everyone who has ever known you has seen that clearly.*

*"For the love of God, Aidan, marry Ashling before you lose her to your false indifference to life. I know you love her, and you know you love her – and I know she loves you. What on earth are you trying to prove by treating her as you do? Do you realize how she misses you when you go out to the bars with your friends too many times a week? Do you know that she loves you despite your failings – yes, you have failings if you have not yet noticed. And get a decent job. You are better than you know, but sometimes I think you have always been afraid to take the big steps you need to become a man of consequence. Working in that liquor store likely does not keep you in touch with the better half of the community. Why not a factory job? You could easily become a foreman like your father, and he's always made good money. If I had my way, I'd send you back to college.*

*"Aidan, the truth is that you have disappointed me and your father for these many years, and I ache for you to snap out of whatever it is that traps you. As I said before, if you are reading this, then I am surely dead. Do your dear departed mother one last favor and dare yourself to be better. Become what you are meant to be, marry that wonderful woman (if she hasn't already left you out of frustration), and have children before you are too old to appreciate their wonder and joy. God knows that your sister has not produced the kind of children I would be proud to call my own, and*

*your brother has produced none at all. Maybe that is a blessing in an odd way. And if your father is still alive as you read this, visit him now and then and perhaps take him to Rhode Island for a visit now and then. He needs to get out of the house. It's not good to live alone as a hermit, as I suspect he might be after I am gone.*

*"You are my beloved son, Aidan. Do these things, not just for me, but for yourself as well. I'll expect a full accounting when you finally arrive in Heaven to join me."*

*"Love,*
*Your Mother (Ellen)"*

Aidan folded the letter carefully and slipped it back into the envelope. He touched lightly the spot where she had written his name. When he looked up, his father was staring at him. Aidan smiled, "It was quite a letter. Quite a letter, for sure."

"What was it that she told you?" Cornelius asked.

Aidan looked down at the envelope and mused for a moment. "Dad, I really think she wanted me to keep it to myself. Sorry."

"Not even a hint?" his father shot back. "She may have been your mother, Aidan, but she was also my wife for all those years."

"A hint..." Aidan ran his fingertips along the envelope. After a moment he looked his father in the eye. "It seems that mom," he said, "knew me far better that I ever knew myself."

Cornelius leaned back in his seat and toyed with his steak knife, sliding it along the edge of his plate. "Your mother and I talked about you often," he said.

"And what did you talk about?" Aidan asked.

His father sipped more of his Jameson and put the glass down. After a while he spoke without looking at his son.

"I remember one time when you were perhaps fifteen, and I came home from work and your mother was in the kitchen, sitting at the table, and crying. You never saw your mother cry, did you?"

"No," Aidan answered. Aidan's mother was as stoic as anyone he'd ever known. If life was difficult, she never let on. If she didn't feel well, it was her secret. If there was not enough money to buy enough groceries for the five of them, she somehow made it seem to be otherwise. The last thought brought memories of her sending him to the corner store to buy one pound of hamburger – one pound, for the five of them – which would be accompanied by boiled potatoes and a small serving of canned peas.

"She was crying because she had become afraid for you," Cornelius said. "She told me you had changed, almost overnight, from a boy who *was smart and good and considerate of people to someone she could not understand."*

*Aidan looked down at the table. After a moment, he said, "I don't remember changing. I was always just me."*

*His father shook his head. "Not at that time," he told his son. "I never really noticed it because I was at work most of the time, putting in all the overtime I could. But she noticed and she became worried."*

*Aidan exhaled in a long slow breath. "What did she say?"*

*Cornelius seemed to be searching for the right words as he twirled his glass of Jameson in the small puddle of water that had dripped from it as the ice melted. "She said this: 'I think Aidan has lost his way. All of a sudden, he seems like he no longer wants to be what he is. It's as if he is trying to shed himself and become someone else. I don't know how to talk with him about this. It breaks my heart because he is such a special boy, and all I can do is pray'."*

*"I just can't recall any of that," Aidan told his father. "I was just being teenager, or whatever it was."*

*His father looked across the table at him. "She was right, you know. I never saw it until several years afterward. But she was right."*

*Aidan felt like he was continuing to open a can of worms that he wasn't sure he wanted to deal with, and he wondered if the turmoil he'd experience on the morning of his birthday was just a prelude to a difficult and stressful year in general. All the same, he said to his father. "What did you see?"*

*"A boy who preferred to avoid his family. A boy who began slipping away from his religion. A boy who was ashamed of the way his parents dressed him and ashamed of where he lived." Cornelius shook his head, but smiled a tolerant smile. "You began take up with boys who went to public schools and who had parents that ate in restaurants on Sundays and shopped on Washington Street in Boston – and not in Filene's Basement. You even began taking on some of their mannerisms, the small bits of self-importance that some of them showed because their dad owned a new car or because they had gone for a summer vacation at a lake in New Hampshire, or some other such thing.*

*"It was as if you had no more pride in your own family, in your own heritage. One day after I got home from work very late, I remember you telling me that you wished I was a supervisor or even a manager and pointing out to me that only the lowest employees had to work so many hours."*

*"I'm sorry," Aidan said after a moment.*

*"You were ignorant of life, then," his father said, as a gentle slap.*

*"I'm hoping you have become less ignorant over time."*

*Aidan began to speak, but his father held up his hand.*

*"I think I can speak for your mother now – as well as for myself – when I say that the way your life has turned out is the only way it could have turned out...because you never allowed yourself to be what you were meant to be. You tried to run away from it all, but all you did was run yourself into a dead end. Did you ever really aspire to be a liquor store clerk all your life?"*

*Aidan stared at his father then slumped back in his seat. With a quick swallow, he finished the little that was left in his glass. "We've got to go now," he said. "It's late, I've got a long ride home, and Ashling is all alone."*

*Cornelius nodded and studied his son's face for a long moment. "You're right, Aidan. We have talked enough for one night. This has taken a lot out of me, as I imagine it has out of you."*

*Aidan took his mother's letter and slid out of the booth. As soon as his father stood up, Aidan crossed to the bar, paid the tab, and followed his father out the door – in silence.*

*After a bit more than ten minutes, Cornelius was safely in his apartment and Aidan was on his way home.*

*The Southeast Expressway was nearly empty of traffic, and Aidan cruised along carefully, aware of the amount of Jameson he'd had to drink. He was amazed his father had been able to keep pace with him at the pub.*

*He and Cornelius had driven to the tenement speaking no more than a half-dozen words between them. Aidan figured his father regretted being so honest about Aidan's shortcomings. For himself, Aidan was simply too tired, too drained to let his mind delve into anything heavier than the time of day or the outside temperature. He saw his father to the door of the apartment and shook his hand before walking slowly down the stairs.*

*"Take care," he said to his dad, without turning around.*

*"Drive carefully," his father said, his words well-blurred by the whiskey.*

*It had always been one of Aidan's gifts that he could wipe from memory anything that made him uncomfortable, or that pained him, or that he simply didn't want to deal with. And already, less than fifteen minutes from his father's home, he found himself fading the evening to a comfortable level that he could tolerate.*

*But that would change, he knew, as soon as he phoned Ashling to report that he was on the way back to Rhode Island. She would be curious about the evening and the conversation, and would expect a full recounting. Despite his wanting reduce the evening's stress, but needing so much to hear Ashling's voice, Aidan flipped open his cell phone and voice-dialed the woman who had been so loyally a part of his life for much longer than he deserved.*

*"It's me," he said when she picked up the phone at the other end.*

*"You're on you way home, then?" she said, her voice hinting that she'd been dozing on the couch. "Are you well enough to drive?" Ashling was well aware that Aidan sometimes drank too much when life pressed him, and she guessed that the evening with Cornelius was not without its stresses.*

*"I'm fine," Aidan said. She expected no other answer from him. "Traffic's light."*

*"So how did it go, luv? Did your father give you the letter your mother wrote?"*

*"Yes."*

*"And you read it?"*

*"Yup."*

*"And...?" Once again, she had to pull at Aidan's teeth to get the least bit of information from him.*

*"What can I say? She wrote a letter and my dad found it."*

*"Had he read it?"*

*"No. It was still sealed." Aidan cruised off the Expressway and headed for the junction with I-95 south. "Dad would never pry into someone else's stuff. He's never been like that."*

*"Did you share it with him?"*

*"Not really."*

*Ashling paused. "Will you share it with me?"*

*Aidan had never expected such a question from Ashling and it took him a moment to formulate an answer. "I'll tell you all about it when I get home."*

*There was a silence on the other end of the connection. Then Ashling said, "She told me about the letter."*

*Aidan was confused. "This letter? The one dad gave me tonight?"*

*"Yes."*

*"What did she tell you about it?"*

*Ashling chuckled. "I'll tell you as soon as you come home. Now keep your attention on the road, luv. The way your words are coming out of your mouth, I'd say you and Cornelius weren't particularly reluctant to hold back on the whiskey."*

*"Tell me now."*

*"No, my sweet man. Not now. Get home safely first." She hung up.*

*With a silent prayer that Aidan made it home without incident, Ashling went to the kitchen to see what she could put together for him to eat when he arrived. Aidan was always hungry and she teased him often about it. She figured she had enough to give him a sandwich along with some fruit.*

*She checked the clock – it was already twenty-minutes before midnight. She guessed Aidan would be home by one. She knew he'd be driving very conservatively, with an eye out for the occasional state trooper that might be loitering on the side of the road with radar aimed at him. He'd been stopped once for driving under the influence, about six months after they'd met. She recalled that he'd phoned her, embarrassed at having had his license suspended, to postpone the Saturday night date they'd planned. She'd gladly done the driving that evening and for the rest of his thirty-day suspension. She had seen no need to caution him about being caught again, but tonight, with his mumbled words, she was worried.*

*Satisfied that there was enough in the kitchen to offer him a bit of a meal, she sat at the table and began musing what his mother had told her about the letter she'd prepared for her youngest child.*

*It was at Thanksgiving, perhaps four or five years before, that Ellen invited Ashling into the kitchen to help cut and serve desserts. As they sliced into the pumpkin pie and the chocolate cake, Ellen asked softly, "Would you marry Aidan if you could?"*

*Ashling, never having had any deep discussions with Ellen before then – except perhaps about the state of affairs in Northern Ireland or the sad decline in the number of people who went to Mass on Sundays – was a somewhat shaken by the question, and it took her some moments to gather herself to answer.*

*As Ellen began wondering aloud about who might want vanilla ice cream with his or her chocolate cake, Ashling leaned on the kitchen counter and thought out her response.*

*Finally, she said, "If Aidan were to ask me now to marry him, I would say yes – instantly. There would be no hesitation whatsoever. We've been together for enough years for me to know I to stay by his side always. But your son – the man I love – has his own pace in life. It's likely I'll have to wait until the moment suits him, and you'll have to wait for whatever grandchildren he and I might be blessed to give you."*

*Ellen smiled, Ashling remembered, as she finished preparing the dessert plates. "Sometimes I think you understand him better than I do," Ellen told her. "Aidan was a handful as a child, and a concern ever since he has been on his own."*

*She put her arm around Ashling. "I would surely love more grandchildren. Ian, for whatever reasons, has never had children, and Margaret's sons will certainly do well in life. But…"*

*"But?" Ashling asked.*

*Ellen looked away, as if ashamed that she had let something loose that should have been kept inside. "We're talking in confidence now, are we not?" she said.*

*Ashling nodded. "Of course. You have my word."*

*"Aidan – there's always been something special about him. Ian and Margaret – yes, I am proud of them and what they have achieved. But they are…so ordinary." Ellen laughed suddenly. "They've always been terribly boring, God forgive me." And she laughed some more.*

*The laughter was contagious and it took a minute for Ashling to catch her breath. At the same time, she hoped that Ian and wife – sitting in the dining room with Cornelius and Aidan – had not overheard the kitchen conversation. Margaret and her family had chosen not to share the holiday.*

*"There is not a chance in heaven that Aidan could ever be boring," Ashling said when she regained her composure. "It's simply not in his blood."*

*"Nor in mine," Ellen answered, adding, "Thank God." Then, smoothing her apron then wiping her hands, she told Ashling: "We had better bring out the desserts before we start hearing complaints. But come back to the kitchen afterwards. There's something I want to tell you."*

*Ashling nodded and picked up some of the plates and pushed through the kitchen door, greeted by the expectant looks of all the family around the table.*

*A half-hour later, after the desserts had been ingested and the men – and Ian's wife -- had gone into the living room to watch football on television, Ashling rejoined Ellen in the kitchen to clean up the Thanksgiving Day dinner debris. For a while, they talked only about how good the turkey was and how delicious the squash tasted, and other things that reinforced the fact that it was, above all, a meal at least as good as all the other Thanksgiving meals before.*

*It was when Ellen was putting away the remains of the turkey that she said to Ashling offhandedly, "Just so you know, I've written a letter to Aidan."*

# Mulligan

One of the few things that have always irritated Sean is a phone call that comes just as he is stepping out his door. It doesn't happen often, but it always presents the same conundrum: ignore it and if it's important the caller will leave a message, or take the call on the very slim chance that it has to do with some kind of emergency. Sean's mother is in good health, so he is not too concerned about her. Yet, he knows he will regret it if the call has to do with something of consequence, so he sighs and closes the apartment door and goes to the phone.

"Hello," he says, ready to fend off a telemarketing call or a wrong number.

A brief silence on the other end. "Hi, Sean. This is Julie." She gives a soft laugh. "Julie Bransfield. You remember me, I hope."

Sean sits down on the couch. He's never been quick on his feet, but he presses himself now. He's known only one woman named Julie.

"I've never forgotten," he says, hoping he's says the right thing. Then memories come back.

He and Julie had met – what? – four years before, at a cocktail party Sean had attended in a professional role. He'd learned that she was a science teacher on loan to the Rhode Island Department of Education for a special project, and by the end of the evening he'd requested an interview with her about the quality of the science curricula in the state's schools, with a focus on those in his town.

The interview, a long one, had turned into an evolving discussion, first in her office then later over drinks at a French bistro near Providence's Financial District. They covered about a dozen topics related to education and young people and politics and the state of the nation, as well as some asides about recipes, restaurants, and favorite books.

After Sean's article was published, Julie invited him to dinner, provided he would bring a couple of copies of that particular issue. The dinner ended with an agreement to have lunch together, sometime soon.

Over the next two years, he and Julie met for lunch a few times, dinner a few times, a couple of shows at Trinity Rep and a Broadway musical at the Providence Performing Arts Center. They'd also shared an enjoyable day at the Newport Jazz Festival, a hot summer day at the Wickford Art Festival, and a trip to Block Island

Julie was delightful company, a great conversationalist, and as bright as Sean wishes he was. But with his broken marriage still a lingering part of his life and his regrets, Sean allowed the growing link between him and Julie to fade and eventually disappear. He'd seen her page on Facebook once and read education-news articles in which she was mentioned, and he'd often thought that she'd be the kind of woman he'd love to have in his life. But she was above him in enough respects that being together was as unlikely as his winning millions in the lottery. The last time he'd been in touch with her – or, rather, she with him – had been long ago enough for him to dismiss any hopes of reviving any relationship. Besides, he didn't consider himself good relationship material. Still, she was someone he found attractive on many levels.

But why on earth is she calling me at this hour?

"It's nice to hear your voice, Julie," he says. "It's been quite a while."

"It has," she says. "I've been wondering how you're doing. I still think about you now and then. You're the only journalist who treated me well in print."

"I doubt that," he says. "I've read other articles for which you were interviewed. You came across well in all of them."

"Following my career?" Julie laughs.

Sean feels his face flush. "I always read about people I've interviewed, or about topics I've covered."

Instead of responding to his response, she says, "So how are you doing? To be honest with you, one of my girlfriends is a nurse at South County Hospital and – without giving me any details, of course – happened to mention you were a patient there not too long ago."

"Sounds like a violation of medical ethics," Sean says, laughing quickly so she knew the hospital leak didn't bother him. "Yeah, I was there."

"Are you okay?" Sean thought he heard real concern in her voice.

"A bleeding ulcer," he tells her. "It sort of exploded on me. I'm okay, though. I need to have some follow-up visits, but I'm feeling fine and I have no restrictions – except alcohol."

"Bummer," Julie says, chuckling. "I was hoping we could have a drink one of these days."

Sean was left speechless for a longer moment that he would have liked. Lamely, all he manages to say is, "You were?"

Sean could almost hear her thinking on the other end of the line. Finally, she says, "It's Friday and the work week is done. What are you doing this evening?"

"Actually, I was just heading out the door to get something to eat."

"Where are you going?"

"Duffy's," he says. "I think I'm in the mood for seafood."

"How about some company?" Julie laughs again. "I know I can be pushy, but – hey – life's too short to have dinner by yourself. And you have to admit that it's been far too long since we've had some good conversation."

Thirty-seven minutes later, waiting in his car in Duffy's parking lot, Sean sees Julie stepping out of a white Volvo.

He's not unhappy that she called and is in fact happy that she's coming, but he's not sure he's ready for company. The ulcer thing has taken a lot of out of him, and he thinks he looks like he's been through hell. Still, Julie is one of those people — intelligent, lively, tuned-in to the world around them, and full of life — that he always found himself drawn to.

All he could think of now, as he watched her scanning the parking lot for him, was why she suddenly called him after nearly two years. Sean has always considered himself no one special. He sees himself as competent at his job and somewhat competent at living out his life. If he had ever developed any social aspirations, they would have been about being personable, charming, fun to be with, and having a gift of great conversation. Julie, on the other hand, was all things that he was not. Yet she had called him – out of the clear blue sky. And, surprising himself, he had agreed to meet her for dinner.

He braces himself – for he thinks himself naturally inept in his interpersonal skills in social situations – and he gets out of his car and calls to her. She turns, smiles, waves, and begins walking toward him.

"It's so nice to see you!" She seems genuinely excited as she comes up to him, smiling brightly, and gives him a quick but enthusiastic hug. Pulling back to take a good look at him, she says, "You look pretty damn good. After you mentioned your bleeding ulcer incident, I thought I'd find you gaunt and wasting away." She laughs and turns toward the restaurant entrance.

"Not me," Sean says. "I'm permanently healthy now."

She hasn't changed a bit, Sean notices. Julie is the kind of woman who has a certain down-to-earth elegance and an easy way of relating with anyone she meets. She still wears her blond hair short – he once thought of her hairstyle as charmingly feisty. And, Sean notes with pleasure, she is still slender and fit, and he wonders if she still runs every morning.

As they reach the door, Sean leans past her and opens it for her.

"Thank you," she says, almost in a teasing way, "I'm not used to having doors opened for me, kind sir."

Sean grins and follows her inside, thinking of a half-dozen questions he could come up with based on that comment, and the wry tone in which it was given, but he still has no clue why she is here. After their phone call was finished, his initial thought was that there was something going on in Rhode Island educational circles and that she might be looking for some journalistic help or advice. If so, he'd be comfortable with that. He could not imagine any other reason she would be turning to him.

Duffy's is already crowded. The tables and stools in the bar area, where Sean normally sat, are all taken, so he leads Julie into the dining room toward the rear of the restaurant. As they pass through the door separating the two sections, Julie says, "Ah, this is so much quieter in here. Better for talking."

"The bar section can get noisy and a little rambunctious sometimes," Sean answers. The hostess spots him and he raises two fingers. She smiles, grabs two menus, and signals him to follow her. A moment later he and Julie are sitting at a corner table toward the back, and Sean tries to put a sentence together to get the conversation going.

Julie, though, speaks first – to his relief. He hasn't felt completely himself since the stay in the hospital, and he's content for her to take the lead.

"We have a mutual acquaintance," she says, "at least indirectly." She smiles at Sean.

"Oh?"

"She's the nurse I mentioned on the phone. Her name is Jane," Julie says, spreading a napkin on her lap. "Her husband is a musician." She eyes him as she finishes her sentence. There's a smile about to light up her face.

Sean stares at her. "Ted's wife?"

Julie laughs. "We've been friends for years. I didn't know you were Ted's friend until Jane mentioned it about a month ago. She was telling me that Ted was really freaked out by his friend's suddenly erupting in blood at a restaurant while they were meeting about some novel."

"This restaurant, in fact," Sean tells her. He indicated the bar section. "In there."

"That must have been frightening," Julie says, sincerely. "Anyway, she never mentioned your name until she was telling me that Ted's been reading a manuscript you're writing. When she finally mentioned you by name, I almost choked."

"Was it a good choke or a bad choke?" Sean says, trying for some humor.

"A good one, of course." She smiles broadly at him, increasing his confusion about her reappearance in his life.

The waitress approaches the table with her rehearsed greeting. "Would you care for a drink to start off?"

Julie points at Sean. "This man cannot have a drop of alcohol tonight, not a drop." She gives him an unsubtle smirk. "I, on the other hand, would love to have a Sam Adams Lager."

"Bottle or draft?" the waitress asks.

"Bottle," Julie says.

"And you?" the waitress asks, turning to Sean.

"Ginger ale will be fine with me."

The waitress smiles a standard smile. "I'll be right back with your drinks." She lays a sheet of paper on the table between them. "These are tonight's specials. The only thing we don't have is the fresh swordfish."

"Gotcha," Sean says as she twirls away from the table and heads for the service bar.

Julie pushes the list of specials toward Sean. "I already know what I would like. Besides, I'd like to make this my treat tonight?"

Sean shakes his head. "No way. I was coming here anyway, and I invited you."

"No. You simply couldn't resist my request to join you. So I pushed you into it. It's my treat, and one of my rules of life is that healthy people should treat the recently ill to a meal of their choice."

Sean has to laugh. "I remember that you were always exceedingly direct." He looks across at her. "You look good, too. When was the last time we saw each other? If I recall, it was over drinks the day after you got that fellowship at the Department of Education."

"Your memory serves you right. What else do you remember?"

More words out of her mouth that make Sean wonder about the reason she called and why she wanted to see him.

He remembers that they had gone to Richard's Pub out on Quaker Lane and had shared a couple of appetizers and a couple of drinks while talking about another educational feature he happened to be writing and about her career in education. At last he says, "We talked, snacked on fried calamari and stuffed quahogs, drank a bit. I think we were there for at least two hours."

"Closer to three. Loosen you up with a drink and you're a great conversationalist." Again she smiles at him. This time it seems almost a smile of appreciation.

"That long, huh?"

"Amazing how quickly time passes when you're having fun."

Julie looks at him, a long look, this time her smile fades to barely a trace. "Do you remember kissing me?"

"What?"

"You don't recall?"

"You're kidding me, right?"

She gives him a most direct look. "I never kid about something so momentous." She lets the words hang in the air, then laughs. "Yes, you kissed me, in the parking lot, just before I got in my car. Surprised the hell out of me."

"Jesus Christ!" Sean says, feeling his face flush as he rummages wildly through his mind for some hint of memory. Finally, sighing, he says, "I remember – jeez! I'm sorry. I was out of line."

"You're sorry?" she asks, cocking her head at him. "Are you telling me you didn't mean to kiss me?"

"We both were drinking…"

"So if you had been sober, you would have definitely avoided kissing me?" She gives him a mock frown, leaving him to wonder where all this was leading.

How could he answer such a question? He can sputter nothing more than, "I take the Fifth."

"The Fifth doesn't work in restaurants," she counters, clearly baiting him. "Are you going to answer my question or not?" Her crooked smile tells him she is taking the matter lightly – at least he hopes so.

Sean sometimes believes in providence – not the city – which in this instance is the waitress's return with their drinks. With exaggerated delicacy, as if handling an exquisite crystal goblet of wine, she places a standard bar mug in front of Julie then carefully pours some of the beer into it. With far less ceremony, she plunks Sean's ginger ale on the corner of his place mat.

"Have you decided?" she asks, pulling out her notepad.

Sean nods toward Julie. "Do you know what you want?"

"I'll have a lobster roll – with fries and cole slaw," she tells her.

"And you?" the waitress says.

"Ditto," he says."

The waitress dutifully jots the orders down and says "I'll get those right in for you" as she spins away from the table.

A second later, Julie says, "That's exactly what you said when we went to Richard's Pub. And that time before that when we went to Café Fresco in East Greenwich."

"I did?"

"You did — 'ditto' each time," she says, with a sharp nod for emphasis. "Are you into the whole 'imitation is the sincerest form of flattery' shtick?"

Her laugh, when it comes in instant later, reminds Sean of why he likes her so much. It's a crystal-clear laugh that imparts nothing more than utter delight in the moment.

"I'm not into any 'shtick'," he answers. "I'm just plain ol' me." An instant later, he adds, "I love their lobster rolls."

"Don't you mean 'lobsta'?"

"I'm not a native Rhode Islander,", he says, chuckling. "I'm not sure I could talk like that even if I tried."

Julie lifts her mug. "To a nice dinner and some fine conversation," she says.

"Seconded," he says, clinking his ginger ale against the glass of beer he so sorely wished he could be drinking now.

Julie leans back in her seat. If there is one thing that Sean really loves about Julie – besides her playful feistiness and her I-can-do-anything attitude – it's her eyes. She has, in his opinion, the kind of eyes that could tie pleasant knots in any man's heart. All the more reason to wonder why she is here with him this evening. Why the hell is he being so damned suspicious?

"So," she says while Sean's mind is still befuddled by her presence, "back to the kiss." She drums her fingers on the table and stares at him as if intending to stare him down. "You never answered my question, dear Sean – and a lot is riding on your answer."

Again the crooked smile and the irresistible glint in her eyes.

Sean picks up his ginger ale. "I wish this was a two-liter bottle of lager," he says.

Julie laughs. "You'd need more than that before this inquisition is over!" Her finger-drumming continues. "Talk to me."

Sean moves his glass of ginger ale in small circles in the puddle of condensation that has slipped down its side. "If it makes you happy, then yes – I would have kissed you even if I – we – hadn't been drinking."

Julie gives him a smug look. "I knew it. It definitely was a kiss that meant business."

Sean feels redness creeping back into his face. He likes it that she is interested in the fact that they had kissed that one time, but he wishes he could change the subject.

He's not sure how to handle the situation and he knows his interpersonal skills – at least on a highly personal level – have not always been among his strengths. He can get along fine with anyone, anytime. But when it comes to something like this, something that broaches the edges of a relationship, he is unsure, unsteady, and maybe unready. Of course, he attributes much of this to the breakup of his marriage and the anger and pain it generated. His ex had demeaned him in every way possible on her way to the marital exit. The hurt and diminished confidence still lingered as strong as ever.

"Is this making you uncomfortable?" Julie asks.

Sean takes a moment to respond. "No. Not really." He doesn't want to get into any discussion of his divorce, his ex, and the overall aimlessness that imbues his life more often than he cares to admit. "I guess I just wasn't expecting kissing to be the topic."

They look at each other for a while, Sean continuing to toy with his glass, and Julie sipping from her beer.

"You're right. I can be a little direct," she says, finally. "It's just my nature."

"It's one of the things I've admired about you," Sean says, giving her a smile intended to reassure her that he isn't upset.

"I didn't mean to make you feel uncomfortable," she continues, the regret clear in her voice. "To be honest with you, I was happy that you kissed me, and I was hoping you would call me so we could go out together again. But you only called me once more – to get some background information some new secondary education grants the Department was rolling out."

For the next few seconds she stares out the window toward the parking lot. "And to be honest with you some more, the reason I called you today is because I enjoyed your company the few times we spent together. And, I enjoyed your kiss. And I was concerned after Jane told me about your ulcer episode. So I decided to get in touch with you to see if you might have at least some interest in seeing each other now and then."

Suddenly it was Sean's turn to be honest. He pushes his glass aside and leans his elbows on the table. "This will either sound stupid, clueless, or immature – take your pick," he tells her.

"I'll bet it's none of the above," she replies.

He shakes his head, then begins speaking.

"I liked you from the start. The first time we met – for that article I was doing – there was something about you that I found very attractive. Not just one thing, but many things together. You're bright and have a fabulous sense of humor. You're assertive and direct in ways that make me envy you. You're charming, smart, well-read, and have the kind of personality that must be an awesome people-magnet. I envisioned you having scores of friends – and most definitely being involved in a serious relationship with someone. I was surprised, actually, that you weren't married or engaged or even dating."

"You checked my ring finger," Julie says, smiling. "You did that the first time you sat me down for an interview."

Sean gives a soft laugh. "How do you know it wasn't a stray glance?"

"I'm a woman – and women notice things like that."

"Oh."

"Continue," she says. Then, almost instantly, she adds. "I'm sorry. I'm being too damned direct again, aren't I?"

Sean waves off her concerns. "It's okay," he tells her. "What I was going to say is that although I thought you were a truly attractive woman, I figured you were out of my league. For some reason, I could see you married to some big-bucks CEO, or a successful lawyer, or maybe a famous surgeon. I could not see you spending time with a feature-writer from a small town weekly. So, even though I kissed you, I thought it was best if I didn't call you again. Nothing ventured, no disappointment."

She smiles at him, genuine pleasure in her eyes. Then she says, "You are an presumptuous and miscalculating ass, Sean O'Connor. So I wasn't worth the risk?"

As Sean is about to answer, Julie burst into laughter. "Don't answer that. I was just busting you. I promise I won't be direct any more – at least for tonight. Just tell me one thing…"

"What's that?"

"Is there any chance you will ask me out after this dinner is done?"

"You just broke your promise," he says with a grin.

"Sorry," she says. "I can't help being who I am."

"If you weren't who you are, you'd be a pretty boring person," he tells her. "And, if I may continue…"

"Please do," she says.

Sean nods. "What are you doing next Saturday?"

Julie reaches across the table and puts her hand on his. "To tell you the truth, I'm probably going to be doing exactly what you're going to be doing."

Sean smiles at her. "It looks like I've sealed my own fate," he says, laughing.

Before Julie can respond, the waitress glides up to the table and begins putting their meals in front of them.

Three hours later, after an unexpectedly delightful evening with Julie, Sean – energized – is at his computer, a half-finished glass of soda next to him, writing again about Aidan. He has a feeling he's going to be writing some good stuff tonight.

***I need to tell you something***

*Aidan walked through the apartment door almost fifteen minutes later than Ashling expected and she hurried to hug him.*

*"I was terribly worried about you," she said, holding him close and kissing his cheek. "You were driving very slowly, were you?"*

*"I was," he told her, his voice holding a trace of the slurring she had heard earlier.*

*"I thank God for that. You've clearly had more to drink than is good for you."*

*"My dad was in worse shape when I left him." Aidan laughed.*

*"That's no matter now," she said, leading Aidan toward the bedroom. ""Let's get you under the covers. You can sleep it off. In the morning, we'll talk about your mother's letter."*

*Aidan allowed himself to be led to the bedroom. He would never admit it, but he was too drunk and too tired to put up any resistance. Ashling always seemed to know what was best for him, and over the last few months he was finally allowing himself to acknowledge the fact.*

*"The letter was interesting," he told her as she gently pushed him to sit down on the bed.*

*"I'm sure it was," she said.*

*"And you knew about it?"*

*"To be honest with you, your mother told me that she had written a letter for you, to be given to you after she passed away – bless her soul." Ashling gave Aidan another shove and he flopped backwards on the bed. She reached down and slipped off his shoes. "She never told me much about what was in the letter."*

*"I'm tired," Aidan said, his voice sliding toward a sleepy mumble.*

*Ashling lifted his feet and swung his legs onto the bed. He could change his own clothes in the morning.*

*"We'll talk when you wake up, luv."*

*"Uh-huh," was all that Aidan could utter in a weakening voice. Then, with a final effort, he said, "Love you…to pieces."*

*She leaned over him, whispered, "I love you to pieces, as well, dearest Aidan." He was already asleep. She kissed him softly on his forehead and left the room.*

*She was tired enough that she should be going to bed as well, but the stress of waiting for Aidan to arrive home safely was keeping sleep at bay.*

*So she sat at the kitchen table, in Aidan's chair, wondering how to approach their conversation tomorrow – for there would definitely be a conversation: about the letter, about the direction of Aidan's life, about her feelings for him and his for her.*

*Her life with Aidan thus far made it impossible for her to leave any of this for Aidan to raise in discussions together. It would likely never happen. It was she who had to be the one – as Aidan's mother had told her more than once – and she decided that tomorrow evening would be the beginning of that special conversation. She crossed herself, whispered a prayer for success to the Blessed Mother, then went to Aidan's cabinet, where he kept his alcohol and took a substantial swig of vodka from Aidan's last bottle.*

*Then she went to bed.*

*Five hours later – for that was all the sleep she managed to get – Aidan was still unconscious and almost in exactly the same position she'd left him when she'd swung his legs up onto the bed.*

*The conversation would, of course, have to wait until evening; Ashling had to get to work, and she was now estimating that Aidan might not wake anytime before noon.*

*She left the bedroom, made herself a cup of coffee and a piece of toast and decided to call Cornelius. She could not be sure that he'd recovered from his drinking/talking session with his youngest, but decided that he'd not answer the phone if he were unconscious as was his son, and would pick up the phone were he up and about as usual. In any case, she decided, it was worth the effort to dial the number. She had many questions to ask him.*

*Cornelius sounded as if the previous evening had never happened – at least with regard to the amount of alcohol consumed.*

*"Good morning to you, Ashling," he said with great – and sober – cheer. "Did Aidan get home safely last night?"*

*"He did," she said. "Although he arrived somewhat later than I expected and I spent some time worrying about him. He's still asleep."*

*"I would have called him a cab, but there was no way that either I or he could afford a ride from Boston to Rhode Island."*

*Ashling had to laugh. "I'm thankful you didn't. It would have been a needless expense. I would have been comfortable knowing he was spending the night with you – although I expect the two of you would have had even more to drink."*

*She heard Cornelius chuckling on the other end of the line. "We had far too much to drink as it was," Cornelius told her. "Still, it was something we both needed, I think."*

*"If I may ask," Ashling said, turning a bit more serious, "how did our Aidan react to the letter Ellen left him?"*

*Cornelius paused, but only ever so briefly. "He told me that his mother's personality shone through, but not much else. Yet from the look on his face as he read it, she must have written things that rang true to him." Again, he paused, this time for a longer moment. "I think Ellen's letter affected him."*

*Ashling, recalling Aidan's "Love you – to pieces," could not disagree. "I think you're right. He seems to have come home a changed man. After he wakes up, I'll have a better idea of what his mother's words might have done to him."*

*She could almost see Cornelius nodding in agreement. Then he said, "I believe he will finally ask you to marry him." There seemed to be a mix of hope and pride in his voice. "It's just a feeling I have," he said, as if trying to reinforce the opinion.*

*"If he doesn't," Ashling said, "I will most certainly ask him to marry me!"*

*Cornelius laughed. It was edifying to hear him sound so happy after the terrible loss of his wife. "Promise me you will. Ellen always knew you were the right woman for Aidan. You can't let him slip away because he sometimes can't see beyond his own nose."*

*"You have my word," she said.*

*"He will say yes," Cornelius stated. "He'd be a fool to deprive me of a daughter-in-law as wonderful as you."*

*"Flattery," she answered, "always wins me over." Her laughter and that of her likely future father-in-law blended together. It was their plot and their plan for Aidan's future that they had agreed upon – and each of them was confident it would all come to pass.*

*After her conversation with Cornelius, Ashling tiptoed into the bedroom to check on Aidan. He was on his back, his mouth agape, snoring mildly, and utterly disconnected from the world. Ashling guessed it might be hours before he would awaken. Sure that he was in no imminent danger of succumbing to excess alcohol, she returned to the kitchen and made herself a second cup of coffee.*

*Then she decided to call in sick so she could tend to Aidan, so she called the office, left a voice message giving a quick synopsis of why she could not come to work, then took her coffee cup to the living room and enjoyed the chance to relax in her pajama bottoms and t-shirt. If the gods of good fortune were truly good, Aidan would wake up before noon. She very much wanted to have the conversation with him.*

*It was actually nearly eleven in the morning when Aidan shuffled out of the bedroom – in Ashling's opinion barely conscious – and attempted to make coffee for himself. She, far more alert than he, intercepted him at the coffee maker and gave him a warm hug.*

*"How wonderful of you to wake up this morning," she said, clearly teasing him. "Do you recall much about returning home last night?"*

*"Do you recall if I was a real ass when I got home last night?" he asked back.*

*She gave him a hug. "The truth is," she said, "that you were quite rational, although exceedingly tired and impressively drunk." She pulled away from him. "I will have you know, luv, that I utterly disapprove of your driving after having had so much alcohol."*

*Aidan regarded her while he tried to gather his thoughts. "It was my father's fault," he said. "He wanted Jameson, and I couldn't let him drink alone."*

*"And I was on the phone with your father less than a half-hour ago. So I know where the truth lies."*

*All Aidan could say was, "Jeez."*

*"However, I am extremely happy that you returned home safely, and I'm delighted you are now awake and reasonably alert." Ashling gave him another hug, enjoying how he felt in her arms. It took a moment, but Aidan returned her hug and held her close to him for longer than she'd expected.*

*"I need to tell you something," Aidan said.*

*Ashling hushed him. "Not now. First, we need to get some coffee in you, then we need to feed you, and finally we need to talk about your mother's letter."*

*"The one you knew about," Aidan said.*

*"Yes," Ashling said, smiling. "The very one she told me about."*

*"So tell me," Aidan said.*

*Ashling pushed him away gently. "First, coffee – exceptionally strong coffee," she told him firmly, "then conversation. I'm not entirely sure that you are not still under the influence."*

*Aidan shook his head. "I slept it off pretty much," he told her, almost apologetically. Although Aidan had always drunk rather heavily, especially when he was with his friends, he'd always made special efforts to keep Ashling from knowing too much about his drinking habits and rarely drank too much when he was with her*

*"Go sit down," she said, giving him a nudge toward the kitchen table.*

*Aidan obeyed.*

*When she brought him his coffee a few minutes later, he cupped the mug in his two hands and sipped the hot brew gingerly.*

*"Thanks," he said after his first swallow. "I need this."*

*He gazed down at the coffee for what seemed to Ashling like a couple of minutes. Lifting his head and looking at her through red and tired eyes, he said again, "So tell me."*

*"And what would it be that I should tell you?" Ashling asked, honestly wondering what he expected from her.*

*"What my mother told you about the letter. I'm sure she didn't just tell you 'I have written a letter to my prodigal son.'"*

*Ashling had always been honest with Aidan about everything. It was in her nature to do so, not just with Aidan but also with anyone else. She sat down across from him and gave him a soft smile. "Your mother told me only that she had written a letter to you, and that you were to get it only after she had passed on."*

*"She must have told you what was in it," Aidan said, confident that he was right.*

*"She never mentioned a word about the contents. She simply told me she had written a letter to you." Ashling leaned her elbows on the table. "So it's your turn to tell me – what did she write in that letter?"*

*Had Aidan not had so much to drink, and had his metabolism had had more time to bring his mind to normal clarity – and had he not been too tired to keep Ashling's curiosity at arm's length, he would have simply said, "She wrote a lot of things."*

*But at the moment he was all the things he wished he were not, and so he told Ashling, "She wrote things about me, that I had been a disappointment to her, but that she had faith in me. And she gave me a lecture – can you imagine? A lecture after she's gone and died on me? – a lecture about what I could be if I tried. She also wrote some things about Ian and Margaret."*

*Ashling pondered what he had revealed. "It sounds like the way your mother would talk about you when she and I were alone."*

*Aidan sat up, his eyes widening. "You and my mother talked about me when you were alone?"*

*"Countless times," Ashling told him. "You were her favorite topic*

*– and her favorite child."*

*Aidan slipped into a slouch in his chair, the coffee forgotten. "She said something like that in the letter," he whispered. After a moment, he shook his head. "I've screwed up my life."*

*Ashling reached across the table and put her hand on his. "No, luv. You've led the kind of life that has led you to where you are now. I have a feeling that you are ready to move forward."*

*Aidan stared at her. "Move forward to what?" He sat up, and took her hand in his. "This is what I wanted to tell you, and you don't know this because I never told you before. But do you remember the morning of my last birthday, when I turned forty-three?"*

*"Ah, I most certainly do. You were, as I recall, as weird as I have ever seen you – although last night you were weird also, but in a rather delightful way."*

*Aidan began to ask what she meant by last night's weirdness, but she plowed ahead with what she was saying.*

*"I recall that you were uncommunicative that morning, perhaps depressed, clearly in need of some alcohol to take care of what the coffee that morning could not relieve, and then you disappeared for the day and part of the evening."*

*"I worked that evening," he said.*

*"So," she said, looking at him with intense caring in her eyes, "what did you not tell me about that happened that morning?"*

*For some reason, Aidan needed to bring Ashling more closely into himself. He sensed that – at this particular moment on this particular morning – he needed to open up to her as he had never done before. It unnerved him; for all these years, after all, he had been deliberately himself and accompanied only by his personal drummer. Ashling had been a fellow traveler, in his view of the world the two of them had shared for all this time. But in the jumble of weeks since he had awakened on his birthday, shocked by the epiphany of seeing himself in a most unflattering light, he had begun to understand that Ashling was with him for something more than the sporadic companionship he was wont to offer. And, after having read his mother's letter, he suddenly could see Ashling in a different light. It was as if he were caught up in a long process of awakening that was being guided by his mother, his father, and Ashling – beginning on the morning of his birthday.*

*Aidan asked Ashling for a second cup of coffee. As she went to the counter and poured it, he began recounting how he had awakened that morning, distressed not so much by having turned forty-three but rather by the realization that he had accomplished virtually nothing in his entire life. He was, he told her, pretty much a loser.*

*"How can anyone be proud of running a check-out register at a liquor store for as many years as I have?" he asked her. As Ashling placed a full cup of coffee in front of him, he added, "And how could someone as beautiful and smart and successful as you put up with someone like me for so long? Most women would have left a deadbeat in a heartbeat. Those are the kinds of things that damn near drove me crazy that morning. I went to Beavertail and I brought some vodka with me. To tell you the truth, I wasn't sure I wanted to be around for my next birthday."*

*His words gave Ashling a chill, but she gave him an empathetic look and waited for him to continue.*

*"Look at Ian, for Christ's sake," he said. "Look at Margaret. They amounted to something. No wonder Ian barely acknowledges me and that Margaret has written me out of her life. I've disappointed everyone."*

*Ashling let Aidan stew in his words for a moment. "You cannot have disappointed your brother or sister because I honestly believe neither of them ever had any respect for you."*

*"Because I fucked up my life."*

*"No, luv. Because you lived your life far more freely than either of them has been able to do. Indeed, they have succeeded in financial terms – fine cars, great houses, exotic vacations, and all the other things that come from having money." Shelia leaned back in her chair. "But those things do not define a good life."*

*She looked intently into Aidan's eyes. "Have you never had any inkling that Ian has always been deeply envious of you?"*

*Aidan laughed, a single explosive "Ha!"*

*"He has, you know," she said, her voice most serious. "I've listened to him and watched him when we've been at your parents' apartment for holiday dinners. I believe he has always had a longing to be you."*

*"He treats me like shit."*

*"Because he's so jealous of you," she said. "How else could he treat you? Remember, you are leading the free kind of life he actually craves. Look at the way he has to live: he is committed to and dominated by the need to come up with new levels of billable hours at work. He is caught in the trap of being unhappy with his work, because it steals so much time from the kind of life he wishes he were living. And he's unhappy with his wife who apparently, in a truly cliché*

*fashion, always seems to want more."*

*Ashling knew Aidan was thinking in the wrong direction. She let him muse about his situation for a moment longer, then asked, "Where is the letter. I'd like to read it – if it would be acceptable to you."*

*It took him a minute to recall what he'd done with it, then he reached into his pants pocket and pulled it out. He'd folded it neatly, but it had crumpled more during the long drive home.*

*"Here," he said, passing it to her.*

*With the letter in her hand, she said, "Would you like more coffee while I read it?"*

*He nodded wearily. "That would be great. Thanks."*

*Soon the coffee was before him, and Ashling sat across from him and carefully unfolded the envelope and slipped the letter out from it. Spreading the letter on the table, she leaned forward and began to read it. Soon she could see that Ellen had written a letter to her son that was clearly intended to turn his life around.*

*Yes, she thought as she read, Aidan and she would have a very important conversation once his mind was clear. For the first time in their many years together, she was truly optimistic about the future of their relationship.*

*She read on, and smiled.*

It is not yet five o'clock in the morning when Sean awakes. He'd spent nearly two hours writing after returning from his dinner with Julie, but now as he lies in bed his thoughts are not – as usual – about the book. They're about Julie and the unforeseen reunion they'd had at Duffy's, and about the amount of honesty he'd allowed himself when they talked. He is typically not especially open or honest about his feelings; being somewhat reticent about things that are so personal can save a lot of anguish down the line – at least sometimes. He wonders, worrywart as he can be, if he may have said too much.

Julie had pressed him so they could meet again, and he was happy to agree on a "date" planned for the coming Saturday. Yet, he half-expects that she will call between now and then to say that something has come up and won't be able to make it.

The thoughts nag at him until he forces himself out of bed and into the shower. He'll get to work early and being busy in the newsroom will settle him down. He'd deal with Julie and her possible cancellation when it happened. If it happened.

He walks to work, briskly, shaking the last of the cobwebs from his mind. The air is refreshing and the morning still and peaceful. As he expected, the newsroom is empty; no one would likely be in for at least an hour. He sits himself before his computer, grabs a file folder that hold the notes he's amassed for the feature he's working on, and shuffles through them. He's already written two pages of the article – this one about an elderly Wickford resident who was cited in a recent issue of "Wooden Boat" magazine for having restored an old Herreshoff sloop, using time-tested boatbuilding skills and techniques.

Sean found he could have talked with the man – Harvey Pease – for hours. And, in fact, Sean spent nearly an entire day listening as the man recounted how he'd stripped the hull of the twenty-five-footer down to its ribs, reinforced the lead keel, and hand-shaped the new planking with tools that were state-of-the-art when the boat was originally built. Through it all, Harvey interspersed stories of life on Narragansett Bay and hurricanes and sailing and fishing and the nuisance of powerboats and the time when the Navy dominated pretty much the entire area until the government began pulling them out in the Seventies. Sean barely had to ask any questions at all.

After spending a few minutes getting himself up to speed, Sean brings his computer to life and begins typing. And the effort begins having its desired effect: his nitpicky concerns about Julie and her motives begin fading away. He writes, unaware of the time, until he hears the door open and Calvin, the sports editor, enters.

"Brown-nosing, huh?" he asks Sean, giving him enough of a laugh to let Sean know that he's just busting him. "What the hell brings you in so early?" Calvin has always arrived at work at seven o'clock promptly, as if he worked for an old evening daily with a ten-thirty morning deadline for the first edition.

"I woke up early, got bored sitting at home, and figured I'd try to get this Harvey Pease feature done early."

"He's the old guy that likes to build dories and fix wooden boats, right?"

"Right."

"Cripes, he's got to be – what? In his late eighties?"

"Ninety-one," Sean says. "But the guy has way more energy that I have."

"That's not surprising," Calvin says, laughing again. "Well, get to it. I've got about six high school sports stories to write. Exciting, eh?"

Sean gives him a thumbs-up and refocuses on getting his story written.

Over the next hour, the rest of the staff drifts in, each greeting Sean and asking how he is feeling, and a few noting with surprise that he is already at work. At nine o'clock, Jeff Gallagher, the editor arrives and slips into his office without saying much to anyone. Fifteen minutes later, he emerges to stand in the middle of the newsroom where everyone can hear him.

"Folks," he says. "Listen up for a minute, okay?" Sean sees that Jeff, normally easy-going, smiling, and virtually always upbeat, is frowning and staring down at a sheet of paper in his hands.

The newsroom comes to a dead stop.

Jeff clears his throat and looks at each of the staff, one by one. Then he speaks.

"I just came from a meeting with Ed Witham. I'm sure you all know that he is the publisher of this paper and of the ones in Warwick and East Greenwich. He has told me that he's sold the papers to another publishing company. The deal will be closed in three weeks."

The staff members exchange glances and mutter questions to each other.

Again, Jeff clears his throat. "Ed gave me some information to share with all of you, and he apologizes he could not be here in person to break this news to you. He is in a meeting with the new owners, and he expects to be tied up for much of the day."

He holds up the sheet of paper. "The new owners have some requests for information so that when the deal is closed they can hit the ground running. If you want to take notes, please do."

A few of the staffers reach down and pick up their notebooks and stand ready with pen in hand. Sean does likewise. Calvin, the sports editor, just parks his butt on his desk and listens.

Jeff says, "Ed is assuring each of us that there will be no personnel changes here at the paper – at least for the foreseeable future. What the new owners want, though, are a listing of any planned news coverage and feature stories, job descriptions for each of you – which I will furnish – and current resumes from each of you, which you will furnish. They'd like this information one week from today at the latest."

Gallagher folds the sheet of paper and tucks it into his shirt pocket. "I'm sorry to bring you the news this way. Any questions?"

The first question is, inevitably: "What do you mean by the foreseeable future?"

Jeff mulls the question for the moment. "To be honest with you, I have no idea. I'm just passing on to you what Ed gave me."

There are other questions that take up much of the next half-hour. Sean asks none. He simply slips back into his seat and ponders the problem of the resume, the need to put factual details of one's past on paper to be evaluated by someone who doesn't know you.

Before he can ponder too long, his phone rings. It's Julie, and she just wants to tell him that she had a wonderful time with him last night. He tells her the same, trying to sound enthusiastic in the face of what could be a change in his employment status in the weeks to come.

"I'm really looking forward to Saturday," she tells him, the smile in her voice more than evident.

"So am I, Julie," he tells her, doing his best to put a smile in his voice as well.

No longer does Sean have to worry that she might cancel. But, as he's learned from many past experiences, one worry fades only to be replaced often by another.

This whole "new owners of the paper" thing has him more than concerned. He tries to be honest with himself, a habit he has cultivated for some years now, but all he can see in the future is the end of his career. Why the hell should college matter so much, when skill and aptitude and achievement are far more important?

That evening, at home, he writes some more, hoping the effort will dull his anxiety about the new owners of the paper and about the resumé they want. And later, as he finally submits to fatigue and heads off to bed, he decides to cancel his Saturday date with Julie. He cannot possibly expect her to enjoy his company when there's an excellent chance that his world will collapse around him. And he truly wants to have her in his life.

For now at least, he decides, it has to be on his terms.

***Before you fell unconscious?***

*It seemed to Aidan that Ashling was taking an inordinate amount of time reading his mother's letter, as if she were parsing every sentence and analyzing every word. He'd already finished his second cup of coffee and had refilled his mug yet again while waiting for her to finish. Seeing the intensity with which her eyes moved carefully along every single line, it dawned on him that even though she'd known about the letter she truly had no idea about what his mother had written.*

*Finally, she laid the letter on the table and leaned back in her chair, nodding her head as she continued to stare at the sheets of paper. Then she looked up.*

*"When your mother told me she had written a letter to you, I had no idea whatsoever that she meant she had written something so rich in feelings and so clear about every point she wanted to make," she told Aidan. "She was a marvelous woman, your mother, and she knew you quite well."*

*She leaned forward in her chair and reached her hand across the table to him, and he slid his into hers.*

*"I know reading the letter must have been an intensely emotional experience for you, luv," she continued. "It has always been one of the things I love about you – that you and your mother were so close. I have no doubt she is watching over you now."*

*Aidan didn't know what to say; his mind was still too fogged to think clearly. So all he said was, "It was quite a letter."*

*"Does your dad know what she wrote? Did you tell him? Did you let him read it?"*

*Aidan rubbed his eyes. "I gave him a bit of an idea of what she wrote. But, no, he didn't read it. He wanted to, though."*

*"I'm sure he'd agree with everything your mother wrote," Ashling told him. She watched him as she spoke. His eyes were bleary, and she could see that he was not interested in talking much about what had*

*transpired last night. "I think I need to feed you," she said. "Would ham and eggs suit you this morning?"*

*Aidan grimaced. "I'm not sure my stomach is ready for anything like that."*

*"Then," she said, cheerily, "it shall be one poached egg on toast. That should be mild enough to your poor, much-disrespected stomach."*

*He let his head fall forward and just waved a hand at her. She took his gesture as a sign of agreement and turned to get his breakfast ready. As she worked, she gave occasional glances toward him, debating within herself whether it was the right time to bring up what she intended to bring up. By the time the egg was poached and placed gently on the piece of multi-grain toast – she had, fortunately, managed to improve his eating habits over the years – she decided it was most certainly time to talk – not because he was in a weakened state, or a vulnerable one, but rather because she hoped that his evening with his father had put many things in perspective for him.*

*She slid the plate onto the table in front of him, provided him with the proper utensils, and gave him a piece of paper towel to use as a napkin. After a moment, he reached for the salt and pepper and applied both liberally, then began eating.*

*When he was taking in his third bite of his breakfast, Ashling leaned on the table and asked him, "Do you remember what you said to me last night, before you fell unconscious?"*

*The question made him raise his head and look at her. It took a while for him to answer, but then he said, with a trace of a smile, "If you mean when I told you that I love you to pieces – yes, I remember."*

*"Do you remember the last time you told me you love me?"*

*"He shook his head and took another bite. "No.*

*"Did you tell me that because your mother said nice things about me in her letter?"*

*He put down his fork and swallowed some more coffee. The caffeine was starting, finally, to have an effect and the world began seeming a bit more real to him. He placed his hands on the edge of the table as if bracing himself. "No," he said. The faint smile was gone.*

*She cocked her head, waiting for him to continue, but there was only silence between them for the next thirty seconds. Eventually, he looked at her and spoke.*

*"How come you've stayed with me all these years? I've been pretty rough on you, carrying on as if I'm the only one that mattered." He turned his head away. "I've loved you pretty much from the beginning.*

*But there was a long time that I thought it would be weakness on my part to tell you how I felt. My mother could understand my feelings better than I could. Hell, even my father saw things for what they are."*

*He pushed his plate to one side and reached across to her, took her hand, and seemed to study it for a while. Then, "I'll say it so I remember it this time: I love you to pieces, Ashling. And I can't understand why I've been so damned stubborn about admitting it to myself and to you all this time. You deserved better."*

*"I deserve you," she said, her eyes wet but a smile spreading on her face. "And I love you more than I've ever been able to say, you sweet but stubbornly clueless man."*

*They locked eyes for the longest while. Ashling broke the trance by telling him, "All these years of effort I've put into you. They've finally paid off, I'd say." Her laugh was warm and happy and nearly giddy.*

*"So my parents knew for a long time how you felt about me?"*

*"Your dear mother did because I told her one day," Ashling answered. "She must have told your dad, else he figured it out himself. He's a most perceptive man, your dad."*

*Aidan waited for her to continue.*

*"In fact, your mother asked me quite a few years ago if we were close to planning a wedding," Ashling said. "I told her that a wedding might very well happen if you were ever to wake up and see the love surrounding you here."*

*Ashling paused. "It has sure taken you a bloody long time to wake up!" Again, the happy laugh.*

*Aidan lowered his head and shook it left and right slowly. "I think I started to wake up on my birthday. And I think I've been waking up ever since."*

*"You are my love, Aidan. It's so good to have you in my life."*

*He looked at her, still amazed that she had somehow stuck with him all this time, amazed that her love for him had remained so strong, and amazed that suddenly life seemed as fine as he could have ever wished.*

*Aidan pushed back his chair and stood and came to where Ashling sat. Taking Ashling's hand, he raised her from her seat, wrapped his arms around her, and held her in warm silence for a long, long time.*

Four days have passed since Jeff Gallagher's bombshell announcement about the sale of the paper, and Jeff wants everyone's resumés in two days. Sean knows that anyone who has never been part of a weekly newspaper's staff could never comprehend the tight and intimate "family" feeling only a weekly could offer. The stress of the impending transfer of ownership has been a growing strain on everyone, leaving Sean and his coworkers on edge and touchy.

Sean has stopped working on his story, leaving Aidan and the others in suspension until he can bring himself to focus again. Stress, Sean knows, has never been conducive to his creativity. Part of his anxiety with everything that is going on is his fear that the story about Aidan will wither on the vine, and once again he will fail to write anything worthwhile.

Since he cancelled his Saturday date with Julie, he has minimized his contacts with her. Still, she's called him a few times, and her calls have forced him to come up with increasingly complex excuses why he and she could not get together, at least for the time being. She, heeding her trusted woman's intuition, has been trying – gently – to wheedle the truth out of him, but he stubbornly holds onto the alibis he's set up. She persists, yet he holds his ground. Sean knows he has precious little time before the budding relationship suffers, and he prays that the issue with the newspaper takeover will be resolved quickly. He'd have a difficult time living with himself if he let a relationship fizzle because he didn't have a college degree.

Sean is smart enough to recognize the signs of depression, and he senses he may already be on a downhill slide. He thinks about calling his doctor for an antidepressant. But life lessons have taught him that the way out of the blues is building a head of steam to push back at whatever is messing him up. He did it when his wife left him. He did it when his father died. He did it again and again when life hurled assorted unwelcome lemons at him. The question is – how the hell can he push back now?

But, he knows, the bigger question is: how the hell can he go to work every day and ignore the possibility that he might be out of a job by the end of his shift?

The answer, whatever it is to be, comes exactly five days after Sean put himself in what has been, essentially, suspended animation.

Without enthusiasm, he awakens, showers, has breakfast, and on this particularly unsettling Wednesday morning, heads reluctantly to work.

At shortly before eleven, after Sean's been trying to focus on his work for nearly three hours, Jeff Gallagher comes over to Sean's desk.

"Can we talk a bit?" he asks.

Sean nods, the unusual request making him nervous.

"Let's go into my office," Gallagher says, leading the way. Sean swallows hard and follows – reluctantly.

As Sean enters and sits in one of the two chairs in front of the desk, his editor closes the door behind him then takes a seat on the chair next to Sean's. Suddenly remembering something, Gallagher gets up, opens the door a bit, and tells his secretary to hold his calls for a while.

Sean is sure of what is to come. The new owners, the requested resumé he hasn't yet begun preparing, the impossibility of making it sound good without listing a college education – the inevitable was about to happen. Since Gallagher's announcement about the sale of the paper, Sean's been trying to remember what was in the resumé he'd submitted to Ransom Coleman, the editor Jeff had replaced six years ago. Did he lie about college? Did he simply present a portfolio of news clips? He can't recall, and it's stoking his anxiety.

What would he do if he can no longer be a journalist?

Gallagher again takes his seat next to Sean's and leans forward, his elbows braced on the chair's arms. After a fifteen-second silence, Gallagher asks, "The new feature coming along nicely, I expect?"

Sean leans forward in his chair as well. "I'll have it wrapped up later today. You should be able to run it in next week's edition." He wonders if his nervousness is apparent.

Apparently, it is. Gallagher reaches out and touches Sean's arm briefly. "Just so you know, they're not going to let you go. I told them about your college education issue – yes, I've known all along that you didn't go to college. Coleman apparently did a background check on you. I also told them that in my opinion you are unquestionably the best feature writer this paper has had in a long time."

Sean stares at his editor, stunned by what he is hearing and not knowing what to say. Finally, he manages to squeeze out a tense

"Thank you, Jeff. That's a relief."

"But they are attaching one condition on your continued employment."

"Jesus," Sean thinks. But all he says to Gallagher is, "And what's that?"

"Well, they've read many of your past features – I gave them about two dozen – and they want you to cut down your hours here."

"Cut back my hours?" Sean feels everything getting shaky again.

"Twenty hours a week."

Sean stares at Gallagher. "I can't do it, Jeff. I couldn't survive on half pay."

Gallagher leans back and smiles. "Relax. This isn't about half-pay. The fact is that they were deeply impressed by your style, your thoroughness, and your dedication to getting the story right. You're pay is actually going up – I think they said by a hundred-fifty a week."

Sean's confusion deepens. He shakes his head as if doing so will somehow clarify what he is hearing. "I don't understand, Jeff. How the hell can they…?"

"They want you to put in twenty hours a week at the daily paper they own over the state line, in Fall River." Gallagher's smile grows bigger. "They need a feature writer who's head and shoulders above what they have now – and they don't give a damn if you didn't go to college. The guy who owns the company that's buying us is a fellow named Harvey Adler. He told me he never went to college either. And he likes it that you've done well on your own."

"Wow," Sean says, his voice trailing off.

"Good news, huh?"

"Damn right!" Sean answers, beginning to laugh.

"Good," Gallagher says, slapping a hand on Sean's shoulder as he stands to signal an end to the meeting.

As Sean gets up from his chair, Gallagher says, "Two things: first, you still have to submit your resumé like everybody else and, second, you will be starting at the Fall River Journal beginning a week from Tuesday. So you'll work here on Fridays, Saturdays, and Mondays. You'll spend Tuesdays, Wednesdays, and Thursdays in Fall River. Feel better now?"

Sean looks Gallagher in the eye. "I feel great. Thank you. I just don't know how you managed to save my job and the other stuff, but…"

Gallagher holds up his hand. "All I did was let them read what you wrote. You saved your own job by being really good at what you do.

You deserve the break. You know, the big time could be beckoning here – if you choose to aim high."

With that, he opens the door and Sean leaves his office, his face beaming. Moments later, he's at his desk, wrapping up his latest feature article. Somehow, his mood invigorates his language and the story almost begins to sing. He makes a mental note to review it – and likely rewrite it – from the beginning.

Before he leaves for the day, he telephones Julie.

"Are you busy tomorrow evening?" he asks. "I really want to make up for canceling our date the other night."

"I hope that part of your atonement will be picking me up at my house."

"No problem," Sean says. "I'd be delighted. You still live at the same place?"

"Yes," she said. "I'm impressed you still remember." Then, "You sound pretty damn cheerful. Did payroll inflate your paycheck this week?"

"Better than that," he says. "I'll tell you all about it tomorrow night. "See you at seven?"

"You bet," she says.

Some days are just plain good.

It's nearly five-thirty before Sean can reach Ted. He knows that Ted's probably spending time with Jane and Allyson before heading out for his regular Friday evening gig at Shoreside and he feels uncomfortable about interrupting his family time. But he needs to talk with his friend.

"It's Sean," he says when Ted answers his cell phone.

"Hey, man. I've been thinking about you," Ted says. "How's the book coming?"

"Good," Sean says. "It's one of the reasons I'm calling you. I've finished a lot of chapters since the last time you read it. Would you have time sometime this weekend if I brought it over to you?"

"You got it," Ted says. "How about coming over tomorrow night for dinner? I'm not playing anywhere and it's been a while since you've spent time with all of us. Allyson asks about you; she says she wants to be a journalist when she grows up – like you."

Sean laughs. "I've never seen myself as a role model. Anyway, I can't. I've got a dinner date."

Sean tolerates the long, deliberate silence that Ted floats between them. At last, Ted says, "You — my friend who swears by the joys of a solitary life — have a date?"

"I've had dates before," Sean says. "No need to be so dramatic."

"Who's the lucky woman?" Ted asks.

"I'm not sure if I should risk telling you."

"How could there be any risk?"

"She and Jane are good friends. You know her."

"One of Jane's friends? Cripes, Sean, don't keep me in suspense. Who is it?"

"Julie Bransfield," Sean says, pausing to wait for Ted's reaction.

"Julie? Wow!" Ted says. "She is one dynamite woman, man. How the hell did you ever wind up with a date with her?"

"I interviewed her for some education-related stuff a few years ago. We actually wound up seeing each other for a while – lunch, dinner, drinks, Newport Jazz festival. That sort of thing."

"And you just tossed her aside?" Ted says. "Hell, if she spent that much time with her, she was interested in you, man. What the hell happened?"

"I wasn't ready for anything. It's as simple as that. Now can we drop the subject?"

Ted is not in a subject-dropping mood. "So if you tossed her aside back then, how is it that you and she have a date tomorrow night? Are you paying her or something?" Ted's laugh borders on gleeful.

"Jesus, Ted."

"Okay, I'll stop busting you. But, seriously, how did she come back into your life?"

"She called me about a week ago. Somehow, Jane told her that I'd been in the hospital and Julie wanted to find out if I was doing okay. We talked a while then she met me at Duffy's for dinner."

Ted paused. "Good for you," he says. "I'm glad you have a date. And if she called because she heard you were in the hospital, she's most definitely interested. Don't let a good woman slip through your fingers."

"One step at a time," Sean says. "Remember, I've been burned before."

"But not by Julie."

It's Sean's turn to pause. "You're right," he says. "Point well taken."

After he and Ted agree on a time that Sean will drop off his manuscript, Sean jumps into the shower. In his heart, he really wants the evening with Julie to go well.

An hour later, he's at Ted's house, standing inside the front door and chatting with Ted and Jane. Allyson rushes down the stairs when she hears Sean's voice.

"I'm going to be a journalist," she tells Sean, a bubbly admission that begs approval from him. "I want to write like you."

Sean puts a hand on her shoulder. "First, you have to learn to write as well as you can. It's not as easy as it looks."

Allyson looks up at him. "I've been getting A's in all my essays ever since I got into high school."

"Then just let me know when you want a job – after you finish college, of course – and I'll do everything in my power to help you get into the business."

"Cool!" she says before her mother slides into the conversation.

"You know I owe you an apology," Jane tells Sean.

"About Julie? A little breach of medical privacy ethics is not going to keep me from dinner," Sean says. "Besides, I wasn't one of your patients, and I am a friend of the family. So, ratting on me is fair play."

Jane laughs. "Thank God!" she says, emoting a huge sigh of relief.

Sean waits for Jane's laugh to subside before handing a thick manila envelope to Ted. "Here's what I've done since the last time we saw each other. Not a lot, but I think it moves the story along fairly well."

Ted takes the envelope and tucks it under his arm. "I'll read every single word," he says. "And, if you don't mind, this time I'll let Jane read it as well. She reads maybe three or four novels a week."

"I want to read it, too!" Allyson says, her voice rising. "I read a lot, and I'm a pretty good writer already."

Sean takes the envelope from Ted and hands it to Allyson. "Tell you what," he says. "You read it first. But don't tell your mom or your dad anything about it. Let them come to it on their own."

"I promise!" Allyson says, hugging Sean awkwardly. Then, after a moment's pause, she says, "What if you get famous for this book. Can I say I knew you when?"

"Of course."

"Cool!" Allyson nearly jumps with excitement. She turns and heads upstairs to her room. "I want to start reading it now!" she calls back.

After Allyson's bedroom door slams shut, Ted says, "She can be a little bit excitable. I wouldn't want her any other way."

Then, he asks, "So where are you and Julie going tomorrow night?"

“Not sure,” Sean says. “Maybe Trattoria Sympatico in Jamestown. The weather should be good for eating outdoors.”

“No,” Jane says, causing Sean to turn his head to her. “I know Julie. Take her to De Pasquale Square in Providence. You can sit outdoors, there’s live music, sometimes dancing by the fountain, great food, and great ambiance. It’s like being in Italy, for Pete’s sake. She would absolutely love that.”

Sean never needs more than one hint. “De Pasquale Square it is, then,” he replies. “Parking okay on a Saturday night?”

“If you park at the far end of Atwell’s Avenue,” Ted tells him.

Jane jumps in: “Walk a few blocks. It makes it much more romantic.” She gives Sean a knowing smile.

“I don’t know about romantic,” Sean says. “She’s pretty good company -- that’s all.”

Ted laughs. “You do understand that this might be a chance of a lifetime for you, right?”

Sean shrugs. “I’m not projecting into the future at all. Julie’s very nice and I enjoy talking with her. She’s smart...”

“And attractive,” Jane interjects. Without letting Sean continue, she adds, “She’s well-read, rather sexy, I would guess, has a warm personality, a great sense of humor, a very nice figure, an excellent cook...”

“Ease up, Jane,” Ted interrupts, chuckling. To Sean, he says, “Jane’s trying to do a good selling job on you. You need to know that she and Julie have discussed you on more than a few occasions. If all this sounds a bit like a plot to trap you, it might well be.”

“Am I so clumsy socially that I need a couple of biased guides to move me in the right direction?” Sean asks the question in mock seriousness.

“Yes,” Jane answers, with Ted nodding beside her.

“Then I’m friggin’ doomed. I suppose I should start planning the wedding first thing Sunday morning.”

Jane looks at him earnestly. “That would all depend on how well things go at De Pasquale Square. You will keep us posted, right?”

“You’re not going to rely on Julie for the details?”

“Of course,” she says. “But we really want your side of things as well. Ted and I expect you will leave nothing out. How about coming here for lunch on Sunday. You won’t be working on then, will you?”

***When you finally wake up…***

*Aidan, on a quiet Friday evening at home with Ashling nearly ten months after his disturbing birthday morning epiphany – if he could ever call it that – picked up the remote control and turned off the television's volume in the middle of an episode of "CSI."*

*Ashling gave him a puzzled look, but he was staring straight ahead at the wall above the television set, a thirty-two-inch LCD set he'd bought her for her birthday using money he'd put aside by drinking less.*

*For a minute or two, she let herself sink in the couch and waited to see what was occupying his mind. Over the past many months, he'd changed – far more substantially than she suspected he knew – and it seemed that the bond between them had grown far stronger than ever before. Not that she'd ever doubted his love; her faith in his feelings for her had ultimately begun to be validated the morning after he'd returned, drunk, from visiting his dad and after reading the letter his mother had written to him long before she died.*

*For the briefest moment as she waited for him to speak, she wondered if he was about to announce that he'd decided to meet his friends for a few drinks. Wednesday evenings had for years been one of his regular nights out with his friends, but for the past four months, to Ashling's delight, he'd abstained from the regular get-togethers. He never explained why; he just stayed home on that first Wednesday evening and had been home each Wednesday evening since. Sometimes they would let the television entrance them, sometimes they would go shopping, sometimes they would sit and talk, and often they would tumble into bed early for some deep loving.*

*It was all good to Ashling.*

*With a slight nod to himself, Aidan turned and looked at Ashling, as if absorbing every detail of her face. To her, it was as if everything were moving in slow motion. He just looked at her. Then he adjusted his position on the couch, and reached out and placed his hand on her forearm. She could deal with it if he wished to join his friends, but she hoped he would not be returning to his old habits. She was growing accustomed to the "new" Aidan. Since reading his mother's letter – indeed, since that strange morning of his last birthday – he had become more of what she had always seen in him. Even his father had noticed how he'd progressed. It was, to her, as if the real Aidan had finally begun to emerge from whatever hole he'd been hiding himself for all this time.*

*Ashling put her hand on his. "What is it, luv?" she asked, her voice soft.*

*Aidan looked away for a moment, then brought his eyes back to hers.*

*"I wish I had the money right now," he said. "I know I'll have a new job soon. That guy from Electric Boat says I should hear sometime next week. But I don't think I can wait any longer."*

*"For what, Aidan?"*

*Aidan suddenly laughed. "God, this seems so damned lame."*

*Ashling waited in silence for him to explain.*

*"Will you do me two favors?" Aidan said, finally.*

*"Of course, luv. When have I not?"*

*"This may be a first time," he said, confusing her more.*

*"Well, if you'd like me to swear on a Bible, I would. But since we have none here, you'll have to take my word for it."*

*Aidan took a slow and deep breath.*

*"Every time I see my father these days, or even talk with him on the phone, I can see how lost he is without my mother. But it's funny in a way, because I never heard him tell her he loved her; and I never heard her tell him she loved him. I never saw them hold hands or saw my father put an arm around her. I never caught them even looking at each other, except when they had to talk about something to do with the bills or us kids – or for an occasional argument."*

*Ashling felt Aidan's hand tightening on her arm.*

*"Maybe one of the reasons I told you only rarely that I loved you was because of how things were at home," he said after a moment. "I regret that. Looking back, I learned a lot from my parents about what to do in life, but I never learned what not to do."*

*Ashling tilted her head as if she didn't quite understand what he was getting at.*

*"I never learned that it was not a good thing to hold back in expressing your feelings for someone. My mother told me once that she loved me – that was when I was about eleven. Even now I remember*

*how special it made me feel."*

*"She only told you that one time?" Ashling asked.*

*"Just once," he said. Aidan let go of her arm and instead entwined his fingers in hers. "I don't want to hold things inside like they did. But it's difficult for me."*

*Ashling put her other hand on top of his. "My parents, alas, were rather mushy with each other when I was growing up." She pronounced the word "mooshy" in her endearing Irish accent. "They were forever kissing and hugging and touching each other every chance they had. Sometimes, it was truly embarrassing."*

*"And so you have no difficult in expressing your feelings."*

*"None whatsoever," Ashling told him. "So I will tell you now, dearest Aidan: I do love you truly."*

*Aidan smiled but kept his silence for a moment. "I was awake a long time last night, after you fell asleep curled up against me."*

*"And..?" Ashling asked.*

*"Look," Aidan said, seeming suddenly uncomfortable, "I know I need to be different than what I've been. And I'm trying to be a better person, even though I'm not sure about how to go about it."*

*He took a deep breath. "I want to be able to tell you I love you – a dozen times a day. But it's like a sinner trying to learn to be a saint. I'm trying to pry myself out of the corner I've been wedged in."*

*Aidan looked at her directly. "I love you Ashling. I love being with you. I love our conversations, our silences, our loving. But here I am, getting on to forty-four, finding myself astounded that I spent so many of my years acting like a high school sophomore. All the years I've made your life less than pleasant; how the hell did you ever find any reason at all to stay with me?"*

*Ashling had been born with certain intrinsic gifts. One of particular value was her ability to empathize. It served her well in her work and in her relationships. She was, to all who knew her, the best and most supportive and most considerate friend anyone could want. And her gift had served her well with Aidan. Almost from the very beginning, that dinner after he'd inadvertently knocked her down in his rush to leave the bank, she sensed what he was missing, what he needed – and what he didn't know he craved. Even then, she knew he had a great deal of growing up to do. But she knew that if she were patient, he would blossom into the man he was meant to be -- although she was never completely certain in her prognosis. So she prayed a lot and bided her time, content to have him in her life.*

*She knew.*

*She just knew...*

*"I'll try to explain what I saw in you from the start," she said, her hands clasping Aidan's strongly as if to reassure him. "But I will be blunt. Are you sure you can tolerate that from me?"*

*Aidan smiled. "I have no choice, do I?"*

*"You most assuredly have absolutely no choice." Ashling laughed. "Sweet Jesus, it seems that I am clearly in charge at this moment."*

*Aidan nodded, his smile one of surrender.*

*She said, "First, after I was dizzied by the initial shock of your assault on my poor self, I saw a man who had the courtesy to help me up from the sidewalk and to apologize for knocking me on my arse. I also saw a man who made jeans and a sweatshirt look chic, despite the three-day growth of whiskers on his face and a goatee that sorely needed trimming."*

*"Go on," Aidan said, slumping into the couch, but not unhappy at all about what she was telling him.*

*"When we went to dinner that first time, I saw a man who had far less confidence in himself than he believed he had, as well as a man who held himself to a higher standard than the others with unshaven faces and untrimmed goatees." Ashling gave him a sly smile. "In short, dear man, I saw someone I could likely mold nefariously into the perfect man for me!"*

*Aidan laughed. "So, have you molded me to your satisfaction?"*

*"Almost," she said smugly. "You do need a bit more refining. Rough edges, and all that."*

*"Are you considering enrolling me in charm school?" he asked.*

*The lightness dissolved from Ashling's face. "No, luv. You are doing quite well on your own. I wish you could stand back and see how much you've grown over the years we've been together -- especially during the past several months."*

*She clasped his arm. "Do you realize that you have truly become a better man than your brother and a better person than your sister?"*

*"It depends on your definition of 'better.'" He waved a hand as if showing her the room. "Do you consider this place better than my brother's? Or the car I drive better than my sister's? Or the fact that I still work at a liquor store?"*

*Ashling regarded him in silence. Then, "I've never been to your brother's house. And I think your sister's Lexus is no more than an affectation that makes her feel better than others. Don't forget that I have a lovely Toyota Corolla that is better than your car. Am I better than you because of that?"*

*Aidan was staring at the far wall.*

*"Look at me, Aidan," she said. Aidan turned.*

*"I have stayed with you because I love you more than I have ever thought I could love anyone," she told him. "And if that is too mushy for you to deal with -- it's your tough luck. I think you yet have a way to go before you finally understand truly who and what you are. When you arrive at that point, you will understand why I've been here for you all this time."*

*Aidan simply stared at her, wondering where this intensity was coming from. There was nothing he could add to the conversation. In fact, he had already forgotten how the conversation had begun.*

*"And, Aidan McCann," Ashling continued, "I have known for a long time that you love me at least as much as I love you, even though you have rarely put it into words, other than an occasional mumble now and then. In normal circumstances, you would have asked me years ago to marry you -- and I would have said 'Yes!' But these have not been normal circumstances. You have been tilting at windmills in your antagonism toward your brother and your sister and whatever internal demons with which you've thought you had to battle. And that has kept you from becoming who you were meant to be."*

*She sat up straight in her seat and pulled back from him, without taking her eyes off his. Aidan opened his mouth as if about to say something, but Ashling put her hand out and placed a finger on his lips. "Hush," she said.*

*Aidan hushed.*

*Ashling reached out and took his hand in hers. "We have a choice here," she said after a moment.*

*Aidan looked at her, puzzled, and nodded as if to encourage her to continue.*

*Ashling took a deep breath and exhaled slowly. "The choice is this: either we continue as we have for all this time -- and I will admit to you that I have a great deal of patience -- or we can take some decisive action to make things the way they ought to be."*

*"Decisive action?" Aidan asked, wondering where this conversation was going.*

*"Indeed," Ashling said. "I learned a long time ago that when a situation doesn't seem to be proceeding to a reasonable conclusion, it's time for decisive action."*

*"Well, are you going to tell me what kind of decisive action we need now?"*

*Ashling smiled. "Of course, luv." Then she fell silent.*

*"Well?" Aidan said, after more time had passed than he could stand.*

*Ashling broadened her smile and slid closer to him,*

*"Aidan, luv," she said, her voice purring. "Are you ever going to get off your friggin' arse and marry me?"*

Sean wakes near mid-morning on Sunday and lays in bed for a while, recalling the enjoyable but somewhat disconcerting evening with Julie -- realizing after a bit that the only thing disconcerting about the five hours they spent together was how much he was enjoying her company, her conversation, her wit, and her interest in him. It was not what he wanted in his life right now; relationships get complicated and he was very comfortable with his life for the time being.

It was his utter enjoyment of their evening together that kept him from sleep when he got back to his apartment. Ultimately, he gave up and sat in front of his computer for nearly two hours, writing again about Aidan and his fictional trials, tribulations, and whatever else was pushing him along to whatever fate awaited him.

Now, with his Sunday morning half-gone, Sean is again at his computer, reading what he wrote before giving in to sleep. After a while, he gives himself a nod of approval -- at least a tentative one -- and decides to begin getting ready for his lunch at Ted's house.

Later, showered, shaved, dressed and feeling still in need of sleep, Sean prints out the few pages he's managed to write since he got home from his date with Julie and slips them into a folder to bring with him.

He looks at his watch and decides to head out. There's a flower shop nearby that is open on Sunday mornings. He will pick a nice arrangement to bring to Jane – a gift for her hospitality, and for boosting him in Julie's eyes.

Jane's De Pasquale Square idea had worked out well; Julie was a big fan of Providence's Italian section and of most of the great restaurants that lined Atwells Avenue. The three-block walk from where Sean parked gave them both time to get an easy conversation going -- about the shops, the restaurants, the people-watching. They walked slowly, side-by-side, talking quietly. At the restaurant, seated outdoors at a table for two not far from the fountain where a trio of musicians played Italian favorites, the conversation continued, evolving comfortably from one topic to another. Sean was amazed at

Julie's fluency in whatever topic they happened to broach.

In deference to Sean's temporary medical prohibition against alcohol, Julie had a glass of cranberry juice, while Sean pretended he was enjoying his ginger ale. Twice they -- first she, and then Sean -- told the waiter to give them more time to decide what they would like for dinner. By their third non-alcoholic drink, Sean was finding himself enthralled by her conversation and by how lovely she looked for their dinner together. He had still not admitted to himself that it was a date. He was more comfortable deciding it was just a get-together for dinner.

Even while eating, the conversation swept onward, as if of its own volition. The longer they spoke, the more humor that crept into their exchanges. By dessert -- a shared lava cake -- they were sometimes laughing so hard that eating was impossible.

On the way back to Sean's car, Julie reached for his hand, and he let her clasp it within hers -- not quite sure how she intended her gesture. He half expected she would assume it might be the beginning of a commitment to a long-term relationship, but then he knew somehow that she could never be so shallow. He decided it was just a friendly signal on her part.

Maybe that was all it was.

He hopes.

His instinct is telling him that something is starting, but he can't predict what exactly it might become or whether he will be able to go with the flow that Julie has initiated.

Sean is stepping out of his apartment when the phone rings, and he turns back.

"Hi, Jane," he says, caller I.D. giving him a heads-up.

"How did it go last night?" Jane has always been direct and to-the-point. "I'm betting you had a great time. But tell me later. I just want to make sure you didn't forget about lunch?"

"I didn't forget," Sean says, smiling. "I wasn't up all night with Julie."

"I know," she says, laughing.

Not very many minutes later, and less-than-thrilled with the prospect of being grilled about his "date" with Julie – especially since Julie and Jane had likely already tittered over all the details of the "date" on Federal Hill -- Sean leaves the flower shop on West Main Street and heads for Tower Hill Road and his lunch with Ted and Jane.

It takes a bit more than twenty minutes of driving before he parks his car in front of their house. And, before he steps out of his car, it takes about two minutes of rehearsing what he will – and will not – tell them about Saturday evening at De Pasquale Square. Finally, steeling himself against the feeling that he was headed into an inquisition chamber, he picks up the bouquet, slips out of his car, locks it, and plods up the walkway to their front door.

To Sean's relief, it's Ted who answers the door – although Sean would have been quite able to deal with Jane's being the one to greet him; he knew he could somewhat withstand her inquisitive looks and probing questions – for a while. At least, he is reasonably optimistic he could.

Until Ted speaks...

"Hey, man. Brace yourself. You are most definitely in for the third degree," Ted says with a look that tells Sean his friend is anticipating enjoying every moment of the evening. "Just between the two of us, Jane and Julie talked on the phone this morning. A very long conversation. I didn't even try to guess what they were talking about."

"Great," Sean says, his inflection flat. He steps through the door, waits until Ted closes it behind them, and follows his friend into the living room.

Jane waves from the kitchen as soon as she sees Sean. "Give me a sec..." she says, pulling something from the oven then adjusting a burner under one of the pots on the stovetop.

Before Sean is settled in the armchair next to the never-used fireplace, Jane enters the living room, bringing him a glass of Sprite, and offers him a warm hug.

"An excellent vintage," she says, pulling back and clinking her glass of wine against his. "Three for ten bucks at the liquor store you go to."

Sean raises his glass. "Here's to good taste." Sean still can't drink alcohol. With luck, his doctor will give him the go-ahead during his follow up visit next week.

Ted, who simply doesn't drink, lifts his can of soda. "I second that. And third it..."

"Since you and Julie had Italian last night, I decided to do roast beef." She gives Sean a look intended to forewarn him that she knows everything about what happened at De Pasquale Square.

And Sean has no reason to doubt her. Still, he says, "Julie misinformed you. She had Italian. I had a steak."

"Beef two days in a row won't kill you," Jane says, blithely. "It'll be ready in about fifteen minutes."

She raises her glass. "Cheers!"

She's barely back in the kitchen when Sean nods toward Ted. "So what did Julie tell Jane?"

"As if I would know," Ted says, a chuckle escaping him. "Jane and Julie are like a closed society. They only let me know what they want me to know. They were on the phone for a long, long time. And Julie did most of the talking, as far as I could tell."

Ted sips at his soda and leans back in his recliner.

"Actually," Sean says, "it was a nice evening. Julie's a very interesting woman."

"Interesting?" Ted asks. "Isn't that like describing the Grand Canyon as a nice riverbed? Remember, I've known Julie for almost as long as Jane has."

Sean shakes his head. "She is interesting. No matter what topic came up, she could talk about it. Intelligently."

"Jane's very particular about her friends," Ted says. "Anyway, I want to give you a head's up."

"Oh?"

"Jane asked Julie to come over next Friday for dinner, and she's going to invite you as well."

"Jesus," Sean says. He starts singing, "Matchmaker, matchmaker, make me a match…"

Ted laughs. "It's not that bad. To tell you the truth, I think you and Julie are perfect for each other."

"You've been brainwashed," Sean says, pointedly. "She's a nice person, and I enjoyed having dinner with her. But it's not going to become a regular thing. I'm not ready for any kind of relationship."

"Once bitten, twice shy?" Ted asks.

"More like a few times bitten," Sean replies. He sips from his soda and stares down at the floor. "Have you ever played Texas Hold'Em?"

"You know me better than that," Ted says. ""No drinking, because that screws up my creativity, and I need — really need — to write music. And no gambling, because when you play local bars and write your own music, you can't count on a reasonably steady stream of income until you have at least one Grammy Award or one Gold Record. I like being frugal."

"I think dating is like playing Hold 'Em. You're always at risk; you never know what the other person has up his – or her – sleeve. If you make the wrong call, you're screwed."

"That's pretty cynical, Sean. You really surprise me. Are you turning into the Ebenezer Scrooge of romance – you know, the whole 'Bah, humbug' bit?"

Sean doesn't answer for a bit. Then, "I hope not. But it's hard being optimistic about a future with someone when things have gone sour more than a few times in the past."

Sean finishes the soda in his glass. "Besides, I'm used to living on my own. In a way, I could call it a blessing. Freedom to come and go as I please."

"And you spend most of your time either working or holed up in your apartment. Hermits never have fun in life."

"And," Jane calls from the kitchen, "hermits never get to spend a lot of time with someone as wonderful as Julie."

"Jesus," Sean says, smiling despite himself. "Yes, Jane. I hear your proselytizing. I assume you're going to keep on topic for the entire evening?"

Ted laughs silently, enjoying his friend's discomfort.

Jane calls back, "I'll keep on topic as long as you are here. The rest of the time I'll talk with Julie about how to hook you and reel you in."

"I want to take a rain check on the dinner, if I may," Sean calls back.

Nearly five hours later, Sean returns to his apartment, determined not to let anything that was discussed during the evening affect his frame of mind toward Julie. On the drive home, he had deliberately turned up the volume on his car radio until the heavy bass nearly rattled the windows as a way of clearing his head. He would think about everything tomorrow.

Jane was a sweet woman, but sometimes she seemed to try too hard.

Tonight, he needs to write – before Julie becomes enough of a distraction that Aidan's story will suffer and his own inspiration will dry up.

***You stubborn mule***

*Ashling let the clearly enunciated question of marriage hang in the air, then gave Aidan a kiss on the cheek and told him she was going off to bed. It was late and she needed adequate sleep before going to work in the morning.*

*"You sit here a while, luv" she said, her Irish accent thick and soothing. "Mull over what we've talked about tonight. And tomorrow, after I'm home from work, we can talk some more. I have a feeling that you have many more things to work out – about your mum and dad, about your brother and sister, and about where life could take you -- and us – if you so choose."*

*Aidan pulled her close and wrapped his arms around her. "How come you can read me like a book?"*

*"Can I, now?" she asked, in her most innocent voice. "I believe it's you who lays open the pages. You are not as you imagine yourself to be."*

*"And how do I imagine myself?"*

*"If you don't know the answer to that, then you've surely been wandering aimlessly in the wilderness all these years," she said, in mock astonishment. Resuming her serious tone, she said, "No, luv, I think you've always known who you are and what you're about, and in many ways I admire the man you are inside. But I think you've never taken the least bit of advantage of your potential, for whatever reasons that have bedeviled you." Ashling paused. "Your mother saw it, and so does your dad."*

*"So you're saying I screwed up?" Aidan was beginning to feel stressed over the direction the conversation seemed to be taking.*

*"Not at all, luv. Not at all. You in fact succeeded in being what and who you wanted to be. But you no longer have to be intimidated by your brother or sister. And I believe you finally understand that you could find far greater satisfaction if you left your old ways behind."*

*Aidan looked away, mulling her words.*

*Finally, he said, "And you'd want to marry me, despite all my aversion to accomplishment and the years of baggage I have?"*

*Ashling laughed. "Remember, I've been part of your baggage for the past many years, and I'm also one of your most important accomplishments. Of course I want to marry you. And you are not unaccomplished at all. You read more than most people I know. Isn't it you who seduced me into going to the library at least once a week? Isn't it you who I've always admired for your ability to talk about any number of topics with just about anyone – and to do so with knowledge and insight. You've never been one of those men who are limited to talking about sports and cars and women – and I thank God for that."*

*"I've always loved reading," Aidan said.*

*"In my opinion, luv, your reading has given you a wonderful college education."*

*"Then why am I living like this?"*

*"Because you have not yet started to build your new life."*

*"So," Aidan asked, "Where do I begin?"*

*"Is not that your own question to answer? I suspect you already know; you have only to bring it to the surface so you can understand it."*

*Ashling stood. "I'm off to bed, luv. Stay here and think these things over, then come to bed whenever you are ready."*

*Aidan glanced up at her and nodded. As she turned for the bedroom, he said, "The job at Electric Boat – that would be a good start, huh?"*

*"An excellent start," Ashling agreed, turning to look at him. "But I think you should make a telephone call tomorrow and ask how the job is coming. It would show that you quite keen about working there."*

*"You think so?"*

*"I know so," she told him. "The jobs go to those who press for them. If you sit back and simply wait, then someone showing more enthusiasm will get the offer."*

*Aidan nodded. "Okay, I'll call in the morning."*

*Ashling resumed walking to the bedroom. "Goodnight, darling Aidan."*

*"'Night," he said.*

*As soon as she left the room, he went to the kitchen and picked up a sheet of paper and a ballpoint pen. Sitting at the table, he wrote a note to remind himself to call Electric Boat's Human Resources office in the morning.*

*A few minutes later, he went into the bathroom, washed his face, brushed his teeth, then entered the darkened bedroom and slipped out of his clothes. When he slid into bed, Ashling turned and snuggled close to him, giving him a soft kiss.*

*"I'm glad you decided to come to bed, Aidan," she said, her voice silky. "I miss you when you aren't here."*

*"I feel guilty," he said, wrapping an arm around her. "I don't understand why, for all these years, I've let you fall asleep alone two or three nights a week – that was stupid of me, and unfair to you."*

*Ashling snuggled closer. "That's in the past. Having you here tonight makes me happy, luv."*

*"Good," he said.*

*They lay together quietly in the dark.*

*"One more thing," Aidan said, his voice a whisper.*

*"And that would be...?"*

*"My father's not getting any younger, and I don't know how long we'll have him. And your parents must be more than anxious for us to make things legal. I don't see any reason to postpone a wedding."*

*Aidan had met Ashling's parents a dozen times since she and he had been together; they lived in Newport News, Virginia, where her father was a project manager for a seaport there, and a year from retirement. They were good people, and Aidan and her father got along well. It was only work schedules that kept them from getting together more often.*

*"Do you think we could do it in two or three months?" Aidan asked.*

*Ashling laughed softly. "Oh, Aidan. Are you sure you wouldn't be traumatized by such a quick and impetuous marriage?"*

*Aidan shrugged. "I'd rather sooner than later. Making you wait this long when you knew, and – to tell you the truth – I knew that I wanted to be married to you."*

*"You knew?" she said. "I always thought you were indifferent to marriage."*

*"Commitment, maybe," he answered. "Or really afraid of messing things up. Remember when we went to Martha's Vineyard two years ago, or whenever it was?"*

*"It was a marvelous day," she said, the smile in her voice vouching for the pleasure the day had given her. "And that fast ferry – I never imagined how fun it would be to travel that rapidly on the ocean."*

*Aidan continued: "When we heading back to Quonset Point, you were standing at one of the windows on the ferry, just watching the sun beginning to drift below the horizon, and I was watching you. And it came to me that you were too good for me, too pretty for me, too educated for me. And I remember asking myself why in hell you stayed with me." Aidan paused, took a deep breath, and continued. "Suddenly I felt that if I tried to bring the relationship to a more serious level – such as talking about marriage – you might decide you'd had enough and would find some way to drift away. So I kept telling myself that it would never work out in the end. I even tried to think of ways to end it between us before it became too serious."*

*"Because you couldn't deal with it?"*

*Aidan was silent for a moment. "No. Because I tried to convince myself that a real man always aimed for a solitary life. Some of my friends always spout off about women being for dating and for living with. They say a guy is crazy if he gets serious to the point of committing marriage. They believe that marriage can destroy an otherwise satisfying life."*

*"That's rather insecure of you, Mr. Aidan McCann, and very Neanderthal of them." Ashling said. "And it sounds very much like sleeping around as long as you don't have to raise the resulting children"*

*"There was a time," Aidan confessed in a quiet voice, "when I was actually thinking that the best thing would be to break up with you, before you broke up with me."*

*Ashling took his hand between hers and squeezed it tightly. "I'm glad you didn't. We'll do well together. Your mother thought so, as did mine – and I, most of all, have always believed that our lives should be entwined."*

*Aidan leaned back. A moment later, he said, "I like that...entwined."*

*Then he switched off the lamp, rolled on his side and put his arm over her. "I do love you," he said, his voice warm.*

*"And that makes me happy," Ashling answered, her voice sleepy. She moved closer to him and kissed him on the cheek. "For such a long time, I've wanted to be Mrs. Aidan McCann."*

*Then she poked him in the ribs, with a giggle. "It's about time you finally came to your senses, you stubborn mule."*

*"Go to sleep," Aidan said, poking her in return.*

Sean surprises himself by calling Julie when he gets home from work on Monday. He rarely keeps his promises to himself, and this particular resolution involved his rationalization that, following their Saturday evening together, it should be up to her to decide about getting together again. Besides, after the many subtle and not-so-subtle comments Jane made during last night's dinner, he felt little doubt that Julie would make the next move.

Still, there was a small knot of anxiety in him that despite what Jane had said last evening, he hadn't really passed Julie's standards test – or whatever women used to deem men keepers or not – during the evening with Julie on Federal Hill.

If there is anything within Sean that drives him, it is his always-lurking fear of what might be. Thus, in high school, he struggled – unsuccessfully, it turned out – to be cool, to be one of the group of students the others envied because he feared being a teenage outcast. In his relationships with people, he was always the one most likely to make the phone call to see how things were going, lest no one call him. He sent out his Christmas cards early, worried that if some of those he knew didn't have his card in front of their faces, they would neglect to send him one.

So now he sits on his couch and phones Julie, after pulling a soda out of the refrigerator and lighting one of the few cigarettes he allowed himself each evening.

All he gets is Julie's voicemail.

He hangs up, not sure what kind of message to leave, but figuring that trying the call again in a half hour would likely find her home.

Then he cheats.

He gets up from the couch and goes to his kitchen. From a cabinet next to the refrigerator, he pulls a bottle Jameson and pours two fingers into a glass.

For the moment, he is ignoring his stomach problems and his doctor's orders.

He spends the next twenty minutes sipping the Jameson and pacing his apartment, waiting to try his call to Julie again, but worried also that she might see his number on her caller ID and wonder why he hadn't left a message.

Two more sips of whiskey later, he drops onto the couch, grabs the phone, and dials again.

Almost instantly, she answers, saying, "I just bet myself a dollar that you would call me tonight. I won!" Her laugh was soft and warm.

Sean, already feeling a little bit whiskey-loose, tells her, "I'm surprised you didn't call me."

"Actually, I was going to call you, but I only just got in the door. I wanted to tell you again that Saturday evening was one of the most enjoyable I've had in quite a long time."

"I enjoyed it, too," Sean says. "You are exceptionally good company."

"You're not going to add 'charming,' 'attractive,' 'tastefully dressed'?"

Sean grins. "You're too impatient. I was just about to bring up those adjectives. They suit you." He can't believe he is speaking so comfortably with her; he's always been more than cautious when the possibility of a relationship loomed.

"Thank you," Julie says, with sincere grace. Then, cutting to the heart of the matter she is most interested in, she says, "So, Sean O'Connor, what did Jane have to say about me yesterday?"

Sean has to laugh at her direct question. "I'm not sure I'm allowed to pass that information on to you"

"That's lame, Sean." Sean thinks he hears the subtle sound of a snicker on her end.

Sean begins pacing the room, the phone to his ear. "She told me what you thought about our evening out."

"And?"

He feels at a loss about how to handle Julie's interrogation, which, he fears, might reach the intensity of Jane's friendly inquisition. He has no choice but to rely on his gut instinct – which is to be honest and open and hope he doesn't say the wrong thing.

"She told me you enjoyed the evening and that she thought you would definitely like to go out with me again." He sips from his Jameson. It's already mostly gone and he's feeling much looser. "And she told me that she thought you and I were absolutely made for each other."

Before Julie could answer, Sean adds, "But I think Jane's concern is that I should not be living a solo life, and not whether you and I are compatible or might even have a future."

"Does that mean you are not interested in getting together again?"

Sean suddenly frets that he's said the wrong things, that he's being too serious when the conversation should be light as air. "Actually," he says, almost lying, "I called you to see if we could get together this weekend. There's a nice restaurant on Jamestown that overlooks the Bay. I think you'd love it."

There is silence on the other end. "Hmmm," Julie says after a moment. "It sounds like it might be doable."

"You have something else that night?" Sean asks.

"Oh – no, not at all," she tells him. "But first, you need to clear something up?"

Again, Sean feels discomfiting warning signals.

"And what's that?" he asks.

"When we were strolling back to your car after dinner, we were talking about what would make life good for each of us. Remember?"

"Sort of," Sean says.

"Do you remember what you said when I asked you what you hoped life would be like for you over the next five or six years?"

Sean rummages through his memories of Saturday evening, but nothing of consequence emerges. "Not really," he says, adding lamely, "but it was late and we were both tired."

"Not I," she says, and again he thinks he hears the subtlest snicker from her.

He waits for her to continue.

Finally, she says, "You said something very interesting, Mr. Sean. You told me that, for you, life would be good if you could write a good novel and if you could get a job with a bigger newspaper."

"I'll take your word for it," Sean says, laughing to show Julie that it was not a matter of great concern to him.

"Then I asked you if you could see yourself sharing your life with someone else."

Sean sips again from his Jameson.

"And?" he asks.

"You said that it didn't matter to you if you shared your life with someone else, or not. You talked about your divorce, and told me that you were content – for the most part – with how your life is now."

Julie falls silent. Sean has no idea how to respond to what she's just said to him.

"Did you really mean that?" she asks, finally. "Would you honestly be perfectly content to live the rest of your life alone?"

She gives him no time to answer. "I'll be honest with you, Sean. I would hate having to live the rest of my life without being connected with someone special. That's what a fulfilling life is all about, isn't it?"

Sean wants to reply, but cannot – at least for this brief moment. When he finally gathers his thoughts, he tells her, "Being unconnected can suck, I guess. But you have to understand that I've been alone for a long time. I'm used to life the way it is – comfortable, actually."

"And you believe nothing could be better," Julie asked, almost before he finished his response.

Sean sighs – and hopes Julie cannot hear him. "To be honest, I don't know what I want or what would be good for me. I go to work every day, and I do what I'm supposed to do. I go home and I work on the novel I'm trying to finish. Sometimes I eat out, but a lot of the time I cook basic stuff here at home. I have one close friend and a couple of other guys I get together with now and then. Life is simple for me. So far, that's been enough."

There's a long silence between them.

When Julie speaks again, she says, "If you're still interested in going out this weekend, let's do it. I don't care if it's dinner or lunch or sharing a package of Twinkies somewhere. I think we need to talk."

Sean says, "I guess…"

Julie interrupts. "Look, Sean. The more we talk, the more I see that you're where I was eight years ago, not long after my husband left me on the flimsiest of pretexts. I've learned a lot since then, and – to be very honest with you – I don't want to lose the chance to spend time with you just because you haven't yet learned the things I did."

Sean says, "Huh?"

"We'll talk about it more when we get together," Julie says, her voice soothing. "How about Saturday evening?"

"Okay," Sean says. "What time would you like me to pick you up?"

"I'll pick *you* up," Julie says. "Give me your address. I've got a GPS thingy in my car."

"What time?" Sean asks.

"I'll be there at six-thirty."

"But dinner will be my treat," he says,

"Mine," she says in a tone of voice that tells Sean she will have her way, at least this time.

Sean gives her his address and she tells him to get busy on finishing his novel.

He finds himself smiling when he hangs up.

***Ashling and I…***

*It was Ashling's idea. And because of it, she and Aidan were about to drive to Boston.*

*Ashling had called Aidan's dad mid-morning, while Aidan still slept. She was sure Aidan had become emotionally exhausted by their deep evening conversation, but she thought their talk had been worthwhile — for both of them. It had been, happily, the kind of conversation she'd hoped would happen one day, and she was pleased it happened the way it had. Aidan had truly come around, he'd embraced the opportunity to make his life a good one, and he'd finally acknowledged what she'd known for a long time: he truly loved her and they really would be better off married to each other.*

*She was thankful she'd been able to be so patient for so long, and for her ability to steadfastly resist the constant low-grade pressure from her parents to get married and have children. As an only child, and as she slipped toward the latter part of her thirties, she could not escape the intense focus of her parents' aspirations for her to be married, and for themselves to become beloved grandparents of however many young ones God would bestow on their daughter. While she empathized with their hopes, she'd long ago carved out her own path to where she wanted to be for the rest of her life.*

*For her parents, the prospect of becoming in-laws, now real, would please them; Ashling would call them after they returned from Boston. Naturally, they would ask with deep anticipation, about when she and Aidan would come to visit them. More likely, though, they would drive to Rhode Island at the first opportunity to share the joy in person with their daughter.*

*About their hopes of being grandparents, the only certainty was that her parents would grill her on her current thoughts about having children, and that the grilling would come within minutes of her announcement of the upcoming marriage.*

*"Are you ready, luv?" Ashling called to Aidan. At last check, he*

*was still in the bathroom, putting finishing touches on himself before they left for Boston.*

*"Another minute," he called back." Brace yourself."*

*"And why do I need to do that?" she asked.*

*"Go sit on the couch," he called. "And close your eyes."*

*"Sweet Mother Mary," she said, "What have your done now?" She sat as directed and closed her eyes. She prayed that he had not decided to shave his entire head as so many men — for whatever odd reasons — had done in the name of looking ugly.*

*From the bathroom, Aidan asked, "Are you on the couch?"*

*"Of course."*

*"Are your eyes closed?"*

*"Indeed they are."*

*"Are you sure?"*

*Ashling gave an oversized sigh. "They are as closed as they will ever be, luv."*

*She could hear Aidan's footsteps as he left the bathroom and approached her. She was sorely tempted to open her eyes just barely to preview what he wanted to show her, but her mature self moved her to keep them shut tightly.*

*When he finally stopped in front of her, she could smell the cologne he'd used as he got ready. It was one she had given him at least three years ago; one he wore only rarely.*

*"Okay," he said. "Take a look."*

*Ashling opened her eyes, first seeing that he had decided to wear khakis and an open-collared blue Oxford shirt. A navy blazer he hadn't worn for at least two years was draped over his left arm.*

*Then she lifted her gaze.*

*"Jesus, Mary, and Joseph," she said in a drawn out whisper. "What on earth have you done?"*

*A look of dejection began to show on his face.*

*Ashling waved her hands at him. "I mean it a good way, luv." She stood and put her hands on his cheeks, making soft sounds of pleasure. "I've never seen you without your whiskers. It's a bit of a shock, but you are even more handsome than I'd pictured you without your beard."*

*"You like it? Really?"*

*She wrapped him in a hug. "I love it, absolutely. She kissed his now clean-shaven face.*

*"And you know what?" she asked, running her hands over the smooth skin where his goatee had been. "It's so much more enjoyable*

*kissing you, now that there are no more of those awful prickly bristles in my way."*

*She pulled back to take a better look at him. "Ah, yes. You've done the right thing." Then, laughing, she said, "Your dad will be rather shocked, I think."*

*Aidan laughed as well. "The last time he saw me without a beard was probably a couple of years before I moved to Rhode Island. He will definitely have a reaction."*

*"Would it not be wise forewarn him? We wouldn't want him to suffer a seizure or something worse when he beholds you in this shocking new condition."*

*Aidan thought for a moment. "Nah. He's tough, and he's had to deal with enough surprises about me over the years."*

*She gave Aidan another hug and a quick kiss. "We'd better go, then. Your dad will be expecting us. Do I look suitable?"*

*Aidan looked at the skirt and blouse she'd chosen. In her high heels and with a tasteful selection of jewelry, she looked stunning, he thought.*

*"You are very beautiful and your outfit is perfect. My dad will likely notice you long before he comes close to seeing my beard is gone."*

*"Let's see, shall we?"*

*Ashling took his hand and they left the apartment.*

*The ride to visit Aidan's dad was always a source of delight for Ashling. She loved Aidan's parents and always looked forward to visiting them. Although the visits lately were bittersweet – Ashling missed Aidan's mother nearly as much as he did – she treasured her moments with Cornelius. He'd never climbed any corporate ladders, and never owned his own home, but he was – to her – the kind of man who had most assuredly earned a special place in the hearts of his family.*

*Ashling even believed that Ian and Margaret revered their father just as much, though their values and the pursuits to which they had dedicated themselves were far removed from his, and from Aidan's and her own values.*

*As they were moving smoothly on I-95 north in Ashling's car, Aidan at the wheel, she reached over and rested her hand on his leg. It was her way of connecting with him when there was silence between them.*

*After a while, she said, "Your dad is going to be happy with what we'll be telling him."*

*"You think so?"*

*"Luv, I know so."*

*"How can you be so sure?"*

*"He and I talk now and then. I've told you that."*

*Aidan turned down the radio volume. "And he said this kind of thing would make him happy."*

*"Yes."*

*Aidan laughed. "The man's desperation to have another daughter-in-law knows no bounds!"*

*Ashling, in response, drove her fingers into his rib cage. "Keep your eyes on the road, luv," she told him as he reacted with a grunt. "Once again you deserve a little poke."*

*"I was joking," Aidan said, putting a sound of pain into his voice.*

*"So was I," Ashling said. "Poking you is fun sometimes."*

*"I should tell my father how you treat me."*

*"I'm certain he'd approve."*

*"Jeez," is all Aidan said.*

*A few minutes passed. Suddenly, Ashling gasped.*

*"You forgot to call Electric Boat. That job could be important for you."*

*"Cripes," Aidan said. "I even left a note to myself. I'll call them first thing tomorrow."*

*"You can be sure I'll remind you. I know you don't want to miss out."*

*He reached over and put his hand on her leg. She covered it with hers. "I won't forget," he promised.*

*A half-hour later, they turned onto the street where Cornelius lived, parking against the curb in front of his tenement house.*

*Aidan looked up at the wooden building, wondering how it was that all Boston three-deckers looked essentially the same. This one, and all the others on the street, had to have been built in the nineteen-twenties or even earlier. And none of them had anything to distinguish it from the others, except perhaps the color of the shingles or the kind of curtains in the front windows.*

*Growing up on this street had not been a bad experience. He'd had friends who were his classmates, and friends who were his playmates. It was a neighborhood where mothers yelled from parlor windows to bring their children home for supper or, in the summer, when the streetlights came on. It was a neighborhood where Irish was the way to be, and thus always filled with much talk about the old country and great emphasis on ensuring that Irish values – hard work and education and deep family loyalty – and treasured Irish traditions were never to be forgotten.*

*Aidan remembered wondering once why his family had never owned their own home.*

*He'd seen single-family homes on television, where children had bedrooms of their own, and where there was an upstairs and a downstairs and a wonderfully landscaped yard, with a picket fence that was always pristinely white. And where there was, of course, a nice car, a mother who's sole responsibility was to cook and keep an nice home, and a father who wore a suit and tie every day to go to work. And he wondered if he would have been more inclined to become a homeowner himself if his parents had been able – or had chosen – to buy a two-story single-family home like the ones he'd seen so often on television.*

*Pushing the thoughts away, Aidan left the car and locked it once Ashling had closed her door. Together, they headed up the stairs and rang Cornelius's doorbell. A brief instant later, which told them Aidan's father had probably watched them arrive, the buzzer rang and they pushed their way inside to the staircase.*

*As they climbed the steps to the top floor, Aidan wrapped Ashling's hand in his. She welcomed the gesture in silence, and simply smiled – all the way up to the third floor.*

*Cornelius was waiting, door open, when they came around to the last flight of stairs.*

*"Come in," he said. "And close the door behind you. I'll make us some tea."*

*"That would be lovely," Ashling said. "But you sit, Connie. I'll be the one making the tea."*

*Without missing a beat, Cornelius said, "That would be lovely. I'm happy you offered. I've never learned to make tea as good as Ellen made it. It's either as weak as dishwater or far too strong for anybody's taste."*

*"We women know the secret to make perfect cup of Irish tea," Ashling said, knowing Aidan's dad would certainly believe her on that particular point. She kissed him on the cheek and headed off to the kitchen.*

*Cornelius patted her on the shoulder as she passed. "You're a sweet one," he said.*

*"I try," she called back.*

*Aidan climbed the last step and shook his father's outstretched hand. "How are you doing, dad? Getting along okay?"*

*"Aches and pains now and then, and I miss your mother always, but I'm doing as well as can be expected. The priest came by last week to ask the same thing."*

*"Father Mulready?"*

*"No, he retired two months ago. This one, Father Donaghue, took his place. He seems a good man, but he never knew your mother."*

*"So he can't provide you with as much comfort as Father Mulready could?"*

*Cornelius directed Aidan to one of the living room chairs, then sat in his favorite platform rocker next to the bay window that overlooked the street. For years, it was the place where he read the daily newspaper and from which he watched television on the nineteen-inch black-and-white set he'd somehow made to last nearly eighteen years. Now, in its place, was a small color set that Aidan's sister had bought for him as a Christmas gift a year before Aidan's mom could no longer be cared for at home.*

*"Your mother loved Father Mulready," Cornelius told his son. "Do you know he was in the parish for almost twenty years?"*

*"No," Aidan said. "I only met him at Mom's wake. He seemed nice enough."*

*"Indeed, he was. This new one," Cornelius shrugged, "he's different, It's almost as if he came calling only because someone told him to."*

*"Priests aren't what they used to be, huh?"*

*Cornelius nodded emphatically. "I think the Church is sorely in need of good priests. But, these days, I don't think they're going to find many. I remember when most families raised a priest or a nun. It was an honor."*

*Aidan nodded in concurrence, even though he didn't believe it was any kind of honor.*

*Ashling returned from the kitchen, carrying a tray with steaming teapot and three cups. She placed the tray on the coffee table. Cornelius and Aidan moved to the sofa. "I'll fetch the milk and sugar," she told them, then turned back toward the kitchen.*

*Aidan and his dad waited until she returned.*

*"It's lovely to see you, Connie," she told Cornelius as she began pouring the tea. She knew enough to add a spoon of sugar to his cup, along with a small amount of milk. She took hers with milk but no sugar, and she gave Aidan a cup with sugar and no milk, though she knew he would have been far happier with a beer or a whiskey or some*

*vodka.*

*"I like it when you visit," Cornelius told her. He sipped from his cup and closed his eyes as he swallowed. "This is exactly as Ellen would have made it. I wish I could do the same."*

*"The secret is in letting the tea steep for the proper amount of time." Ashling said. "I'll show you before we leave."*

*Aidan's dad sipped again then placed his cup in the saucer. "Are you both doing well these days? They say the economy is not well at all, and sometimes I worry about you."*

*"Things are very good," Aidan said. He sipped again at his tea and put the cup down. "We have some news for you."*

*Cornelius leaned back in his chair. "News?" he said. "It's good news, I hope."*

*Aidan looked at Ashling. "Should you tell him, or should I?"*

*Ashling waved a hand at him. "For the love of God, Aidan, you're his son and he's your dad. It should be you who tells him."*

*Cornelius looked at both of them with concern and confusion on his face. "Well," he said, his voice anxious, "I hope one of you will speak up before I get too nervous."*

*Aidan waved his hand as if to say, "Calm down." After inhaling deeply, he said, "Ashling and I are going to be married."*

*Then he waited for his dad's reaction.*

*For a few brief moments, his father sat there – first staring at Aidan, then scrutinizing Ashling. Then he put his teacup into its saucer on the coffee table and nodded.*

*"It's about time you did the right thing," he said, looking directly at Aidan. "Your mother always said that you would be married to this wonderful young woman one day. What on earth took you so damn long? Do you realize how happy your mother would be now if she were with us?"*

*Ashling jumped in. "She knows," she told Cornelius.*

*"She knows?" he said. "And how does she know that?"*

*Ashling looked at Aidan and then at his father. "Because I promised her that Aidan loved me and I him – and that she had to know that he'd never make such a foolish mistake as to let me go."*

*Cornelius laughed. "She believed you, you know. I remember she told me once that this son of mine would come to his senses and realize you were good for him."*

*Ashling gave Aidan a sidelong glance. He was smiling.*

*"I feel like the victim of a conspiracy," he said, with false dejection.*

*"No," she said. "We simply agreed on what was good for you."*

*Cornelius added, "I'll be invited to your wedding, I hope."*

*Ashling laughed as Aidan shook his head.*

*"Dad," Aidan said, "the wedding would be nothing without you. The truth is, I'd like you to be my best man."*

*Cornelius sank back in his seat. "Best man!" He slapped his knee with pleasure. "This woman," he said, pointing to Ashling, "She's turned you into a very special fellow, I think."*

*"Almost," she said. "He's a work in progress, but I believe I have everything under control." She gave Aidan a wink.*

*"Jesus H. Christ," Aidan said, then asked if his dad had any whiskey he could borrow for the rest of their stay.*

*His father laughed. "It's not whiskey you need. It's this lovely woman." He got up from his rocker. "But I think a bit of whiskey in celebration would not be a bad thing."*

*He turned to Ashling. "What would you like?"*

*"If I'm to be celebrating with my favorite men, it's only right that I have whiskey as well. Thank you."*

*As his father turned toward the kitchen, Aidan said, "There's one more thing to celebrate – at least for Ashling and me."*

*"And what's that?" Cornelius asked, turning to face his son.*

*"I've applied for a new job – a good one. And I think I might have a good chance of getting it."*

*Cornelius smiled and nodded at his son. "That's great news as well. Let me get the whiskey and then I want to hear all about it."*

*As he walked into the kitchen, Aidan and Ashling heard him say in an excited whisper, "Ellen, I wish to God you could be here."*

For Sean, Fridays come all too slowly when his weekdays are going poorly, and all too quickly when he wishes Monday through Friday could drift endlessly along.

He is looking forward to his dinner tomorrow with Julie, yet the small amount of pressure he sensed from her during their last phone call concerned him. He is in a relatively comfortable place in life. He'd shaped his post-marriage life into an orderly thing, predictable for the most part, and needing very little additional direction from him. Julie seems at least somewhat inclined to press him on decisions and wants and needs, and whatever else is important to a woman like her.

But he knows only two things for certain: he likes her, and he is afraid of a sudden acceleration of this budding relationship, or whatever else it may be.

These thoughts seep into any vacuums in his day while he works at the newspaper. Despite his best efforts – and sometimes he wonders why he even bothers to try otherwise – Julie keeps infiltrating his mind. Her face, her smile, her voice, her laugh – she keeps swirling within his brain the moment he stops focusing on the things he needs to do to earn a living.

Somehow, though, he makes it through the day.

On the way home, he stops to buy some groceries for the weekend, the visit to the store more a way of easing his worries about tonight than something he needs to do. He also stops at the small liquor store in Wickford. He had intended to buy beer, despite doctor's orders, but at the last instant decides to emulate Aidan, so he buys a bottle of Jameson. He needs to write tonight. And he will drink. And the bottle of Jameson he has at home is nearly empty.

He also needs to talk with Ted.

Later, at home, Sean pours himself a Jameson on the rocks and sits back on his couch. The small sips of Irish whiskey and finally feels himself beginning to relax — at least a little bit. As the whiskey sinks in, he picks up the phone and dials his friend.

Jane answers, as usual. Ted is either working on a song or an arrangement or spending time rebuilding an antique BMW motorcycle, a hobby he's had for years. Sean has always envied Ted's ability to be so meticulous about so many things.

"Has Julie tamed you yet?" Jane asks as soon as Sean responds to her "hello." Jane hardly ever pays attention to Caller I.D., instead preferring to be surprised by whoever may be on the other end of the line.

"Tamed?" Sean asks back. "You underestimate my ability to resist wanton women."

Jane laughs. "And should I tell Julie you consider her a wanton woman?"

"Is she?" Sean asks. Then, quickly, he adds, "Don't do that. Please. She's a nice person."

"She's only 'nice'?" Jane seems determined to tweak Sean's nose a bit. "I'll have to tell her to make a greater effort to subdue you."

"Jesus," Sean says, laughing. "You're starting to seem like a lobbyist for Julie.

Jane laughs back. "She pays me well."

"Is Ted there?" he asks, finally. He enjoys Jane's sense of humor, but he needs to be spending his energy speaking with Ted.

"He is," Jane answers. "You know I can't resist busting you."

"I accept my fate," Sean says.

Julie laughs. "Just a sec. I'll get him."

Sean sips and waits. A few moments later, Ted picks up the phone.

"Hey, man. Are you still single? What's happening?"

"Come on," Sean says. "You sound like Jane. Is my fate sealed already?"

"If it was up to Jane and Julie, it would be a done deal," Ted says. Sean takes Ted's laugh as an unnecessary punctuation mark.

"Thanks, friend."

"Hey, I'm on your side. I keep reminding Jane that she's the one who roped me in."

It was Sean's turn to laugh. "I think you're right."

"Heck," Ted says, "you didn't even know me back then. Jane and I were still in Pennsylvania."

Sean agrees. "Okay. But I've got a different problem."

"With Julie or with your book?"

Sean pauses. "With both," he says, after a moment.

"Is it something we can do on the phone?"

"I don't know."

"That tells me it has to be an in-person thing."

Sean sighs. "You're right again."

"Hold on," Ted says. Sean hears Ted call out to Jane. "You okay if I meet Sean tonight?"

Sean hears Jane's muffled voice, "Of course. He needs you. Go."

A second later, Ted says to Sean, "Where and when?"

"You're not working tonight?" Sean asks, surprised. Ted is almost always working on Friday nights.

"Lately I've been taking one Friday off each month. So no problem in getting together tonight. Where do you want to meet?"

"Duffy's – in a half hour?"

"You got it, man." Ted says. "And I want you to listen to a couple of new songs I'm working on. Okay?"

"Of course."

"See you in a bit," Ted says.

Sean turns off the phone and lays it on the end table. He sips the last of his Jameson and slumps on the couch.

He really wants Ted to read – and react to – his latest chapters. More than that, though, he needs Ted's guidance on how to deal with Julie.

Long ago, his divorce still stinging, he convinced himself that he can survive forever without any one else in his life. Lately, though, in the moments when he is being honest with himself, Sean's gut feeling is that Julie may well be the woman he's hoped for.

And he's not yet sure if whether it is a good or bad thing.

He gets up from the couch and enters his dark office. Once his computer boots up, he prints out the pages Ted has not yet read and tucks them into a manila folder.

He looks at his watch. It will take him less than four minutes to get to Duffy's. Ted is likely already on his way.

Sean resists the urge to have another sip or two of Jameson, instead heading to the bathroom to pee.

After zipping up, he picks up the folder and heads for the door. He'll be waiting inside for Ted to arrive. Sean has never wanted to keep people waiting.

The drive to the restaurant is too short to give Sean any time to worry about anything more than how parking might be. He enters the parking lot, finds a spot immediately – Fridays mean that Duffy's is usually packed – and enters the bar side of the restaurant.

He chooses a table far away from the bar stools – the same table, he remembers a bit later, where his bleeding ulcer, not so long ago, blared out its existence in a most embarrassing and frightening way.

In memory of the event, he orders a Jameson as soon as the waitress approaches, and tells her that his friend will be arriving soon. He will drink some more tonight.

He places the folder to his right and focuses his attention on one of the television screens nearby, one that shows images not matched at all by the sound coming from another over the bar. He is content to watch the visuals, imagining what the narration might be.

His drink comes, he sips, and he is content for the moment. His times with Ted have always been good ones. He glances toward the door, in case Ted might walk in momentarily.

Moments later, Sean is submersed in his thoughts about Julie, and life, and his future, and her voice, and his concerns, and her smile, and his stupid fears, and her impeccable logic, and so much more.

He is still embroiled in his thoughts when Ted slaps him on the shoulder. "Wake up, man!"

Sean is startled and nearly jumps to his feet. "Christ, don't scare me like that!" he tells his friend. "You damn near gave me a stroke!"

Sean, too late, realizes he'd raised his voice a bit too much. Several of the bar patrons have turned to look at him.

"Roaming around in Neverland?" Ted asks.

"Just thinking," Sean answers.

The waitress comes over. Ted orders tonic water with lime. The waitress gives him a disappointed look. Sean orders another Jameson.

"Not following doctor's orders?" Ted asks.

"I'm feeling fine," Sean answers. "If I want to drink, I'll drink. It helps me write."

"So you think," Ted says. "I write music and I don't drink."

"But you've got talent. I'm just faking it."

Ted ignores Sean's self-deprecation and reaches out to tap Sean's folder. "That's it?"

Sean nods. "Its what I've done since I saw you last. I just keep waffling about whether it's good or not, and it's driving me nuts sometimes. But I want your advice about Julie, too."

"I'm pretty good with music, and pretty good with reading manuscripts," Ted said, smiling. "But I'm not sure I have much expertise when it comes to women who are pursuing my best friend."

"Whatever," Sean says. "I'll take whatever input you can give me."

"How about we do that after we eat? I'm thinking that you'll be talking more loosely once you finish your drink and have some food in your belly." Ted gives Sean a reassuring look.

"Fine by me," Sean tells him, considering that this might be a night where yet another Jameson might be necessary.

"Mind if I read while we eat."

Sean slides the folder to his friend. "You'd better start now. It'll take a while. I wrote a lot since the last time."

Ted slides to folder to his side of the table and opens it. As he begins to read, he tells Sean, "Order something for us. Anything is fine with me, as long as it's not something raw."

"Seafood or regular food?"

"A burger would be fine."

"You got it." Sean begins looking to catch the waitress's eye. He sips once more at his Jameson, anxious to be home again writing. Somehow, Ted's judgments about his story always seem to repair his sometimes-sagging confidence. It will happen again this time, Sean expects, and he knows he will be staying up late into the night, writing as much as he can before fatigue pressures him off to bed.

While Ted reads, Sean begins mulling what he wants to write tonight.

***Not at all about the past***

*Aidan and Ashling arrived home just before midnight after having visited Cornelius. They were tired, and rode most of the way without speaking. Once in the apartment, Ashling asked, "How about a cup of tea before we go to bed?"*

*Aidan nodded. "I'd like that. Let me put the kettle on."*

*"Thank you, luv. I've got to visit the bathroom."*

*When returned to the kitchen, Aidan said, "My turn. The water should be boiling in a bit." Then he hurried to the bathroom.*

*Ashling noticed he'd already set up teacups for both of them and had already prepared the loose tea to be steeped in the kettle. Whenever he made tea, he'd always done as he'd seen his mother do so many times when he was a boy. Tea bags were not welcome.*

*She pulled a half-loaf of bread from one of the cabinets, then retrieved some strawberry jam from the refrigerator. She placed both items on the table, then fetched a dessert plate and knife for each of them. Bread and jam and a cup of tea would be a perfect nightcap.*

*The kettle began to boil just as Aidan returned to the kitchen and he lowered the heat so the tea simmered for a bit. In a move that surprised Ashling, he approached her from behind and gave her an enthusiastic hug and brushed her neck with a kiss.*

*"And to what do I owe this particular honor?" she asked with a pleased laugh.*

*Aidan held her more tightly. "I know there are a lot of things I've never said enough, but I promised myself to be better." He let go of her and she turned to face him, her smile making her even prettier.*

*"Such as?" she asked, with as much impishness as she could muster at this late hour. She locked her arms around his waist and leaned back to study his face as he responded.*

*"I never thought I could be this much in love with someone..."*

*Ashling opened her mouth to speak.*

*"Don't interrupt me when I'm on a roll," he said, touching a*

*finger to the tip of her nose.*

*She nodded and kept looking into his eyes.*

*"I never thought I'd find someone I could happily devote my life to, someone who fits my heart and my soul the way you do."*

*Aidan looked away for a moment. "I saw a movie once, a long time ago. Clark Gable and Marilyn Monroe...I think it was called 'The Misfits'.*

*The water in the kettle was making comforting simmering sounds. Aidan kept talking.*

*"Clark Gable was beginning to fall in love with Marilyn, who'd just gotten a divorce in Nevada. Anyway, they were driving in an old pickup truck, going down a desert road or something, and he looked over at her and said, 'You shine in my eyes.'"*

*Aidan leaned down and kissed Ashling lightly on her mouth. "You truly shine in my eyes. I'm sorry I never told you so before."*

*Ashling put her arms around his neck and pulled him down for a deeper kiss.*

*"Life does become good, does it not?" she said when their lips pulled apart. "We will have a fabulous future together, dear man."*

*Then, playfully, she poked him in the ribs. "Are you not going to take care of that boiling water so your true love can have her cup of tea?"*

*They sat at the table talking until nearly one in the morning: he trying to make up for his past cluelessness, she allowing herself to bask in the love emanating from him. They talked about everything they wanted in their coming lives, and talked not at all about the past. Finally, exhaustion setting in, they curled up in bed together, too tired to make love, and slept until morning.*

*When Aidan's eyes opened, Ashling was laying on her side, facing him, her eyes studying him. Without a word, she moved closer and kissed him, then rested her head on his chest.*

*When they finally got out of bed and showered and dressed and made themselves ready for whatever portion of the day remained to them, Ashling suggested that they spend part of the afternoon close by the water's along Narragansett Bay.*

*Aidan, managing one surprise after another for the past many weeks, offered to put together a picnic lunch.*

*"I figure we can spend some time along the sea wall in Narragansett," he explained, "and then we can have a picnic lunch down by Point Judith lighthouse."*

*"It will likely be nearly time for dinner by the time we get there," Ashling said, teasing him. "But it would be a great time for us. I'll help with the sandwiches."*

*As they were working side-by-side in the kitchen, Ashling slicing ham for sandwiches and Aidan gathering condiments, Aidan said, "I called Electric Boat yesterday...about the job I applied for."*

*"You did, did you? And?" Ashling seemed more focused on sandwich making than on Aidan's future.*

*"I called this guy -- Phil Moretti. He's in human resources. I asked him if I got accepted for the training program."*

*"And?" Ashling said, slathering mustard on multi-grain bread.*

*"He said I should be getting a letter from them in the next two or three days. I'm going to be in the program."*

*"Utterly wonderful!" Ashling said, ignoring the sandwiches and wrapping her arms tightly around Aidan's neck. "You've done it, luv! I'm so proud of you!"*

*Aidan could manage only, "I hope so." Then: "It's going to feel really weird not working at the liquor store any more."*

*"That will surely be a good thing, won't it?" she asked.*

*"Oh, yes," he said, kissing her upturned face. "Let's make this a picnic to remember."*

*"I haven't heard a better idea in a long time," she said. They unwrapped themselves from each other and got busy.*

*Together, rummaging through the refrigerator and kitchen cabinets, they organized a picnic of sandwiches, potato chips, pickles, chocolate chip cookies, and some soda – caffeine-free for her, high-test for him. Packing it all in a large brown paper bag surrounded by Ziploc bags filled with ice cubes, they left the apartment and headed south on Tower Hill Road.*

It was not unexpected: Ted's assessment of how Sean was progressing with the story was, overall, a good one. Still, he wishes Ted could have shown more enthusiasm about the latest chapters. But it was not Ted's way; he was more laid-back and less flappable than Sean could ever hope to be, giving Sean another reason to envy his friend. Yet, Ted's comments gave Sean more impetus to keep the story alive.

Sean had managed to spend more than two hours writing after he and Ted left Duffy's. By the time he was ready for sleep, he felt as if he had completed a worthwhile number of paragraphs.

He awoke well after nine on Saturday morning and spent a half-hour waiting for sleepiness to give way to some degree of alertness. Writing into the wee hours was not made any better by having a Jameson or two – after the ones he'd already downed during his visit with Ted at Duffy's.

He had awakened with a nudgy feeling that he needed to get everything under control; for too long he'd allowed the story to build in whichever direction his mind took him. He sensed now that he needed to bring more discipline to the process. He knew that some authors created outlines of what they wanted to write; others created timelines of events; and still others developed detailed profiles of the characters that would populate their stories.

Sean though – at least until now – had simply placed his hands on his keyboard and let the story proceed on its own, wherever it seemed to want to flow. Now, unexpectedly, he was feeling that his effort would suffer if he failed to do more to plan the course of his story.

After a bowl of Cheerios and a piece of fifteen-grain toast, Sean slaps some cold water on his face, dries himself with a towel, and heads off to his rudimentary office, dim and cave-like even on this sunny morning.

He calls up a blank page in Word and touches his fingers to the keyboard. Many minutes later, the page is still empty. Instead, he's been trying to decide what form the outline should take, and how much detail he should include, and whether or not he'd actually be able to follow the direction he outlines. It just doesn't feel a comfortable way for him to produce the story. Until now, when he's sat at his computer, it has mostly been with a kernel of an idea for moving the story forward. And once his hands have begun churning out words, the story has always seemed to move in a good direction. But is that the best way?

He's willing to give it a shot. His decision has little to do with a hope that his story might be easier to write if he knew in advance each step in the plot. It's much more about fear — that by not attempting an outline, he might miss out on his only remaining good chance to be a published writer.

So he types:

*Aidan and Ashling spend time watching the surfers at Narragansett Town Beach, then head to Point Judith lighthouse to have their picnic...*

*After they eat, Ashling tells Aidan there is something she needs to tell him...*

*She is not sure how he will react, but she decides the time is right to tell him...*

*Must make sure that Aidan is utterly clueless about what Ashling is going to tell him...*

*Does Cornelius know yet about what Ashling will tell Aidan?....no (save that for later)...*

*How about if Aidan has a...*

After spending less than ten minutes working on the rough outline, Sean throws up his hands. Planning, at least on this project, will be a wasted effort. It's not the way he does things – certainly not in terms of what he is writing now. The story has gotten to the point where it is almost writing itself; the characters he has created have pretty much have lives of their own. An outline or a plot, or whatever else, will not make the story any better, he decides. He needs to trust his instincts and his mind's ability to take the right course.

He deletes the outline and calls up his manuscript. For the next three hours, he reads what he has written thus far.

It's after one o'clock when he finishes, and he's hungry. Moving to the kitchen, he pulls out a loaf of bread and a package of sliced ham he has in the refrigerator. A sandwich and a can of soda would take care of him for now.

He's putting the finishing touches on his sandwich when the phone rings. When he sees the caller I.D. information, he smiles.

"Hey, Julie," he answers.

"Did I just wake you up?" she asks. "Your voice sounds pretty froggy."

"No. I've been up for a few hours. But I had a long night."

"Writing?"

"Writing, and reading, and – if I can get the energy – trying to do even more of that today."

"You won't be too tired for tonight, will you?" she teases him.

"No way," he tells her, wanting to talk with her some more but growing hungrier for his uneaten sandwich.

"I put your address in my GPS. I'll pick you up promptly at six," she says.

"Where are we going?"

Julie pauses. "You'll see," she says, flatly. Then she laughs. "You'll enjoy the evening, I promise."

With a quick "See you soon," Julie hangs up, leaving Sean wondering if Julie had conspired with Jane on the evening's agenda. Having Jane and Julie sharing such a close friendship left Sean feeling that Jane had become Julie's informer in all things having to do with Sean. And then there was Ted. Although Sean was confident Ted would never share anything about Sean with Jane – at least nothing that might make Sean uncomfortable for whatever reason – there was always a chance that Ted could blurt out something or other unwittingly.

Sean sighs then heads back into the kitchen to grab his sandwich. He has a few hours before he has to get ready for Julie's arrival. He needs to spend the time writing, if he is ever to be able to finish the book.

A minute later, he is in front of his computer, ready to write, praying that whatever he types will be good, solid writing.

**He is what he is**

*It was the following evening when Ian telephoned Aidan.*

*Aidan's first reaction was one of anxiety. Ian never telephoned him unless there was something wrong. The last time they had spoken on the phone was when Aidan's mother had died.*

*Ashling had answered the phone and now came to get Aidan from the bedroom where he'd been putting away his freshly washed clothes; helping Ashling in her chores was another thing he'd learned over the past months.*

*"It's your brother who's calling," she said, her voice not much more than a whisper, although the telephone receiver lay on the kitchen table several paces away. "There's something in his voice. Please God let it not be anything about your dad." She was visibly fretful.*

*"Jesus, I hope not," Aidan said, going around her to get to the phone.*

*A moment later, he picked up the receiver slowly and put it to his ear.*

*"Ian?" he said. "What's up?"*

*"Dad told me."*

*"Told you what?"*

*"About you and Ashling, getting married."*

*"That's right. We want to get married."*

*Aidan could have sworn that he heard an exasperated hiss of air coming from his brother's mouth.*

*"I hope you're calling to congratulate us," Aidan said, knowing full well that his brother would likely have great difficulty wishing Aidan the best of anything.*

*"Actually," Ian said, "I just wanted to let you know that you upset dad with your announcement."*

*"Upset him? How?" Aidan was silently congratulating himself on once again predicting accurately that his brother was genetically loath*

*to support him in anything at all.*

*"He's hoping for a big wedding and that he'll have a chance to dance and socialize and see his friends and our other relatives." Ian was talking as if that sort of enjoyment should not be anything an old man like their father should be exposed to.*

*Of course, Ian's attitude peeved Aidan to no end. "And what the hell would be wrong with a nice wedding with fun for everyone."*

*Ian could not miss the edge to Aidan's words. "Look," he said, "you're not a twenty-something who needs to have an exuberant wedding celebration. You're middle-aged, for Christ's sake. The best thing would be a quiet wedding with immediate family in attendance. That way, dad wouldn't stress himself out so much, and everything would be much more seemly."*

*"We haven't even made any wedding plans yet," Aidan said. "We will have the kind of wedding Ashling wants – and we will likely not take into consideration any of your opinions on the subject."*

*"Don't you..." Ian said sharply before Aidan cut him off.*

*"You will be invited if you stop being a friggin' jerkweed about so many things. So will Margaret, if she can get off her high horse long enough to acknowledge that she can be a real sister to me instead of a snotty phony who thinks she is so far better than peasants like me and dad and mom."*

*"You won't even consider what that kind of stress will do to dad, will you?" Ian said.*

*"I see dad far more than you do. And Ashling and I talk with him on the phone at least once or twice a week. We're pretty sure we know what will make his life fun."*

*Aidan paused. "Tell me the truth, Ian. When was the last time you spent more than five minutes with dad?"*

*Again, Aidan heard what sounded like a hiss from Ian's end of the line. "I see him every week."*

*"Whether you need to or not," Aidan said with much intended sarcasm. "But when was the last time to sat with him and talked with him about anything under the sun? When was the last time you took him out to lunch or dinner, or tossed back a drink or two with him at one of the places where he likes to meet his friends sometime?"*

*Ian didn't respond. Finally, just about the time Aidan was going to ask if his brother was still on the line, Ian said simply, "We'll talk later," and hung up.*

*When Aidan replaced the receiver, Ashling came up behind him and wrapped him in her arms.*

*"Your brother was being himself again, was he not?" she said.*

*Aidan let himself be absorbed in her hug.*

*"He is what he is," he said. "The thing is that I think he'd be treating me the same way even if I had become a vice president of some big company."*

*Ashling released him and put her hands on his shoulders, turning him to face her.*

*"He needs to be that way to you so he can feel better about himself," she said. "It really has nothing to do with you or who you are or what you have achieved in your life. It's about how poorly he feels about himself."*

*Aidan pondered her words for a bit. There was some sense in what she said. But there was no way he could imagine his brother feeling poorly about himself; after all, he was successful, relatively wealthy and secure, and had a large circle of friends and acquaintances.*

*"If that's the case, I just wish he would stop taking things out on me."*

*Ashling looked at Aidan as if she were studying the depth of his soul.*

*Then she nodded. "Perhaps it would be best if you take the offensive from now on," she said. "You should become the positive one, and perhaps rescue him from the trap of negativity in which he's found himself all these years."*

*"I should be nice to him?" There was more than a hint of incredulity in Aidan's response. "You're kidding – right?"*

*"Flies and honey," was all she said.*

*"Right," Aidan said, dismissively.*

*"For all the time we have been together, luv, you let your brother dominate you with his disrespect for you, his criticisms of you, his imperious treatment of you. Yet you let him continue to do these things over and over again. And you've allowed your sister to do the same." Ashling was planting her feet firmly in this discussion. "So he completed college and you didn't. So what? So he became a lawyer and you didn't. So what? Are you truly unwilling to stand up for yourself?"*

*"It's complicated," he said.*

*Ashling reached up and took Aidan's face between her hands. "You, luv, are a far better man than Ian could ever be. Do you not understand?"*

*Aidan turned his eyes away for a moment.*

*"Then what should I do?"*

*Ashling already had an answer for precisely that question.*

*"We should invite Ian and his wife to join us for dinner one evening. Perhaps on Federal Hill in Providence. We need to create an environment where you and he can speak civilly for a while."*

*"He'll just laugh and tell me to go to hell."*

*"No," Ashling said. "Not if you ask in the right way."*

*"You invite them, then," Aidan said. "You seem to have the right touch with people."*

*"But the invitation will be worth nothing if you are not the one to ask them."*

*Aidan turned away and wandered to the far side of the kitchen.*

*"What the hell would we talk about?"*

*Ashling approached him and took his hand.*

*"We'd talk about whatever topic arose," she said, calmly. "It will be a start, at least."*

*Aidan became quiet, thinking about what she was telling him, picturing how it could be, and wondering if it ever could be possible for his brother and he to have a reasonable family relationship.*

*To Aidan, it seemed as if his older brother had been dominating him ever since Aidan himself had graduated from diapers to big-boy underpants.*

# Mulligan

A few minutes before five on that Saturday afternoon, Sean leans back in his chair in front of his computer. He's managed to produce almost four pages that seem to be as good as he can manage on this particular day.

Aware that he needs to clean up before Julie arrives to take him wherever she's decided, he hits "save" to protect his manuscript and pushes away from the desk.

A few minutes later, he is lathering up under a stream of hot water, his mind focused less on showering than on what the evening with Julie might become.

For whatever reasons, her "You'll enjoy the evening, I promise" made him somewhat uncomfortable. He has a feeling that Julie is into relationship building while he's just tap dancing around the possibility of having a potential dinner companion now and then.

What she meant by her statement, he can only guess. He hopes that she does not intend to seduce him tonight. He misses sex, but he doesn't want to fall into some emotional trap simply because he is needy. So, if that's what Julie has in mind, he will have to find some way of letting her down without upsetting her – and without destroying the potential for a fine relationship in the future.

Julie is attractive, vivacious, charming. She is a great conversationalist. She is…fun!

Sean, though, feels far away from any decision about embracing a new relationship – especially one that might come with long-term potential. He knows that he's being a bit irrational about the whole thing. But the lesson he's learned from his failed marriage – and from the single entanglement he found himself involved in since then – is that he needs to move carefully and gingerly into whatever life might offer him. At least in terms of life with a woman.

If that means keeping Julie at arm's length, then it's the way it has to be. At least for the time being.

He shuts off the water and leaves the shower. Minutes later, he's shaving in front of the mirror, looking at his forty-something face with its new creases, wondering what the hell Julie sees in him. Suddenly, he wishes he were better looking and maybe more stylish. He will dress in khakis tonight with a light sweater and boat shoes. But somehow that doesn't seem to be enough. He hopes he will impress Julie even further. A brief moment later, though, he is reiterating to himself his position that he's almost definitely not ready for a relationship that calls for anything more than superficial fun.

Ten minutes before Julie is due to arrive, Sean is ready to go. With nothing else to do – writing some more is out of the question because he simply has not enough time – he paces in the apartment, waiting for the doorbell to ring.

Unexpectedly, he is embarrassed about where he lives. The apartment is nothing – as plain and simple and sparse as anything someone could imagine. He rushes about, pulling sheets of paper into neat stacks, tidying his pile of unopened mail, grabbing a sheet of paper towel and swiping surfaces of dust straightening the cushions on his couch. Turning off overhead lights and relying on two table lamps to provide low-level illumination to help camouflage the apartment's flaws.

After one last look around the place, he is moderately satisfied Julie will not be dismayed by what she sees.

When the doorbell rings, Sean presses the buzzer and opens his door. He can hear Julie closing the outside door behind her and beginning her climb to his place. He debates whether he should descend the stairs to meet her partway, then decides that he'll stay put.

As she comes into view at the bottom of the last flight of steps, he says, "Welcome to my world."

Julie looks up, smiling. "No wonder you seem to be in good shape. Three flights of stairs will do anybody a lot of good."

Sean laughs.

Brief moments later she is on the landing outside his door, barely out of breath. He begins to gesture for her to enter when she gives him a small hug and a light kiss on the cheek.

"It's great to see you again," she says, delight in her eyes. "I've been looking forward to this evening."

Sean smiles back. "So have I." He puts a hand on her shoulder and guides her into the apartment. "Come on in."

She crosses the threshold, her head turning slowly to take everything in.

"It's not much," Sean says, apologetically. "But it's close to work and close to the water. I can see part of the harbor from my living room. I've been thinking about getting a better place. This place is old and not exactly presentable, but…"

Julie turns and puts a finger on his lips. "Shush," she says. "I love it. It's cozy and warm. Mine's a bit too vanilla for me. Show me where you write."

"Would you like some wine," Sean asks.

"Not really. We'll be having…or at least I'll be having a drink at dinner. I don't want to overdo things. Now show me where you write. I want to be able to say that I was in the room where a great novel was written."

Sean laughs. "Great? I don't know about that." He leads her to his office. His computer is still on, the computer monitor playing a geometric screen saver. He leans over his chair and turns on a lamp. "It's not much, but it serves my purposes."

"Please stop with that 'not much' nonsense," she says with a mock frown mixed with a soft smile. "Your apartment seems perfectly fine, and your office is the kind of eclectic place I love to see. All that counts is that you are comfortable writing here."

"I am," Sean says, realizing he might not be as comfortable anywhere else.

"Jane tells me that Ted is reading your book as you go along, and that he's quite impressed." She puts a hand on his keyboard and the screensaver disappears. "Oops, sorry," she says. Then, "Let's go to dinner. I've picked a place I think you'll love. Then I have a surprise for you after dinner."

Surprises have a way of unsettling Sean. All he says is, "Oh?"

Julie catches a look in Sean's face, so she adds quickly, "It has nothing to do with snuggling or dancing or whispering sweet nothings. That's all I'll say for now." She gives a laugh, twirls away from him, and heads for the door.

"Shall we go?" she asks.

Sean nods. "Of course. Let me grab my keys."

"I'm driving," she reminds him.

"And I'm locking my apartment door," he says, smiling.

As they descend the stairs, Julie says, "I hope you'll let me read your book one day."

Sean thinks for a moment. "I don't want to say the wrong thing here," he says. "I'm not sure I'd be comfortable letting you see it when it's still incomplete."

"Whatever your decision," Julie says earnestly, "I won't be

crushed. I'm a patient person."

A half-hour later Julie and Sean are being seated at Mediterraneo on Federal Hill, getting a corner table.

As the hostess leaves, Julie says, "You love seafood, so I know you'll love this place. They have a seafood dish here to die for."

"Really?" Sean says, his eyes taking in the place, guessing that this place has to be one of the more expensive ones on Atwell's Avenue. He's heard of the place, of course, though only in general terms, and he and Julie passed by it when they spent the evening at De Pasqaule Square, but he's never been here.

"Their seafood dish — it's got lobster, fish, shrimp, clams, mussels, and scallops, and they always do it to utter perfection," Julie says. "By the time you finish, you'll be addicted to the place."

"Duffy's does a good job with lobster and clams and that stuff," Sean said.

"Duffy's is down-and-dirty seafood," Julie says. "This is seafood raised to haute-cuisine".

The waiter comes. "I'm Michael and I'll be your server this evening. May I get you drinks while you look at the menu?"

Julie pauses for a moment, thinking, "I'd love an apple martini, please."

"Of course," Michael says. "And you, sir?"

Sean looks across the table at Julie, "I'll explain in a moment." Then, to the waiter, he says, "Jameson on the rocks, please."

The waiter gives a small bow. "I'll have your drinks in a moment."

Julie leans back in her chair and gives Sean a serious stare. "Jameson, Sean? Your doctor cleared you? You're ulcer is all healed?"

"Close enough," he tells her. "I just feel like celebrating a bit tonight," he says, quickly adding, "I'm not making a habit of it." Immediately, he is worried Ted might tell Jane about his recent drinks and Jane might tell Julie. He looks away for a moment. "This is quite a place," he says, lamely trying to initiate a new topic.

"I've always loved it here," she says. "But I only eat here two or three times a year. They are excellent at everything they do, but there's a price for excellence, especially here on the Hill. I'm usually more than happy to settle for very good, and much lower prices."

"We could have gone to a very good place," Sean suggests.

"I wanted this to be special."

Again, a bit of discomfort digs into Sean. Julie has something planned; she's already admitted that. He wonders if he should try to explain to her how he views their relationship.

Julie interrupts his train of thought. “The first time I came here was when my brother and his wife took me out to celebrate my divorce.” She waits to gauge Sean’s reaction. He is simply nodding gently, waiting for her to continue.

“I told you I was divorced, didn’t I?” she asks. “It was almost eight years ago.”

Sean shakes his head. “You told me your husband had left you. I guessed you got a divorce at some point.”

She reaches across and touches his hand lightly. “The divorce sucked, but it was the best thing that happened to me — in retrospect. He married his honey and they divorced two years later. He married a third time, with the same outcome. Anyway, I was more than happy to celebrate when our divorce was final. It was all good.”

“No need for details,” Sean tells her. “All that’s in the past.”

“I agree,” Julie says. “Anyway, that’s how I discovered Mediterraneo.”

“Thank you for introducing me to the place.”

Michael appears with the drinks, placing them carefully on the table.

“Are you ready to order?” he asks.

“I need more time,” Julie says.

“Take all the time you need,” Michael says, backing away from the table.

“I hope you’re not starving,” she says to Sean. “I just want this dinner to be long and leisurely. Is that okay with you?”

Sean nods. “I’m very much okay with that.”

He lifts his glass.

“Cheers,” he says. “It’s very nice seeing you again.”

Julie clinks her glass against his. “I’m glad we could see each other tonight.” Her eyes catch his and linger just long enough to let him know she is sincere in her pleasure with his company.

He takes in her gaze and her smile, and as they sip their drinks, he begins to wonder if he might ever let his guard down as far as Julie is concerned. In her presence, and even when they are apart, there is something about her that entices him – in a good way.

He puts his glass down and wonders what the rest of the evening will bring, and what her ‘surprise’ might be. All the while, in the undercurrents swirling in the back of his mind, he is thinking about what he wants to write when the evening is over.

***Beating Ian's butt***

*There were three things about himself that Aidan knew with certainty: he was not a quitter, he was stubborn, and he was a decent human being. There were other things he considered himself to be: caring, respectful of others, capable of doing better, and a failure as responsible adult who could have fulfilled what could have been bright potential had he not been so damned intent on living life the way he thought he wanted.*

*The telephone call from his brother, clearly intended to intimidate Aidan into doing what his brother considered to be the only honorable thing to do in light of the fact that Aidan had shown himself – to Ian and Margaret, at least – to be a loser, settled like a stone in Aidan's gut the way a bad meal would.*

*At another time in his life, Aidan would have let his brother's arrogance seep into him and eat at him. He'd be pissed off, he'd curse Ian, but he'd settle into a passive aggression that accomplished nothing more than increasing his frustration with his snotty siblings.*

*This time, though, he no longer wanted to roll over and accept whatever his brother — or his sister — lobbed his way.*

*Maybe Ashling was right. Perhaps he should arrange to meet with Ian – and with Margaret, as if that were remotely possible – and have an adult conversation about the planned wedding and Aidan's future and their father's take on everything. Perhaps it was time for Aidan to let his brother and sister know about the letter their mother had written him long before she died. Perhaps, as Ashling had hinted so strongly, it was time for Aidan to stand up for himself and end the disrespect that his brother and sister had for so long seemed to enjoy slinging his way.*

*He had gone to work at noon that day, thoughts about his family's dynamics popping up between his interaction with customers despite the ongoing trite banter with this guy and that guy and the alcoholics and the wine snobs and the kids with phony IDs.*

*He wasn't going to hand in his notice until Electric Boat confirmed that he'd passed the physical and the other tests. But the realization that he might only have to be behind the counter for another two or three weeks was liberating. For the first time, it dawned on him how monotonous and draining this job had been for all these years. And how much ground he'd lost.*

*It was a minute after nine when he left the store and headed home. Ashling had gotten into the habit of having a cup of tea ready for him after work; since he no longer spent time with his friends at the pub, she could count on his being home right after work – and she could count on being able to curl up with him as she fell asleep.*

*When he entered the apartment, Ashling greeted him, as usual, with a warm hug and a kiss. Taking his hand, she led him to the kitchen table where she'd place his cup of tea and a ham sandwich she'd made for him.*

*"If you'd like a second sandwich, tell me," she said, knowing one sandwich was not usually enough for him after a long day. "Anything exciting at work?"*

*"Boring," was all he said. He took a hearty bite from the sandwich and chewed slowly. After he swallowed, he said. "I want to call Ian tonight. I want to do what you said. If he agrees to go out to dinner with me – with us – I want it to happen."*

*"What about Margaret?" Ashling asked.*

*"I'll call her after I talk with Ian."*

*Ashling leaned back in her chair and sipped her tea.*

*"Make sure you plan precisely what you're going to say to him," she said. "You know how he can be – debater-in-chief whose main concern always is winning. He's likely to want you as another trophy, even though you're his flesh and blood."*

*She shook her head. "I am constantly amazed that you and he came from the same parents."*

*Aidan smiled. "I think he's a genetic throwback to some medieval blackguard in the family tree."*

*Ashling laughed and Aidan continued to eat.*

*Fifteen minutes later, Aidan had his hand on the phone. It took him another five minutes before he dialed.*

*It took four rings before Ian answered.*

*"McCann here," his brother said, in a most businesslike voice.*

*Aidan let a moment pass.*

*"Ian, it's me."*

*"Aidan?" his brother asked. I thought you usually work nights."*

*"I do, but I got out at nine."*

*It was Ian's turn to pause briefly. "I see."*

*"I'm glad you see," Aidan said.*

*Again Ian paused, as if unsure of what was going on with his substandard brother.*

*"Am I to take it that you've considered what we talked about last night?" Ian had an uncanny ability to sound pompous, no matter what the circumstances. Aidan's mind suddenly flipped off in another direction and he wondered if Ian and his wife were pompous in bed. He quashed the thought immediately.*

*"You're absolutely right. I did consider it," Aidan admitted. "And the reason I'm calling is that Ashling and I would like to get together with you for dinner one night this coming weekend. You're wife is included in the invitation. We'll even drive up to Massachusetts. We want to discuss what you were talking about last night."*

*Silence from Ian.*

*Aidan had a feeling that all lawyers had a compulsive need to take a moment or two to formulate foolproof answers to whatever questions they were asked or whatever suggestions were put before them – even something as simple as "how do you like this great weather?"*

*At last, Ian said, "You'd rather not talk about it on the phone?"*

*"Not really. Besides, the last time we saw you was at mom's funeral. It'd be nice to get together with you again." Aidan struggled to keep a snide tone out of his voice. "We're planning to invite Margaret and dad as well."*

*Again, Ian took a leisurely moment to create his response. "I'm not sure we need to involve dad – at least not now. As far as Margaret is concerned, I doubt if she'll want to come."*

*Aidan began to get the vague feeling that perhaps he was, for the first time ever, almost in control of a conversation with his brother.*

*"Come on," Aidan said, hoping he was pushing some of his brother's buttons, "dad loves to go out to eat. And I'm sure he'd enjoy having us all together. And I have a feeling that Margaret will like to get in on this."*

*The predictable pause from his brother. Aidan waited patiently.*

*"Okay," Ian said, "let's get together. When and where?"*

*"Do you have any favorite restaurant that you and your wife like?"*

*"I'm not planning on bringing her along."*

*"No?"*

*"This is a family thing, Aidan. She doesn't need to have a say in any of it."*

*"Sorry to hear that," Aidan said, trying to put disappointment into his voice. "Well, pick a place, then."*

*"When do you want to come up?"*

*"Friday, Saturday or Sunday. Whatever is good for you."*

*Ian thought for a moment. "Sunday is better for me. I think we've got plans for Friday and Saturday."*

*Aidan said, "Sounds good. Name a place."*

*Ian named a restaurant in Boston and gave its Newbury Street address. Aidan knew that any restaurant in that section of the city was incapable of being modestly priced, and he knew that Ashling would probably insist that he and she pick up the tab – if only to irk Ian.*

*"We'll be there," Aidan said. "Six o'clock okay?" We'll have a long ride back home. We don't want to stay too late."*

*"Six is fine," Ian said, without enthusiasm.*

*Aidan couldn't say that he was excited about driving to Boston on Sunday. Had he been able to avoid this meeting with his brother, he would have. But Ashling had convinced him it was his only alternative; and Aidan knew that Ashling had the wisdom he himself lacked.*

*A half-hour later, Aidan dialed and Margaret's husband, Kenneth, answered Aidan's call and said nothing at all after Aidan said he wanted to speak with his sister. Aidan heard the phone being placed on the table or desk or whatever and waited at least two minutes in silence before Margaret said, "Hello, Aidan. Is there something wrong?"*

*Aidan outlined the plans to meet with Ian in Boston. Not surprisingly, Margaret told him she and Ian had just discussed the Aidan's idea of a dinner in Boston. Surprisingly, she said she'd be delighted to attend. And, no, her husband would probably not be joining them.*

*With one last phone call to his father, Aidan had Sunday evening completely booked. The next day, he booked a reservation at Chez Albert, feeling uneasy about what dinner would cost him.*

*Aidan and Ashling arrived on Newbury Street shortly after five-thirty, Cornelius seated comfortably in the back seat and looking forward to the Chez Albert experience.*

*After looping a couple of blocks in search of a parking place, Aidan finally surrendered to reality and parked in the Boston Common underground garage. It was maybe five blocks away from the restaurant his brother had chosen. Thankfully, it was a pleasant late afternoon, and the walk was enjoyable.*

*Aidan had stopped at an ATM machine before leaving town and took two hundred dollars – which made an unwelcome dent in his checking account. Ashling had two hundred in her purse and reassured him that the dinner would not take all their money. It was, she tried to convince him, an investment in a better future for themselves.*

*"If we conquer Ian – and, hopefully, Margaret – we will be far better off, luv," she said as they drove toward Boston. "Believe it or not, I think Ian likes me – although he would never admit it."*

*Aidan laughed. "I think he's jealous that you and I have each other, he's stuck with his wife. I wonder if he knew before he married her that she would turn out to be such a snot."*

*"I'm certain there was some attraction," Ashling said. "Whatever brought them together, I believe your brother got exactly what he wanted and what he deserved."*

*"I feel sorry for him in a way," Aidan said, grinning. "But not too sorry."*

*Ashling chuckled. "Be serious now. We are about to become involved in a debate with your brother – who, we both know, engages in debate for a living – about some very important matters. And Margaret will likely take his side, making it the two of them against us."*

*Aidan looked at her. "You know what? I have a gut feeling that tonight we can beat his butt in debate."*

*"And how's that?" she asked.*

*"Because I understand real life, and I don't think he has any clue at all."*

*Ashling took his hand and pulled him close. "I think, luv, that you have finally come to understand yourself."*

*"I don't understand," Aidan said, seriously.*

*Ashling looked at him, her brows furrowed. "You live in the real world, luv. His world is far more artificial – money, large houses, upper-crust friends who put on airs, fancy cars, a keep-up-with-the-Rockefellers mentality. I would never want to live that way."*

*"I've never been to his house," Aidan said. I wonder if he has a staff at his service."*

*Ashling poked him. "It's no matter if he has butlers or maids or valets. All that counts is that he is human like you and shares the same roots. It's he who has chosen to stand off from the family because he needs to feel as if he's climbed a very important ladder. And he's done it by throwing aside important parts of who he is. You have chosen to be you – and I'm sure he is exceedingly envious of you."*

*Cornelius was waiting for them, and it took less than two minutes until they were all in the car and heading toward what Aidan called a "family dinner to end all family dinners."*

*Throughout the fifteen-minute ride into downtown Boston, Cornelius spoke with joy about the wedding and the dancing and the friends and anything else that might make the event perhaps the most memorable ever.*

*Aidan and Ashling let him talk on, both of them spending much of the ride with smiles on their faces.*

*They walked slowly from the parking garage; Cornelius commenting on places they passed and reminiscing about the occasional visits he and Ellen had made to Boston when they were younger and had a bit of money for fun.*

*When the three of them arrived at the restaurant, Aidan took in the elegantly understated façade and peered through the window. Inside, as far as he could see, there were only eight tables. Five of them were occupied and one of the remaining three was set for six. Aidan reported on what he saw.*

*"I'd wager that must be our table," Ashling said.*

*Cornelius moved closer and stared through the glass, almost wide-eyed, and finally said, "Your brother picked this place? It looks far too expensive for the likes of us. I think your brother likes spending more money than necessary."*

*"He's got the money to spend," Aidan said, looking for a menu posted outside the entrance. There was none. His faced creased in worry. "But we're paying for the dinner," he told his father.*

*"We can afford it," Ashling added, trying to ease Cornelius's concern. "Besides, if we take care of the bill, we don't owe anything to anyone."*

*Cornelius nodded. During his phone call inviting his father to dinner with them, Aidan had mentioned that Ian had some concerns about the wedding without mentioning specifics. Cornelius had little to say on the topic during the ride into the city.*

*Aidan put an arm around Ashling and pulled her close for a quick hug. Then he put his hand on his dad's shoulder. "Thanks coming with us," he said. "We can use your support."*

*Cornelius gave him a look. "Support for what?"*

*"It all depends on Ian and Margaret," Aidan said.*

*Before Cornelius could say anything more, Aidan said, "We might as well go in. There's no telling when Ian or Margaret might show up."*

*As he opened the door for his father and Ashling, the maître 'd, in a tuxedo, greeted them warmly, verified that they indeed had a reservation, and led them through the dining room that was several light years removed from any other restaurant in their experience.*

*Aidan began having a waking nightmare about what the exorbitant tab would be by the end of the evening.*

*Ian, not surprisingly, was more than late, arriving nearly twenty after six. With only a half-sincere apology for his tardiness, he greeted his father with some warmth, commented in passing on how lovely Ashling looked, and shook Aidan's hand, saying, with little enthusiasm, that it was great to see him again.*

*"One of my favorite places," Ian said as he sat. "My office is not far from here."*

*"On this street?" his father asked.*

*"No, on Boylston Street."*

*"So you come here a lot?" Cornelius said, trying to get a sense of how much his eldest spent on restaurants.*

*"Four or five times a month, that's about it. Usually for business lunches."*

*Cornelius looked at the leather-bound menu before him. The least expensive appetizers started at twelve dollars. The entrees started at thirty-five dollars. "Then they must be very expensive lunches," he commented.*

*Ian laughed. "The lunch prices are much lower than those on the dinner menu," he said, as if that would reduce his father's menu-shock.*

*"Still," Cornelius said, "I can't imagine anyone in his right mind paying that much for food."*

*Ian was about to answer when Ashling, who was seated facing the entrance, said. "Here comes Margaret."*

Once again, Sean and Julie's time together included discussions that spread over multiple topics and included lively exchanges and more than enough humor to enliven an already lively evening for the two of them.

Finally, sipping the restaurant's wonderful limoncello after the dishes had been cleared away, Julie says, "I promised you a surprise tonight. Are you ready?"

"Depends on how life-threatening the surprise is," Sean says, grinning. "As long as it doesn't include nighttime sky-diving, I'm game."

"I'm more of a bungee-cord person," Julie says.

"You're kidding!"

"I've only done it twice. Believe me, that's enough."

"Not my kind of thing," he says, instantly wishing he had said something that made him seem less of a wimp.

"I wouldn't recommend it."

"Then why did you do it twice?"

"I really don't know," she says, laughing.

She finishes the last of the limoncello, picks her credit card and receipt from the folder the waiter had put in front of her. She gives Sean a broad smile.

"Shall we see what the evening has in store for you?"

"Let's," Sean says.

He rises from his chair and gestures for her to precede him as they leave. She, however, takes his hand as she passes and leads him out of the restaurant.

The sidewalks of Federal Hill are busy with people walking, talking, leaning on utility poles, hunkered over round tables on the sidewalks. Sean can hear music from De Pasquale Square over the sound of traffic cruising Atwell's Avenue.

Julie gives her valet parking ticket to the attendant and she and Sean lean against the side of the restaurant, people-watching and commenting discreetly about the people passing by.

When the car arrives, Julie hands some folded bills to the valet. She and Sean get in, fasten seat belts, and Julie drives off toward downtown Providence.

"Do I get to know where we are going?" Sean asks. "Or do I have to wait to see."

She gives him a sidelong look. "You have to wait approximately seven minutes."

"Seven?"

"I try to be precise when someone has an urgent need to know what's next."

Sean laughs. Julie's company is more refreshing than he could ever have anticipated.

A few minutes later, they are in the heart of the city, Julie turning right here, left there. Finally, they arrive just off Davol Square and Julie parks in a lot close to the Point Street bridge.

Sean, who willingly admits he is not a city denizen, asks, "Where are we?"

"Julie gives him a conspiratorial grin. "You'll see in a minute."

Before he can respond, she leaves the car and slams the door.

When he gets out, she waves him over to her side of the vehicle. Again, she takes his hand and leads the way.

"Have you ever been to Retrograde?"

"What's that?" he answers, his ignorance honest.

"A club," she says with an exaggerated sigh. "One of the great ones in Providence."

"Oh," he says, wondering why she's taken him here.

"Who's your favorite group?"

Sean thinks for a moment. "Outside of Ted, I don't think I have any local favorites."

"I'm not talking local." Julie says. Just outside the entrance, she stops. "Who is your favorite group, bar none? Tell me."

Sean thinks for a moment. "'April Morning'," he says, then adds quickly, "I have a lot of favorites, but I have their CDs. Sometimes I listen to them in the background when I'm writing."

Julie chuckles and squeezes his hand. "Surprise number one, Sean: April Morning at Retrograde – two nights only. My treat!" she added with a dash of feigned smugness.

Sean says, "Holy shit."

Julie laughs.

"Jane and Ted, right?"

"Right."

Julie raises herself on tiptoe and plants a quick kiss on his cheek. Before he can react, she reaches for the door and pulls him in behind her.

Except for the times he has headed to Matunuck or wherever else to meet Ted, Sean hasn't been in a club for maybe twenty years. It's not his style. He's always pictured clubs as full of twenty-somethings more interested in hooking up than in much of anything else. Sean is not a meat-market kind of guy.

Tonight is different. Nearly an hour into the evening, he is comfortable sipping the tail end of another Jameson, and content with Julie's hand still holding his.

There's a dance floor, a small one, but Julie has not given any indication of wanting to dance. Sean, if it were up to him, would prefer simply listening to the music. He's never been much of a dancer.

When April Morning finishes their first set, and silence drifts over the place, Julie signals the waitress for another round of drinks, then leans back in her chair, a crooked smile on her face.

"Having fun yet?" she asks. She has, Sean has noticed, an uncanny ability to inject playfulness in to whatever words come out of her mouth.

He smiles and nods – and squeezes her hand. "This is fabulous," he tells her, adding, "I mean it, Julie. This is one heck or a great surprise. Thank you – so much."

She shakes her head. "No. Thank you for your company tonight."

The waitress brings the drinks and places them on the table.

"Can I bring you anything else?" she asks.

"We're fine for now," Julie says. "Thank you."

The waitress wiggles away and Julie lifts her glass.

Sean follows suit and they clink the glasses together, then sip in silence for a moment.

"I promised you surprises tonight," Julie says, "not just one."

"Surprises?" Sean asks, smiling. "I should hope you'd have at least a few for me."

Julie pretends to glare at him. "I'm wondering if you can handle more than two surprises from me in one evening."

Sean takes another sip from his Jameson, welcoming the illusion of inner strength it is giving him.

"Well," he tells Julie, "Go for it."

Julie slouches in her seat and gives Sean a probing look. "You're sure?"

"Yup."

"Absolutely?"

"Of course," Sean replies, although he is experiencing a small surge of uncertainty.

She sits up in her chair, leans forward, and takes both of his hands in hers.

For the briefest instant, Sean is afraid that she is going to propose marriage to him or, at the least, will ask him to agree to sleep with her tonight. He is not ready for either scenario.

"Surprise number two," Julie tells him. "Maybe you've already guessed it, but here goes: I really, truly like you, Sean O'Connor. Honestly, I don't think I've ever met a man like you, and I just want you to know that I hope you and I can go on seeing each other again and again and again."

Sean stares at her, then looks away, then stares at her again.

"Surprised?" she asks, with a crooked grin.

Sean tries to pull himself together. Suddenly, instead of simply being in a you-are-good-company mode, real emotion has been introduced into the mix – not something for which Sean is even remotely ready. It's not that he doesn't want her to like him, it's that he's done without for so long that he's assumed that such a thing would not be in the cards for him — ever.

The real problem is how much he likes her.

Julie searches his face. Finally, probably in self-defense, she says in a calming voice, "Look, I understand how it can be. I've been alone for a long time. And for ages I thought I'd never find someone I'd love and who would love me back – at least, not the kind of guy that I'd see as a perfect fit."

"It's not that," Sean interrupts, squeezing her hands for emphasis.

"Let me finish," Julie says. "Please."

Sean nods.

"I gave up eventually. Actually, it was a relief to give up. No longer did I have to live my life based on potential contingencies that may or may not arise. Dating was out; occasional get-togethers with friends were in. Jane and Ted have always been so good about inviting me to spend time with them. I was content with my life – not perfectly content, but content enough."

Julie lets go of Sean's hands and leans back in her chair.

"Then Jane mentioned you one day when she and I were shopping. Over the next few months, she'd pass along various tidbits about you, about your personality, about your life."

Sean has to laugh. "She really betrayed me to you, didn't she."

Julie shakes her head. "No betrayal at all. Jane's not like that. She wants happiness for me, and I think she kept suggesting you as good remedy for my situation. I hope I haven't made you feel too uncomf…"

Sean raises his hand. "Julie, I like you, too. A lot more than you may know. And the way you just described how you were living your life – well, that's how I've been living mine. It's not particularly satisfying. You find a groove that is tolerably comfortable, and you go with the flow while avoiding anything that might change the way you've structured the days and weeks and months of your existence."

It's Julie's turn to laugh a bit. "Predictability has its comforts, but a whole lot of disadvantages."

"I'll drink to that," Sean says, raising his glass.

After they put their glasses back down on the table, Sean reaches again for her hand.

"I suppose this means we're likely to be seeing a lot more of each other," he says.

"I'll pencil you in," Julie answers.

In Julie's car, later, as they are heading from Providence back to Wickford, Sean finds himself looking at Julie as she drives. He makes a mental note to thank Jane and Ted profusely for interfering in his private life.

He is content, no longer worried about what Julie thinks of him. For the first time in a very long time, he is beginning to feel energized about his future.

He leans back in his seat and watches the traffic ahead. It won't be easy to get to sleep tonight.

He needs to write to settle himself down. It might be a long night.

***Margaret said…***

*Margaret brushed by the maître 'd and headed straight for the table where the rest of her family sat. She was the kind of person who was sparing in her smiles and tended to spend most of her waking hours in serious focus on one issue or another. Aidan had always wondered if she ever found any joy in living. Now, she reserved her first half-smile for her father who she greeted with reasonable warmth and a kiss on the cheek. Next she put an arm on Ian's shoulders and kissed him as well.*

*When she was seated, she gave Aidan a perfunctory greeting and told Ashling that she looked good.*

*"Have we begun the conversation yet?" she asked, donning her glasses and opening the menu.*

*"Not yet," Aidan said, preemptively taking his brother out of the start of the conversation. "By the way, Ashling and I are treating tonight, and I think it might be nice to start with a drink and a couple of appetizers."*

*Margaret raised an eyebrow and Ian did a barely perceptible double take.*

*"I hope they have ordinary food," Cornelius said.*

*Aidan smiled. "I'm sure you'll enjoy your meal."*

*"Thank you, Aidan," his dad said.*

*Ian raised his water glass. "I thank you as well," he told Aidan.*

*Margaret nodded. "It's very nice of you both." She left her water glass where it was.*

*When the waiter came, they ordered drinks and Aidan told him to make sure that he got the tab.*

*"It's been a long time since we've sat around a table together," Cornelius said. "I wish your mother was here; she'd be very happy, indeed. It would be nice if we could do this more often."*

*Margaret looked away. Ian said, "Maybe we could – now and then. Aidan?"*

*"I'd love it," Aidan said.*

*Ashling added, "I hope we do. And I hope you can join us Margaret, when we get together." The sincerity in her voice was clear.*

*Margaret studied Ashling for a moment. "If my schedule permits, I think it would be something to consider. We don't meet as a family very often." There was less sincerity in Margaret's words. She gave Ashling a half-smile and returned to perusing the menu.*

*Cornelius must have noticed Margaret's coolness because he gave his daughter a look that she didn't see.*

*Aidan changed the conversation to how much downtown Boston had changed over the years.*

*Finally, the waiter returned and, with a certain élan, placed the drinks before them. As he left, Aidan lifted his glass.*

*"To our little family reunion," he said. "It's good to have all of us together. Thank you for coming."*

*Glasses were clinked together, sips were taken, and a quiet moment passed.*

*Before anyone else could speak, Aidan laid his hands on the table and spoke to his father.*

*"You probably know that the reason we're here tonight is because Ian has some concerns about our wedding," he said. Looking toward his sister briefly, he added, "I'm not sure if Margaret holds the same opinions as Ian, but I think that we need to talk things through."*

*Cornelius looked at Ian. "Why should you have any concerns over your brother's wedding to Ashling?" He looked over at Margaret and then back at Ian. "Your mother and I always thought they belong together."*

*Ian leaned back. His face, Aidan thought at the moment, probably looked the same when he was reacting to some surprise setback in one of his legal cases.*

*Ian lifted his glass for another swallow of the very expensive scotch he had ordered. When he put it down, he leaned on his elbows and clasped his hands together.*

*Margaret did not seem especially at ease.*

*"After you told me the other day about Aidan's wedding plans, dad," Ian said, "it just seemed to me that it would be inappropriate that someone Aidan's age should opt for anything more than a quiet ceremony in a chapel. I didn't mention the issue to you because I assumed Aidan and I could agree on something less grand. Besides, dad, I was concerned that a long evening of dancing and drinking might not be good for you. After losing mom, we'd rather not lose you as well." Ian smiled at his father.*

*"I was concerned, too," Margaret said, with a sidelong glance at Ian. "I agree that Ian's concerns have a good deal of validity. A small, quiet ceremony would be far more dignified."*

*"But it's to be a celebration," Ashling interjected. "We will be celebrating the love that has bound us together all these years, and celebrating the promise of our future years together. And we want to celebrate it with your dad and the both of you and your families and all our friends."*

*Margaret was about to respond when Cornelius raised his hand. "You and Ian discussed this together?" he asked her.*

*"Of course," she said, suddenly speaking condescendingly to her father. "We're concerned for you in this situation. Weddings can be stressful, and sometimes weddings between older people can turn out rather embarrassingly. Aidan has been known to drink more than he should. If I recall, he was drunk at mom's funeral."*

*Cornelius reacted immediately. He pressed his hands against the table and glared at Margaret and Ian.*

Sean crushes his half-puffed cigarette in the ashtray. He is upset to the point of no longer feeling fatigued. He'd prefer to be drinking now, but drinking would just complicate things for him.

He's been sitting at his keyboard for over two hours – two frustratingly unproductive hours – and he's managed to produce barely more than three pages. His mind refuses to focus…or he is unwilling to allow his mind to focus. For every two or three sentences he writes, he spends ten minutes thinking about Julie and the evening they shared.

He is clearly distracted. But he senses that it's not the wonderfully fresh memories of Julie's company that are making it difficult to write. It is something deeper and more disconcerting: a fluttering worry that his writing – when he finally has to let her read it – will cause her to be disappointed in him. The fretting has become a slowly evolving undercurrent since he first admitted to himself that he likes Julie, perhaps more than he should. But part of the worry also comes from not knowing what Jane or Ted have told Julie about his story, and from concern that Julie might be expecting a tour-de-force from him.

It also comes from the fact that he feels now, in these suddenly sullen post-midnight hours, that he will likely not be able to live up to the expectations of those who know what he's trying to do. It's as if his confidence has inexplicably begun leaking out of him and he is beginning to founder.

He frowns at his computer screen.

He should never have let Ted or Jane read the manuscript. He should have done all his writing in seclusion. If it had turned out to be a pile of crap, he could have simply tossed it away – and no one would have been aware of his final failure.

He gets up from his chair and paces the room. He no longer has any sense of time.

Then, against, his better judgment, he goes to the kitchen and pours himself a Jameson. The clock above the kitchen table is pointing closer to three in the morning. When he again sits in front of his computer, he lights another cigarette. Unintentionally, he begins to inhale, but the action makes him cough. He puts the cigarette down in the ashtray and takes a hefty swallow of his whiskey.

"So where the hell do you go from here, Sean?" he asks himself aloud. "Any bright ideas?"

Another puff on his cigarette, another sip of Jameson. The words on the computer screen give him no inspiration, no direction – no salvation.

It's as if the spark is suddenly gone.

But he is stubborn, he knows, even though his stubbornness rarely gained him any rewards. He will write some more tonight. Even if he has to force it, one word at a time.

He will do this, damn it!

Sean sips again. Inhales once without choking, and almost dares the computer screen to intimidate him. He takes long moments to read what he has written already tonight. His train of thought might have evaporated, but he is capable of putting one word after another, and capable of writing coherent sentences.

"Fuck it," he says aloud.

He begins to write again, picking up where he left off, and it is difficult. But he needs to do this.

***Dancing the polka***

*It took Cornelius long moments to digest what Ian and Margaret had said and to bring his anger under control. He was upset with their attitude toward the wedding, but angered at Margaret's assertion that Aidan had been drunk at Ellen's funeral. His face tightened and he took a healthy swig of his Jameson, then began to speak in strict, measured tones.*

*"Your mother and I," he said to Margaret, keeping his voice low so as to not cause any embarrassment, "we never raised you to become arrogant. How is it that you've become so?" He shook his head as if trying to figure things out.*

*She tried to speak, but he raised his hand.*

*"I was the one who was drunk at your mother's funeral," Cornelius told Margaret. "Well, half-drunk, in fact. And if Aidan was drunk too, then it was my fault." Cornelius chose not to mention the post-breakfast drink he'd also shared with his son, instead telling Margaret, "We stayed up late, Ashling too, and drank and talked about your mother. How else could I face the nightmare of having to bury my wife?"*

*He looked at Ian. "I'm not much surprised that you, too, have become arrogant over the years," he told his eldest son. "You showed arrogance even as a child, God forgive me for saying so. But I never expected you to reach the point where you thought you had the least right to have a say in your brother's life."*

*Ian began to speak. Cornelius shook his head and Ian fell silent.*

*Cornelius composed himself. When he spoke again, his voice was soft and even.*

*"Believe me when I tell you both that I am happy that Aidan and this wonderful and loving woman are to be married. They have shown more care and compassion for your mother and me than any parents could hope for. Ashling and your mother could have been sisters, they were so close to each other. Aidan, though he lives so far away, spent as much time as he could visiting your mother and me. Ashling has spoken on the telephone with me – and with your mother before I had to put her in that home -- perhaps two or three times a week for many years."*

*Ian spoke, with no pomposity: "I work about sixty or seventy hours a week, dad. I wanted to be able to visit more, but I..."*

*"It's not about that," his father said. He looked at each of his children. "I'm not exactly sure what it's about. But I know this: your brother has been more than good to me and to your late mother, and I fully intend to be good to him in return. I want him and Ashling to have a wonderful wedding and I want to dance at it and I want to drink at it."*

*Suddenly, Cornelius laughed. "I love dancing the polka. I hope Aidan and Ashling will let me bring a friend who loves to dance as well."*

*Ashling smiled and reached out to put her hand on his. "Of course," she said. "We'll invite your friends."*

*Before the conversation could resume, the waiter returned. Three minutes later, he had their orders and withdrew from the table.*

*Then there was silence.*

*Aidan had expected strong protest from his siblings – mostly about the fact that he had outmaneuvered them – but the entire table had fallen quiet.*

*It was Ashling who finally spoke.*

*"Have either of you been to the north of Ireland?" she asked, her gaze sweeping from Ian to Margaret and back again.*

Sean can no longer stay awake. He's sipped another of Jameson and has had four more cigarettes than he's ever allowed himself. He turns away from the computer and plods to his bedroom and strips to his boxers and crawls into bed. If he can write again, it will have to wait.

Seconds later, he is unconscious.

When Sean's eyes open, the glow of daylight has been slipping through the slats of his window blinds for hours. He grabs his watch from the bedside table and squints at its face. Noon is only a few minutes away. If he were a believing person, he would be disappointed probably that he'd missed morning Mass. He feels as if he should spend some time praying.

He'd spent the rest of Saturday night, first enjoying the afterglow of his time with Julie, then later at his computer trying to write. Earlier yesterday, he was rich in ideas of where to take his story. By the time three in the morning passed him by, he was still sitting in front of his computer, his sudden inability to pick up on the story digging into him. At least a half-dozen times he read the last ten chapters, trying to recapture the story-generating energy that had brought him thus far. His loss of his bearings not only frustrated him, but also began to scare him. How many times in the past two weeks had he felt ready to begin bringing the story to a solid, satisfying conclusion? The end of the story was even more important than the beginning, he believed. If he could not find the proper resolution to the story line he'd crafted thus far, he'd only reaffirm the needling and barely suppressed feeling that this effort, like the others, would be another waste of time.

Only utter fatigue forced him into bed shortly after dawn. Even then, his frustration – could it simply be writer's block? – kept sleep at bay for at least another hour.

Exhausted and craving far more sleep that he's had this morning, Sean crawls out of bed, shuffles to the bathroom to pee, then heads back to the comfort of his blankets. He lies there, staring at the ceiling, feeling almost paralyzed and unable to focus.

For a time, he thinks he should force himself to the computer and simply type what comes to mind. Perhaps he'll be able to grasp onto a thread of narration that will revive him. But he is far too tired.

How in hell could he have suddenly lost his way?

The story had been going well, and each time he sat in front of his keyboard, he did so with confidence and the story would flow from him in a way he'd never experienced before.

What the fuck has happened?

More important: what in God's name can he do to bring it all back?

After a long while, he again gets out of bed and slouches to the kitchen. He needs coffee — badly. While the coffee-maker is dripping into the pot, he decides to focus on Aidan; perhaps rehashing Aidan in his mind will help him regain his story line. After all, he knows Aidan nearly as well as he knows himself. He knows where Aidan has come from, and – at least until twenty-four hours ago – where his main character was likely going.

He fills an oversized mug with coffee, adds a bit of sugar substitute, then slumps at his kitchen table.

He is utterly lost. And, whether it is his intense frustration or his painfully deep fatigue, he feels tears welling up in his eyes.

"Jesus H. Christ," he says into the empty apartment.

He seems to be slipping downward and there's nothing to grab onto to halt his slide.

Then the phone rings, the sharp sound jangling him. Through his fog of worry, he suspects it's either Julie or Ted calling him – or perhaps Jane. He cannot answer and wishes the ringing would stop. The only comfort he is finding now is in the quiet of his apartment and in the steaming coffee in his hand. There's no way he can talk with anyone now. He is feeling far too lost.

By late afternoon, his phone had rung four more times, and each time he has let it ring until the apartment turns quiet again. He had not yet bothered to dress and still sat at his kitchen table in boxers and a t-shirt. The coffee was long gone and he had poured himself a Jameson, not giving a damn if he had one or if he had ten. He was trying to lose himself in some muddled pit of consciousness, as if losing himself that way would help him magically find his way again.

He stares at the wall, his mind obsessed with reliving Aidan's life and Ashling's life and Cornelius's life – and those of Ian and Margaret and everyone else he'd already created.

He sees only bleakness.

He sits a while longer, having two fingers more of Jameson, which he finishes in three fuck-the-world swallows.

Feeling anguished, he gives up and heads back to bed. For now, at least, he will not be writing – or even trying to write. The whiskey is bringing him down. Soon, he is asleep again, feeling his consciousness fade to black just as the phone rings one more time.

His sleep is restless and haunted. When he wakes, it's with a start, and he lies under his blanket, his heart pounding, his breathing heavy. It's dark now. He's been dreaming – about the story, of course. It's bedeviling him to the point where it seems it's the only thing he can focus on. But now, he feels he has simply run out of steam, and he has almost agreed with himself that he should end it.

The easy way out, he muses, is sometimes the best way out.

At one point, as his mind rambles this way and that, Sean laughs bitterly to himself: he created these people and he has every right to kill them off, one by one, without remorse or penalty.

He wishes that were the case. If he chooses to kill them off, he will be killing himself in a way. At least, he'd surely be killing the last creative sparks he would ever have again. But doing so would be a relief. There would be no more dreams of publishing, no more hopes that he might have what it takes to tell a great story, no more vanity about his writing skills.

He is trying to think things through when he drifts off to sleep once again.

It's the pounding on his door that rouses him, although from a great distance. He waits for a moment, barely awake, to see if the noises are nothing more than a dream threading through his inner darkness, but the pounding resumes – this time with greater strength.

Sean pushes himself to a sitting position on the edge of his bed and, with great difficulty, stands.

Only now does he realize how drunk he's become, and whatever additional sleep he's managed to get has not diminished his blessed intoxication.

Carefully, he walks to the door and reaches it just a fresh flurry of fist thumps shake the door and dun his ears. He turns back the deadbolt and opens the door and stares straight ahead with only partial comprehension.

All he can say, his voice rusty, is, "What time is it?" as he squints into the lighted hallway and sees Ted and Jane – and Julie.

For a confusing moment, he assumes he is dreaming. He mumbles something to that effect and begins closing the door.

Ted keeps the door from closing. "Hey, man, it's nearly ten o'clock. What the heck's going on?"

"We've thought you were sick or something," Jane adds.

"When I couldn't get you on the phone. I didn't know what to do, so I called Jane," Julie says.

Jane puts on her mother voice. "And I tried to call you at least four more times. And Ted tried. And Allyson was worried about you."

Ted says, "Jane and Julie were afraid you had another bleeding ulcer thing and were on the floor here, bleeding out."

Sean is catching most of what they are saying, but is having difficulty absorbing it all. He wants another drink, but is afraid to put his craving into words.

"I'm okay," is all he can tell them. He turns and heads toward his kitchen. Ted and the women follow. Jane immediately sets about making coffee. Julie helps Sean sit down and then pulls a chair to sit next to him. Ted remains standing, trying to figure what Sean's been up to. He's never seen his friend in this condition.

No one speaks until Jane has the coffee pot rinsed out and producing another pot. Then Ted leans down on the table and catches Sean's eye. "Talk to me, man, he says. "What the hell is going on? You look like you've gone off the deep end. Come on, talk to us."

Sean lifts his head and looks at the three of them. He is suddenly embarrassed that Julie is seeing his in this condition. Looking down at himself and recalling that he hasn't dressed or showered or shaved or brushed his teeth, he asks Jane to get a blanket off his bed so he can cover himself.

"I'm sorry," Sean says. "I'm sorry you have to see me like this. I never thought you'd come pounding on my door." Sean tried to smile, but the effort failed.

Jane returns with a blanket and wraps it around Sean's shoulders. He pulls it closed to cover himself from neck to foot, embarrassment beginning to seep into his consciousness.

For a while, each of them peppers Sean with twenty different questions, most of them making no sense to him. He is aware only that when he tries to answer, his voice simply drifts off and the questions remain unanswered.

After a while, Ted pours coffee for each of them and puts the mugs on the table.

"You're drunk, man," Ted says, in his genially direct way. "You can be drunk all you want. But I've never seen you *this* drunk. So what's up?"

Sean sips at his coffee and it nearly burns his lips. He coughs. "I felt like it," he says.

"Bullshit," Jane says, shocking Sean. "You have never been the get-drunk kind."

Julie reaches out and touches Sean's hand. "We care about you, Sean," she says in a soft and encouraging voice. "What's the matter? Please tell us."

"I'm tired," Sean says. He shakes his head. Long seconds pass. "I think I've lost it," he says, at last, looking at Ted and afraid to look at Julie. "Lost it," he says again, his voice trailing off.

He rises from the table and goes to sit on the sofa. The others follow in to the living room.

Julie sits next to Sean. Ted and Jane pull chairs out of the kitchen and sit across from the sofa.

"I sure as hell have lost it," Sean says yet again, staring at the floor.

Jane, Ted, and Julie look at each other. They're not sure what Sean means.

"Lost what?" Jane asks.

"I don't want to talk about it," Sean says in an unconvincing voice.

Julie takes his hand in hers. "Maybe all of us here at once are a bit much for you. If you want, I can leave, or Jane can leave, or Ted can leave. But one of us is going to stand by you tonight. We can't help unless we know what the problem is."

"Please stay," Sean says to Julie. A moment later, he tells Jane and Ted that he wants them to stay as well. "The three of you got together to come and see if I was okay. I can't kick you out."

Ted leans forward. "Then you need to tell us how we can help."

"When was the last time any of you felt like a loser?" Sean asks them.

With that, the conversation was launched.

It takes not much more persuasion from Ted and the two women before Sean begins to open up. At first, he speaks only in bits and pieces, his train of thought falling apart now and then. In a while, he is talking more, trying to spill out what has dropped him into this pit, hoping to make enough sense so that they will understand that his problem is his and his alone and so they will then go home and leave him alone.

The point Sean is trying to make to his friends is, it seems to him, a simple one: he has given all he has to the story, but he's finally run out of steam. Despite what he's written in the last two or three chapters, he has no idea of where the story should be headed. It's as if he's been faking it over the past few weeks, putting words down hoping they might somehow coalesce into a personal yellow brick road that would lead to the story's excellent conclusion and wonderful book reviews.

But it hasn't worked; he is sure of that. Therefore, he is depressed about his failure, unhappy that he even decided to try writing a novel, and wanting only to find his way out of this mess.

It's Julie who speaks first. She reaches out to take his hand.

"Would you take 'suck it up' as useful advice?" she asks gently. She doesn't wait for him to reply. "You know you're not a quitter, Sean. I'll bet you never quit on anything in your life. Why now?"

Sean shrugs and simply looks down at her hand clasping his. He opens his mouth as if to speak, but remains silent. His friends wait.

"I've quit way more times than I can count," he says, his voice barely more than a whisper. "I have a long trail of failed fiction. I quit my hopes of going to college. I quit trying to climb in my career. I quit obeying my doctor's orders about drinking. And I'm pretty sure I quit believing in myself.

An hour after midnight, Jane and Julie apologize to Sean. They need to get home to sleep so they can function at work in the morning. Julie will drive Jane. Ted offers to stay with Sean if Sean needs to talk some more.

Sean declines the offer. "I appreciate it that you tried to come to my rescue," he says, smiling awkwardly. I'll be okay, I think."

Sean gets up from the sofa.

To Julie, he says, "I'm sorry you had to see me this way. I guess this ruins my image as a suave and refined Adonis, huh?"

She laughs and leans in to kiss him on the cheek. "Everything's good, Sean. At least I now know you are human."

Before he can speak again, she says, "How about dinner at my place Tuesday evening? I think some good home-cooked food and a bit more pep-talk might be just what you need."

Sean nods. "Sounds good to me, but no need to do any pep-talking."

"Right," Julie says, rolling her eyes.

After they leave, Sean closes the door and walks toward the couch. Instead of sitting down, however, he turns and goes to his computer. He's not tired, at least not yet, and he wants to read what he's written, perhaps as a way of trying to find out if there's anything at all he might be able to do to salvage his story.

Through tired eyes and fading confidence, Sean calls up his manuscript and reads the last four chapters, examining the sentences, looking for some reason to keep moving forward. He knows the problem lies within himself and not with the story he's trying to tell. Another of his failures of confidence – something he came to believe long ago was a trademark of his life. As he reads, he knows the only solution is to pull himself out of the funk that has overtaken him. It's the only way he will be able to avert one final failure. Despite the discouragement that has seized him, he is beginning to heed the faint but insistent part of him that is refusing to lie down and die on this issue.

Sean pulls a cigarette from the pack on the desk and lights it. As usual, he takes a drag and puffs the smoke up and away, without inhaling. Then he sits and stares at the computer screen.

It takes a long time before he begins tentatively to type again, trying to pick up where he left off – and hoping it will all make sense. Eventually, struggling, the words begin to come, and he lets them come, whether they flow swiftly or painfully slow. He has no idea if any of words will make sense when he wakes up in the morning. He is afraid to let go of this small breeze of momentum.

***This has to stop***

*"It's a lovely place, the North of Ireland," Ashling was saying, "despite the many, many years of Troubles. Have either of you ever been?"*

*It was Margaret who answered first. "You know, I've always wanted to go, but I've never had a schedule that would allow me the time. Surgery, patients – I really can't afford to take much time to myself."*

*Ian chimed in as he nodded in agreement with his sister. "Same here. I guess I've been putting it off until I had somewhat less pressure in my life. But the workload never really eases up."*

*Ashling gave a small smile. "I grew up there, as you perhaps know."*

*"If we didn't know, your accent would give you away," Ian said, trying with little success to lighten the mood.*

*"I grew up in a small village near Newry that perhaps had five hundred people in it, and one very cozy pub," Ashling continued. "My father worked as a supervisor in a factory in Newry; my mother was a seamstress and, on occasion, cleaned the houses of those with money – most of them Unionists — Protestants.*

*"What made our lives special there was our family. Blood can be so strong. I was blessed to have five aunts and four uncles and a lot of cousins, all living close by, as well as my grandmother on my father's side, and my grandmother on my mother's side. My mother's father was killed by Unionists when he fought for the IRA before I was born. They blocked the road one day as he returned from the village and shot him. My father's dad, who to me was the most wonderful old man in the world, died of a heart attack two years before we moved to this country."*

*Ashling paused, as if to assure herself that Ian and Margaret were listening.*

*"Leaving my aunts and uncles and grandmothers behind was the saddest thing I've ever had to do. But the Troubles were not making life easy for any Catholics. There had been rumors that my father was in the IRA, and there had been frightening threats against him on a number of occasions.*

*"Several months before we came to America, someone in the IRA accused my father of telling the Brits about something the IRA were supposed to have been planning. Of course, he would never have betrayed anyone; if anything, he was somewhat sympathetic to the IRA's cause. Yet, he was branded a traitor and they began threatening him as well. He left suddenly one night while I was sleeping. In the morning, my mother told me what had transpired. Believe me, I wept for days."*

*Ashling paused again, trying to tamp down the emotions that were rising in her. The memories of separation were not easy to deal with.*

*Her eyes swept around the table and she looked at each of them in turn.*

*"Many months later, we were finally able to come to America to join my father; he had made safe passage after fleeing to London. It was, to say the least, a great relief to be all back together again – although it would have been far better if we could have brought everybody – my aunts and uncles and my cousins – with us."*

*Ashling waved her hands in front of her. "I'm taking too much time, and I apologize. All I want to say is this: in my experience, there is nothing in life more precious than family. And families stick together and support each other, even when they butt heads over one silly thing or another."*

*Again, she gazed at Ian and Margaret. "Look at the wonderful family you have," she said. Indicating Cornelius, she told them, "Your dad and your mum had to leave their family members – cousins and aunts and uncles and grandparents – so they could give their children better and safer lives. And they were not yet twenty when they left.*

*"And look at the wonderful lives you have now. It's true that you worked hard to live so well, but I doubt if you would have succeeded as impressively without the guidance and encouragement that your mum and your dad gave you along the way."*

*Again she paused. No one gave any indication of wanting to interrupt what she was trying to say.*

*When Ashling spoke again, she said, "Aidan – well, Aidan is different than either of you. His mother recognized that early on, as she wrote in the letter she left for him. He is a good man and a loving man. Yes, he chose a different drummer than either of you would have heeded, and yes" – she reached and took Aidan's hand, smiling at him – "he has begun coming into his own later than most."*

*She stared down at the table for moment. "I know of no other way of putting it," she continued, raising her eyes to Ian and Margaret. "If you are family – and an Irish family, at that – then I would think that you'd want to behave as such, and give each other the family support that each of you deserves. This squabbling, this being in a snit over one thing or another, this not wanting sometimes to be in the same room with one another, and this looking down your noses at your brother – all this has to stop. For Ellen's sake, and for the sake of your wonderful father, this has to stop.*

*Ashling let the words sink in. Then she smiled at them all. "And a beautiful way of signaling that all that petty stuff is over and done with is to support Aidan – and me – in our wish to have a memorable wedding celebration."*

*There was an awkward silence around the table. Aidan, for one, was not going to try to add anything to what Ashling had said. Cornelius sensed that Ashling had gotten the upper hand and was content to let these particular chips settle where they may. Ian was actually twiddling his thumbs, looking down at them because he did not want to look directly at anyone just now. Margaret simply stared blankly at Aidan.*

*The silence hung over them until the waiter returned to the table.*

*After a time, a rivulet of small-talk began flowing between them, beginning with Ashling's admiring comments about Margaret's outfit, to which Margaret replied that she loved the way Ashling wore her hair.*

*"I've always wished my hair was a thick and wonderful as yours," Margaret said.*

*Then their topic switched to which clothing stores Margaret liked to patronize.*

*Soon enough, while the two women were talking, Ian began some small-talk of his own with Aidan.*

*"How are things going for you guys down in Rhode Island?" he asked.*

*"Pretty good, actually," Aidan told him. "I think I have a new job. I'm just waiting for a letter of confirmation and a starting date."*

*Ian look surprised. "When did all this happen?"*

*"I applied a while back. The job's with Electric Boat, about ten minutes from our apartment. I'll be training to be a welder. The pay and benefits are supposed to be good there. I figure I'll be starting in a couple of weeks or so."*

*"Good for you," Ian said. "That's where they make nuclear submarines, right?"*

*"Well, they make parts for them. One of my customers at the liquor store gave me the tip about the job."*

*Ashling interrupted her conversation with Margaret. "And it means he will have regular hours, finally," she said, "No more working odd hours depending on the day of the week, and no more working at night." She gave Aidan a brilliant smile.*

*"Congratulations," Margaret said, reaching across the table to shake her brother's hand. Cornelius was leaning back in his chair, grinning. After a moment, he said, "I can barely believe it. My children are actually speaking to each other!"*

*The mood at the table had grown substantially more comfortable.*

*Dinner was excellent, probably the best meal Aidan and Ashling – and certainly Cornelius – had ever had. Cornelius was utterly impressed by the service, by the fine settings on the table, and by virtually every single bite of food he ingested.*

*Throughout the meal, the light conversation continued. For a time, there was no stress, no airs, no attitudes or egos to spoil the evening.*

*At one point, just before a busboy appeared to clear the table of the dinner debris, Ian looked across at Ashling and Aidan and said, "I apologize about trying to tell you how to set up your wedding. You have every reason to celebrate. I hope we'll be invited."*

*Aidan nodded, impressed that his brother had gone so far as to apologize in front of everyone. Ashling was about to say something when Margaret said, "I'm with Ian on this, Aidan...Ashling. We'd love to be part of your wedding. We want dad to have a great time, and he's always loved weddings and dancing."*

*Ashling smiled. "Thank you," she said. "It's good to have your support, and it is so very good that the three of you are talking again."*

*The busboy arrived and assiduously cleared and tidied the table. On his heels, the waiter returned, asking if anyone might be interested in coffee, dessert, or an after-dinner liqueur. Cornelius, of course, requested tea, as did Ashling and Margaret. Ian and Aidan chose coffee.*

*Ian was the first to speak as the waiter left. Looking at Ashling, he said, "I hope you can believe me when I say I wasn't trying to spoil your wedding. Aidan is my little brother and I've always felt responsible for him. I wanted him to do well. I wanted him to succeed. I saw myself as his pathfinder. I was in a position to tell him how to navigate high school, how to make the most out of college. Heck, I even think I gave him advice on dating and cars and how to pick good friends."*

*Ian shrugged. "I guess I let the 'big brother' role get out of hand. And I apologize. I never imagined that I'd been arrogant or that I have ever bullied Aidan to go in any particular direction. I knew that mom and dad valued good education and valued high standards. I thought I was just helping Aidan live up to their hopes."*

*Aidan smiled. "The way I saw it, you had decided that since you were the big brother, you had the right to keep pressure on me to become just like you. You did a damn good job of being arrogant and bossy."*

*Ashling laughed. "And you've probably learned over time, Ian, that Aidan has always insisted on being most assuredly himself."*

*"He's been himself, for sure," Ian said, with a chuckle.*

*Margaret looked at her youngest brother. "And I am sorry, too, Aidan," she said. "I allowed myself to become frustrated by, and perhaps jealous of, your easy-living way. It was simpler for me to simply keep you on the far fringes of my life because I thought you had let our family down. I apologize for my attitude."*

*Aidan nodded, smiling at his sister.*

*The waiter came with the coffee and the tea, in china cups. After being assured that none of them needed anything else, he left and headed for the kitchen.*

*Margaret was the first to speak after the waiter left. She sipped at her tea and said to Aidan, "So what's this about a letter that mom left you?"*

Late in the afternoon, Julie calls. Sean has been awake for perhaps an hour and is still groggy.

"I would have called earlier," she tells him, "but I had meetings all day, and I figured you'd be dead to the world until at least noon."

"Try three o'clock," he says, happy to hear her voice.

"Rip Van Winkle, huh?" Her laugh is soft and warm. "No work at the newspaper this morning?"

"I called my editor a half-hour ago. He was not especially happy," Sean says. "But he won't make an issue about it."

"So," Julie asks in her typically direct way, "have you decided to scuttle your story?"

"No," he says. "I actually wound up writing last night, after you guys left."

"You did?" she says, her voice excited. "You got over your hurdle?"

"I don't know – I haven't read it yet. I'm hoping."

"May I come over and read it with you?" Julie asks. I'll be leaving the office in about an hour. We could do dinner — or, in your case, a late day breakfast — at that nice restaurant on Post Road, just south of Quonset Point."

Sean doesn't hesitate. "I'd like that."

He hears Julie laugh. "You're supposed to say that you would *absolutely love* that."

Sean laughs as well. "Okay, I would truly and absolutely love that."

"I'll pick you up," she says.

Sean agrees. When they hang up, he checks to see if he has clean clothes to wear for dinner, then heads for the shower. When he's done, he revs up his computer and prints out the entire manuscript.

It makes no sense to let her read a single chapter. He has decided, somewhat nervously, to let Julie read the whole thing.

At five-thirty, Julie arrives at Sean's apartment. Two minutes later, they're heading for Sonoma Grille.

Julie says, "So what's that package you're carrying?"

"My manuscript," Sean tells her. "I want you to read it."

"All of it?"

"Well, all I've written so far. I've still got a really long way to go."

Julie is quiet for a moment. Finally she says, "How about if we get some pizza and go back to your place? I could read it while we eat."

"And I could sit there like a bump on a log?" Sean laughs. "I'd rather spend my time talking with you." He taps the oversized manila envelope on his lap. "You can take this home with you."

She grins at him. "You realize, don't you, that if I start reading it and end up loving it, and therefore stay up much of the night, I'll have to call in sick tomorrow."

"Such is life," he says.

The restaurant is not crowded. Most restaurants are lightly patronized on Mondays. Sean knows the owner well enough to engage him in a brief chitchat before he shows them to a nice corner table, away from the handful of other diners.

After they are seated, Sean tells Julie, "This is one of the locales in my story, but I call it the Porthole Grille."

The waitress appears, smiling "Hi, Sean. I haven't seen you here in a while."

"I'd eat here a lot more often, Laura. But you guys are damn expensive."

Laura laughs. "It's because the wait staff is totally upper crust."

Sean introduces Julie. "We've actually started dating," he tells Laura.

"You're kidding me – right?" She turns to Julie. "It's nice meeting you. Sean is a nice guy. You have good taste."

Sean points a thumb at Laura. "She is shameless, really. She'll do say or do anything for a nice five percent tip."

Laura and Julie share a look that puts Sean in his place very effectively.

Sean is sipping a Jameson on the rocks and Julie is savoring a chocolate strawberry martini. Laura has taken their food order, and now they are simply enjoying each other's company.

"I'm glad you got some good sleep, even if you slept until three. I wish I could have done the same."

"Thanks," Sean says. "But now my sleep/wake cycle is all messed up. I am so, so very wide awake right now."

A moment later, he says, "Look, I really need to apologize for the way I was last night. I've never been that messed up before."

Julie smiles at him and reaches across the table for his hand. "Life's like that sometimes. You don't have to apologize. We all have great days and awful days. I just hope that the three of us helped you out of your funk."

Sean nods. "You did, actually. The fact that I was able to write anything at all last night was really because of you and Jane and Ted. I really appreciate it that you came to check up on me."

"Whether you know it or not, you are rapidly becoming my best friend, Sean O'Connor. How could I not make sure you were all right?"

Sean sipped from his Jameson and grinned at her. "Best friend, huh?" Pause. "I like that."

"That makes two of us," she says. "And I hope this means we can begin seeing each other more often."

"I'd enjoy that."

"We already have a date for tomorrow night," Julie says. "You probably don't remember; you were in kind of a fog last night."

Sean tries to remember and shakes his head. "I can't remember. Sorry."

"I offered to cook for you, and you accepted my invitation. Are we still on?"

"Of course," Sean tells her with much enthusiasm.

Julie's smile grows. "So what kinds of food do you absolutely love? I'm pretty good in the kitchen. So your wish will be my command."

Sean shrugs. "I'm pretty much omnivorous, although I don't especially care for foods that are spicy enough to cause internal injuries."

"Because of the bleeding ulcer you had?"

"No. Just because I haven't met a super hot pepper or hot sauce that I've ever liked."

"Then I will stay away from gustatory nuclear weapons and will prepare you a meal you can really enjoy."

"Sounds good enough for me," Sean says, the needling worry arising again in the back of his mind if Julie's plans for the home-cooked dinner also includes moving their budding relationship to a higher level.

When Laura returns with their meals, his concern fades — for now.

Over coffee, after the table had been cleared, Julie asks Sean about the book.

"Ted and Jane haven't told me anything about it, although Ted has said he loves what you're doing with it. Can you give me a quick synopsis before I read it?"

Sean thinks for a moment. "No," he says.

Julie gives him a look. "No?"

"I'd like it if you read it with an open mind. If I tell you what it's about, you'll be biased to the way I see the book… and I'm not sure what's on paper is really what I'm trying to accomplish. So you understand?

"You want me to read it so I can tell you what I see in it?"

"More or less." Sean sips coffee. "I guess I just need to know if it makes sense, if the story line is good, if the characters are real enough so you can touch them – and if I have screwed up in any way at all."

"What do Ted and Jane tell you?"

"Ted always says he likes it, although now and then he'll point out something that I need to fix. I'm honestly not sure how much Jane has read, although I told her and Allyson that I'd be happy if they read it."

Julie gazes at Sean. "I promise you that I'll be totally honest about your story."

"But not brutally so, I hope," Sean says with a crooked smile.

"I'm not taking 'brutally' off the table," Julie laughs. "If you really want me to be a critic, then I will be an honest critic."

Sean gives her a thumbs-up. "Go for it," he tells her. "I need honesty."

After dinner, they drive to the center of Wickford and walk along the quiet streets and spend a while sitting on a bench by the harbor, relishing the solitude and the soft sounds of the water washing ever so gently against the town dock and the seawall behind it.

They sit in silence for a long time. Finally, Julie says, "I have a feeling that your mind is drifting somewhere else."

Her words pull Sean back into the moment. "I'm thinking about the story," he tells her.

"Are you always thinking about the story? I've never spoken with an author. I'm not sure how they go about developing their stories."

"I don't know either," Sean tells her. "I'm just trying to find my way."

After a moment, he says, "To answer your question, it's not that I'm thinking about the story all the time. It's more like the story is percolating in the back of my mind, and now and then it pops into my consciousness for a while."

"So does that mean your writer's block, or whatever it was, is disappearing?"

Sean nodded. "God, I hope so. That little episode I had — that was scary."

"Maybe you'll be able to write tonight."

After a pause, Sean says, "I'm starting to think that I just might be able to. Sometimes things about the story are so tenuous, especially now, and I don't want to lose the chance to keep it alive."

"Write, then," Julie says. "I can wait until tomorrow to talk with you again."

"Maybe you'll be able to read some of the manuscript by then." Sean looks at his watch.

"Itching to get home?" she asks, a wry smile on her lips. "Want me to drive you?"

"I'd love it. But since I live maybe two minutes from here, I'll probably be in my apartment before you get back on Post Road."

She laughs, then get up from the bench. Sean takes her hand and walks with her to her car.

"This has been a very nice evening, Sean. Thank you."

"I thank you for making it enjoyable," he says. "I'm looking forward to dinner tomorrow night."

"Six-thirty," she tells him.

Sean nods as she beeps the locks on her car.

"One more thing," she says.

Sean is caught flat-footed as Julie wraps her arms around his neck and kisses him, a soft, gentle kiss that lasts a but a second or two.

"Life is good, Sean," she says after the kiss, keeping her arms around him. He puts his arms around her. It feels comfortable.

She gives him one last peck on the lips, and then lets go. Sean exhales loudly and smiles at her. "It sure is beginning to seem that way."

Glad to be home again, yet wishing that his evening with Julie had lasted far longer, Sean pours himself a small Jameson on the rocks and sits at his computer. After fifteen minutes of meditating on where the story might go from here — if he can yet salvage it — he begins typing. Without any hesitation, he writes for nearly two hours, his thoughts interrupted every now and then by the memory of Julie's unexpected kiss. His progress is slow, but he is content.

***She had faith***

*At the mention of the letter his mother had left for him, Aidan looked at Margaret and merely shrugged, not sure how to tell her about what their mother had written.*

*Cornelius, sensing Aidan's discomfort, stepped in.*

*"I found the letter in your mother's things after she died," he said to Margaret and Ian. "I have no idea when she wrote it, but it must have been before that Alzheimer's thing began taking her away from us. Had I to guess, I would think she might have written it a four or five years ago – certainly well after Ashling and Aidan had begun seeing each other. It was addressed to Aidan, so I gave it to him."*

*"That was the only letter she left?" Ian asked.*

*"I've found no other," Cornelius said.*

*"Did you read it, dad?" Margaret asked.*

*"Why would I do such a thing?" her father said, as if shocked that she should even consider doing that. "It was for Aidan, not for me. But Aidan told me at least some of what your mother wrote."*

*There was a silence at the table.*

*Then Ashling spoke. "Aidan let me read it after he'd done so. It was a lovely letter, and I think it did Aidan a world of good."*

*Again, silence settled over the five of them.*

*Ian cleared his throat and looked at his brother. "Would you mind sharing what she wrote?"*

*The question filled Aidan with unease. There had been little in the letter that said anything good about his siblings. And there was his mother's warning about striking him down should he discuss the letter with Ian and Margaret. Sitting across from them, Aidan was wishing in futility that the topic of the letter had not come up.*

*Even if he chose to tell them something of what the letter contained, he had utterly no idea where he should begin. And if he didn't share a thing about the letter, his brother and sister were not likely to leave him unscathed, and the tentative détente they were experiencing would vaporize before they left the restaurant.*

*For the sake of his father, he felt he had to let them in on some of what his mother had written. But what?*

*Ashling put a hand on his arm. "May I tell what I thought about the letter, my sweet?"*

*Aidan leaned back with relief. He trusted Ashling to put things in perspective.*

*He nodded.*

*Ashling spoke simply and straightforwardly.*

*"Your mother had strong feelings about Aidan," she said to Ian and Margaret. "As you two were, perhaps, and as your father certainly was, she was deeply worried about the course in life that Aidan had chosen."*

*Ian nodded sagely; Margaret looked at Aidan then folded her arms and sat back in her chair to hear more.*

*"The best way to summarize what she said is this: she had faith in Aidan to make a life for himself, although she knew somehow that it would take him longer to find himself than it had taken the two of you.*

*"She let him know what she saw as his strengths, his virtues, and his potential. And she wished him well in finding the kind of life and the kind of success he was meant to have.*

*"And," Ashling said, smiling, "she told him that he'd be a fool if he didn't marry me."*

*Aidan and Cornelius laughed. Ian and Margaret smiled but were clearly still focused on what else the letter may have contained.*

*Ian began to speak but Aidan raised his hand.*

*"The only time she mentioned you and Margaret in the letter was when she said that she had not written letters for each of you," he said, avoiding mentioning the critiques of Ian and Margaret that his mother had included.*

*"She didn't explain why she didn't write to either of you," Aidan added.*

*Ian and Margaret looked at each other, suddenly seeming hurt by having been ignored by their mother in that way.*

*"I'm sorry," Aidan said. "I wish she had written to you, too."*

*When they finally left the restaurant, Aidan aching from the price of the meal, they stood outside for a time, the traffic on Newbury Street moving casually past them.*

*Ian asked Aidan, "You're driving dad home?"*

*Aidan nodded. "It's more or less on the way for us."*

*Margaret approached and hugged her father, then – surprisingly –*

*hugged both Aidan and Ashling.*

*"Can we do this again sometime?" she said.*

*"We'd love to," Ashling told her.*

*Margaret looked pleased.*

*Ian offered his hand to Aidan and they shook. "Do you play golf?" Ian asked.*

*"A few times a year, usually," Aidan said, "but the last time was about two years ago."*

*"I'd like it if we could do a round of golf sometime. I think it would be good if we had a chance to do a lot more talking than we've done in the past."*

*Aidan agreed.*

*Ian continued, looking somewhat abashed. "I do have to apologize to you and Ashling about this wedding thing. But I think, more importantly, I also need to apologize for the way I've treated you over the years. I see how it's hurt dad, and I think that it's maybe why mom didn't write a letter to me or to Margaret. I hope you will accept my apology."*

*"And mine," Margaret said, in her typically brusque way. "Maybe it's not too late to mend fences."*

*"It's not," Ashling said. "It would be nice if we could start fresh, all of us."*

*Cornelius was grinning broadly, looking as pleased as he ever had.*

*"Sweet Jesus, Mary, and Joseph. My children are finally showing some common sense," he said, jubilation in his voice. "I hope you're looking down and seeing this, Ellen!"*

*As they part, Ian calls out to Aidan. "Let me know how the new job is going. You've got McCann blood; I think you're going to be all right."*

*Aidan smiled and said he would. As they left for the parking garage, he shook his head, not quite able to believe that his brother was talking to him in such an encouraging way.*

*Or that his sister had actually opened up to him and Ashling.*

*It was as if the whole world had gone upside-down.*

Sean's messed-up sleep cycle kept him awake until nearly two in the morning after his evening with Julie. When he finally fell asleep, he slept dreamlessly until his alarm roused him at seven.

He'd work today at the Wickford newspaper. Tomorrow would be his first day being the Fall River Journal's new feature writer.

When his editor had first told him about the opportunity, Sean had felt uncomfortable about the arrangement. He'd always avoided working at larger newspapers, afraid his educational shortcomings would be found out and unsure whether he could deal with the pressures of producing articles at a daily. As it was, he had the luxury of spending even three or four days or more working on an article. Meeting his weekly deadlines was never an issue. Meeting daily deadlines, if that's what he was facing, was daunting.

But he would give it his best shot. The new owners of the Wickford paper were willing to offer him such an opportunity. He'd be a fool not taking it.

After showering, shaving, and making himself ready for the world, he fries an egg and microwaves some bacon, makes some toast and coffee, and spends fifteen minutes reading what he wrote last night. It needs work, he knows, but it's enough to encourage him. He might well be back on track, after all. The thought lifts his spirits.

When he arrives at the newsroom, Jeff Gallagher spends ten minutes with him, first giving him a half-serious lecture about calling in sick after having already failed to report to work, then giving him tips on what to expect at the Fall River paper tomorrow. Sean apologizes again for missing work, and once more thanks Gallagher for the help he has been giving him.

"You're a good man, Sean," Gallagher tells him. "You've got the talent and the ability. You're a really good writer. You'll do fine, as long as you have faith in yourself."

The day is busy and productive. Sean wraps up two articles he's been researching, gives some editorial tweaks to another he completed a few days ago, and begins some preparatory research on another article that Jeff Gallagher had assigned him for next week.

The split schedule between the two newspapers would mean that Sean, at least for a time, would have to work perhaps six days a week – three at Wickford, and three in Fall River.

For the extra hundred-and-a-half a week that Gallagher had mentioned, Sean was happy to take on the job; a seventy-eight-hundred pay bump would make life a good bit better.

Julie calls at three.

"I've decided tonight's dinner will be seafood – baked stuffed shrimp, to be precise. Suitable?"

"The way to a man's heart…huh?"

Her laugh makes Sean feel good.

"Be here at six-thirty at the latest. You will *love* this meal."

A half-hour later, Sean's phone rings again.

"Sean?"

"Speaking," Sean says. The voice sounds vaguely familiar, but he can't place it at the moment."

"Pete Ferrini, Fall River Journal. I just want to remind you to stop in at Human Resources before coming up to the newsroom tomorrow. They've got a few things for you to sign, and you'll be getting your ID badge as well.

"Thanks for calling, Pete. I'm looking forward to getting started," Sean tells the managing editor.

"You met our city editor, Vin O'Brien, right?"

"We had a nice chat after I met with you."

"He's anxious to have you onboard, finally. He's been hungry a long time for a good feature reporter."

"I'll be doing my best," Sean says.

As much as he is anticipating the new opportunity in Fall River, his mind is dealing with his anticipation of the coming evening with Julie. And as much as he is looking forward to sharing dinner with her, his mind is also dealing with the lingering apprehension that the evening might turn into more than he is ready for.

It's not that he hasn't thought about the possibility that he and she would end up in bed together at some point. She's beautiful, charming…and sexy in an excitingly different way.

He was thinking of her this morning as he got dressed for work. He knows enough about her that she likely would not blindside him with a sudden seduction. On the other hand, she's shown she can surprise him. As he walked to work, he was trying to figure what he should say to her if the evening began to make him uncomfortable.

Damn -- he wishes now that he had more experience dealing with this sort of thing. The fact is that he had settled placidly and uncomplainingly into a solitary life after his divorce, never considering that some woman somewhere would be interested in more than a friendship with him. He was just an average guy, and he figured that didn't count for much.

Now, it seems, a woman is interested in more – if Julie's hints and comments over the past couple of dates were meant to tip him off about where she wanted things to go.

Even then, he was not sure if the things she said were hints and comments having to do with moving the relationship to the next level. Subtleties often eluded him, and sometimes it made him feel dense.

His ex-wife had always told him that men were pretty much tone-deaf when it came to relationships with women.

"It's a chromosome thing," she'd tell him, derisively.

He has to force his mind to focus on his work for the last hour of his workday. He wants to make sure that everything is ready for him to hit the ground running when he comes back to the Wickford paper on Saturday. He makes a list of things he needs to do when he returns, checks with Gallagher about any possible upcoming features he might tackle, then does a final review of the articles for this week's paper. He hits "Send" and his day is done.

Ten minutes later, he's in the shower, refreshing himself for his visit to Julie and trying to decide what he'll wear. Probably khakis and a light sweater. Then he changes his mind. An Oxford shirt would be much better…easier to take off.

Immediately, he berates himself: he can't let the evening to move to the next level. That will have to wait. It's the right thing to do, he decides.

Julie's house is in East Greenwich, on a serene street just over a mile from downtown, a white colonial that she got as part of her divorce settlement. Husbands who cheat tend to lose a lot when the divorce process runs its course.

Sean had been there only twice. Once to drop Julie off after an after work cocktail party, when her ride left without her, and another time when he and she had gone to dinner together a long time ago.

Sean's memory called up the easy conversation on the front steps and the light goodnight kiss on the cheek. Until Julie's recent reentry into his life, it was the last time they had seen each other.

She had invited him in on that last visit, but Sean had demurred; it was late, he told her, and he had to be up especially early the next morning.

It was not exactly true; he was simply – and frankly – nervous. And cutting the evening short was his best option

Now, as he pulls into Julie's driveway once again after all this time, he is far less nervous. The setting sun is shooting rays through the trees – lush oaks and maples and cedars – that surrounded her house, making the place seem warmly inviting.

When Julie answers the door, she is wearing an a red and white apron that declares "It's My Kitchen – So Back Off, Sucka!"

"You found your way," she says, smiling. "You have a good memory. It's been a few years."

"One of my two or three good qualities," he says. He scans the apron. "So you're a fiercely territorial woman, huh?"

Julie laughs. Her laugh is hearty and infectious. "I'll share my kitchen with you. No worries."

She takes his hand and brings him in, closing the door behind her, then leads him into the kitchen. She points at the center island. "See what I got for you?"

Sean sees the bottle of Jameson, sitting next to a squat crystal glass and an ice bucket.

"Thank you very much," he says. "But how did you know that I'd want to celebrate tonight?"

"Celebrate?" Julie says.

Sean grins at her. "My doctor has officially cleared me. No more ban on alcohol."

"Congratulations," Julie says, giving him a hug. "Then pour yourself a drink while I tend to my kitchen duties. And if you pour me a glass of wine – the bottle is in the refrigerator – you win brownie points."

Sean grins. "You've got it. I'll be the bartender."

Julie turns back to the counter to finish some of her dinner menu details. By the time he's poured her wine and his Jameson, she is shedding her apron.

"We'll eat in forty-five minutes or so," she tells him as she accepts the glass of wine from him. "The shrimp doesn't take long, but I think both of us can use some relaxation before we have dinner. Let's do the chat-in-the-living-room bit."

She hangs her apron on the back of a chair, then raises her glass and leads the way.

For a while, the conversation between them hovers around photos on her side tables and on the mantel above her fieldstone fireplace. Photos of friends and family; she has no children.

When they finally sit, they sit together on the sofa, Sean at one end with his drink on a coaster on the coffee table, Julie leaning back on plush pillows in her corner, sipping her wine.

"So how was your day, dahling?" she asks, clearly playing with him.

Sean laughs. "My day, dahling, was perfectly predictable," he says, imitating her mock hoity-toity accent. "And yours?"

"Quite satisfying," she replies, her accent out-Britishing his. "My days always go well. I insist on it."

Again, she makes Sean laugh and he is grateful. It takes the edge of his anxiety.

"I'm starting the new job tomorrow," he tells her. "The one I was telling you about, in Fall River."

"I'm impressed. One journalist – two newspapers. I think you may be a rarity."

"I have no idea. But my editor thinks it's a good thing, so I'm going to give it a shot."

"I'm sure you'll do fine."

"I hope so," Sean says. "Working for a daily newspaper is far different from a weekly."

"More pressure?"

"More pressure. At least that's the way at my first job," he tells her. "There's no time to mess up. You need to do it right the first time."

He pauses, sips, and puts his glass down again.

"The good thing is that the new job will be limited to feature-writing," he continues. "The real pressure at a daily is writing news and beating the next deadline. I'll have deadlines for the features, but they won't be nearly as tough as the daily ones. I'll be working there Wednesdays through Fridays."

"And you'll be working in Wickford how many days?"

"Three," he tells Julie. "I can deal with a six-day week."

"You'll do fine," she tells him again. "I know."

"You do, huh?"

She takes a long sip of wine, and he sips from his Irish whiskey.

"Yes, I know," she gives him a direct look. "I've read a good part of your book. In fact, I was up until nearly two this morning. Based on that, I have no doubts whatsoever the you can succeed as a writer, no matter what the circumstances."

Sean looks at her. "You like it?" There is a perceptible tone of disbelief in his voice.

"Have faith in yourself, Sean," she tells him. "Your story is great. Of course, some spots need to be cleaned up, some parts of the story line need tidying. But you've got a really good story going. Stick with it…dahling."

"Thank you," Sean says. Then, "…dahling."

Julie smiles at him and reaches out with her glass. Sean raises his and clinks it against hers.

They talk beyond the whatever-number-of-minutes Julie had planned, and cover a satisfying range of topics from politics to groceries to movies to delightful – or strange – people they've met over the years.

By the time Julie notices the time, it's nearly eight.

"My tummy is telling me it's feeding time," she says. "Yours?"

"I'm very ready," he tells her.

"Let me get the oven started. It'll take only fifteen minutes for the shrimp. The rice pilaf and the steamed veggies will be ready in no time. Thank God for microwaves."

She stands and reaches out for Sean's hand. Grasping his hand firmly, she leads him back to the kitchen and tells him to sit on one of the stools at the center island.

"Can I help with anything?" he asks.

"Nope," she says, curtly. "I'm the boss of the kitchen and I have everything under control."

She turns on the oven, pulls a foil-covered baking dish out of the refrigerator, and then asks Sean to refresh their drinks.

As he pours, she sets a pot on the stove for the rice pilaf and gets a steamer bag of mixed vegetables from the freezer.

"I was going to make a salad tonight," she tells him as she arranges things next to the stove. But I have something better, if you don't mind helping me out."

"What's that?"

She comes to the center island and lifts her wine glass. "Fresh cherrystones," she says. "I know you love seafood."

"Wow," he says. "That's a nice treat.

"Are you good with a clam knife?"

"I am," he tells her.

"The clams are in the meat drawer in the refrigerator. If you do the honors of preparing them on the half-shell, I'll finish with the cooking chores here."

"My pleasure," he says.

She looks at him with a sly look on her face. "The way to a man's heart…" she says.

When you are enjoying good company and good food and good conversation, there is no room for worries. Sean, however, is enjoying all three and is still worried. After the cherrystones, more great conversation, and an absolutely great dinner, Sean is again sitting with Julie on the sofa. This time, though, Julie is sitting next to him, her hand on his arm, drinking after-dinner brandy, and they are talking in soft tones.

It is seductive and Sean can imagine sitting here with Julie evening after evening, exploring in conversation an almost inexhaustible range of topics. Sharing stories together, smiling together, laughing together, planning together, and enjoying each other.

Still, there is the specter that is clouding his enjoyment of the evening. He fully expects Julie to ask him to spend the night, and he has no idea how he will be able to decline without hurting her feelings.

They continue talking and laughing and sharing quiet moments until it's nearly eleven.

Eventually, Julie pulls away from him ever so slightly and looks into his eyes for a long time – long enough to make him blink more than a few times.

Finally she begins speaking, and Sean's worries increase.

"Some decisions are more difficult than others," she says.

Sean gives her a concerned look.

She shakes her head. "Don't worry. I'm not about to announce Armageddon."

Sean exhales exaggeratedly.

Her laugh calms him.

"This is the decision, Mr. Sean. "Over the past few days, I've considered asking you to stay with me tonight. But I don't think either of us is ready, at least not now. I believe that timing is important and I don't believe in forcing things to happen."

Julie looks at him, probing his eyes.

"I agree," he says.

"Good," she says, smiling. "I was afraid you'd be disappointed."

Sean reaches out for her hand. "I'm not. I'm just happy that we can spend time together." He's not about to tell her how deeply relieved he is.

Julie gives him an impish smile. "Then you won't mind if I pencil us in for a tryst sometime in the next week or two?"

Her laugh is hearty and unfettered and Sean is drawn into it.

"Penciled-in for sure, right?"

"Penciled-in. I promise. No ink."

She leans over and kisses him on the cheek. "You are a wonderful man, Sean."

Before he can answer, she leans closer and kisses him on the mouth, a lingering kiss that catches him off-guard. In a moment, though, he lets himself be absorbed into the moment. For the next hour or two – Sean loses track of the time – they remain curled up together on the sofa, embracing, kissing, talking in whispers.

When he returns home, later than he had hoped and facing early rising tomorrow morning, he is unable to unwind. There so much to think about, so much awakened emotion, so much relief and yet so much anticipation of what might yet develop between Julie and him.

He goes to bed, hoping that somehow he will find at least a passable amount of sleep. But time passes, and he can't get comfortable, and he finds himself no closer to sleep than he was when walked in the door of his apartment.

Irritated with himself, he gets out of bed, grumbling. He'll write a bit tonight, and maybe that will settle his mind enough to give him a night in peace.

He plods to his office and calls up the notes he typed before leaving for Julie's house. Then he calls up his manuscript, tries to force himself into his writing zone, and begins typing.

***Bed, sleepyhead?***

*Two days after their dinner on Newbury Street, Aidan returned home after his liquor store shift and walked into a hug from Ashling.*

*"You will never believe what has just happened," she told him. "I could barely believe it myself."*

*"Well...?" Aidan asked, enjoying the great gleam in her eyes.*

*"Your sister – yes, your very own sister – has actually offered to help us plan our wedding. She asked if we were considering having the wedding in Massachusetts because your dad has many friends there. I told her I would check with you. And she said it didn't matter where we held it; she would be most happy to help us out."*

*Aidan smiled. "Talk about a total one-eighty," he said to Ashling. "A week ago, we were practically family outcasts in her eyes and in Ian's eyes. This has to qualify as a miracle, or else I'm dreaming weird dreams."*

*"You are most certainly not dreaming, "Ashling said. "Anyway, luv, I told her we'd let her know about where we would like the wedding to be. And I told her I was very happy to accept her generous offer to help us plan our special day."*

*Ashling led Aidan to the kitchen table. "I made a beef stew, and I expect you are probably quite famished. Would you like a bowl?"*

*"Feed me," Aidan said, grinning.*

*Ashling went to the stove where the pot of stew was simmering gently. As she prepared a bowl, Aidan said, "You're a very remarkable woman, you know. You take care of me, you put up with me, you nudge me through life in your own subtle way, and you want to marry me."*

*Ashling turned away from the counter, the bowl of stew in her hands. "Would you care to thank me now for being such a wonderful human being?"*

*Aidan took a long look at her, and they cracked up together, laughing and unable to speak. When they had settled down, and the steaming bowl was safely on the table, Aidan pulled her toward him and had her sit in his lap. Then he wrapped his arms around her and kissed her deeply.*

*"God I love you, Ashling," he said, holding her close as if hoping they would merge into one, then and there.*

*After a long silence, Ashling pulled back and looked at the man she loved. "Sweet Aidan, I love you far too much for words. I can't wait for us to be husband and wife. And I promise you that I will make your life as happy as I possibly can."*

*Again, they kissed – a long and lingering kiss. And again, they snuggled in silence on Aidan's chair.*

*After a bit, Ashling whispered, "I could stay in your lap forever, but your stew – over which I slaved for a good two hours – is getting cold, and I am sure that my weight has already numbed your legs. Shall we make a date for more snuggling in bed this evening?"*

*Aidan nodded. "Sounds good to me, my sweet Irish colleen."*

*Ashling got up from Aidan's lap and pulled the salt and pepper shakers closer to him.*

*"Eat your stew," she said. "Would you like some bread with that? I bought a loaf of French bread on the way home from work."*

*"That would be great."*

*"And I have a blueberry pie for dessert."*

*At nine o'clock, Ashling phoned her parents. Aidan watched her face as she spoke, first to her mother, and a while later to her father. Ashling's smile always made her look ten years younger, and tonight her smile didn't wane a bit.*

*The conversation continued for over a half-hour, Ashling giving her parent, in turn, details about the decision to marry, the wedding hopes, Cornelius's reaction to the announcement – all such things clearly in response to questions they were asking. When the questions ran out, Ashling volunteered that relations between Aidan and his brother and sister had improved to a surprising degree, about Margaret's offer to assist in planning the wedding, and about Aidan's new job.*

*Moments later, she called Aidan to the phone.*

*"My dad would love to talk to you about your new job," she tells him. "He's in shipbuilding, if you recall, and he says he knows quite a bit about Electric Boat."*

*"Great," Aidan said. He got up from the kitchen table and took the phone from Ashling.*

*"Mr. McManus, how are you doing?"*

*"Quite well," Patrick McManus said, his voice jovial as usual. Aidan envied his thick brogue, and wished he himself had such a jovial personality. "And I imagine that now there's a wedding in the future, and*

*a new job, you are doing quite well also."*

*"I am," Aidan responded. "I find myself wishing that we had tied the knot a long time ago. Ashling is such a special woman."*

*"Certainly, I have to agree with you." Ashling's dad laughed. "I always expected you would discover that for yourself sooner or later."*

*"I've been very lucky to have her in my life."*

*"Yes, you have," Patrick said, laughing again. Then, "Bernadette and I would like to come up to Rhode Island to visit you and Ashling. Perhaps this weekend, if that would be acceptable to you."*

*"We have nothing planned," Aidan said. "Even if we did, we'd cancel the plans. It would be great to have you visit."*

*"Wonderful," Patrick said. Then he cupped his hand over the telephone mouthpiece. Aidan heard muffled conversation. When Patrick spoke again, he said, "We'll probably drive up on Friday. Bernadette is suggesting we stay at least four or five days – she wants to see more of Rhode Island, and we both would love to meet your family."*

*Suddenly, Aidan felt embarrassment running over his skin. "That's right," he said, feeling the words come out lamely," "I never introduced you to my family. I apologize for that."*

*"No need for apologies. Bernadette and I figure that sons and daughters are reflections of mothers and fathers. We are deeply sorry that you lost your mother, but we are excited about meeting your father, as well as your brother and sister."*

*"I'd like that very much."*

*"Well, then, we shall make the arrangements. As soon as we have the details, we shall call you and Ashling."*

*"Ashling and I wish you could stay with us, but we don't exactly have room for guests."*

*"It's no bother," Patrick said. "Bernadette likes making our travel arrangements. I'm certain she will find accommodations that will suit us quite well."*

*"I'm looking forward to your visit," Aidan said. "It's been a long time since we've spent any time together."*

*"Far too long," Patrick said. "We'll make up for lost time, all of us."*

*"Yes, we will."*

*"So, tell me all about your new job. I understand you'll be working for Electric Boat. From what I know, it's a superb company to work for. Welding, is it?"*

*It was well past ten when Aidan concluded his conversation with Ashling's parents – Bernadette McManus also wanted to spend some time speaking with her future son-in-law. When he finally hung up the phone, Ashling was dozing on the couch, her head tilted back, her breathing regular.*

*Aidan leaned over and kissed her softly on the mouth, instantly aware that it was something he had rarely done in all the time they'd been together. It was Ashling who had usually initiated their romantic times together.*

*Ashling stirred a bit then her eyes opened ever so slightly. "Mmmmm," she said.*

*"Shall we get to bed, sleepyhead?"*

*She gave him a lazy smile. "Did you and my dad have a good conversation?" she mumbled, without stirring from her spot.*

*"They're coming up this weekend. And, yes, we had a good talk."*

*"Good," she said. "They like you, you know."*

*Aidan smiled. "I'm surprised," he said.*

*"And why would that be?" she asked, her eyes opening wide as she moved to sit up straighter. "They have always thought quite highly of you."*

*"Right," Aidan said with an exaggerated nod. "Aidan McCann – liquor store clerk, ne'er-do-well, high-school educated, whiskey-drinking half-man. How could anyone think highly of that?"*

*"They have a certain acumen about people," Ashling said, calmly. "If they had not seen your potential to be a wonderful mate for their favorite daughter, they most certainly would have pressured me until I was forced away from you. Besides, I am sure they knew that if I was so in love with you, you must possess at least a few socially redeeming qualities."*

*She giggled as she watched his face.*

At seven-fifteen on Wednesday morning, Sean is already headed eastbound on I-195, in light early morning traffic, heading for Fall River. The managing editor told him to arrive at eight, but Sean wants to be early. It's his nature.

He still doesn't feel especially confident about the new job or — as he's begun thinking of it — the additional job. Weekly newspapers have always been comfortable for him; dailies are more worrisome. Despite his efforts to quash his self-doubt, he continues to fret that he might not be able to live up to whatever expectations Gallagher had given these people. He wishes he could stop worrying so much about so many things.

He arrives and parks in a small lot a block from the newspaper's building. He finishes the last cold sip from the hot coffee he'd bought at the donut shop in Wickford, takes a deep breath, and leaves the security of his car.

He wonders if life will ever be the same again.

The human resources office is on the first floor of the building. As Sean arrives, a young woman is unlocking the door.

"Hi," she says, giving him a brilliant smile.

"Hi," Sean says, trying to give an equally bright smile. "I'm Sean O'Connor. I'm supposed to..."

"I figured it was you. I'm Erin," she says, her smile still brilliant. "I've got your paperwork all ready for you. Mr. Costa will be in any minute – he's the boss. He wants to see you. But we can start with your paperwork now."

"Sounds good to me."

In the five minutes it takes to sign the various forms and paperwork that Erin put in front of him, two other women and one middle-aged man arrive for work. Sean is ready to stand and introduce himself to the man, but Erin shakes her head and watches as he leans back in his seat again. The man is not Mr. Costa. Sean has to wait another fifteen minutes. By then, he's checking his iPhone for messages and peeking at his email, and he's unaware of the Human Resource director's arrival until he hears a hearty voice say, "Sean?"

The man in front of him is perhaps five-foot-six, burly, with a luxuriant head of black hair, a bushy mustache, and a grin that unselfconsciously exposed his yellowing teeth. Sean guesses that the man is a smoker.

"Mr. Costa?" Sean says, standing quickly and extending his hand.

"Manny," the HR director says. "Call me Manny." His handshake is more than firm and Sean is glad it didn't last long.

Manny makes a gesture toward an office behind where the women and the other man are sitting. "Let's go into my office. We have some paperwork for you."

"Erin already gave me a few things to sign."

Manny looks toward Erin. The young woman gives him a thumbs-up. Manny nods.

"That young lady is always right on the ball," he tells Sean. As they near the door to the office, Manny gestures for Sean to enter first.

Once they are seated, Manny behind his desk and Sean in chair with chrome arms and legs, Manny says, "Since the paperwork is signed, I just want to fill you in on a few of our policies and procedures – in relation to HR, of course. Then, I'll have Erin bring you to the newsroom upstairs."

A few minutes before eight, Erin guides Sean to the lobby elevators.

"Everybody says Mr. O'Brien is a nice guy," she says about the managing editor, making small talk while awaiting the elevator. "Everybody says he's like an encyclopedia. Really! I mean, ask him a question about anything at all, and he'll give you the right answer. Everyone says he should go on *Jeopardy*." She laughs.

"Has he been here long?"

"Someone told me he's been here twenty-five years, or something like that."

The elevator arrives and they step in.

"He must be a good city editor," Sean says as the elevator doors slide shut.

"Everybody likes him," Erin says. "I've only talked to him a few times, but he really seems like a nice guy."

"Cool," Sean says.

When the elevator doors open, Erin points to the newsroom. "That's Mr. O'Brien, over there at the big desk. I've got to get back downstairs."

"Thanks, Erin," Sean tells her. "I appreciate your help."

"Good luck in the new job," she says, with another brilliant smile.

The newsroom is a sprawling space, compared to the cozy confines of the small quarters in Wickford. Sean counts at least fifteen desks with two thirds of them occupied by reporters. The large semi-circular city desk occupied by the editors and headline writers is at one end of the newsroom, just outside a door labeled as "Managing Editor." Seated in the center of the city desk, in seat that gives him equal access to the six men and one woman sitting around the semi-circle, is Sean's new boss – Vin O'Brien.

The pace in the newsroom, at this hour, seems slow – or at least slower than Sean expects a daily newsroom to be. He's barely through the door before O'Brien gets out of his chair and heads toward him.

"Sean," he says heartily, gripping Sean's hand with equal enthusiasm. "Welcome aboard. Come along and I'll show you where you'll be sitting."

As they cross the newsroom, Vin says. "I don't have much time to get you settled right now, but as soon as the we get by the first deadline, I'll introduce you to some of the folks you need to know."

"Fair enough," Sean says.

Vin stops at a desk next to a window that offers a view of part of the downtown area. On the desk are a reporter's notebook, a couple of pens and pencils, and a computer workstation. O'Brien picks up a sheet of paper that's sitting on the corner of the desk.

"Here's what you need to know to get logged on to the computer." He scans the paper. "Yup, they've given you a login name and password."

He passes the sheet to Sean then calls another reporter over. The man is maybe thirty, tall and lanky, with wire-rimmed glasses and a crooked smile.

"Fred Goddard, this is Sean O'Connor, our new feature guy," Vin says. "Can you take a few minutes to show him where we put each reporter's assignments, then take him to meet Jake?"

Fred reaches out to shake Sean's hand. "Not a problem," he says. "Welcome aboard."

"Thanks," Sean says.

Vin turns to Sean. "Jake Varga handles all our reference resources, mostly back issues and that sort of thing. Years ago we kept clippings of everything we printed, along with all the photographs we ever published. Now everything is on digital files, and Jake's responsibility is to make sure everything is included and that all the files are protected. You can access them all from your workstation. But I want you to get to know Jake because he's been around here for forty-two years, and he knows just everything that anyone needs to know about Fall River and its history."

With that, Vin shakes Sean's hand again and leaves him in Fred's capable hands.

Without wasting a second, Fred points to a corner across the newsroom, indicating a stack of open-ended cubes, about a dozen across and eight high.

"That's where you'll find your assignments usually," he tells Sean. "I'm sure your name is already on one of them. They really could just send them to you via your terminal, but Vin likes the old-fashioned touches so, for some material that would have to be scanned, the cubes remain." He chuckles.

At the cubes, Fred scans the nametags. "Here you are," he says, pulling a manila folder from the bottom cube in the fourth column. He taps the top edge of the cube. "That's yours," he says, handing the folder to Sean.

"Thanks," Sean says.

"Vin told me that there's enough in there for you to hit the ground running. I've got to get back to my desk. Let me know if you have any questions, or if I can help in anyway. We've got a good crew here, for the most part. You'll feel right at home in no time."

"Thanks again," Sean says. With another handshake, Fred heads off and Sean makes his way to his own desk.

When his cell phone rings at around noon, he knows it's Julie who's calling him. A quick glance at the screen confirms his guess.

"Should I call you Clark Kent – mild-mannered reporter for a big city newspaper?" she says. Sean can swear he can hear her giggling.

"Let's wait until we find out if I can carry this off," he tells her.

"I hope I'm not interrupting you. I just figured this might be your lunch break. How's it going so far?"

"Pretty good, actually. They've given me two assignments – one they need completed in about ten days; and it's going to take about ten days' research if I'm going to get it right. The other is supposed to be a three-part feature that will probably take me most of the month."

"Sounds challenging," Julie says. "Tell me about them at dinner tonight."

Sean is confused for a quick second. "Do we have a date planned?"

"Now we do," she says, in her impish tone of voice. "I want to treat you to dinner to celebrate this new milestone in your life."

"What if it's a millstone around my neck?"

"No way," Julie says, firmly. "You've got what it takes, Sean. And I have enough confidence for both of us."

Sean laughs. "That's reassuring."

"I've made reservations for us at the Pot au Feu restaurant in Providence, that nice French restaurant with the fabulous atmosphere. Six o'clock sharp. I'll meet you there."

"Great," Sean says after a pause. "It'll be nice to spend time together again."

Sean has spent most of the morning gathering information, lining up contacts, checking with other reporters and a couple of the editors about potential contacts for his features, and scoping out how the story might be structured. As soon as he wolfed down a grinder from the pizza shop next door, he spends the rest of his day with Jake Varga in the newspaper's archives, gleaning from the older man everything he might be able to offer in the way of background information that could help Sean find ways to flesh out the feature. The man, probably a tick of the clock away from retirement, seems to know more about everything in Fall River than can be held in a terabyte hard drive.

Sean wants to spend as much time as possible with him over the coming months.

At Jake's suggestion, Sean introduces himself to Dick Thibodeau, one of the paper's four photographers. "You're going to need good shots for your features," Jake tells Sean. "Dick can give you want you want. Besides, he probably knows more about our photo library than I do. I know the pictures that have been published; he knows all the additional photos that were taken."

Thibodeau and Sean, roughly the same age, hit it off immediately, and talk for about fifteen minutes. But Sean, pressed for time, schedules another meeting where he can talk more with the photographer.

There's less than an hour left to the day, and Sean spends it at his work station, making lists of some of the key things he's learned, and noting whatever details he's been able to scrape up so far, and creating list of questions to which he will need to find answers.

It's shortly after five when he leaves. Back at his car, he phones Julie.

"I can be at the Pot au Feu in about twenty minutes," he tells her. "Want to meet me there early? Maybe they can seat us ahead of the reservation."

Without hesitation, Julie says. "Last one there buys the first round of drinks."

She always has a way of making Sean laugh. "You're on," he says. "I'm starting my car now."

"Not fair!" she says. "I'm still in my office."

"Such a shame," he says, laughing, then clicking off his phone to end the call.

As he pulls out of the parking lot, Sean finds himself anxious to be with Julie again. Now, for the first time, he needs her company, her smile, her always-wonderful conversation. Yet, as he begins to drive away, he is suddenly immersed again in his story. By the time he is crossing the Braga Bridge and heading toward Providence, he is already composing in his mind what he will write tonight about Aidan and Ashling and the swirling of their lives. His mind keeps working at the story until he pulls into the parking garage a block away from the restaurant. He knows exactly where the next chapter will go.

***Fear not, Aidan***

*Five days after the McCann family dinner in Boston, three days after Margaret offered to help Ashling plan the wedding, two days after Aidan finally received the letter he had been anticipating from Electric Boat, and one day after Aidan received an unexpected phone call from Ian with an invitation to play golf tomorrow – which Aidan, with real regret, had to decline because of the imminent arrival of Ashling's parents — Aidan and Ashling were sitting together on the couch, sharing wine, and talking about what their wedding might be like.*

*"I am not inclined to draw out all the planning," Ashling was telling Aidan. "We know we want to be married and we know who we want to invite."*

*"We just have to decide when and where," Aidan said.*

*"I think we should marry in St. Mark's Church, in Dorchester, the one your parents attended for so many years. That way, your dad's friends can attend if they so choose. Our friends from here are young enough to be able to tolerate a drive."*

*"There's a veterans' hall a couple of blocks away. We could have the reception there."*

*"Will you be wanting to wear a tuxedo, Aidan?"*

*He smiled. "Not really. I'm not the tuxedo type. But I probably should buy a new suit."*

*Ashling nodded. "And I think elaborate wedding dresses and long trains are a waste of good money. Besides, there's no one who knows us who would even begin to assume that I have any shred of virginity left. So white is clearly out of the question."*

*Aidan agreed. "A decent suit for me, a very nice dress for you, and some gorgeous flowers for you to carry down the aisle. Life will be good."*

*"I think your dad is very happy that you've asked him to be your best man," Ashling said, reaching for Aidan's hand.*

*"Who do you have in mind for maid of honor?" Aidan asked.*

*Ashling pondered for a few moments as she sipped her wine.*

*"Perhaps we should keep it in the family," she said. "I should like to ask my mother."*

*"I bet she'd love to do it." Aidan looked at his watch. "Speaking of your mom and dad, they should be here within the hour if they haven't run into any traffic problems. You're dad said they'd be leaving no later than nine o'clock. It's a long drive — probably eight or nine hours at least."*

*"They might not arrive until seven or even eight o'clock tonight. He drives so slowly," Ashling said, laughing. "I remember driving with him on the highway, and he always insisted on traveling five miles per hour under the speed limit. I was terrified we'd be overrun by one of those great trucks. He said the lower speed was safer and driving in that way saved gasoline."*

*Aidan laughed. "Just like my dad," he told her. "But my dad sometimes actually stopped in the middle of the highway — really! — to point something out. Talk about terror!"*

*"So our pasts have much in common," Ashling said. They laughed, the memories for each of them almost as fresh as yesterday.*

*"Hey," Aidan said when the laughter eased into a comfortable silence, "your parents will probably be hungry when they get here. How about if we take them to Dugan's?"*

*"I spoke with my mother yesterday while you were at work. She promised they would call us as soon as they checked in at the motel," Ashling said. "I'll ask them then. But I'm certain they'll want to do so, whether they're hungry or not. They're anxious to spend time with their delightful daughter." Her not-very-subtle grin was priceless.*

*Aidan reached out and pulled her close.*

*"We're very lucky, you know," he said.*

*"I've known it for a long time" she said, grinning again. She put her hand on his chin and turned his head toward her and then planted a soft and warm kiss on his lips.*

*It was just after six-thirty when the telephone rang, and Ashling hurried from the couch to answer it.*

*"Dad!" she said after listening for a few seconds. "You've arrived safely! Have you checked in to your room yet?"*

*Ashling listened for a moment.*

*"Wonderful. Aidan and I figured that perhaps you and mom would be hungry. There's an ale house nearby, and we would love to treat you to a welcome-to-Rhode Island dinner."*

*Another pause.*

*"You would? That's wonderful. If you like, Aidan and I will pick you*

*up in fifteen minutes. Would that give you time to refresh yourselves?"*

*Again she listened.*

*"Fifteen minutes it is, then. There's no reason to dress especially for the restaurant. Everyone who goes there dresses quite casually."*

*After listening for another moment, Ashling said, "We can't wait to see you." Then she hung up the phone.*

*Turning to Aidan, she said, "It will take us only five minutes or so to the motel, so we'll wait a bit before leaving." She looked down at herself. "Do I look all right for our evening on the town?" She was wearing a lovely pair of jeans and a green scoop-neck top, both of which enhanced her nicely proportioned figure.*

*"Beautiful and tastefully dressed as always," he said, getting up from the couch.*

*"You know what they say about flattery," she said, moving toward him and capturing him in her arms.*

*"I sure hope they're right," Aidan said, looking at her with his best imitation of an undisguised leer.*

*As they were leaving the apartment to pick up Ashling's parents, Aidan said, "I'd rather not invite them back to the apartment after dinner. If they see how their treasured daughter is living, they might well want you to cancel the wedding."*

*Ashling looked at him. "My parents are not so superficial that they would take issue with where I live with the love of my life. If they would like to visit with us this evening, we'll gladly welcome them and not feel badly that we don't live in a mansion on the water."*

*Aidan, reluctantly, agreed with her — but it didn't make him feel any less uncomfortable.*

*Patrick and Bernadette McManus were waiting under the portico just outside the motel's office as Aidan and Ashling arrived in her car. Aidan had barely stopped the car when Ashling jumped out and ran to her parents, bestowing excited and hearty hugs upon each of them.*

*"It is so wonderful that you have come to visit," Ashling said as Aidan got out to greet his future in-laws.*

*As Aidan approached, Ashling's dad took the initiative and strode in Aidan's direction with a beaming smile and an outstretched hand. "It's wonderful to see you again, Aidan. Our visits with you have been far too rare."*

*Aidan was about to respond when Ashling's mother came over and gave him hug that took the words out of his mouth.*

*"You look wonderful, Aidan," she said, her face as smiling as any could be. "And I agree with Patrick – it's been far too long since we've seen the two of you."*

*"It's great that you could come up to see us," Aidan said. "But we should get you fed. If you're ready, let's get in the car and head off for some food."*

*Patrick clapped Aidan on the shoulder. "Sweeter words I have not often heard," he said.*

*In many ways, Dugan's Ale House was plain and simple, with no pretenses at all – except that of being an "authentic" Irish pub. But the place did have good food, and served some outstanding bangers and mash as well as an Irish mixed grille that always satisfied.*

*The four of them were given seats in a booth not far from the bar, with a view out the window, although the view consisted primarily of light traffic on Post Road.*

*Aidan had stopped by the day before to alert Michael, the owner, that he and Ashling would be hosting her very Irish parents. Could they get some additional attention at their table? It would be good for Ashling and him if her parents ended their meal with a very favorable opinion of the food and the service. Michael, who'd known Aidan for years, told him, "We'll make a great impression on them," he told Aidan. "I promise."*

*Though the place was busy, their waitress appeared at the table less than a minute after they were seated. As she slid menus in front of each of them, she asked, "Would you like to start with something to drink?"*

*Aidan spoke up, addressing Ashling's father. "I'd be honored if we could drink Jameson together. It's the only whiskey I'd ever drink."*

*Patrick smiled. "That would be lovely. I'd be delighted."*

*Aidan turned to Ashling's mother. "They have several good drinks here that I understand are very popular with women."*

*The waitress – who had introduced herself as Kelly – addressed Bernadette. "One of our drink specials tonight is a chocolate-strawberry martini. It's absolutely to die for. And we also have a pomegranate martini that's almost sinfully delicious. Of course, we have a nice selection of wines and beers as well."*

*Ashling reached across the table to take her mother's hand. "Should you choose a chocolate-strawberry martini, I'll be obligated to have one as well." It seemed to Aidan that these few minutes with her parents had already begun to enrich her Irish accent.*

*Her mother smiled, got a nod from Patrick, and Aidan ordered the drinks for everyone, then reminded the waitress that the tab for the dinner should come to him.*

*"And why should it be that you pay for the meal?" Patrick asked, as the waitress headed for the bar. "This should be a treat for the both of you. After all, it's your engagement and coming wedding that we're here to celebrate."*

*Ashling spoke up. "No, dad. We want to do it because the two of you have been so very supportive all during the time Aidan and I have been together. You are lovely and loving parents, and we want to show our appreciation."*

*With the talk turning to parents, Patrick looked at Aidan and said, "Bernadette and I are so sorry that you lost your mother, Aidan. We would have loved to meet her. The good qualities of our mothers show in ourselves. She must have been a saint of a woman."*

*"Thanks," Aidan said. "She was a good mother. I couldn't have asked for anyone better.*

*"We will be meeting your father while we are here?" Bernadette asked, as if to confirm what had already been part of the agenda for their visit.*

*Ashling responded, "He's expecting us Sunday afternoon. Aidan's dad is a most delightful man. I've always thought of him as a dear friend as well as the father of my late-blooming love." She gave Aidan a light poke in the ribs and laughed softly.*

*Aidan knew that Ashling had often talked with her parents about his once less-than-serious ways. Her attitude was that her parents needed to know, because they would find at least a bit of comfort in the fact that* she *knew all about his shortcomings. And because of their faith in her, they would trust that she knew what she was doing.*

*Bernadette reached across the table and patted Aidan's hand. "Fear not, Aidan. Ashling has always told us that you are a good man, and we've always had faith in our daughter. Besides, I for one decided the very first time I met you that you and Ashling were very likely made for each other."*

*"We're very truly happy for both of you," Patrick said. To Aidan, he added, "Ashling is a very remarkable young woman. We have been surely blessed to be her parents."*

*Ashling cocked a thumb in Aidan's direction. "He knows I am extraordinarily special and I know he counts his lucky stars every single day," she said, mostly to lift the mood from serious talk to topics lighter and more delightful.*

*It worked.*

*By the time the drinks came, the conversation at the table had become a comfortable banter, as if they'd been coming to dinner together for years. Patrick listened as Aidan described his new job at Electric Boat and his hopes for the future. And Bernadette listened as Ashling began giving her details about the kind of wedding she and Aidan wanted.*

*They paused only to decide what they wanted for dinner – Patrick picked baked stuffed shrimp, Bernadette chose baked haddock, while Ashling opted for chicken Marsala, and Aidan chose Irish mixed grille.*

*As they waited for the food, Ashling's parents talked about Patrick's upcoming retirement. Though he could have been retired by now, he'd chosen to stay at work another year and would be retiring shortly after his sixty-sixth birthday. "But I am hoping to pick up some consulting contracts" Patrick said. "It would be a shame to not put my skills to good use as long as I am alive." Ashling's mother explained to Ashling and Aidan why she would most likely keep working – she'd worked for the past sixteen years as a part-time real estate agent – after Patrick's retirement. And she talked brightly about satisfaction and accomplishment and added income. To Ashling, though, it seemed almost as if both of her parents were afraid of having to deal with all the spare time of retirement. It didn't surprise her; both had always had substantial difficulty sitting still.*

*When the conversation tipped away from Ashling's parents, Aidan began to talk in greater detail about his family, trying to put his brother and sister into as good a light as he could, and talking about his family's roots in the Northern Ireland, as well as their lives in his country. Ashling voiced her unadulterated praise for Aidan's family and stated that she and Aidan were delighted that Aidan's siblings had been pleased to hear about the wedding.*

*"You will surely love Aidan's dad," Ashling told her parents. "He's the perfect Irishman: outspoken, strong, faithful to his church, fair and loving with his children, and a hardworking man the likes of which is not easy to find anymore."*

*"He's retired now," Aidan said. "He and my mother got a later start than the two of you. I was born when my mother was nearly forty."*

*"Do you see him often?" Bernadette asked.*

*Ashling answered for Aidan. "We used to visit Aidan's parents nine or ten times a year, but we go there much more often now that Aidan's mother is gone. You will love that man, just as I do. He and I talk on the phone often, usually while Aidan is at work. But soon Aidan's crazy work hours will be a thing of the past, and he and I can talk together to his dad."*

*"I'm looking forward to meeting him," Patrick said. "I'm always happy to be able to talk with someone from Ireland. It's one of the pleasures I've missed since we came to this country. You're dad grew up in*

*Silverbridge, you say?"*

*"On Carnally Road," Aidan told him. "Born and raised in one of those classic two-room thatched-roof Irish cottages, as far as I know."*

*"My family lived near Newry, not that far away from Silverbridge," Bernadette said. "And Patrick's family lived at Ballymoyer. I had one cousin who grew up in Crossmaglen, nearby to where your father grew up. It's a lovely area there."*

*"I've never been," Aidan said. "I'd like to be able to go someday and take my dad with us. He's not getting any younger, and I feel like I owe him such a trip for all he's done for me – for us – lately."*

*"I assure you that you will have a fabulous time," Patrick said. "Do you have any relatives still there?"*

*"My dad talks about his sister, Minnie, and my mother's sister, Alice, who are still alive, and some nieces and nephews – my cousins – who live in that area. The rest of his brothers and sisters – as well as my mother's – are dead now. A couple of them came over here to visit with my parents years ago, when I was very young. I loved meeting them."*

*"Your dad must be excited about going back," Bernadette said.*

*"I haven't talked to him about it yet, really," Aidan answered. "I'm planning to tell him before the wedding. With my new job, we'll be able to afford the trip within the year."*

*Ashling put her hand on his arm. "We'll manage the trip far sooner than that," she told Aidan.*

*"And how's that?" he asked, giving her a look.*

*"Well," she said, stretching the word out significantly, "I've been thinking."*

*"Oh, dear," her father said, chuckling. "You must know by now, Aidan, that when this young woman thinks, there are always repercussions."*

*"I've learned," Aidan said, with a wry smile.*

*Ashling gave him a light slap on the arm. "Mind what you say about your beloved," she said, her smile impish as usual.*

*"So," Aidan said, "what have you been thinking about?"*

*"Hear me out," she said, talking more to her parents than to Aidan. "We have been talking about a honeymoon in Bermuda. For me, though – and, I am sure, for Aidan as well – a trip to Ireland would be a truly memorable honeymoon for the two of us."*

*She turned to Aidan. "You've always said that you'd do anything to be able to visit the land of your parents, and I've been wanting for a long time for us to be able to experience Ireland together."*

*She smiled brightly at him. "And we can take your father with us."*

*Aidan locked his gaze on her. "My father?"*

*Ashling laughed. "Look, luv, my parents know and your father knows that we have been living together for all these years. Our honeymoon does not have to be one of those traditional marriage initiation rites that are reserved for the very young. And it's not like your dad would be sharing a room with us. Besides, it would not cost us a great deal more than going to Bermuda, and I have some extra savings."*

*"Why, that sounds like a marvelous idea, Ashling," Bernadette said.*

*Patrick nodded and smiled at Aidan. "Think of how your father could enrich your trip to Ireland, all his memories, all his history, and all his contacts with his nieces and nephews."*

*Bernadette spoke: "You will have a great honeymoon while your father has a great homecoming. What could be better?"*

*Aidan shrugged, then smiled. "You know, that might work out pretty well."*

*"We could go for two weeks," Ashling said.*

*"I won't have that much vacation time at my job by then," Aidan told her. "I'm not sure I'll even have an entire week."*

*"Then we will talk with your new employer," she said. "I'm sure they are reasonable people."*

*"It doesn't work that way," Aidan said.*

*"It will," she said, her voice emphatic.*

*When the food came, the four of them had not come close to becoming talked out. Each topic that arose simply led to another, then another. Aidan was truly enjoying Ashling's parents. His unspoken worries about how they might react to him once they had an opportunity to spend such a great amount of time with him – well, those concerns disappeared as fast as the food on their plates.*

*And, once desert came – pie for Aidan, cake for Ashling's dad, the women refrained – the conversations continued for an hour more.*

Julie stirs in Sean's bed and makes a small sleepy, mewing sound as Sean begins to wake. For a while, he lays there, still half-submersed in sleep, loving the warmth of her body next to his.

Eventually, he opens his eyes and turns his head to check the clock on his bedside table. The sun is already brightening the room.

Six-thirty-nine, the clock tells him. He needs to be at the Fall River paper by eight. It's a forty-five minute ride – without traffic.

Jesus H. Christ…

He is about to slip out of the bed when Julie rolls over and snuggles herself tightly against him, her arm slung over his ribcage.

He remains still for maybe fifteen seconds, then begins sliding out from under her arm.

As soon as he moves, Julie stirs and moves yet closer. Then, in a croaky voice, she says, "I know you have to get to work. Can we do this another time soon?"

Sean aborts his exit and turns back enough so their faces are nearly touching nose-to-nose. "I'm not sure how *this* happened, but…wow," he says, his voice a whisper.

"Wow is right," Julie says, her voice still infused by sleep. "I think we seduced each other."

Sean kisses her forehead and lingers close, enjoying the scent of her skin and her hair.

"I absolve myself of all responsibility," he says in a voice that she can't mistake as anything but an attempt at keeping the pillow chat comfortably light.

"You took advantage of me," she says lazily, after a while, the wry humor yet showing through clearly. "I had two glasses of wine, and…"

"Three glasses," Sean corrects her. "And remember that after-dinner liqueur."

"I don't remember that," she says. By now, Julie is approaching full wakefulness and pulls Sean closer for a deeper kiss. "I think you planned this whole thing in minute detail."

"Whoa," Sean responds after the kiss reaches a crescendo and eases off like a thunderstorm pulling away rapidly. "You're the one who invited me to dinner and plied me with liquor. And I, being tired from the deep stress of my first day on the new job, was pitifully unable to resist your charms – or you're nefarious actions after you followed me home."

Julie looks at Sean and laughs. "I didn't follow you home," she tells him.

"Sure you did," Sean says.

"Okay," she says, tossing the challenge into his lap. "Then where's your car?"

Sean, at first, is confused by her question, and he's about to tell her that his car is downstairs, in the parking area for the apartments. He has no answer. His mind is still cobwebbed.

Julie taps a finger lightly on his chest. "You do realize that we left your car in the parking garage around the corner from the Pot au Feu? We drove home in my car."

"No," Sean says.

"Yes," she says. "Both of us agreed that I was less under the influence than you, ergo I drove. "So if you're going to be on time for work, we both need to get out of bed and get moving. If we hustle to Providence, you might actually get to Fall River on time."

"Christ!" Sean says, rolling out of bed, his stress showing.

Julie laughs. "Our first morning together is beginning to show some signs of a comic adventure."

Sean head off for the shower, apologizing for his haste. "I don't mean to shower first, but I'm already behind schedule. Make some coffee, if you want."

"Shower and shave and whatever," Julie tells him. "I'll clean up when I get home."

Sean calls a "thanks" over his shoulder as he disappears into the bathroom and closes the door.

Twenty minutes later, Sean exits the bathroom and pulls out some clothes appropriate for the newsroom. Julie is already dressed and is sitting at the kitchen table, a cup of coffee cradled in her hands. She has prepared another cup for Sean, and it sits there waiting for him.

"I'm sorry we have to rush so much," Sean tells her, downing as much coffee as the hot brew will allow him. Four swallows later, Sean says, "Let's go."

As Sean is backing the car out of his parking spot, he says, "You're right. My car's not here. I can't believe I forgot that you drove me home."

"Well," Julie says, "you had two Irish whiskeys, then two glasses of wine with dinner, and a liqueur afterwards."

"Sorry about that," Sean says. "I don't usually have that much when I'm…"

"No need to be sorry. Somehow, unlike most men, you are quite adorable when you're a bit under the influence." She laughs softly, then says, "I really like spending time with you, Sean. And I'm really happy we could spend the night together."

"Now *that* I remember very clearly." He turns to look at her. "We've taken a big step, huh?"

Julie muses for a moment. "A big step, yes. But the right step, as far as I'm concerned." She reaches out and touches his cheek. "We're very lucky, I think."

Within fifteen minutes of arriving in Fall River for work, Sean is fully immersed in the first feature article he's been assigned. Yesterday, he had planned out the research he'd have to do, had made two appointments to interview potential sources, and had gotten a lead on some background files that could be important.

The day would go by quickly and would help him to keep his mind occupied and away from the lovemaking he and Julie shared last night.

He did not regret for one instant that they'd wound up in bed together. And he already admitted to himself that he wanted this relationship to continue and to grow. He just needed to get accustomed to feeling wanted again, and to come to terms with the notion that his life could be very, very good once more. Yet it was not easy to simply accept such possibilities, not after so many years of doubting that he'd ever find such good fortune in someone so special.

Julie had already told him that she had a meeting to attend in the evening, and told Sean that she was disappointed that they could not see each other. Sean was disappointed, too, but Julie's schedule gave Sean an opening to get together with Ted. It had been far too long since Sean had shown Ted the new material in his story, and he needed his friend's input. True, Julie was reading his manuscript as well but, for now at least, it was in Ted that Sean's real trust rested.

As he drives home from work, Sean pulls out his cell phone and dials his friend.

"Hey, man," Ted answers. "Where have you been?"

"Busy," Sean says. "I started that new feature-writing job in Fall River, and the dating situation is showing potential."

"Really?" Ted says. "Jane's been talking with Julie, but she doesn't let on very much about what the two of them discuss. Woman-talk, you know."

"I'm not surprised," Sean says, chuckling. "Why I called is, I was wondering if you're tied up tonight? I'm on my way home from Fall River."

"Actually, no. Jane and Allyson went off to do some girly shopping, and I expect they'll stop somewhere for a cozy mother and daughter dinner."

"You've got time for me, then?" Sean says. "I want to give you the new stuff I've written since the last time we got together."

"Sounds good to me. Where?"

"You pick a place this time. We're always ending up at places that I suggest."

"There's that Italian place on Kingstown Road, south of the university. I haven't been there in a couple of years, but the food has always been good."

"Perfect," Sean says. He peeks at his dashboard clock. "Six-thirty? I need to stop by my place to pick up the manuscript."

"You got it, man," Ted says. "See you there."

Traffic congestion as he passed through Providence on his way home to pick up his manuscript put Sean ten minutes behind. He dislikes being late. When he reaches his apartment building, he jogs up the stairs, grabs the manuscript and heads downstairs two steps at a time.

Ted's car is already in the restaurant parking lot by the time Sean arrives. He takes a slot three places away. Out of habit, he checks his watch as he reaches the door: six-forty-three. He curses the traffic as he opens the door.

Ted is seated at a high-top across from the bar and spots Sean immediately.

As Sean sits, Ted reaches out to shake his hand. "It's great to see you, man." He looks at the manuscript. "Wow. That looks like double the number of pages since the last time I saw it."

"At least double," Sean says, placing the folder to one side of the table. "I've been able to put a fair amount of time into it over the last few weeks. The parts you read already are still pretty much the same – some editing changes here and there and some polishing in the places that really needed it."

"Now I'm going to have to spend four or five nights reading it," Ted says, his tone becoming one of a man facing drudgery.

"Bastard," Sean says, laughing.

Ted signals the waitress who's returning from another table.

"You drinking the same?" Ted asks Sean.

"Wine tonight. Jameson doesn't pair well with Italian."

The young woman approaches and pulls out her order book. "I'd like a coke," Ted tells her.

"A merlot for me," Sean says. "The house merlot is fine; I'm not even close to being a connoisseur."

"And can we have menus?" Ted asks.

"Of course," she says, her smile genuine but tired.

After she leaves, Ted questions Sean about his part-time job at the Fall River newspaper.

"The only thing really exciting about it is that I've been there two days and nobody's made a move to fire me," Sean says.

"No one's going to fire you," Ted says. "Cripes, man, you're talented."

"But daily newspapers are way different from weeklies. The pressure is there. Plus, I'm now working a six-day week. I'm hoping I can deal with it. I mean, they're paying me good money, and I still have my job in Wickford for as long as I want it."

"Two magic words for you," Ted says. "Optimism and Confidence. You've got those in your arsenal."

"Right now, they aren't especially strong. I'm already making some progress, though. Today, I connected with a couple of really good sources, and I managed to dig up a lot of reference material for the story they want me to do."

"Sounds like a good start to me."

"We'll see," Sean says in his typically cautious way.

By the time the waitress returns with their drinks and menus, Ted has already begun probing Sean about how things are going with Julie.

"Jane shares some things with me – about Julie, I mean — but not a lot," Ted was saying. "I know you guys are still seeing each other, and I know that you two went to Pot au Feu last night. So fill me in." Ted gives Sean a conspiratorial smile and Sean wishes he had ordered a Jameson instead of the wine.

"You already know about our date last night?" Sean says, hardly believing how fast Julie and Jane shared information.

Ted smiles again. "Just fill me in. I won't tell a soul."

Sean gives a sardonic laugh. "Sure," he says. "And there is no way at all that whatever I tell you won't get back to Julie – via Jane."

Ted grins. "You know I can't promise that. Besides, I'd only pass on information that would help you with Julie."

"I don't need any help," Sean says. "I'm a grownup; I'm pretty sure I can take care of things on my own."

Ted sips from his soda. "How long has it been since you had any kind of potentially serious relationship?"

Sean shakes his head. After a moment, he says, "Not since I got divorced."

"That's why you need my skilled guidance."

"Right," Sean says. "Your whole focus has always been on Jane. You're about as qualified to opine on relationships as I am to instruct you on successful song-writing techniques."

"I'm insightful," Ted grins.

"Bull. You just want to know everything that's going on with me and Julie."

"Is that an issue?" Ted asks, clearly tweaking his friend.

Sean has to laugh. "Jeez, you never give up."

"I give up," Ted says. "Jane and Julie never give up. Jane didn't have to say anything, but it was obvious that she — and probably Julie as well — wanted me to quiz you tonight until your head spins."

"Tell them I refused to submit to torture."

"Okay," Ted says. Then, "For my own benefit, though, how are things going with Julie?"

"You won't pass this on to Jane?"

"Not a chance."

Sean relaxes and sips from his wine. "Better than I would have thought a few weeks ago. I like her. A lot."

"I'm happy for you. You need someone in your life before you become a shriveled-up lonely old geezer."

"Thanks," Sean says.

"I'm guessing that you guys are at least committed to dating for the foreseeable future."

"It seems that way." Sean smiles. "There's something about her. I'm not sure how to describe it. It's as if she and I are naturally on the same wavelength."

"Go for it, man," Ted says. "She feels the same way about you. To tell you the truth, I know both of you and I think you guys are a damn good match."

The waitress returns, ready to take their order. Sean orders frutti di mare; Ted orders linguine with Bolognese sauce. Sean asks for another glass of wine.

The waitress twirls away from the table.

Ted taps the thick folder that Sean has brought him.

"I'll probably start reading it tomorrow," Ted tells him. "I've got that new gig right through Sunday, so I won't be able to finish it any time soon."

"Not a problem," Sean says. "I still can't figure how you do it. I mean, you play three or four nights a week and you still work first shift at Electric Boat. Don't you ever want to ease up on the gigs a bit? I'd be exhausted if I tried to do the same thing."

Ted looks a Sean, the looks down at the table. It takes him a long moment before he speaks.

"I'm going to ease up," Ted says. "One of the reasons I'm glad we got together tonight is that I wanted to tell you what's happening."

Sean gives Ted a quizzical look.

"I'm giving up my job."

"You're kidding me," Sean is astounded. Suddenly it dawns on him. "You're going into your music full time?"

Ted nods. "Pretty much. It's something I've been wanting to do for a long time."

"I'm really happy for you," Sean says.

Ted hesitates.

"But I'm not going to do it here," he tells Sean.

Sean is flabbergasted by Ted's announcement.

"What do you mean?"

"We're moving to Charleston, South Carolina – Jane, Allyson, and me. There's a great music scene down there, and I think that's the kind of environment that can help me a lot."

"Jesus," is all Sean can say.

"Besides, I've got a deal on a possible album."

"An album? That's fantastic." Sean tries to convey an excitement for his friend that he is not especially feeling at the moment. They've been getting together two or three times a month for years. "You deserve that kind of break."

Ted nods and Sean falls silent. Then, "So when are you moving?" Sean asks.

"I gave my notice yesterday. I'm heading down in two weeks to find a place for us to live. We'll probably move as soon as I find something."

"Oh."

When the waitress brings their food, Sean is no longer hungry. He orders a Jameson on the rocks and tries to digest what Ted has sprung on him.

***Five Jamesons coming up***

*On Saturday afternoon, Aidan and Ashling picked up her parents at the motel. Aidan had already spoken to his dad and told him to expect them about four-thirty, assuming traffic on the Southeast Expressway was relatively sedate.*

*On the ride to Boston, Aidan drove while Ashling caught up on family affairs with her mother and father. The aunts and uncles in Ireland were all doing fairly well, given their ages and the economy and the weather and other such things. Uncle Peter, her mother's brother, had broken a leg trying to perform a repair on the roof of his house, but he was mending properly. Aunt Minnie, her father's sister, was apparently beginning to become a bit senile but still managed in her small cottage. One of the cousins had begun a high-level job on the Continent – in Amsterdam, in fact – working for a large import-export company.*

*For her turn, Ashling filled in the details about the life she and Aidan shared together, about her job which she found especially fulfilling, about how much she enjoyed life in Rhode Island, and about the hopes she and Aidan had for the future.*

*Bernadette knew better that to ask if children were part of the plan. It had nothing to do with whatever limit there might be to Ashling's childbearing years; it was more a matter of feeling it would be unfair to put such pressure on them.*

*When they arrived and parked in front of Cornelius's apartment, Ashling said, "He's a very sharp man, Aidan's dad. I believe we are about to experience a fabulous evening of conversation."*

*Aidan added, "I made a reservation at Murtaugh's, a restaurant that my dad loves." After they got out of the car, Aidan added, "I've got to warn you. This could very likely be a long evening. Dad loves to talk."*

*"And so do we," Patrick said.*

*Cornelius had outdone himself in preparing his apartment – and himself – for visitors. The living room and the kitchen were spotless, and he was wearing good slacks and a white shirt with a necktie. Normally, Aidan's dad dressed that well only for church and weddings and funerals.*

*"Snazzy, dad," Aidan said.*

*"Stop it," his dad said, only half jesting. To Ashling and her parents, he said. "Please come in." He backed away and opened the door wide.*

*"Dad," Aidan said, "I'd like you to meet Patrick and Bernadette McManus, Ashling's mother and father."*

*The handshaking was vigorous and the smiles were universal. Ashling stepped through the door and gave Cornelius a hug.*

*"You're looking very well," Ashling told him.*

*"I'll never look as lovely as you," Cornelius said.*

*He closed the door behind them and indicated they could take any seats they chose in his living room. Patrick and Bernadette chose to sit side-by-side on the couch. Aidan picked a rocker in one corner, Ashling an armchair in the other.*

*Cornelius was about to sit in the well-used brown recliner Ellen had bought for him at least twenty years ago, when he caught himself.*

*"Would you like to have a drink before we go to dinner? We have plenty of time. I have Jameson and I have beer." He thought for a moment. "I might even have some wine left over from the funeral."*

*Aidan nodded. "We've got nearly two hours before our reservation. I'm going to have a Jameson, as will my dad, I'm sure. Would you like one, Patrick?"*

*"I will, indeed."*

*And my mum and I will perhaps have some wine," Ashling said.*

*"Nonsense," her mother said instantly. "I'll have a Jameson as well."*

*Ashling tilted her head at her mother. She'd had no idea that her mother ever drank whiskey of any kind.*

*As if reading her mind, her father said, "Your mother and I will have a Jameson together now and then."*

*Ashling shrugged. "Well, if that's the case, then I might as well have one, too."*

*Cornelius clapped his hands. "Five Jamesons coming up."*

*As he left for the kitchen, Aidan jumped up. "I'll help you, dad."*

*The conversations over the Irish whiskey bounced from one topic to another, and between one family and the other. Patrick and Bernadette answered Cornelius's questions about their lives in Ireland before they came to America. And Cornelius told Ashling's parents about his and Ellen's experiences after leaving Ireland. At one point, Cornelius went to the dining room sideboard and brought out a box of photographs of Ellen and of the children when they were younger. There weren't many;*

*photographs were a luxury during many of Aidan's growing-up years.*

*Murtaugh's had saved for them a table for five in a quiet corner, away from the normal cacophony that surrounded the bar, which occupied the heart of the place.*

*The conversation started in Cornelius's apartment had continued during the drive over, and continued still when they were seated at their table. The topics had ranged from talk of Ireland to talk of life in America, from talk of family to talk of the state of politics in Ireland and in America, and from talk of perhaps being able to spend more time together in the future (meaning Cornelius and Ashling's parents) to talk about the upcoming wedding.*

*"I know Aidan has talked about having the wedding fairly soon," Cornelius was saying over the round of drinks Aidan had ordered. "I suppose it doesn't matter if it's next month or next year."*

*Bernadette looked at Ashling. "You and Aidan are planning a July wedding, are you not?"*

*Ashling nodded. "We wanted to marry sooner, but the Church has rules about that. These days, they are wanting to make sure that the couple has every chance for a successful and blessed marriage. So we have to wait and go through the counseling and all else they require."*

*"July," Patrick said. "That's yet some time away. You shouldn't have any problem arranging for a reception hall and the other niceties.""*

*Aidan spread his arms wide. "I called Danny Murtaugh a week ago. He said we can have the reception here in the pub."*

*Bernadette looked around. There were plenty of tables, an area that could be used as a dance floor, and a bar. "This looks perfectly suitable," she said. "Quite appropriate, actually."*

*"And we've talked with the pastor at St. Mark's, not far from here," Ashling said. "That's where Aidan went to church as a boy, and where Cornelius and Ellen have always gone. He agreed to let us have the wedding there, even though we are not parishioners, because of Mr. and Mrs. McCann. It has been their church for so long."*

*She turned to Aidan, her grin lopsided, "But we didn't tell him that we've been living together for all this time. He might have objected."*

*Cornelius rolled his eyes. Bernadette took a deep breath. Patrick thought for a moment then said, "It seems to me that if you are serious about being married in the eyes of God, your love for each other and your sincerity are the only things that matter."*

*He looked at Ashling. "We're very happy that you and Aidan are to be married in the Church."*

*"We would have it no other way, dad," Ashling told him.*

It's been two days since his meeting with Ted — and the impact of Ted's bombshell — and Sean has found himself without the ability to concentrate on what he needs to write.

This thing — this friggin' moving-to-Charleston issue with Ted! — has handed Sean a complete loss of focus. Hell, he can't even remember where he'd wanted the story to go from where he left off.

He sits for a long empty time in front of his computer, sipping at a cold beer, then paces his apartment, and finally settles down enough to read the last thirty pages he's written. But he finds nothing there to unlock him. He is feeling discouraged.

The phone rings. Sean's first inclination is to ignore it and he slouches on his sofa until the ringing stops. Seconds later, his cell phone rings. This time he decides to at least check on who's calling.

It's Julie.

Sean's not even sure he wants to be with Julie tonight. Solitude seems to be right for him this evening. But he can't leave her hanging, so he answers.

"Hey, Julie," Sean says, trying to put a smile in his voice. "How was your day?"

She begins to say, "It was pretty productive, actually." She hesitates, then asks, "Are you all right, Sean? You don't sound like yourself."

"I'm okay," he tells her, trying to hide what he is really feeling. "I've just got a lot to do, and I'm feeling pressure at work to get everything wrapped up. New job and all that."

A less sensitive woman might have let things pass. But Julie is not like that. Something else is going on, she senses, and she begins to feel badly that Sean is not letting her help.

Then it dawns on her.

"You've talked with Ted, haven't you?" she says, concern in her voice.

Sean's silence is protracted. Finally, he says, "So you know already?"

"I talked with Jane last night," Julie tells him. "I never expected them to leave Rhode Island. I'm guessing that's what's got you bummed out."

Sean exhales, relieved he can open up to her. "Bummed out is an understatement. Ted and I have been buddies for – God – fifteen years."

"It's been eleven years for Jane and me," Julie says.

"It's not easy to deal with."

"Let's deal with it together," Julie says.

Sean gives a sober laugh. "I figure I'll be bad company, the mood I'm in."

"Then we can be bad company together. How about if you drop your 'I've-gotta-work' excuse and we go to Sonoma Grille for a really good dinner and enough drinks to dull our pain?"

Sean doesn't hesitate. "What time?"

"I can be on my way in about two minutes," she tells him.

"Okay, I'll meet you there," Sean says, trying for more enthusiasm than he's feeling.

Sean is in the parking lot when Julie arrives. He leaves his car and walks over to meet her as she emerges from hers. She gives him a long, warm hug and kisses him. Holding each other eases his stress and he wishes the hug could last ten minutes longer.

When she slips out his arms, she says, "I need a martini. Thank God they make good ones here."

He reaches for her hand and they walk toward the entrance. "This could be a long evening," he says.

"I don't care how long," she tells him. "We've got a lot to deal with."

As they enter, Julie says, "Let's sit at the bar. The way I feel tonight, the bartender is going to earn his keep."

"Limits," Sean says. "We've both got to drive home after we finish here."

Julie looks at him, her grin sly. "How about if the one of us who is most sober drives the other one to his or her residence?"

Sean wraps an arm around her shoulder and guides her into the bar. "We'll see," he says. "It depends on whether either of us is able to drive."

"Then I'm okay with calling a cab."

Sean shakes his head. "I don't think it'll come to that," he tells her.

The bar is sparsely occupied; it's nearly seven. Most of the diners are nearing the end of their meals, and most of the bar patrons have finished their post-work drinks and have left for home. Sean finds a high-top in a quiet corner. The bar waitress arrives just as they've made themselves comfortable.

"Hi, folks. What can I get for you?" she asks.

Julie speaks up immediately. "A Blue Sapphire martini – very, very dry."

"A Jameson on the rocks for me," Sean says. "Make it a double, please."

"I'll have those for you in a minute," the waitress says. "Would you like menus?"

"Please," Julie answers. As soon as the waitress leaves, Julie adds, "I'd rather just sit here with you and drink until we're numb, but the food will help delay the numbness."

For a time, Sean and Julie sit in silence. Sean's eyes are on one of the television sets, but he's not seeing anything. Julie is staring off into nothing.

"I just can't believe they're moving away," Julie says at last, her voice laced with a mix of anger and disappointment.

Sean says nothing, because at the moment he can't voice his feelings. He has had friends all his life, although they have been few – by choice. Ted, however, has been his *only* best friend for the past many years. It has always been Ted to whom Sean turned when he felt uncertain about something, when he needed some perspective on an issue that was digging into him, when he simply needed a boost, or when he simply wanted enjoyable company. And Ted had always been there, without reservation. In many ways, Sean felt Ted had saved him from himself. Where Ted was confident and optimistic, Sean had always been less so, and had envied the certainty that Ted always seemed to exude.

A kick in the gut could never come close to how it felt to hear Ted announce he was moving away. To South Carolina, for Christ's sake.

The waitress brings their drinks, asking cheerfully if they might like an appetizer.

Julie gives her a serious look. "We'll order later. Right now, we need only the drinks," she says. "Bring another round in fifteen minutes."

"Yes, ma'am," the waitress says.

As she leaves, Julie says, "I fucking hate being called ma'am."

Sean hesitates for only a second. "So do I."

Julie looks at him. Slowly, as if her face were gently evolving, she begins to smile, then her smile changes into a chuckle, and finally she erupts in a full and hearty laugh.

As her laughter slowly fades, Sean stares at her. As she regains her composure, Sean says, "I figure we needed something to cheer us up a bit."

Julie lifts her martini. "Your timing is perfect, sweet Sean. We might mope all night long, but at least we had one good laugh."

"With luck, we'll have more," Sean says as they clink their glasses together. "Sooner or later."

They drink, swallow, then fall silent again.

Finally, Julie says, "What do you figure our chances are to convince them to stay here in Rhode Island?"

Julie is leaning on Sean as they wait for the taxi to pick them up. A two-minute discussion convinced them that it would be unwise for either of them to attempt to drive.

"This will be the second night I've spent at your place," Julie says, leaning in to plant a soft kiss on his cheek.

"You almost spent a night there when I had that crisis of confidence or whatever it was."

"Almost doesn't count."

The taxi pulls into the parking lot and stops in front of the entrance. Sean holds the door for Julie, then walks around to the other side to climb in. He gives his address to the driver. As the driver pulls out, Julie whispers to Sean, her words slightly slurred, "I wish we could make love tonight."

"Fat chance," Sean replies. "With luck, we'll still be conscious by the time I put the key in the door."

Julie gives a giggle, then snuggles closer to him. "Wake me when we're there."

***Feeling stupid***

*On Wednesday, after her parents concluded their visit to Rhode Island, an evening when Ashling had shut herself in the bathroom to relax with a long, warm, sudsy bath, Aidan's brother Ian telephoned.*

*Although Ian had called twice since the dinner in Boston with their dad, Aidan was still startled to hear his brother's voice when he picked up the phone.*

*"Oh, hey Ian," Aidan managed to say. "What's up?" He kept his voice neutral. Despite the seemingly warmer relationship between him and his brother and sister, Aidan was nonetheless wary. The long history of antagonism from his siblings had made him cautious. While he was hopeful – far less so than Ashling – he kept his reservations to himself.*

*"I'm just calling to see how you two are doing," Ian said, "and to see if you might be interested in a round of golf Saturday. From what I've been able to find out, the North Kingstown golf course near you is a pretty good place."*

*"I went there once or twice," Aidan said. ""But that was a long time ago. Most people I know think it's a great course."*

*"So the question remains," Ian said, his voice more than pleasant. "Golf on Saturday?"*

*"What time?"*

*"I could be down there by ten," Ian said. "Weather's supposed to be good. And I can reserve a tee time from here."*

*Aidan paused. "I think it's better if I reserve the tee time. We get preference over non-residents."*

*"So we're on?"*

*Again Aidan paused. His brother had never suggested that they do anything thing together. Aidan had always felt like an outrider as far as Ian's life was concerned. But Aidan sensed that refusing his brother's invitation would serve no purpose other than to destroy the détente that had developed over the past few weeks. In his mind, accepting his brother's invitation would ensure their father could enjoy the reunion of his children. And that, to Aidan, was all that mattered.*

*"Let me check with Ashling," Aidan said. "I don't think she'll mind. I've just got to dust off my clubs. I'll call you back in a while."*

*"Then it's good, right?"*

*Aidan found himself smiling. "Yeah, it's good."*

*Ashling, when Aidan told her of Ian's invitation, was thrilled. For her, the encouragingly positive interactions between Aidan and his sister and his brother – and their father – were good and boded well for the future.*

*"It's very simple, luv," she told Aidan, a towel wrapped snugly around her torso, her hair still wet from her bath. "Golfing with your brother is another step in the right direction for the two of you."*

*Aidan gave a weak laugh. "It's been damn near forever since I've spent that much time alone with him. I'm not sure I'll be able to take it."*

*Ashling moved close to him and wrapped him in her arms. "You'll find out only if you accept his invitation.*

*"I've already accepted – sort of," Aidan said, his face against her damp hair.*

*"Then you've done right." Ashling lifted her face toward his and kissed him, a quick kiss on his cheek.*

*"We should make love," she said, giving him the inviting look that she knew he could not possibly ignore. Then she slipped out of his arms, took his hand, and led him to the bedroom.*

*Aidan did not resist.*

*Aidan handed in his notice at the liquor store on Thursday morning when he arrived for his nine-to-five shift. His announcement left everyone unhappy – his bosses, his co-workers, and the few special customers he alerted about his imminent departure from what, in many ways, had become his second home.*

*The initial shock slowly turned into warm congratulations and heartfelt wishes that the new job would turn out exceptionally well for him. It took only minutes before Angie suggested that they all get together to set up a farewell party for Aidan. Of course, Angie loved parties and regarded them as an excuse to exceed the boundaries of civilized behavior – as long as his wife was not present.*

*Lou, who came out of his back office just as Angie was making his party suggestion gave a thumbs-up and put Angie in charge of making it happen. "You guys arrange for the food and I'll supply the beer and wine," Lou said.*

*"How about you supply everything, Lou?" Angie said, laughing. "It*

*would save me a hell of a lot of work."*

*Lou's response was no more than a look. Angie shut up.*

*Aidan spent the rest of his shift feeling guilty about abandoning his job there and leaving behind everyone associated with it. All of them had given him so many good years. Yet, as he reflected on things in the down time between customers, they might have been good years, but they were pretty much wasted years.*

*Suddenly, the cost of his years-long stubborn refusal to push himself to whatever he could become was bearing down on him.*

*Reflecting, he felt stupid.*

*Aidan's old golf clubs were in bad shape, or at least dust-covered and looking more like antiques than anything golfers would use here in the modern era. He took them out of the bag, one by one, and polished them as best he could for the morning's round of golf with Ian. In a side pocket he found a handful of tees and three golf balls, each of them scuffed with grass markings and one that had a cut in its surface. He decided he'd get to the golf course early enough so he could buy a few more balls and more tees. He didn't want his brother arriving to find him with meager equipment. Most things didn't embarrass Aidan, but this particular thing would – probably because he was hoping to win more respect from his brother. Would he best his brother with his golfing? Likely not. But he wanted simply to be able to hold his own. Besides, he had a gut feeling that Ian was more interested in talking than in golfing. Probably because of his lawyerly background, Ian's idea of conversation usually amounted to a series of probing questions. Seldom did he state his positions or his views. He was, Aidan thought, prosecutorial – or at least he had been in the past.*

*Still, although he was not especially anticipating a fun round of golf with his brother, Aidan was inclined to give Ian the benefit of the doubt in terms of how he and Aidan would interact on the course.*

*The North Kingstown Golf course, a few minutes north of Wickford, had once been a Navy golf course when Quonset Point – now an industrial park – was known as Naval Air Station Quonset Point, a place where aircraft carriers docked during the second world war and where aircraft were repaired and maintained, and where Navy pilots learned to fly. Quonset abutted Davisville where the Navy Seabees were headquartered and where the Quonset hut – ubiquitous during World War II – was designed.*

*After the Naval base closed, the golf course was turned over to the town and was turned into one of the state's finer courses. Aidan had never golfed there before, and felt more than a middling amount of anxiety about teeing off with his brother's eyes on him. He knew, from occasional reports from his parents, that Owen played golf often and had entered more than a handful of tournaments over the years. Nevertheless, Aidan resolved to be philosophical, no matter what happened. Ashling was right when she pointed out that playing golf with Ian would go a long way to strengthening the family ties that had frayed almost beyond repair over the past many years.*

*The parking lot at the clubhouse was nearly full when Aidan arrived. He found a spot for his old car in a far corner, slung his bag over his shoulder, and headed off to locate the pro shop.*

*Before coming, he'd asked to borrow forty dollars from Ashling, apologizing for having forgotten to get extra cash yesterday. "I've got enough for the greens fees, I think, I just don't want to have him pay for me in case he wants to have lunch or a drink or two afterwards."*

*Ashling gave Aidan four fresh-from-the-bank twenties. "You treat him," she said. "He needs to know that you are doing well."*

*Aidan hugged her in thanks, amazed as usual that she gave him all the support he needed, no matter what.*

*As he approached the pro shop, he searched around for Ian. He would have looked to find Ian's car in the parking lot, but he wasn't sure what kind of car his brother drove.*

*Seeing no sign of his brother, Aidan entered the shop. Three other golfers were there, dressed – Aidan guessed – the way golfers should be dressed. Immediately, he felt discomfort. In his jeans, boat shoes and deep blue t-shirt, he felt out of place. It took him only a few moments to decide that golfers who kowtowed slavishly to ridiculous golfing dress codes were not due much respect from him.*

*At the counter, he bought eight golf balls and a package of tees. Figuring he'd lose at least four balls along the way, he'd have a comfortable supply in reserve.*

*Tucking his purchases into the pouch of his canvas bag, he went out of the shop and found a bench. He'd wait there, trying to relax in the sun, until his brother arrived.*

Alcohol sometimes brings regrets, and Sean becomes aware of the regrets when he awakes just before three in the morning, stirred out of sleep by an uncomfortable pressure on his bladder.

As he rolls clumsily out of the bed, his head swirls and he has to grab onto the bedstead and wait for a few seconds until he feels he can safely make the walk from bed to bathroom. He feels shaky and knows that morning will not find him feeling well.

Julie is asleep, curled on her side, breathing in soft snores that he, for some reason, finds comforting.

Once he regains his equilibrium, he pads quietly to the bathroom where he avoids the risk of toppling over by sitting on the toilet to pee.

When he is done, fighting to stay awake and upright, he tiptoes back to the bedroom, slips quietly into the bed, and moves as close to Julie as he can without waking her.

Julie rouses just after six. Sean is flat on his back, his snoring jagged. She edges closer to him and kisses him gently on the cheek. In the softest of whispers, she says, "I love you Sean."

Seconds later, in the midst of beginning to rue how much they imbibed the night before, she is again in deep sleep.

It's nearly nine when Sean stirs again, his head not feeling well, his stomach feeling less well, and wishing he could sleep another dozen hours.

When he finally manages to open his eyes enough to glance at his alarm clock, he curses under his breath. Damn! He's supposed to be at the Wickford weekly wrapping up one of the features he's promised for next week's edition.

He moves swiftly to get out of bed, the dull ache in his head and the vague nausea in his belly not helping his cause. In the bathroom, he showers and shaves as quickly as he can, his actions clumsy – almost as if there is a great residue of alcohol yet in his bloodstream. When he's dressed, he moves back into the bedroom and kisses Julie awake. She looks at him with lazy eyes and stretches and murmurs something he doesn't understand.

"I'm sorry, Julie," he tells her. "I work on Saturdays, remember? Part of my deal for working on the Fall River paper too."

"Poor baby," she says, her voice croaking with sleep. "You must be exhausted."

"Hung over is more like it," he says. "I'll be all right."

Sean leans down and kisses her, and she wraps her arms around his neck and kisses him back.

"Look," he says, "you go back to sleep. Just lock the door when you leave, okay? I'll call you later."

"What time will you finish work?" she asks, her arms still keeping him close.

"I figure I can wrap everything up by two or three this afternoon."

"Good," she says, her sleepy smile tugging at Sean.

"Good?"

"I'll wait until you get out of work." She lets her arms slip away from him. "No reason why our entire Saturday should go to waste just because you have to work for a bit."

"I'd like it if you're here when I finish at the paper."

"You are so sweet," Julie says. "I'm pretty damn lucky. And I'll be here waiting for you."

Sean allows himself a laugh that won't make his head hurt more than it does already. "We're both lucky," he tells her.

He leans down, gives her another kiss, smooths out the blanket covering her and, wishing he could stay, leaves her to sleep some more.

Just as he is about to leave the apartment, Julie calls out.

"The cars!" she says. "We left them at the restaurant."

Sean stops abruptly and mentally slaps himself in the forehead. He turns back to the bedroom. Julie is already rolling out of bed.

"Jesus," Sean says. "I could have left you stranded here."

Julie laughs as she dresses. "Just because you can walk to work from here doesn't mean I want an early two-mile walk to get my car."

Sean gives her a look that approximates repentance, then calls for a cab. He'll have a late start to his day, but he figures he can wrap up his work at the paper by early afternoon – and he won't have to worry about getting his car after his day is finished.

There is nothing much to tell Julie about his abbreviated workday when he gets home just before two-thirty. She is sitting in his den, in the old recliner that is his comfort spot on the rare times he spends watching television. She's wearing jeans and a teal pullover.

As he closes the door behind him, she gets out of her chair to greet him. "I'm so glad you're back."

"I'm glad I'm back, too," he tells her. "You look elegant," he says.

"Maybe not elegant," she replies. "But I had to drive home after we picked up the cars. You probably would have tossed me out on the street if I were wearing the same clothes two days in a row. I picked an outfit for a casual afternoon and brought some extras in case we want to go out to someplace a bit more formal tonight."

With that, Julie moved into Sean's arms, and they stood together in his living room enjoying the closeness without any need to speak.

Finally, Sean asks her, "Is there anything special you'd like to do? Other than drinking, of course."

"I was thinking of a few things while you were gone. And there is one thing I think we *should* do."

"And that is...?"

"We should go see Jane and Ted," Julie says, adding quickly, "As upset as we are that they're moving away, I want them to know that we understand and that we support them."

"It's tough to give support when their moving away will have such a big impact on us."

"It's about what's better for them," Julie says. "It's about Ted maybe getting a good deal for his music and his talent. And that would be great for all of them, although I'm not sure how Allyson will react to having to leave her friends behind."

Sean couldn't argue with Julie's point. "We could always visit them in Charleston," he tells her after a pause. "And there's the phone and email."

"How many times do you usually see Ted in person?"

"Before I got him involved in reading my manuscript, we'd see each other maybe a couple of times a month."

"Other than that, you guys would talk on the phone, right?" Julie says. "It's the same with me and Jane. With them in Charleston, it will be more inconvenient, but not the end of the world."

Sean cannot disagree, but it doesn't make him feel any better.

While Sean goes to his bedroom to change out his work clothes, Julie telephones Jane.

Within seconds of arriving to visit Ted and his family, Julie and Jane are embracing tearfully just inside the front door, clinging together as if confirming their everlasting bond, Jane apologizing for the abrupt change in the course of their lives, and Julie reassuring her that everything was all right and that they needed to put more focus on Ted's promising career

To Sean, shaking hands somberly with Ted, it seems that the rest of this day cannot avoid being one of reminiscences, sadness, and mutual promises that the relationships they've so long enjoyed between each other would never wane.

As Ted and Jane lead them into the living room, Sean hopes that despite all that likely would be said today, his friends would not soon, inexorably, begin to fade out of his and Julie's life.

***An asshole for way too many years***

*Ian did not disappoint Aidan.*

*As Aidan expected, his brother arrived at the golf course dressed like a PGA Tour professional, his clothes impeccably chosen, his clubs gleaming in what looked like an impossibly expensive bag, his golf shoes protocol-perfect, his walk – a strut, really – intended to exude the kind of confidence Aidan could only hope to have on the course.*

*"Have you been waiting long?" Ian asked, tucking a scorecard into his pocket.*

*"Maybe ten minutes or so."*

*Ian looked up at the sky. "Couldn't ask for better weather for a round. I love this time of year."*

*"You got that right," Aidan replied. The exchange of small talk felt odd to Aidan. In his memory, his brother had always favored lectures over chitchat.*

*"How long since you golfed the last time?"*

*Aidan pondered for a moment. "Maybe two or three years, at least. There's a par-three course on the other side of town. A couple of friends of mine and I used to play there a few times a year."*

*Ian was looking out to the practice green and, beyond that, to the last hole on the back nine. "This looks like a nice course," he proclaimed. "Well maintained."*

*"It used to be a Navy course along time ago."*

*Ian pointed down the path to the right. "The guy in the pro shop says there's a driving range over there. I'm figuring you could use some practice – and I can use some warming up. Is that all right with you?"*

*Aidan coughed up a sharp laugh. "Practice is not going to improve my game at all, at this point. But, sure, let's hit a few. Maybe I can at least make sure I can still manage to connect with the ball."*

*Ian said, "Let's go, then." He pointed at the rows of golf carts. "Let's pick up our fairway limo. I rented one."*

*They were nearly through the bucket of balls they decide to share. Out of fifteen strokes, Aidan had manage to hit three balls straight out from the tee. He sliced most of the rest left or right and clipped the top of the ball twice in a row, sending it skittering over the grass for maybe thirty yards.*

*Ian swung like a professional, his shots putting the ball out near the extremes of the driving range, that majority sailing straight as an arrow. The two or three slices he hit were, to him, a reason to focus more intently on his next shot.*

*Aidan slipped his driver back into his bag. "Finish the bucket," he told his brother. "I don't want to exhaust myself before we hit the first tee."*

*Ian chuckled. "You'll survive. I only signed us up for nine holes." Then he tossed the remaining handful of balls down on the grass, selected a nine iron from his bag, and proceeded to chip each of them down the range. Perfectly, Aidan guessed.*

*The ride in the golf cart, from driving range to the first tee, took only a minute. Aidan and Ian rode in silence. Once or twice during that minute or so, Aidan opened his mouth to speak, but couldn't decide what to say to his brother. It dawned on him then that he really didn't know much at all about his brother or his brother's life, except for the crumbs of hearsay he'd picked up from his father and mother. He shook his head subtly and whispered to himself, "How friggin' sad."*

*The first tee was theirs for the taking. Aidan could see a foursome well ahead of them. Turning, he saw no one behind them, for the moment.*

*Ian pulled a driver from his bag, then drew a tee from one pouch and a ball from another.*

*"You want to tee off first?" Ian asked.*

*Aidan shook his head. "No. You go first. I'm still trying to wrap my mind around this."*

*"You're sure?"*

*"I'm sure. Go for it."*

*The way Ian sought out a sweet spot on the tee and the way he bent over to set up his ball and tee told Aidan with great certainty that his brother played golf at least a couple of times a week, weather permitting. Although, watching the great care his brother was taking before teeing off, Aidan could imagine Ian playing on rainy days as well. Ian came across as a very practiced golfer, and that made Aidan even more self-conscious about his own skills.*

*At last, Ian set his club behind the ball, head down, arms straight, back straight. Then, with a graceful arc, he brought his club back as smoothly and as far as it could reach, hesitated for only the briefest instant, then accelerated on the downswing until the club struck the ball perfectly, with that unique on-target sound, and sent it at an optimum angle down the middle of the fairway. Seconds later, the ball touched down, bounced aggressively several times, and finally rolled to a stop an impossible distance from the tee – or, at least, that's the way Aidan saw it.*

*Ian stood there in silence until the ball stopped its motion. He said nothing at first, but simply nodded to himself.*

*"Better than I expected," Ian said, turning to Aidan. Smiling, he added, "Your turn, Aidan."*

*Aidan took a driver from his bag, grabbed a ball and a tee, and proceeded to set up. The fairway looked disturbingly long, and too closely encroached upon by maples and oaks and evergreens.*

*He set the ball upon the tee then stepped back and took some practice swings. Frankly, he didn't give a damn what his brother thought of his golfing ability – or lack of it. If he was honest with himself, his only thought was of being able to say he had given this his best shot. His "screw-it" attitude had served him reasonably well over the years, and this was a good time to implement it once again.*

*He approached the tee, took a couple more practice swings, then lined-up his club with the ball. His focus was so intense that for a moment he forgot his brother was there, watching him.*

*Aidan muttered a prayer, raised his club, and swung it downward with great ferocity, surprising himself that the club made contact with the ball. Quickly, he raised his head, searching for the ball's trajectory.*

*"Jesus," Ian said.*

*Aidan finally spotted the ball, flying high and straight, as if chasing Ian's ball. Then it began curving ever so slightly to the right, but not so much as to put it in among the trees. Finally, still holding his breath, he saw the ball fall to earth, bounce, bounce again, and yet again, and finally roll to a stop perhaps thirty feet beyond his brother's ball.*

*"Jesus," Aidan said.*

*Aidan could have guessed at Ian's performance on the first hole. Ian made the green on his second shot, then sank a sixteen-foot putt to make par. For himself, Aidan managed to reach the green in two, but he needed three putts to put the ball into the cup.*

*By the fourth hole, Aidan was feeling less embarrassed than he'd anticipated; bogeys on both the second and third holes and, at the moment, looking at a possible par on the fourth — depending on his luck in making the six-foot putt to sink his ball.*

*"The green curves a bit to the left," Ian said as Aidan studied his prospects.*

*Aidan crouched, trying to see what his brother meant. Crouching and studying had never helped him much in the past; he had only a scant idea of what he should be looking for.*

*Aidan stood and positioned himself next to his ball. "I should maybe hit it in this direction?" he asked Ian, using his left hand to indicate what he meant. "But not too hard?"*

*"You've got the right idea," Ian said, sounding surprisingly patient, and perhaps even supportive. "Give it a shot. That's the only way to find out if it will work."*

*Aidan nodded then brought his putter to within inches of the ball, trying to make a correlation between the angle of the club and the direction he thought the ball should go.*

*"Go easy on the putt," Ian warned, his voice quiet.*

*Aidan set his feet, then reset them. He took a couple of practice swings close to the ball. In his mind, he was trying to imagine how the ball would travel once he hit it. And in his mind, it looked as perfect as it could ever be.*

*Slowly, he brought the putter back perhaps a foot. Doing his best to focus on the ball and on his swing, he said a silent prayer. For some reason, this particular putt was the most important one yet in this game between him and his brother. He blocked out everything: the sounds of nearby golfers, the sounds of the birds in the trees that lined the course, the feeling of the warm breeze on his skin — and the fact that his brother was standing no more than a dozen feet away.*

*He reassessed his position, his stance, his grip, and even his posture. Then, because he had to, he brought the club forward with measured speed, made contact with the ball, then held his breath as it began moving in the direction of the hole.*

*For the three seconds it took for the ball to move from the putter to the hole, Ian was silent and Aidan was desperately trying to will the ball into the cup. He stood immobilized in place as the ball began to lose speed, slowing too perceptibly as it moved toward the rim of the cup. Then, with a clunk that left Aidan breathless, the ball coasted over the edge of the cup and, in the slowest of motions, rolled in.*

*"Christ," Aidan said. "I was afraid it was going to just stop on the edge."*

*"Great shot," Ian said. "You made par."*

*Aidan laughed. "First time in a long time. Believe me."*

*Together, they moved to the next hole, the golf cart bouncing along the path, the sun getting warmer, a breeze kicking up off the Bay. The rides from hole to hole had been thus far been in silence, Ian likely planning how to attack the next hole, and Aidan simply trying to recall what he'd learned in the one-day of golf lessons he'd taken maybe fifteen years ago.*

*At the fifth hole, they had to wait. They had caught up with the foursome ahead of them, and the golfers were only now beginning to take their second shots. Ian pulled the cart into the shade under an oak tree and he and Aidan sat there, each sipping from bottles of water Ian had bought at the pro shop.*

*After a bit, Ian said, "I wonder why we've never done this before."*

*Aidan examined Ian's comment, then said, with a gleeful laugh, "Probably because you've been an asshole for way too many years."*

*Then there was silence. Ian said nothing, nor did he look at his brother. For long minutes, he simply stared ahead at the foursome as they moved further along on the course.*

*Finally, Ian chuckled, then said. "You may be right."*

*With that, he gestured toward the tee and said, "We're up." Ian got out of the cart, circled around to his bag and grabbed a driver and a tee. To Aidan, he said. "You go first. We both made par on the last hole, and I don't mind hitting last."*

*Aidan set a tee into the ground and balanced a ball on it. With an amateur's nonchalance, he set his stance, took stock of the fairway before him, and turned his attention to the ball.*

*Suddenly, Ian spoke. "I forgive you."*

*Aidan stepped away from the tee. "You forgive me?"*

*"Yeah," Ian said. "For not telling me a long time ago that you considered me an asshole. Although I wish you had chosen a more charitably chiding term."*

*Ian grinned, then laughed. "You're a good brother, Aidan. And you've been a good son to mom and dad. I thank you for that."*

*Aidan, smiling back, said, "You're welcome. Can I tee off now?*

*"Go for it," his brother said.*

*Aidan returned to his stance. He took careful practice swings inches from the ball. He checked the breeze, not that it would help anything, and he spread his feet just so. Moving the club right behind the ball, he brought the driver back, hesitating only a second at the top, then brought it down as swiftly and as smoothly as he could.*

*It took only milliseconds to realize that he'd badly hooked the ball and he watched as it curved sharply away, heading toward brush and trees.*

*Even before the ball disappeared, Aidan cursed. "Shit!" he said, almost spitting in frustration. "Goddam it!"*

They are sitting together now around the kitchen table, Ted and Jane occupying one corner, Sean and Julie the other.

The women's tears have nearly dried. Sean and Ted are facing each other but looking down at the table, neither inclined to break the ice. Jane is boiling water for tea for Julie and herself. Sean asked only for a glass of soda. Ted has a glass of ice water in front of him.

"We drank a bit too much last night," Julie tells Jane.

Jane says, "You both look like you've been through the mill — if you don't mind my saying."

Julie smiles, barely. "You can say it. It's the truth."

"Celebrating?" Jane asks.

Julie looks down. And Jane understands.

Another silence settles between them.

Julie pours the tea and the women each bring a steaming cup to the table, handling them carefully so as not to spill.

As Jane sits down, Julie speaks. "I've heard that Charleston is a beautiful city. And it really sounds like a good deal for both of you." There is no conviction in her voice.

A long silence drifts in the air between them.

Ted says, his voice soft, "I really need to give it one big push," he says. "My music, I mean."

He takes a swallow of ice water and shrugs. "Rhode Island — we love it here. Hell, I've always got a full house when I'm playing at Matunuck. But it's not the kind of music venue that's going to help us out. Charleston, though — that's something else."

Ted's voice turns apologetic. "I know this is going to disrupt everything. This is the only home Allyson has ever known. Julie and I have you guys in our lives, a stone's throw away if we ever want to get together. But I need to see if I can really make it with my music. I really do."

Sean says nothing. He just watches his friend, his expression neutral. Julie is the one who responds. "We're disappointed, to say the least. But we're really happy for you guys. We know you wouldn't be moving down there if there wasn't a chance for things to work out for Ted."

Jane's eyes begin again to well up. "We hate to leave here — and we sure as heck hate to leave you two behind. But you can always visit us…and we'll come back to visit you whenever we can."

"Is it okay if we visit five or six times a month?" Julie asks, her attempt at a laugh crimped by new tears.

Jane tries to laugh back and reaches across the table for Julie's hand. "We really hope you two will come visit us often," she says. And we'll do our best to come back often."

Silence again. Julie and Jane are looking down at their cups of tea; Ted is staring at the wall beyond Sean. Sean is wondering what to say next. He hasn't said much of anything yet, but knows he should be saying something.

Finally, tentatively, he speaks up, addressing Ted. "Wouldn't it be great if I get my book published and you put out an album while you're down there? Maybe we could exchange autographs."

Ted laughs, Sean smiles.

"Freebie autographs?" Ted asks. "Or do I have to pay you for yours."

"It depends on whose autograph is most in demand." Sean says, relieved to be talking about something less depressing.

Julie jumps in. "I think Sean will have a national audience, so I'm betting you're going to have to pay for his autograph. The only question is 'how much?'"

Sean says, "Ted's going to be the one with the national audience. I'm not sure my book will appeal to a wide range of people."

"I hope you're right," Ted says, his laugh genuine.

With that — thank God — the conversation takes off.

An hour later, the mood has become far more comfortable. Jane and Julie are talking about what Charleston has to offer and the kinds of things that Janc can get involved in. Ted and Sean have become entwined in a deep conversation about what it takes to write music or a novel.

Just before six, Sean checks his watch. "You're playing tonight, right?" he asks Ted.

"I start at nine. We've got lots of time to talk."

"I was thinking that I'd like to take all of us out to dinner. To celebrate. We could go to the Coast Guard house. If you take your car, you could leave from there for your gig, and we could take Jane home."

Jane says, "Why go out to eat? I can whip up something here. It would be easy and a lot less expensive."

Sean shakes his head. "No. You guys — and Julie — have done so much for me, I really owe it to you. Let me treat tonight."

Julie nods at Jane, as if to say, "he needs to do this."

Jane gives a nod to Ted.

Ted says, "Sounds great. We haven't been to the Coast Guard House in maybe three years.

Sean gives a thumbs-up. "I'm honored to be the one to give you a luxury dining experience."

Ted laughs. "So, doing two jobs is making you wealthy, huh?"

Sean rolls his eyes. "It means only that I can afford, just this once, to let you and Jane have absolutely anything you want. No limits."

"You're living dangerously, Sean," Jane says. "A long time ago, I offered to treat Ted to lunch at a nice steakhouse in Warwick. He ordered a gourmet hamburger and fries. Darn near ruined my credit rating by the time the meal was over. And not only that, but he had two sodas, for God's sake."

The unfettered laughter is welcome. Sean looks at Julie. She is relaxed now, enjoying her time with Jane. Sean himself is starting to feel comfortable that life will work out and they will sustain the ties that they've shared for such a long time.

The meal nears an end just after sundown. Through the large windows of the Coast Guard House, in the fading light, they watch gentle swells approaching the shore, growing higher as the water grows shallow, then curling into small walls of splashing froth and sea foam before washing over the rocks that line the shore in front of the concrete sea wall

Julie and Jane are engaged in quiet conversation, mostly reminiscing about the years of friendship they've shared in Rhode Island.

Ted and Sean have confined their conversation to Ted's music and aspirations, and to Sean's hope of completing and publishing his novel — and perhaps writing another one sometime soon. Neither of them has any certainty of succeeding — a fact each of them grasps midway through their conversation.

It's Sean who says, "What if things don't work out in Charleston?"

Ted shrugs. "Then I'll have to try something else," he says. "But there's no way I'm going to give up on my music. If things don't work out in Charleston, then I might try Austin, or Nashville, or New York City."

"You'll do fine," Sean tells him. "Your music is a damn sight better than a lot of stuff I hear these days."

"That's the way I feel about your book," Ted says. "From what I've seen, it's better than a lot of things I've read. Jane thinks so, too. I think you've got a winner."

"Winner?" Sean laughs. "I'm not sure what it is, but I can't let it go.

It's like I'm challenging myself to finish it," Sean says. "It's getting scary now, because I feel like I'm getting close to wrapping it up, but I'm still not clear about how it's going to end."

"For that matter," Ted says, "I'm not clear on how this move to Charleston will end."

Sean says, "If things don't work out down there, will you guys come back to Rhode Island?"

Ted laughs, "Only if you become rich and famous in the meantime. Once you hit the big time, you could promote my music. You know, tell the people who interview you that you always listened to my songs when you were writing."

Sean smiles at his friend. "Agreed," he says.

Outside the restaurant, Jane hugs Ted before he heads off for his evening gig, then Sean and Julie drive her home, making small talk. Afterwards, Sean and Julie head back to Wickford, each immersed thought. They're traveling slowly along Boston Neck Road. Occasionally, through breaks in the trees or between houses, they can see the bay and the lights of the bridges connecting to Jamestown and to Newport.

"I really love Jane and Ted," Julie says as they near Wickford. "We've been very lucky to have them around here for so long."

"No doubt," Sean says. "But it sucks big time that they're going to be leaving."

They say nothing more until they enter Wickford.

Sean's making the turn onto Brown Street when Julie asks, "Can we spend the night together again?"

***Returning to the tee***

*Aidan turned away and headed off the tee, shaking his head, his frustration obvious. He's never been a great golfer, but he's always been pretty competent teeing off. He's hooked the ball before — who the hell hasn't? — but today, in front of his brother, his crappy swing has upset him.*

*"Wait up," Ian called after him as Aidan headed for the golf cart.*

*Aidan stopped and turned.*

*"You can take a mulligan, you know," Ian told him, his voice earnest. "It's like that first shot never happened."*

*Aidan knew about mulligans, though he'd never presumed to take one before. If you're a mediocre golfer, he figured, mulligans do nothing to erase that fact. He'd always been determined to play through thick and thin. If the ball landed in the rough, he played it. If it landed out of bounds, he dropped a ball and played it from wherever. Even if it landed in the crotch of a tree twenty feet off the ground, he would play it aggressively, no matter what happened. For all his faults, Aidan counted all his shots and lived with the bad news — except for the two times that he'd made par when playing with friends.*

*"Come on, Aidan," Ian said. "It's a do-over, a gift — how often do you get second shot?"*

*Aidan looked at his brother, surprised by his Ian's encouraging tone. He nodded and almost smiled. He continued to the golf cart, grabbed another ball from his bag, and returned to the tee.*

*He was aware that Ian was watching him closely.*

*This time, he took more time to set up his shot, took two or three additional practice swings, set the club precisely behind the ball, kept his head down, focused until he could focus no more, drew his club back with great deliberation, then swung.*

All things being equal, Sean likes to think that he rarely sleeps beyond sunrise. It's not entirely true, though; winter or summer, he rarely sleeps beyond five-thirty in the morning — and sunrise varies greatly in its arrival in New England. It's been his way since he was a child. His father believed that sleeping away any small part of the morning was as close to a mortal sin that anyone could get. Thus, with rock-solid predictability, his father would wake him — even on Saturdays and Sundays — at the proverbial crack of dawn.

Despite Sean's childhood frustration with his dad's compulsion to shortchange his son's sleep, the childhood regimen ingrained itself in him. Even now, unless he has had too much to drink, he wakes predictably when most sane people are still sleeping soundly.

This morning, not surprisingly, despite the fact that he and Julie tapped into his bottle of vodka before heading off for sleep, Sean's eyes open when daylight begins intruding through the bedroom blinds. His first awareness is that of Julie's being snuggled against him, her arm over his chest, her face nestled against his shoulder, her breathing slow and relaxed.

For a long time, he lays there, fearful any motion might disrupt her. Soon, though, his need to pee exceeds his whatever concerns he has for Julie's sleep.

With slow, careful, subtle movements, he gradually slides out from under her arm and inches toward the edge of the bed. Finally, the covers slip off and her arm drops away from him. She stirs briefly, but then settles back into her rhythmic breathing pattern. Sean sits up on the edge of the bed then stands, again as quietly as he can.

When he returns, the pressure on his bladder blessedly relieved, he eases onto the bed and lies on his side, looking at Julie as she sleeps. Somehow, having her there comforts him and makes him realize how much he's truly missed having someone in his life.

Yet he's not sure he's ready to let her know what's really going on in his head.

He stares at Julie's face, happy that she has chosen to be with him, and wondering why he has suddenly become so lucky.

"I like watching you sleep," Sean tells Julie.

They are still snuggled together, an hour after Julie woke up, and maybe fifteen minutes after they finished making love. The sun in the east is slamming sunshine against the pulldown shades, filling the bedroom with a golden light that caresses everything.

She nuzzles his neck then kisses his cheek softly, her lips barely brushing his skin.

"I like making love with you," she replies. "No. Correct that. I *love* making love with you."

"I guess that makes two of us," Sean says.

"I might be wrong, but it seems to me that we've crossed some kind of threshold."

Sean looks up at the ceiling and laughs softly. "You think so, huh?"

"Yup."

A long moment elapses.

"So do I," he says, at last. "So where do we go from here?"

"I suggest we go out for breakfast," she replies, laughing playfully. "That little place south of town hall. My treat, of course."

Sean feels comfortable enough with her to respond, "Wow. I must have been really good last night."

"Goodness has nothing to do with it," Julie answers, trying for the last word.

"That's from an old Mae West movie, if memory serves me right. You're plagiarizing."

"Smarty pants," Julie says, reaching over to pinch his belly.

Sean drinks coffee, but usually not much of it. A cup when he gets breakfast in the morning and maybe another at work — that's generally enough. This morning, though, he's had two cups even before the waitress lays their breakfast platters on the table, and soon asks for a third.

"Going for a caffeine high?" Julie asks.

Sean shrugs. "I think I need the buzz to help deal with the Ted and Jane thing. It's too early to pour a nice, stiff Jameson."

Julie toys with the slice of ham on her plate. "We need to be supportive. That's what friends do."

Sean nods. "Oh, I'll be supportive. I'm just going to miss them one hell of a lot. I mean, Ted and I got together now and then every month. That leaves about twenty-seven or twenty-nine days that we didn't see each other. But it was all about having him and Jane and Allyson nearby. If we wanted to get together, it could happen any time at all. No travel plans needed."

"So now we'll need travel plans," Julie says, calmly. "I think we've grown up enough to handle travel arrangements any time we need to." She reaches across the table and places her hand on top of his. "As my mother often told me when I got into a snit: 'it's not the end of the world.'"

Sean toys with his food, then sips his coffee and leans back in the booth. Of course, Julie is right, and Sean knows he has no reason to begrudge Ted and Jane and Allyson the potential for new opportunities. But he can't help being upset, and he knows he'll likely be upset for quite some time. Ted and his family had become family to Sean. How else could he be expected to react to the news that they are going away?

Breakfast finished, Julie convinces Sean to hike the mile-long trail from Boston Neck Road to Rome Point where they can stroll along the bay and spend time with the soft slushing of waves on the wave-smoothed stones that cover the shore. They walk in silence for a long while. Then, impulsively, Sean turns to face Julie and wraps her in his arms.

"I'm glad you phoned me out of the blue that day."

"So am I. I did it on a whim, you know."

"You mean it wasn't something you plotted over a period of weeks"

She grins. "That's for me to know, Mr. O'Connor."

They continue walking, hand-in-hand, their chitchat settling comfortably into the mundane.

Eventually, Julie asks, "Are you in the mood for writing today?"

"Why?"

"You didn't get much chance yesterday," she tells him. "Or the day before that."

"My story can wait," he says. "I'm not sure I'm in the mood."

"You realize, of course, that I get involved in serious relationships only with men who are published authors."

"And you, of course, must realize that I've been published every single week for years."

"Newspaper articles don't count," she says. "Only novels count."

Sean finally says, "You've got things to do today? Is that why you're wondering if I'm planning to write?"

She looks up at him. "I'm sorry to say that I do," she says, true regret coloring her voice. "Things I needed to do yesterday — I need to do them today. And I've got other things to get ready before I go to work tomorrow. All play and no work is fabulous, but it doesn't wash in the real world."

Sean looks at her. "How about if we get together tomorrow after work?"

Julie smiles at him and nods, and they head back up the path to the car. Sean will write today.

***It's Ian, luv***

*In early March, just months after he and Ian played the one round of golf together — an outing that showed Aidan how woefully limited his golfing skills were and, surprisingly, revealed his brother to be someone who was not the pompous jerk Aidan had long ago deemed him to be — the telephone rang just as Aidan and Ashling were heading off to bed.*

*Aidan's first thought was that it might be Ian. He'd been calling Aidan once a week since the golf game, mostly to chat and reminisce about their childhoods and to pass along news about their cousins in Ireland and things happening in Boston.*

*Ashling was closest to the kitchen, so she turned and answered the phone. Aidan lingered by the bedroom door as she listened to the call.*

*"When did this happen?" she asked. The look in her face gave Aidan concern. His first thought was that something had happened to Ashling's father or mother.*

*"How did you find out?" she asked whoever was on the other end. She had not yet signaled Aidan to indicate who was calling.*

*Again, she listened. Her expression concern began growing more serious.*

*"Where is he?"*

*She listened for a moment, then she said, "Let me put Aidan on the phone."*

*Her words chilled him, and he reluctantly began walking toward her.*

*"It's Ian, luv. Your dad is in the hospital."*

*Aidan grabbed the phone, alarmed. "Ian, what's going on?"*

*"We're not sure yet," Ian said, keeping his voice even, although Aidan could detect the stress his brother was feeling. "Dad was outside clearing the snow off his car — we had about four inches of snow up here today. As he was heading up the steps to the front door of his building, he collapsed."*

*"Is he okay? Heart attack? What happened?" Aidan couldn't get the questions out fast enough. "Where is he?'*

*Ian tried to calm his brother. "Take a deep breath, Aidan. He's okay for now. He cut his head pretty badly when he fell. I talked with one of the doctors a half-hour ago. Dad's conscious but confused. They ran some tests, and it seems he had a heart attack, but the mental confusion is of concern. It could be because of the head injury. It could be that he threw a clot when he had the heart attack. They're trying to figure it out."*

*"Where is he?" Aidan asked again.*

*"Carney Hospital. Dorchester Avenue. You and I and Margaret were born there."*

*"I remember where it is," Aidan said. "I'm coming up tonight."*

*Ian said, "You might as well wait until morning. I'm not sure they will allow anyone to visit tonight."*

*"I'm coming up," Aidan said again.*

*"They probably won't let you see him."*

*"I'll find out when I get there," Aidan said, adamant.*

*"Fine," Ian said. "Do whatever you want."*

*"You're not going to the hospital by yourself," Ashling said as soon as Aidan got off the phone.*

*"I'll be okay," he told her. "You need to work in the morning."*

*"It has nothing to do about whether or not you will be fine, and it has nothing to do with whether I work or not," she said. "I'm worried deeply about your father, too. We can call in to our jobs in the morning."*

*She stood in front of Aidan then hugged him, a hug meant to reassure him and make his world seem safe. But, to Aidan, the hug could mean nothing until he knew how his father was doing.*

For Sean, the whole process of creating Aidan's life has been sometimes satisfying, often frustrating, and never without inner battles to maintain his confidence.

With Julie gone home to work on whatever she needed to prepare before Monday arrives, Sean has managed to spend a fair part of Sunday afternoon moving the story along in a direction that seems to make sense. For the next few hours, allowing himself one modest Jameson for the day, he sits at his desk and reads his story from the beginning.

The reading goes quickly; after all, he knows the plot and the characters. He's really beginning to look for careless flaws and dumb mistakes and whatever glaring gaps he might have left in the thread of the narrative.

For the first time since the beginning, he knows the story is nearly done. As he reads, he makes notes about what to change, what to add, and what to delete. By the time he finishes, his Jameson is long gone and it's already dusk.

Sean leans back in his chair, the glow from the computer screen the only light in the room. He finally understands how the story will end. For the moment, he almost allows himself a sense of satisfaction.

He stands and moves into the kitchen. There isn't much in the refrigerator, although he finds a couple of slices of ham he bought maybe a week or so ago. If he has any bread, he'll make a sandwich. In the end, he eats the ham slices alone, along with some snack crackers. It will be enough for now.

As he eats, his mulls what he'll write next. He feels good about the direction he's planning to give to the story. It's a matter of resolving the various issues that have suffused the story so far, but it's also a matter of weaving his words into descriptions and actions that satisfy the reader. The end of the story, he knows, needs to be strong and memorable. And it needs to leave readers — if there will ever be any beyond his circle of acquaintances — feeling so satisfied that they will hope that he will soon produce another novel.

Tonight, he will try to being doing just that.

Before returning to his manuscript, Sean telephones Julie. He is almost ready to assume that she's not home when she finally answers.

"Sorry about that," she says, breathing as if she'd rushed to the phone. "I was downstairs loading up the washer. I just remembered that I have nothing ready to wear to work tomorrow."

"Jeans and a t-shirt wouldn't be acceptable?" he teases.

"We in education need to set proper standards for the rest of the population," she answered, in a snooty tone that made Sean laugh.

"So," he says, "did you have a productive day so far?"

"Pretty good, in fact. I'm all caught up on things I definitely need for tomorrow. Once I get the laundry going, I want to prep for two meetings I have on Tuesday. I'll probably be done by nine. How about you?"

Sean tells her about the new chapter he's written, and that he knows how he wants to end the story.

"That sounds great," Julie says. "But do you think that's a fair way to leave Aidan? I mean, you've brought him a long way."

Sean pauses. "What do you expect in the conclusion of novel? I don't want to leave readers feeling let down. At the same time, I want them to be thinking about Aidan and his life and his family and his future — about all those things. I guess what I mean is that I would like the readers to decide what they want to take from the story, instead of my telling them what they should think."

Julie answered, "Maybe it's just me, but I think if a writer creates characters and a world for them to inhabit, he needs to bring the reader from a realistic beginning to a realistic end. He can be cryptic or simply stingy with the details he uses as a framework for the story, but I really think a writer ought to leave the reader saying 'Wow, what a book!'"

"So I should reconsider what I'm thinking about doing?"

"Sean," Julie says, "you need to do it the way you think it ought to be done. It's your book, and you need to write it so that you're satisfied that you've done your best. If the ending you described to me is the one you think fits perfectly, go for it. If not, have a Jameson, then sit back and let your brain churn on its own. I've got a feeling it will come up with the best solution."

Sean digests what Julie has said. After a bit, he tells her, "I think you could be a valuable muse. Thank you for putting this in perspective for me."

"Anytime. I am perfectly willing to be your personal critic as well."

Sean laughs. Then he tells her, "I wish we could hang around together tonight."

"So do I. But you need to write some more and I need to work some more. Let's get together tomorrow night. I'd love to read the latest stuff you've written."

"Call me when you're leaving work", he says.

"I'm penciling you in as we speak." Sean can hear the smile in her voice.

"You make me feel so special," he tells her.

Julie's laugh as the conversation ends leaves Sean smiling broadly.

The phone call finished, Sean pours himself a second Jameson and heads back to his desk. He's ready to begin the ending. And for the first time in a long time, he's truly excited — about the book and about having Julie in his life.

Tonight, he will spend however long it takes to develop the final chapters of the book.

***Stepping softly***

*Carney Hospital has expanded since Aidan's only visit there, when he was nine, for a broken ankle incurred when he tried to prove he could jump from a back porch into a pile of autumn leaves. The new additions to the hospital were impressive, but the main building looked unchanged.*

*Aidan drove into the visitors' parking lot and parked. It was nearly an hour before midnight when he and Ashling arrived, but Aidan was determined to see his father before the night was out. He and Ashling would sleep in the car, if necessary; there was no way he was going to be far from his dad. Not now, at least.*

*Aidan got out of the car and waited for Ashling to join him. It was cold and the March snow that had hit Boston, but not coastal Rhode Island, was still on the ground. Ashling clung to his arm as they moved toward the main entrance.*

*The lights in the main lobby were dimmed, and the receptionist's desk was unattended. Aidan looked around, searching for signs of life that might mean he'd be able to find out where in the hospital they were keeping his father. A minute went by with no signs of life. Aidan, impatient, wandered beyond the desk, peering down corridors, hoping someone might appear. The hallways were empty.*

*"Perhaps there's another desk," Ashling suggested. "It's likely they don't expect ordinary visitors at this hour of the night."*

*"Let's find the emergency room," Aidan said. "There was a sign when we arrived. It has to be to the left of where we came in."*

*"Let's go then," she told him.*

*By the time they rounded the building and arrived at the emergency entrance, after minutes of walking in the cold and the too-brisk wind, Ashling was shivering and Aidan's hands were nearly numb.*

*"Christ, it's cold," he said. "It was always too cold here in winter."*

*Aidan pulled open a door and let Ashling enter first. In the first corridor they found, a doctor was leaning on a counter, speaking with a nurse who was standing on the other side. Aidan and Ashling headed for them.*

*The nurse spotted them first.*

*"May I help you?" she asked. She was in her forties and, to Aidan, looked like she belonged on one of those television medical dramas.*

*Aidan stepped up to the counter. "My dad was brought in today, and we just found out. I need to see him. His name is Cornelius McCann. We just drove up from Rhode Island." The words tumbled out, and Aidan was unable to conceal his anxiety.*

*"Aidan's brother called," Ashling added. "He told us that Aidan's dad had a heart attack and perhaps a stroke. It would be a relief to Aidan and to me if we could see him, even if it's only for a moment or two. Can you please help us?"*

*The doctor spoke up. "With an Irish accent like that, I should think that we can make such an arrangement for you," he said in an Irish brogue that rivaled Ashling's.*

*The nurse smiled then clicked through some files on her computer terminal. "Let's see what we can do," she said. She punched the phone keypad, waited a few seconds. "Cornelius McCann — the gentleman we admitted this afternoon. Is he in ICU?"*

*She listened for a moment. "His son is here. Drove up from Rhode Island. Would it be all right for him and his wife to visit for a moment?"*

*She listened again, her expression neutral. Then she said, "Hold on for a second."*

*Pushing the mute key on the phone, she looked up at the physician standing next to Aidan. "Maybe a word from you would be helpful."*

*The doctor nodded and took the phone.*

*Thirty seconds later, Aidan and Ashling were thanking both him and the nurse and were heading for the intensive care unit.*

*When Aidan and Ashling stepped off the elevator, they spotted the nursing station to their right. There were four nurses behind the counter, eyeing monitors, filling out paperwork, checking doctors' orders, or whatever they did when everyone else was sleeping.*

*Aidan neared the counter, Ashling clutching his hand and trailing a half-step behind. A nurse with white hair looked up. She reminded him of a kindly woman who had lived next door when he was growing up. The nurse's name badge said she was Margaret Bresnahan, R.N.*

*"The nurse and the doctor in the emergency room said we could see my dad for a bit," Aidan said. "Cornelius McCann. I wouldn't usually do this kind of thing...visiting hours and all... but I need to see him. We've*

*come a long way."*

*The nurse nodded. "I understand."*

*Ashling interrupted. "How is Aidan's dad doing?"*

*The nurse pulled a folder from a rack to her right. It took a minute for her to review the information the folder contained. Meanwhile, Aidan's anxiety far from abating. Then the nurse looked at the screen in front of her and clicked the computer mouse a few times.*

*"He's likely to be asleep now. He was restless earlier — maybe an hour ago — so we gave him something to relax him." She looked at Aidan. "He's doing relatively well. Of course, at his age, it's a bit more difficult to predict how he will fare tomorrow or the next day."*

*"My brother told me he had a heart attack and maybe a stroke, too."*

*"He did have a heart attack," she told him. "But it doesn't appear to have been too serious. We checked him and found some arterial blockage. But, again, it doesn't seem to be too severe. His doctor can give you more information if you come by tomorrow morning."*

*"What about a stroke?" Ashling asked. "Did he in fact have a stroke along with his heart attack?"*

*"Actually, we're not sure yet. He presented with some signs that suggested a stroke when they brought him in. But he's scheduled for some tests tomorrow. So, we'll know better then."*

*Ashling put her arm around Aidan's waist. "Let's go see him, luv. If he's asleep, we'll come back in the morning. If he's awake, at least you will be able to talk with him a bit, and perhaps that will put your mind at ease."*

*Aidan nodded. "Where is he?" he asked the nurse.*

*"Third room on the left," she said, pointing toward the corridor on their right."*

*"Thank you," Aidan said.*

*"Thank you so very much," Ashling said. "You have been most kind."*

*With Aidan leading, they walked slowly long the corridor, stepping softly as if afraid they might wake other patients.*

*There were four patients in the room, each of them hooked up to wires and IV bags and, one of them, a respirator. The two beds on either side of the doorway were occupied by men, both of them old, one extremely obese, and the other appearing to be at least in his nineties. The air was filled with small beeping sounds, and display screens jiggled with heart rates and respiratory rates and blood pressures and whatever else they were capable of checking. The room smelled...medical.*

*Moving toward the far side of the room, they found Cornelius in a bed opposite a woman who appeared to be shrunken and not likely to be alive in the morning. The sight frightened Aidan. Despite his mother's death, he had not been able yet to face that particular finality of life. Seeing the woman at the edge of her existence heightened Aidan's anxiety about his father.*

*Cornelius was hooked up to monitors, oxygen, and an IV bag. He appeared to be sleeping, his breathing slow and regular. He looked older than he had when Aidan visited him last, as though the episode with his heart had taken extra years from him.*

*Aidan walked to the side of the bed and looked down at his dad. It would be unfair for the fates to take his father away so soon after he and his dad had finally become comfortable with each other. Aidan found himself whispering a prayer to himself, addressing whichever saints might deign to pay attention to someone like him, trying to revive memories of the prayers he'd recited as a boy.*

*His dad had to live to be Aidan's best man at the wedding.*

*Ashling, able always to sense Aidan's mind and his heart, came to stand next to him and wrapped an arm around his waist. "Are you praying, luv?" she asked in a whisper.*

*Aidan nodded.*

*"That's good. You and I should keep praying," is all she said.*

For the first time since he began the story, Sean has become acutely aware of the importance of the last chapters he is about to write. For several days, now, he has been toying with possible final touches he might put on the lives of Aidan and Ashling and Cornelius, as well as on Ian and Margaret.

He has stopped writing for the moment because he has suddenly found himself having to make some key decisions before he can continue the narrative. There's the matter of Aidan's father's hospitalization, for one, and the related interactions between Aidan and Ian — and the need to bring Margaret into the dialogue at some point.

Then there's the wedding.

For a while, Sean paces slowly back and forth in his living room, mostly gazing down at the floor, as he attempts to assemble bits and pieces in his mind. He ends up standing in the doorway to his office, looking across the room toward his computer. A page of his story glows on the screen, appearing from this distance to be no more than a set of illegible horizontal lines. He takes a step toward his desk when his cell phone rings. He pulls it out of his pocket and answers.

"I'm almost home," Julie says. "Are you still writing?"

"I was just about to sit down again," he tells her. "I needed to take a break to sort things through a bit more."

"Can I bring you anything to eat? I don't think starving artists have enough strength to produce good stuff."

"Thanks, Julie. I ate something a while ago."

"What did you have?"

"A couple of slices of ham, along with a couple of crackers."

He hears Julie sigh. "And you expect to be able to write with almost nothing in your stomach? You need to take better care of yourself, Sean."

"I'm doing fine," he tells her.

"Look. I know you want to focus on writing tonight, and I want you to take all the time you need to write well. But I'm about a block away from that sandwich shop on Post Road. I'll pick up something for you — and for me — and I'll bring it over." She hurries to add, "And I promise I'll stay only as long as it takes me to eat. Is that okay with you?"

Sean isn't about to refuse. Julie has been cropping up in his mind all day. Frankly, he misses her. Being able to spend some time with her tonight, however little, is bound to energize him.

"I'd like that," he tells her.

"Good," she says. "What kind of sandwich would you like?"

"Surprise me."

"I will," she says, laughing. "I should be there in less than a half hour."

After Julie hangs up, Sean sits down at his keyboard. He will write more after Julie goes home. Now, though, he selects the chapters he's written since he gave her a copy of the story, loads paper into his printer, and hits "Print."

As sheets of paper begin feeding into the printer, he leaves his office to make sure his apartment is relatively ready for her visit. As he gathers up already-read newspapers, wipes down the kitchen counters and table, sweeps the kitchen floor quickly, and runs a piece of paper towel over the furniture to get rid of any dust, he decides that if his book does become published and he earns even a modest sum from it, he will move into a much nicer apartment.

The last few pages slide out of the printer just as Julie knocks. In two quick paces, he's opening the door for her and reaching for the bag in her hands. She enters and closes the door behind her as Sean brings the bag to the kitchen table. As he turns, she throws her arms around his neck and gives him a welcome happy-to-see-you kiss. Sean is happy to reciprocate.

"Have you written a lot today?" Julie asks.

"Enough to feel as if I've accomplished something." He doesn't want let go of her. "Are you hungry now, or would you prefer to wait?"

"Actually, I'm kind of hungry," she says.

"Then, let's eat. I'd rather spend time with you than having staring at my computer. My brain needs to process the story some more before I start typing again."

Julie gives him another quick kiss then slides out of his arms. "Want to see what I got for us?"

"Show me."

Julie reaches toward the table and opens the bag.

"For you, I've brought a meatball sandwich; you need something hearty and filling to sustain you as you write tonight. And for me," she says, reaching again into the bag, "I got a luscious veggie pocket, with all the fixings."

"Does 'all the fixings' mean extra veggies?"

She cocks her head and looks at him. "You are absolutely correct. I try to eat healthy most of the time."

Julie reaches into the bag once more and pulls out a bottle of lemonade and a bottle of diet soda. "Take your pick," she says, placing the bottles on the table.

"You pick," Sean says.

"Lemonade for me," she tells him.

They share small talk while they eat, Julie talking about her day at work, Sean talking about his work both at the Wickford paper and the one in Fall River.

"Working those kinds of hours doesn't leave me as much time as I'd like for my story," he says. "But I'm actually managing to be somewhat productive."

He takes another bit of his sandwich, thinking as he chews. "It's funny," he tells her. "I hope I can sell the book when it's done. But the main reason I'm hoping I can get it published is so I can quit my job — jobs, I mean — and write full time."

"How long will it take to get published?" Julie asks.

"I've been doing some research. In fact, I talked with a fellow I interviewed about ten years ago who had his second novel published."

"And?"

"There are a couple of ways I can go. If I go the traditional way, I need to submit a synopsis and some sample chapters to publishing houses." Sean pauses. "The only problem with that approach is that not many publishers pay any attention to new authors. And some of them — at least according to the writer I told you about — resent it if you submit to more than one publisher at a time."

"So it could take months," Julie says.

"Or years," Sean tells her.

"That sucks."

"But..."

"But what?" she asks.

"I can self-publish. There are some online sites where you can self-publish and sell your books. I've done some research on those, too. I could actually have the book on the market in less than a month after I finish it."

For the next twenty minutes, Sean tells Julie about the benefits of self-publishing and the royalties he might be able to collect. As he speaks, she becomes more excited about his prospects.

"You've got a really good story, Sean," she says. "Based upon what you let me read, I can't imagine anyone not liking it."

"Thanks," he replies. Then, "Before I forget, I printed out the new chapters I've written since I gave you a copy of the story. Remind me to give them to you before you leave."

"Do you want me to leave so you can keep writing?"

Sean shakes his head. "No. I'd really like you to stay a while longer, if you can. Sometimes, my mind needs to mull things quite a bit before I can write more. You're just the kind of sweet distraction I need right now."

"I'll stay for a while, then."

Sean stands and begins to clean up the table. "Go relax on the couch," he tells Julie. "I'll be there in a minute."

"Okay," she says. "I have to warn you, though: cleaning up after me is a good way to spoil me forever."

"It's a risk I have to take, then," Sean tells her.

"Yes," Julie replies. "The way to a woman's heart is through dedicated spoiling."

***Chilling Aidan's spine***

*Months ago, Cornelius had given Aidan a key to his apartment in Dorchester, in case there were ever an emergency.*

*This was an emergency, Aidan decided.*

*After leaving the hospital, he and Ashling drove to Aidan's dad's place to spend the night. Again, they used Aidan's old bedroom, falling asleep within mercifully brief moments of getting under the covers.*

*When Aidan began to awaken, his mind was still in turmoil over his father's situation. In his half-sleep, he tried to chase away disturbing fragments of a frightening dream he'd had. It left him feeling more anxious than he had been in a long time.*

*He checked his watch. It was already nearly nine. Ashling was on her side, pressed up against him, breathing softly. He tried to remember — vainly — if he'd seen any signs indicating visiting hours at the hospital.*

*Feeling badly that he'd dragged Ashling to Boston so late in the evening, he was reluctant to wake her. Yet he wanted to get to the hospital as soon as he could. He needed to see his father and make sure his father had survived the night. Phoning the hospital would not do.*

*Moving with slow urgency, he slipped away from Ashling and climbed out of the bed. He was thankful that Ashling had insisted on bringing a change of clothes with them before leaving Rhode Island. He found the bag she'd brought in and pulled out fresh underwear. The shirt and jeans he was wearing last night would be adequate for today. He made his way to the bathroom and showered, then used his father's razor to shave. He took care of his teeth with a dab of toothpaste on his finger; he'd need to buy a toothbrush if they were to stay another night.*

*When he returned to the bedroom, Ashling was sitting on the edge of the bed, her hair mussed, her eyes sleepy. When she spoke, her voice was croaky. "I'm going with you, luv. Please wait. It will take me only a few moments to freshen up."*

*While Ashling got ready, Aidan telephoned his brother.*

*"Ian," he said, when his brother answered on the fifth ring. "It's me. We're at dad's place."*

*"I'm glad you came up to Boston," Ian said. "Are you going to visit him?"*

*"We saw him last night briefly," Aidan said. "He was sleeping. We didn't want to disturb him."*

*"He needs his rest."*

*"Anyway, Ashling and I will have some breakfast and then we plan to go back to the hospital. Are you planning to visit him this morning?"*

*"I cancelled most of my appointments. There's only one I need to attend to, but I should be free before noon."*

*Aidan nodded, as if his brother could see him. Then he said, "What's your sense about how dad is doing? He looked as if he was sleeping comfortably, although his color wasn't great."*

*"I actually called the hospital around seven-thirty and managed to speak to the nurse on the floor. She told me he's awake and reasonably alert. She said he had a good night."*

*"Is he still confused?"*

*"She said he's doing better."*

*Aidan digested what his brother told him. Again, he nodded, as if Ian were standing in front of him.*

*"Okay," he said. "We'll see you when you get to the hospital, then."*

*Aidan hated hospitals nearly as much as he hated funeral homes. Much too late in life, especially after his mother's death, he'd managed to become somewhat able to keep his feelings in check. The two places were necessary evils, in his view. In this case, however, the frightening aspects of hospitals could be pushed aside now that his father's life depended on the care they could offer.*

*When they entered the hospital, Ashling led the way to the elevators.*

*"Let's talk with the nurses, if we can, before going to your father's room," she suggested to Aidan as they entered the elevator car. "It will be better if we understand what's going on."*

*Aidan nodded. On the way to the fourth floor, he said nothing. Ashling understood that he was tangled in thoughts.*

*The elevator doors opened upon bustling activity, unlike the serene scene they encountered late last evening. Nurses and aides and phlebotomists and doctors were in every direction, some conferring, others walking slowly while scanning charts, and still others busy with paperwork. Ashling took Aidan's hand and walked toward the nursing station where overhead monitors tracked the status of each patient and where, this morning at least, there seemed to be little time for the staff to do anything but tend to whatever urgencies were presently at hand.*

*As they approached the counter of the nursing station, a forty-something nurse with warm brown eyes looked up.*

*"May I help you?"*

*Aidan spoke. "My father was brought in yesterday; Cornelius McCann. We'd like to see him, but I need to know how he's doing before we go in."*

*A chill passed down Aidan's spine as he spoke. He was afraid — despite Ian's assurances over the phone that his father was doing relatively well this morning — that the nurse would say that his dad had passed only a few moments ago.*

*The nurse reached for a folder, browsed through it briefly, then looked up at the monitor above her head.*

*"He's doing well," she said. "Have you had a chance to talk with his doctor?"*

*"No," Aidan said.*

*Ashling jumped in. "We found out about his dad last evening, and we came right up to see him. We haven't really spoken with anyone yet."*

*"His doctor is on the floor right now. Would you like to speak with him?"*

*"Yes," Aidan said. "Yes, please."*

*The nurse turned to another nurse behind her. "Could you tell Dr. Kelliher to come by the desk when he finishes with Mr. Adler?"*

*The other nurse said she would and left the station.*

*Minutes later, Dr. Kelliher, younger than Aidan and looking as if he probably ran marathons in his spare time, approached the desk.*

*"This is Mr. McCann's son," the nurse told him.*

*The doctor looked at Ashling and then at Aidan. "I see the resemblance. You look like your dad," Dr. Kelliher said, shaking Aidan's hand. Turning, he shook Ashling's hand and said simply, "A pleasure to meet you, Mrs. McCann."*

*Ashling shook her head and laughed softly. "It will be a few more months yet before it becomes Mrs. McCann."*

*"Forgive me for assuming," the doctor said. "My mother always insisted that I should never assume. Of course, I never listened to her."*

*Dr. Kelliher took at least five minutes to describe in detail what he believed had happened to Aidan's father. It was much as Ian had said when he called Aidan in Rhode Island.*

*"It was a small heart attack, an infarction. The kind of thing that is*

*more of a warning than a threat to his life." The doctor asked the nurse for Cornelius's chart. When he had it in hand, he opened it and reviewed two or three sheets of paper. "When he was admitted, he was confused. For a time, he was unsure of his name or where he was. Now the confusion could have been a result of the infarction — perhaps reduced blood flow to the brain — or simply a result of the stress he was feeling. Less likely is that as a result of the infarction, a small blood clot entered the brain and blocked some blood flow temporarily."*

*"Is he still confused?" Ashling asked.*

*"Actually, he seems to be doing much better this morning," Dr. Kelliher told her. "He's not out of the woods yet. We want to do a few more tests before we get ahead of ourselves."*

*"What kind of tests?" Aidan asked.*

*"A brain scan for one," Dr. Kelliher said. "And we'll take a closer look at his heart to check arterial blockage. Until we do that, we can't devise a treatment plan for him. He's scheduled for both tests this afternoon."*

*Aidan nodded, as if satisfied with what he was hearing. Ashling took his arm and stood close to him.*

*"I'd like to see him," Aidan said.*

*The doctor smiled. "Be my guest. Third room on the left."*

*Cornelius was awake and looking bored, his eyes glued to nothing special on the television set. As soon as he saw Aidan — and especially as he spotted Ashling — his mood changed dramatically.*

*"You've come!" he said, clearly happy to see them. Then he added quickly, "I'm sorry to cause you a lot of trouble. When I got the chest pain, I was afraid, so I called for an ambulance."*

*"I'm glad you did, dad," Aidan said as neared his father's bed. He reached for his father's hand and took it in his own. "And we're so glad that you're doing pretty well."*

*"What do you mean, 'pretty well'?", his father asked, with some alarm.*

*"Dr. Kelliher says you're doing quite fine," Ashling said quickly. "He seems like a very competent doctor, and he simply wants to conduct a few more tests to make sure you heal properly."*

*"They said I had a heart attack."*

*"A mild one," Aidan said.*

*Cornelius nodded, seemingly lost in thought for a moment. Then he said to Ashling, "Hearing the way you speak makes me think of Ellen. I miss her."*

*The sound of footsteps made Aidan turn. He barely completed his turn when his sister Margaret wrapped her arms around him. The only thing that popped into his mind was, "Will wonders never cease?"*

*"Thank you for coming, Aidan," Margaret told him, her subdued smile sincere. Then, turning to hug Ashling as well, she said, "I wanted to call you last night, but Ian insisted on making the call himself. Sometimes, he insists on being more bossy than normal."*

*"Not a problem," Aidan reassured her. Then, "Dad seems to be doing well this morning."*

*"I don't intend to die now," Cornelius said, in a particularly feisty tone. "I'd love nothing better to be with your mother now. But I have a wedding to attend, and I pray I can be around for an additional grandchild."*

*"You'd better be," Ashling said. "Aidan needs a good best man."*

For three days, Sean hasn't written a word — or, at least, anything good enough to spare it from deletion — and his frustration is digging into him. This drought, whatever its source, has also crept into his work at the newspapers and he's managed only perfunctory progress with his assignments. In the newsroom in Wickford, Jeff Gallagher sat on the edge of Sean's desk and asked him if everything was okay; at the Fall River paper, Vin O'Brien pulled Aidan aside and wondered if he was unhappy with his job there. Although Sean reassured both men that he was perfectly content with his journalistic work, he is trying to fathom if his newspaper slump is impacting his novel, or vice versa.

He feels lost.

On this evening, one where Julie needs to attend a function in Providence that will probably last until ten o'clock — followed by an almost obligatory after-function drink with colleagues and professional acquaintances at an upscale local bar — Sean decides he won't even bother trying to write a single word.

Back in his apartment after finishing a disappointingly unproductive day, he eats a tuna salad sandwich, catches the local news on television, then fills a tumbler with ice and pours himself a too-healthy dose of Jameson.

He needs to meditate.

Turning off the television halfway through the sports report, he kicks back on the couch, takes a long slow sip of the Irish whiskey, and tries to let his mind drift into emptiness.

Six or seven sips later, the whiskey is nearly gone and his mind is still not at rest.

He knows this is happening because he has been pressuring himself: the conclusion of the story is where everything hangs in the balance. A vapid ending would make the story eminently forgettable. It's not a matter of finishing the story; doing so is simply a matter of typing words until there's nothing more to add. Sean's stress comes, again as it has in the past, from wavering confidence. What if, in the end, he is unable to give his story the rich ending he believes it deserves?

He needs to kill the pressure, so he drains his glass and moves into the kitchen to refill it. What he's had to drink so far has only just begun to take some of the edge off of what he's been feeling. The bottle of Jameson is nearly empty and, for a moment, he debates whether he ought to leave his apartment now to buy some more. He cuts the debate short and decides to sit in his office, in the dark. If he can't force his brain to quiet down, he can at least sit in silence and darkness and let it roam around. Perhaps it will follow its own internal twists and turns and, with some luck, lead him to the direction he needs to follow.

It doesn't. At the end of an hour, he's as empty as he was at the beginning.

He wishes he could phone Julie, or spend some time with her. But he knows he won't hear from her until tomorrow. Whatever balm she might provide to soothe his anxiety is, for now, out of reach. At this moment, he sorely needs her encouragement and her confidence that what he's writing is good.

The ice clinks against his glass as he lifts the Jameson to his lips again. He swallows, places the glass on his desk, and picks up his phone. He needs to talk with Ted.

Sitting in silence can only be tolerated for so long, Sean decides. He looks at his clock; Ted is probably in the middle of his first set at the Ocean Tides. Pushing his drink aside, he grabs a light jacket, makes sure he has his keys, and does something he would otherwise never do: drive under the influence.

When he gets behind the wheel, keys in the ignition, he hesitates. He begins to consider whether this is a good idea, but cuts off his thoughts before they can become too rational. He starts the car, backs out of his parking spot, and heads toward Matunuck. As he drives out of Wickford, he begins chanting, "Failure is not an option. Failure is not an option. Failure is not a fucking option!" He feels silly, but the chanting seems to be making him feel better.

Sean opts for keeping to the side roads, assuming that any police on the lookout for weaving drivers will be focused on the busier roads. Besides, he doesn't want to risk driving at higher speeds — and the more leisurely pace along the curving back roads seems more suitable for his chanting.

Nearly forty minutes later, he finds a parking place at a lot near the Shoreside. When he gets out his car, he can hear Ted's music penetrating the walls, the rhythm pulsating, making the evening seem alive. He makes his way toward the entrance, very anxious now to make it to the men's room, before seeing Ted. Beer might make you want to pee sooner, but any alcohol creates strong urges in due time. He cuts his way through the crowd, praying that he wouldn't have to wait for a turn. When he gets to the entrance to the men's room, he finds that God must have been listening to him. He heads for the first urinal and stands there, a deep feeling of pleasant satisfaction wrapping itself around him as he finally, thankfully relieves himself.

The place is crowded, as always, with most of the people letting Ted's music wash over them while they drink and talk and strut and flirt and lose themselves before tomorrow comes.

Sean finds a tight spot at the bar where he can place an elbow to prop himself while waiting for Ted to take a break. About five minutes later, one of the bartenders asks Sean what he wants to drink. The right answer should be a soda or a class of tonic water, but Sean orders more Irish whiskey.

Ted performs two more numbers before he sets his guitar down. Sean makes his way toward the low stage, waving his arm at his friend. Ted is shaking a few hands as he heads for the nearest exit and, as one fan is patting him on the back, notices Sean.

"What's up, man?" Ted says as he finally gets close enough shake Sean's hand. "Good to see you." He indicates a door twenty feet away. "Let's get out of here. I need some quiet."

It's a calm evening, cool but not too chilly. Ted, predictably, pulls out a single cigarette and lights it. He knows better than to ask Sean if he wants a cigarette as well; Sean smokes only when he is at home.

Sean looks out to where the gentle waves hitting the beach are so dimly lit that they look like ghosts curling up to the sand. "Do you ever start writing some lyrics and then can't seem to come up with the right ending?"

Ted laughs. "I have a special wastebasket for songs without endings." Then, letting the laugh fade, he asks, "Having an issue with your story?"

"It's been three days since I've managed to write anything that isn't trite or worn or just this side of crap. I don't know what to do, to be honest with you."

"Where are you in the story?"

"A few days ago, I thought I could wrap it up in maybe two good chapters." Sean sips from his beer. "Right now, I just don't know."

Ted puffs his cigarette and ponders. "Trying too hard?"

Sean thinks for a moment. "Possibly. I know I've been pressuring myself. But it's almost as if something in the back of my brain is making me afraid of coming up with a good ending."

"Well, you've always been pretty critical of yourself," Ted says. "Maybe, somehow, you're persuading yourself that you can't do it."

Sean shrugs. "I wish the hell I knew. The words aren't coming. Until now, even when I had that bad spell when I thought I'd have to kill the whole story, I sensed that the words would eventually come back to me once I sat down at the keyboard. But now? Nothing, zero, zip. Not even a hint of how the book should end."

The two of them stare out into the offshore blackness.

"The only thing that has ever worked for me is persistence," Ted says, at last. "You asked about not being able to come up with a good ending for a song. If I think the song has good potential, I'll keep trying for an ending. It might take me days, weeks, or even months. But sooner or later, I get the kind of ending that makes the whole things work."

Sean sips again from his whiskey. People are beginning to move inside, anticipating the start of Ted's second set.

"Persistence," Sean says.

"I call it mental elbow grease," Ted replies. "You don't have any specific deadline for finishing the story, do you?"

"No. I have enough deadlines at work."

"Then just put the story aside. Take a week or two off from writing. Have fun with Julie. Go somewhere for the weekend." Ted takes a final puff from his cigarette then plunges it into a bowl of sand filled with three-dozen other butts. "I'll bet that will do the trick."

Three days later, Sean and Julie leave for a weekend in Bar Harbor, Maine.

Sean begins writing again when they return.

***Who told you I love lobster?***

*One month after Cornelius was discharged from Carney Hospital, feeling healthy and healed, Aidan and Ashling arrived in Dorchester to pick him up for a promised Sunday ride.*

*For Cornelius, getting out of his apartment and getting out of Dorchester were blessings. He'd spent most of the month at home and doing nothing, eating only the healthy foods the doctor had suggested, taking the new medications that were now part of his daily life, and letting his body heal. He was pleased with his progress, though wishing he could have healed with the zest of a twenty-year-old. And he was pleased that he no longer had any bouts of confusion, aside from the kinds of mental lapses that most of his friends suffered far more than he.*

*Aidan drove, his father in the front passenger seat, and Ashling content to sit in back.*

*"We thought we'd take you for a day in Rhode Island," Aidan said as he pulled away from the curb. "This kind of good weather, it would be a shame to waste it in the city."*

*"And," Ashling said from the back seat, "we will take you for the best lobster dinner you've ever had."*

*Cornelius laughed... "And who told you that I love lobster?" he asked.*

*"And why is it that you think anyone had to tell us?" she replied, adding, "You do love lobster, don't you."*

*"I have had lobster five times in my life, and I loved it every single time," he said. "And I can tell you where I had it each of those times. It's very expensive, though."*

*"Don't worry about it, dad," Aidan said. "My new job pays pretty darned good. Now that I'm finished with the training program, I got a raise."*

*Cornelius thought for a moment. "Your mother would be proud of you, just as I am proud of you."*

*From where Ashling sat, she could see a tear welling his Cornelius's eye.*

*The ride to Wickford took just over an hour. They stopped first at Dugan's Ale House.*

*"It's our version of an Irish pub," Aidan said as he held the door for his father to enter. "Not as good as Murtaugh's, but the menu's decent."*

*"Is this where we are having the lobster?" Cornelius asked.*

*"No," Aidan said. We'll have a sandwich now. The lobster is for dinner, much later this afternoon.*

*"Dinner as well?" Cornelius said, smiling as he nodded his head. "We'll be eating out twice today?"*

*Ashling spoke. "Aidan wants to treat you to lunch. I want to treat you to dinner. We'll be going to Duffy's, not to far from here."*

*Cornelius laughed. "Imagine that. Two restaurants in one day."*

*When they were seated, in a booth by the window, Aidan told his dad that he could order whatever he wanted.*

*Cornelius, already studying the menu intently, said, "My doctor says I should stay away from fatty things. My heart, you know." Then he grinned at Aidan and Ashling who sat opposite him. "My doctor be damned!"*

*Ashling reached for Cornelius's hand. "You should really take care of yourself. It hasn't been that long since you've been in the hospital."*

*Cornelius looked at her in a fatherly way Aidan hadn't seen in a long time. "It doesn't matter, really. I will live as long as God wants me to live. I have great faith in that. I also have great faith in a man's right to enjoy himself when his son and his son's future wife take him to two restaurants in the same day. I only wish Ellen could be with us."*

*Ashling squeezed Cornelius's hand and whispered to him, "We both love you dearly, you know, and we miss her terribly."*

*Cornelius smiled. "I know. And I thank you for putting up with me as you do sometimes."*

*Aidan stepped in. "How about some Jameson, dad?"*

*"Would the doctor object?" his father asked.*

*"Who could object to fine Irish whiskey?" Aidan replied as he signaled the waitress.*

*Their luncheon conversation entwined the three of them for nearly two hours. For Aidan, it was a further opportunity to learn about his father, and all the difficulties his father and mother had dealt with from the time they left Ireland to the time Ellen died. Ashling was a curious as Aidan, and listened intently as Cornelius patiently — and happily — spun the story of his and Ellen's lives.*

*When they left Dugan's and Aidan was driving along Rhode Island's scenic coastline, Cornelius said to him, "There was a time when your* mother and me were deeply sad about the life you had chosen for yourself. Had it not been for your mother, I would have likely taken a fist to you in the hopes of waking you up. We didn't know what to do about you, and we couldn't understand why you had become the way you were."

The words cut into Aidan nearly as deeply as those in the letter his mother had left for him. He sensed his father needed this opportunity to vent some deep feelings, and he expected a long lecture. So he drove on, listening to his father, his mind barely focused on the road ahead, and feeling a new surge of regret building in his soul for having let his parents down.

"Did you know that your mother worked an extra day each week so we could pay your college tuition? I did the same. Your brother and sister had scholarships, and they worked during the week to help with their college expenses. You had not scholarships. Yet, your mother and I were prepared to make whatever sacrifices we had to make so that you could have the kind of education we never could have dreamed of for ourselves. We just couldn't fathom why you chose not to work hard at college, or why you decided to give up on getting a good education. Your mother cried after you told us you were leaving school."

Cornelius fell silent. Aidan drove on, staring straight ahead. In the rear seat, Ashling watched Aidan's eyes in the rearview mirror; they were moist. She knew she could not speak for him, but she could speak about him.

"Aidan's a far different person now," she said.

"I know," Cornelius answered, his tone conciliatory. "Ellen and I always thought that you would bring him to his senses sooner or later."

He turned toward Aidan, who kept staring straight ahead. "I am not being critical, Aidan. You've had to find your own way in more ways than one. Your mother and I only wished for your own sake that you could have found yourself earlier."

He paused. "I need to be quiet now," Cornelius said, sounding embarrassed.

Ashling spoke quickly. "Aidan will make you proud."

Cornelius turned in his seat to look at her. "Yes. He is already making me proud."

Looking into the rearview mirror. Ashling could see Aidan's eyes begin to smile.

Nearly four hours later, with Cornelius marveling at the beauty of the Rhode Island shore, Aidan parked the car in Duffy's parking lot. The three of them ambled in, enjoying light banter, and — Aidan thought — being in *total harmony for the first time ever.*

*After not much of a wait, Cornelius was in his glory enjoying Duffy's triple-lobster special.*

Ted is sitting in Sean's makeshift office while Sean is trying to cobble together a coherent ending to his story. Ted is sitting on a kitchen chair Sean brought into the room, sipping on a glass of ginger ale. Sean, focused on his computer screen, is having a beer.

He knows he is trying too hard, but he doesn't know how to try less hard.

For the past hour, between bouts of trying to explain his creative process to Ted, combined with the basic elements of a male-only bull session covering everything from women to sports to work to what-the-hell-is-life-all-about, Sean has been pressing himself to write at least one damned sentence that will launch his final chapter — or chapters — so he can bring phase one to a close and then embark on phase two: rewriting and editing and self-criticizing and trying to keep the spirit of his story intact all the while.

"What I really don't know," Sean is saying to his friend, "is how this thing will finally end. I've got a dozen different endings sloshing around in my head."

Ted thinks for a moment. "Maybe you should decide if you want to pander to people who love predictable stories, or if you want to write something that makes people think."

Sean ponders what Ted has said.

"You know what I hate?" Sean says after a while. "I hate reading a book that has a wishy-washy ending. It always makes me think that the author got tired of writing and just wanted to wrap it up as quickly as possible. I don't want to do that to whoever might read my story."

Julie phones just as Sean and Ted are standing in the kitchen, each with a lighted cigarette, and Ted taking occasional sips of some pomegranate juice blend that had caught Sean's attention at the supermarket a few days before.

Sean needed to step away from the keyboard while he and Ted discuss the ending of the story, and Ted is trying to relate Sean's challenge to his own approach to finishing a song.

The discussion is suspended as Sean picks up the phone.

Sean says, "I miss you too," as Ted lowers himself onto one of the kitchen chairs.

"Actually, Ted's here now. We're talking about the best way to finish my story." Sean listens for a minute then turns to Ted. "Julie says — and I quote — "leave the creative genius alone!"

"Tell her I respect her intellect, too," Ted says, with crooked grin.

Sean listens as Julie speaks. After a couple of moments, he says, "I hate to say it, but I really need to spend tonight trying to figure out how to make this story end just right. How about if we go out tomorrow after work? I want to take you to Junction Pizza."

Again Sean listens. "It's not just a pizza place," Sean explains. "It's got great Italian food and seafood and other stuff."

Sean falls silent as Julie speaks.

"Okay. I'll pick you up at six." Pause. "Yes, I'll tell Ted to give me only gold-plated advice." Then, "I'll call you at work tomorrow." Pause. "Me, too."

Sean is smiling when he hangs up.

"Sounds like you and Julie are more than casual acquaintances," Ted says. "Jane predicted this, you know."

Sean shrugs. "Things are going fine," he says, adding, "And it wouldn't cause me any heartburn if Jane is right."

"You should tell Jane so she can pass it on to Julie." Ted chuckles and gets up from the chair. Putting his empty glass on the kitchen counter, he says, "Let's get back to talking about an ending for your book."

An hour later, Ted is doing most of the talking and Sean is doing most of the listening and nodding. Sean's beginning to feel an edgy urge to get back to his keyboard, but he wants to hear his friend out.

"When I read a book," Ted is saying, "I look at it this way: in the first few chapters, the book is making me a promise about how much it will capture my attention. If I get to the end — maybe the last two or three chapters — and if the author breaks that promise, I'll never read him again. It's as simple as that."

Sean mulls what Ted has said

"So I'm screwed if I can't nail the ending."

"Pretty much."

Sean falls into thought. Finally, he says, "So where to I go from here?"

Ted lights the last cigarette he will have today. "You write your ass off. It's as simple as that."

Sean looks at his friend. "Another blatantly simplistic solution from my buddy the music-writer."

"But I'm selling albums," Ted says, chuckling.

"Bastard," Sean says, smiling.

***Like I was the family pet***

*Two weeks before the wedding, Aidan and Ashling shared a Saturday lunch with Margaret and Kenneth, her husband, and their two sons at a restaurant in Lexington, not far from Margaret's home.*

*Aidan had never spent much time with the two boys — Thomas, now nineteen, and Timothy, seventeen — although he had seen them on occasion years ago when he visited his parents during the holidays, before Margaret began making a point of staying away if Aidan was going to be present.*

*Over the past three months, through a couple of visits he'd arranged with his sister, Aidan had had the opportunity to get to know the boys better. The elder boy was nearly a clone of his father, tall, pleasant in a serious kind of way, and seeming more interested in achieving success in life than in enjoying it. Timothy, in many ways, reminded Aidan of himself. He looked like his mother, and thus looked a lot like Aidan; Margaret and Aidan were obviously brother and sister, while Ian strongly resembled an overfed Cornelius. And Timothy seemed to have Aidan's sense of humor and free-spirited attitude toward life.*

*Aidan wondered if Margaret was aware of that particular resemblance. He'd seen nothing in their family dynamic that indicated that she loved her younger son less because he resembled her prodigal brother so much.*

*During lunch on this Saturday, conversation ranged between school, sports, the boys' girlfriends, Kenneth's work, Margaret's most recent honor in Neurology, and plans for the summer. Soon enough, the conversation shifted smoothly to the wedding.*

*"Do you know yet how many are coming?" Margaret asked Ashling.*

*"Thirty-four will be there, if all decide to attend. All of you in Aidan's family, my parents, some friends Cornelius wanted to include, two or three of Aidan's friends and their wives, and a few of my girlfriends and their husbands. It will be a small gathering."*

*Margaret looked at Aidan. "Ashling and I have been working on the menu and the music. I think you'll like it." It was almost as if she was hoping for his approval.*

*"I hope so." Aidan smiled at his sister. "She's been keeping me in the dark. It's still at Murtaugh's, right?"*

*Ashling elbowed him. "No, luv. We've changed it to one of the most expensive restaurants in Boston. Your father insisted."*

*Timothy gave a teenage thumbs-up to Ashling. "All right! You gotta live it up when you have the chance."*

*"She's making a joke," Margaret told her son, giving him a look that ensured his silence. To Aishling, she said, "Ignore him...please!"*

*Kenneth, mostly silent except for a few agreeable grunts and still sipping the vodka martini he'd had in front of him for the past half-hour, said, "It'll be a good wedding. If Margaret is excited about it, then it means nothing will go wrong. She's very good about that."*

*"Ignore him, too," Margaret told the others, making sure she punctuated her directive with a broad smile.*

*When the food came, the six of them settled into enjoying the meal, keeping the conversation and comments to a minimum until they began to fill at least moderately sated. Aidan had a second Jameson, only because Kenneth ordered a second martini. Ashling declined the waitress's offer to bring her another glass of Chablis. Margaret abstained.*

*"I'm on call," she said.*

*"That sucks," Aidan said.*

*"She loves the attention," Kenneth said, laughing*

*Then, again in silence, they picked at the scraps on their plates.*

*Aidan leaned back in his chair, looking as if he was thinking about something. After a moment, he said, "You know what, Margaret?"*

*"What?" she asked.*

*"You always pissed me off when I was little. You and Ian. You always made me feel like I was the family pet: train me, give me treats to keep me quiet, and make sure I spent very little time inconveniencing anyone. It sucked being the youngest."*

*Margaret looked at him, her head tilted, concern in her face. It seemed as if she was trying to formulate a response to a grenade attack.*

*Aidan preempted.*

*"I used to think that you were a bitch and Ian was an asshole," Aidan told her.*

*Thomas, the elder son, quipped, "My mother was a bitch?"*

*Margaret silenced him with a look that could have killed.*

*Aidan paid the boy no attention and kept talking.*

*"But I'm starting to think that it was me, in a way, who was a bitch*

*and an asshole," Aidan told her. "Do you realize that the only time you and I had a serious conversation — at least when we were growing up — was that time when mom was in the hospital for something or other and you lectured me on how to be a responsible son when mom was incapacitated. Other than that, you hardly talked to me."*

*Margaret smiled, "But you were young."*

*"Young doesn't mean stupid," Aidan said. "I was so scared about mom being in the hospital. There was no way I was going to upset her when she got home."*

*Margaret reached across the table and touched Aidan's hand. "I was young, too," she said. "I suppose I was trying to take care of the family while mom was sick. I'm sorry if I made you feel as if I was bossing you around."*

*Aidan nodded. "Apology accepted.*

*"Is there anything else you need to get off your chest?"*

*"Not really," Aidan said. "I just want to apologize for not being the kind of brother you could be proud of."*

*Kenneth raised a hand as if he was about to speak, but fell silent when Margaret told him, "Finish your martini. This is between Aidan and me."*

*Margaret looked at Aidan for a long time, then sighed. "You and Ian and I, I don't think we ever felt the kind of brother-sister bonds most people experience. I've always wished we could have been closer. But that never happened."*

*"It may be starting to happen now," Ashling said to Margaret. "As I hear the two of you speaking, it seems that you both are trying to build something you never had."*

*The table was silent. Then Margaret said, "It's about time." As she smiled at her brother, there was a tear welling in her eye.*

*After a bit, Aidan said, "One question."*

*"Yes," Margaret said.*

*"How come you always insisted on being called Margaret instead of Margie or Peggy?"*

*"Do I look like a Margie or a Peggy?"*

*Aidan laughed. "No. You definitely look like a Margaret."*

*The waiter arrived to clear the mealtime debris from the table. As he worked, conversation died and each of them stared elsewhere.*

*When he was finished, Aidan and Margaret began a conversation about Ian. Ashling and Kenneth and the boys began a conversation about things that both Margaret and Aidan weren't listening to.*

*"There's always been something about Ian," Margaret was saying to*

*her brother. "If you think I was bossy toward you back then, Ian was always far more bossy with me. I know now it was the age difference between him and me; he thought he was in charge of me. Needless to say, he infuriated me all too frequently."*

*Despite what Margaret was saying, the look on her face was one of fond remembrance.*

*"The worst time — the most embarrassing time — for me was when Kevin Flaherty, who was a year ahead of me in high school, came to pick me up for a double date. Ian answered the door and — for whatever reasons — decided that James was not suitable for me and chased him away. Literally!"*

*"You're kidding me," Aidan said.*

*"I think if you ask Ian, he'd be proud to tell you how he defended his sister from an insidious boy who was threatening a double date."*

*Aidan couldn't help laughing. It was easy to picture Ian as presenting himself to the boy as a gatekeeper of sorts. In his own younger years, Aidan always thought Ian seemed intent on developing an intimidating persona. Despite Ian's best efforts to present himself master of everything about him, Aidan always saw Ian as a chubby and pompous older brother who would always need an excess of self-importance in order to cope with life.*

*"I called Ian earlier today," Aidan told his sister. "I told him that Ashling and I want to go to dinner with him and his wife. I expect there'll be voicemail from him when we get home."*

*"Are things becoming more comfortable for you two?" Margaret asked.*

*"Passably. We've golfed together. He phones now and then. I have no doubt that he's trying to make things work between us, but I'm not sure that he'll ever be able to relax enough to make that truly happen."*

*It was Margaret's turn to laugh. "He's always been so formal." She paused. "No, that's not the word. He's always been so rigid."*

*Aidan nodded in agreement. "I used to be pissed at him most of the time when I was growing up. It was like he saw the world structured in a certain way — one that suited him, of course — and couldn't tolerate any deviance from the way things ought to be, in his view."*

*"Maybe he's a victim of an regressive gene," Margaret said, with a soft laugh. "God knows mom wasn't like that, and neither is dad."*

*"Or you," Aidan added. "I think the way you behaved toward me was just because you were upset that I was throwing away a good education and wasting my life by working in a liquor store."*

*"That's over now," Margaret said. "The past is the past. I'm really*

*glad that we've reconnected — thanks to you and Ashling."*

*"No," Aidan said. "Thanks to mom."*

*Only Kenneth and the boys opted for dessert. Ashling and Aidan both had a cup of tea, and Margaret was sipping black coffee. The five of them had settled into an easy banter about nothing important.*

*For Aidan, life had become very good. His family was coming together and he was savoring the moment. Ashling and Margaret were engaged in chitchat about various aspects of the wedding, and Margaret asked if she might be able to raise a wedding toast to Ashling and Aidan. Ashling gave her a hearty "Of course!"*

*The two women had moved on to talking about each other's childhoods, with Margaret enthusiastically interested in what it must have been like growing up in Ireland.*

*Ashling was flattered by the interest and was telling Margaret about the "Troubles" that sometimes made the lives of her parents and her uneasy, to say the least.*

*"There was a time when the IRA set off a bomb on one of the main roads to Newry," she was saying. "This happened about ten minutes after my dad left the house to drive to work in Newry. It took us nearly a hour to..."*

*Aidan's phone rang.*

*"...find out if my dad was safe," Ashling said, finishing her sentence.*

*"Dad?" Aidan said into the phone. "What's up? We're coming to see you after we finish our dinner with Margaret and Ken and..."*

*"What?" Aidan's face sagged. "Say it again."*

*Margaret was staring at her brother. Kenneth put down his fork. Ashling looked afraid. The boys suddenly looked uncomfortable.*

It's two hours after midnight before Sean finally steps away from his keyboard.

After Ted left, Sean sat on his couch for a long time, letting his mind sink into a place he called a Zen state, considering what he needed to do to finish the story. It was nearly eleven o'clock before he got up, walked into his office, a cold beer in his hand, and sat in front of his computer. No matter that he had to be at work in the morning; what he had to do tonight could not wait. But the very act of sitting in front of his computer screen, the cursor in Microsoft Word blinking at the top of a blank page, has suddenly roused in him the same fear of failure he'd felt so many months ago when he began the story of Aidan's awakening.

By the time Ted left, Sean was feeling optimistic, with threads of a possible dynamite ending floating around in his mind. But no sooner had he closed the door behind Ted than his optimism began to fade in a sudden surge of self-doubt, draining much of the positive feeling he'd had only moments before.

He reads again the last chapter he wrote, hoping to seize upon a starting point — and an ending point — for the final chapter. For a time, he considers taking a sheet of paper and a pencil and sketching a timeline, a plot line, or whatever it might take to help him get over this final hurdle. But he's never been able to work like that, he's learned. It only works if he builds the story as he goes.

He searches within himself, but there are no easy answers, nor are there any difficult ones. There are, however, expedient ones. But those, he knows, are not worth pursuing, because they will only prove that he in incapable of being a seriously good writer.

He sits there for a long time, not paralyzed but stymied, and again very afraid of failure. And it is only in a desperation brought upon by fatigue, frustration, and deep worry that he's lost his way completely so very close to completing the story.

It is only then, in desperation, that he picks up his phone and calls Julie.

It's a sleepy voice he hears when she answers.

"Hello?" she says, her voice raspy.

"I'm sorry to disturb you, Jules," Sean says.

He hears rustling, then Julie says, her voice sounding afraid, "Sean? Is everything okay?"

"I'm okay," he says. "I'm so sorry I woke you. I'm lost."

"Lost?" Julie sounded as if she was trying to find her bearings.

"God, I feel like an absolute idiot," Sean says. "Look, go back to sleep. I'm so sorry. We can talk in the morning."

"No," Julie says, her voice sharper. "What's going on, Sean?"

He exhales slowly, then begins to tell her about the hurdle he is facing, and about his intensifying worries.

When he finishes speaking, Julie is silent for so long that he assumes she has slipped back into sleep. Then she says, very simply, "You can do it, Sean. Take a deep breath, then write the sentence that comes logically after the last one in the last chapter you wrote. Then write the next logical one. And then picture yourself writing toward an ending that would impress your friends — Jane, Ted, me. Don't worry about the faceless ones out there who might or might not read your book. They don't count. Right now, only we count, because we believe in you. And you count because you've got more than enough talent to make this happen. Impress us, in whatever way you see fit. That, sweet Sean, is all that matters."

"That's heavy stuff for the middle of the night," Sean tells her.

"But you understand what I'm telling you, right?"

"I think so," Sean says after a moment. "Maybe I'm just too tired to write tonight."

"Then get some sleep."

"I don't know if I can," Sean says. "I'm so damned wound up by this whole thing."

Sean hears Julie rustling in her bed. "I'll be there in a half hour," Julie says. "Forget about writing tonight."

"No," Sean says. "Go back to sleep. You've got to work in the morning."

"So?" she replies. Then — click.

When Julie arrives, a small bag of clothes and toiletries in her hand and clothes for work slung on hangers over her shoulder, Sean lets her in, apologizing again for waking her.

Julie drapes her clothes over the arm of his couch, puts her bag on the floor, then wraps her arms around him.

"So, have you decided to give up trying to write tonight?" she asks.

"No," he replies. "I'm afraid that if I give up, it'll be harder to get back on track tomorrow." Then he adds, "You didn't have to come over."

"Yes, I had to come over," she tells him. "I've got a remedy for writer's block." He is unable to answer because she is literally in his face, kissing him deeply.

When she pulls away, Sean is unable to say anything.

"You need some lovin'," she tells him. "Let's put you to bed."

In the morning, closer to ten than to her normal eight o'clock starting time, Julie slips her phone from her bag while Sean still sleeps beside her.

To the woman who answers, Julie says, "Gloria, tell Andy that something's come up and I need to take today off and tell him I apologize for not calling in sooner".

Julie listens for a moment. "Thanks, I appreciate that," she says. Then, she puts her phone away and gently moves closer to Sean and listens as he breathes softly in sleep.

At just after eleven-thirty, Sean wakes to the smell of breakfast in the making, the aromas of coffee and bacon making their way through the apartment.

When he shuffles to the kitchen, Julie is just about to break eggs into the skillet.

"Good morning, Mr. Author," Julie says. "I'm glad you got so much sleep."

Sean looks at the kitchen clock. "Oh, shit! I've got to get to work."

Julie comes over to him and wraps her arms around his waist. "You, sweet Sean, are officially sick today. Your employer has been told that you have a fever and are most definitely under the weather."

"You called the paper?"

"Yes," she says, with conspiratorial smile. "So you can relax. Breakfast will be ready soon, now that you're awake. And then we can get busy psyching you up for writing. Fair enough?"

Sean shook his head. "You are something else," he tells her, a contented smile on his face. "I think I like you."

"I was hoping you were getting close to loving me," she says, only barely teasing him.

Sean holds her to him more tightly. "I think I am," he says.

"Then my 'hurry-to-Sean's-rescue' ploy last night really worked, huh?"

Sean can't keep a straight face. "It did — if that makes you feel smugly satisfied."

Julie rises up on tiptoe and kisses him. "It certainly does. Now go sit down. Breakfast will be on the table in less than four minutes."

When breakfast is over, Julie showers first. By the time Sean finishes his showering and shaving, she is dressed and sitting on the edge of the bed

"I wish we could have the rest of the day together," Sean says.

"Just so you know," Julie tells him, "We do. I called my office earlier."

Sean smiles. "So we're both bunking school today, huh?"

Julie comes up behind him as he is finishing dressing. "Bunking school? Yes. Goofing off? No."

"So what do you have in mind?" Sean asks.

"I intend to spend the day being your muse," Julie says. "You are going to write a great ending to a great story. And I will kick your butt if you slack off. Fair enough?"

Sean spits out a laugh.

"You really are something else," he says.

"I'm glad you appreciate me," Julie says, smugly.

An hour later, Sean completes a fifth difficult sentence to continue the thread of the last chapter he wrote. It's progress, albeit extremely slow.

Julie reads his words then makes a couple of suggestions. Sean counters with some ideas beginning to take shape in his mind. As they continue to exchange thoughts, it seems to Sean that he is beginning to feel 'unlocked.' It's the only way he can describe it. Suddenly, words seem ready to flow, and the narrative of his story seems ready to move forward.

"Just type," Julie says. "I'll be in the living room. When you want me to read something, let me know."

Sean leans back in his chair and looks up at her.

"Thank you," he says.

"Go for it," she says, leaning over and wrapping her arms around his neck. "You'll do this. I have faith."

Sean nods. "I'll do this."

Julie slips out of his office and heads for the couch, and Sean begins typing — and praying.

***This is it***

*Ian was dead before he hit the pavement in the parking lot.*

*At least that's what a doctor said once the family had gathered in the emergency room at the hospital where he'd been taken.*

*Ian had been at a local garden shop picking up flowers his wife wanted to plant around the extensive patio behind their home. From what witnesses told the EMTs, he paid for the flowers and was pushing a flatbed cart to his car when he suddenly stopped, gasped, and dropped to the ground.*

*One man performed chest compressions, and another tried — although half-heartedly — mouth-to-mouth respiration. But Ian was already dead, at fifty-two years old.*

*At the emergency room, Cornelius and Aidan and Ashling were huddled in a corner of the waiting area while Margaret was badgering people for whatever information she could squeeze from them.*

*Kenneth and the two boys were slouched in chairs against the far wall of the room, Kenneth looking as if he were texting people who worked for him. Thomas was focusing on a game on his phone to block out the fear. Timothy looked stunned and simply stared into the distance.*

*Ian's wife, Anne, was — as far as anyone knew — with her husband, or at least with her husband's body. She had yet to come to the rest of the family for whatever comfort they could give. Margaret and Aidan had both tried to find her, but the busy ER staff pushed them away gently. One nurse told them, "She needs time to say goodbye. I'll make sure she knows you're here."*

*"Thank you," is all that Aidan said.*

*Cornelius was pale and silent. For the past twenty minutes he had been sitting in an uncomfortable chair, pondering the loss of his son.*

*He'd said nothing as Aidan and Ashling drove him to the hospital. Once, when Ashling turned to look at him in the back seat, he had tears in his eyes. When they arrived at the emergency room, he remained silent and let Aidan and Ashling and Margaret do the asking and the talking.*

*It seemed like hours had passed before a doctor entered the ER waiting area and approached the family.*

*"I'm Doctor Doberstein," he said, his voice gentle, his look sad. His eyes settled on Cornelius. Cornelius straightened in his chair, as if about to be led before a firing squad.*

*"Are you Mr. McCann?" Doberstein asked.*

*Cornelius nodded reluctantly.*

*The doctor crossed the room and took a chair next to the one Cornelius was sitting in.*

*"I know that you've been told about your son's death," Dr. Doberstein said, his voice calm and quiet. "I'm deeply sorry that we could not save him. Apparently, passers-by performed CPR on him, and the EMTs who responded to the call used every measure available to them. They did what they could to restart his heart and maintained continuous CPR until they arrived here and our team could take over. We worked for over a half-hour, hoping that we could save him. But we failed."*

*Cornelius simply nodded, and Dr. Doberstein reached out and put a hand on Cornelius's shoulder.*

*"Would you like to see him?" he asked Cornelius.*

*Cornelius nodded again. "I would," he said in a weak and raspy voice. "Yes."*

*The doctor looked around the waiting room. "Are you family as well?" he asked as his eyes scanned them.*

*When Margaret answered, "Yes," he invited them as well to see Ian if they so chose.*

*"His wife is with him now," the doctor said. "It might be good if you all could join her."*

*"We'll do that," Aidan said, his voice firm, as he took Ashling's hand.*

*Kenneth stood, the boys begged not to be included — and Margaret agreed. Then she came to stand where Cornelius still sat and reached out her hand to him. Aidan mirrored her gesture, and the two of them helped their father to his feet.*

*Walking haltingly, they followed Dr. Doberstein to where Ian lay.*

*At the wake for Ian, three days later, held at the funeral home where Aidan's mother had been waked recently enough for the memories to add to the hurt, well more than a hundred people drifted through to pay their respects. Many, by dress and demeanor, were clearly some of Ian's professional acquaintances and colleagues. Others, less businesslike, were likely neighbors and family friends. The rest seemed to be friends of Cornelius and Ellen, who had also come to offer comfort when Ellen died.*

*Ian's widow, Anne, was standing where Ian had stood to receive those who had come to pay respects to his mother. Cornelius was next to her, his face ashen, his grieving gaze focusing on his son's body in its bronze casket; there was no way he could avoid reliving the nightmare of seeing his wife in her coffin. Next in the receiving line were Margaret and her husband, then Aidan and Ashling, each of them speaking softly and briefly with those who had come to honor Ian.*

*Anne was holding herself together admirably. Although Aidan didn't know her well, his father had often described her as a strong and stoic and pious woman. "Much like your mother," he'd told Aidan once.*

*Aidan, holding Ashling's hand the whole time, had not expected to feel the kind of anguish that had flooded into him when he and Ashling entered the viewing room before the doors were opened for the respect-payers. When Aidan approached the casket, nearly engulfed with flowers and wreaths and proclamations of love and sorrow, he knelt before it, crossed himself, said a prayer for his brother, then felt tears welling in his eyes. After a long moment, Aidan whispered, "It isn't fair, Ian." Then he stood and helped Ashling to her feet to go stand with Cornelius, Margaret, Kenneth, and Anne.*

*Aidan was astounded at the number of people who told Anne that Ian "looked good," and tried to recall if some had said the same thing about his mother's corpse placed out for viewing. By the time the fifteenth or sixteenth person uttered those words, Aidan was ready to indulge in assault and battery. His mother did not "look good" in the coffin that she was posed in. And Ian looked like shit — made up with a flawless complexion and made to have a vague smile on his lips.*

*"Being dead would not make Ian smile," Aidan hissed to Ashling after a while. "He'd be so pissed off. Jesus H. Christ — people are so fucking ignorant!"*

*Ashling shushed him. "We can vent about this later, luv. We're here for Anne and for your father." Then she squeezed his hand and laid her head against his shoulder.*

*They stood in the receiving line for nearly three hours. The endless stream of people had the desired effect: Anne and Cornelius and Margaret and Kenneth and Aidan and Ashling were as numb as they could hope to be. When the last person left the viewing room, the funeral director walked soberly toward them and gave each his deepest condolences. That done, he explained what would happen in the morning before the funeral Mass, and told them what time they should arrive at the funeral home.*

*When he left the room, Anne approached Aidan and Ashling. Her voice was a bit shaky, and her eyes were red — not from crying, but more likely from trying not to cry. Cornelius was hovering close by. Margaret and Kenneth were on the fringe of the circle of conversation.*

*"Ian," Anne started, "never had much of a sense of timing. You know that he was looking forward to your wedding. And I hope you know that he was so happy that the two of you had found each other."*

*Anne stopped and took a deep breath. "Two nights before he died, Ian told me that he was sorry he'd been so hard on you, Aidan, and that he sorely regretted that he never got to be as close to you and Ashling as he could have been. His words were, 'I wasted a lot of years being a bastard to them.'"*

*Again, Anne stopped to breathe and brace herself. "I wish," she said, her voice earnestly sincere, "that both of us — Ian and I — had been more like a real family. You know: sticking together, helping each other out, arguing, laughing, supporting each other no matter what. He and I failed to be like that. And it is something I will always regret."*

*Anne smiled a deeply rueful smile and, for the first time since they arrived at the funeral home, there were tears in her eyes.*

*"I have thought this through," Anne said. "There is nothing Ian would have hated more than to have anyone blame him for something that went wrong."*

*Cornelius looked puzzled. Aidan and Ashling, both with furrowed brows, waited for Anne to continue. Kenneth had a vacant look on his face, but Margaret managed to spit out, "What on earth did he do that was wrong?" The question came out as if implying that there might be some kind of scandal lurking behind Ian's death.*

*Anne looked down at the carpet, a mournful color of deep blue. Then she looked at Aidan and Ashling.*

*"You may not know it, but Ian had decided to offer to pay for your wedding — knowing you might very well refuse. So he was about to do two things."*

*"What things?" Aidan asked. Then he added, quickly, "You're right. We wanted to pay for the wedding ourselves."*

*Anne reached out and placed a hand on Aidan's arm, then she placed her other hand on Ashling's shoulder.*

*"This is what he would have done," Anne said.*

*Cornelius drew closer. Margaret and Kenneth hemmed him in.*

*"And this," Anne said, raising a finger to emphasize the point, "is what I am going to do — for Ian and for you. And please do not even think of denying me and Ian of this.*

*It took less than five minutes for Anne to explain what she was going to do to fulfill Ian's somewhat-spoken wishes.*

*When she was done, it was Cornelius who spoke first — probably because Aidan and Ashling could do nothing more than stare at Anne. Margaret and Kenneth clearly could not even come up with words to suit the occasion.*

*"So," Anne was saying in a voice she was trying to imbue with a strong tone of authority, "this is what I know Ian would want, and what I am urging you to accept, for his sake."*

*She took Ashling's hand. "Your husband-to-be can be a stubborn man. Cornelius knows, Margaret knows, and Ian knew. It's not a debatable point. So I hope you will help me to prevail on this."*

*Ashling stared at her and nodded, slowly.*

*Anne then took Aidan's hand.*

*"I know — knew — Ian's mind. Surviving with Ian and his strong ego could not be possible without understanding what was driving him. Do you know what that was?"*

*Aidan shook his head. It felt odd to be ten feet from his brother's body and listening to his widow expounding on what her late husband would have wanted.*

*"Fear of failure. That's what tortured him all his life," Anne said. "He told me once, not too long ago, that it was his fear of failure that made him be so tough on you. In the end, though, he found that he was tough on you in the wrong way."*

*"So," Anne said, "he decided he would make up for whatever discomfort or pain he had cause you, Aidan, or you, Ashling."*

*There was a long silence before Cornelius said, "And what is that?"*

*Anne almost smiled when she looked at Aidan and Ashling. "Do not postpone your wedding. Ian wanted to be there, and I know he will be there in spirit. So, please, do not postpone it. That's the first thing."*

*"And the second?" Margaret asked from the backside of Cornelius's shoulder.*

*"Ian wanted to pay for your honeymoon, as long as you took it in the north of Ireland. I intend to fulfill his wishes, and so I will pay for you, Aidan, and Ashling and Cornelius to spend two weeks there."*

*Aidan could say nothing. He had assumed, and Ashling had agreed, that Ian's sudden death meant postponing the wedding at least for a few months. They were to telephone Murtaugh's after the funeral to cancel the reception.*

*"We can't," Aidan said. "Ian's gone. We can't celebrate a wedding*

*when my brother has died."*

*"Who says?" Anne gave Aidan a stubborn look.*

*While Aidan fumbled for a retort, Cornelius spoke up. "We would be heartless if we ignored Ian's wishes."*

*"Those were his wishes," Anne said, emphatically. "Please."*

*The room was void of sound as the family struggled with the notion of celebrating marriage while mourning for Ian, and while sharing the pain that was torturing Anne.*

*No one spoke for the longest time. Nor was anyone anxious to break the silence. Each of them was contending with Ian's death and Anne's proposals in his or her own way.*

*"We will honor Ian's wishes," Aidan said, finally, with no enthusiasm or joy in his voice.*

*Having said that, Aidan turned to Cornelius. "I remember mom telling me, much more than once, something that I've never forgotten."*

*"And that is?" Cornelius asked.*

*"She always said, 'Whatever is meant to be is meant to be.'"*

*Cornelius nodded, smiling. "She said that often. And she was right, you know. At least, it always seemed that way."*

*Ashling jumped in. "Why else would I have stayed so long with this man," she said to Cornelius, "if I hadn't been certain that it was meant to be." She put an affectionate arm around his waist.*

*Aidan could do nothing but look at Anne and give the best sorry smile he could, considering that Ian's body was in the middle of the flower-smothered display nearby.*

*"Maybe this is what's meant to be, Anne," Aidan said. "Irish fatalism or Irish optimism — take your pick. It makes me feel uncomfortable, but I will honor Ian's wishes, if that's what they were."*

*Anne stepped closer to her brother-in-law and wrapped her arms around him. "Thank you, Aidan. Thank you so very much."*

*Ashling stepped close to Anne and took her in her arms. "You will be at the wedding, won't you? I have a feeling that Ian will be there in spirit and we want you there as well."*

*Anne lowered her head, as if in thought. "I will be there," she said, at last, raising her head to look at Ashling. "I promise."*

*Eleven days later, at the altar, Aidan said, in words he had written himself, "I most certainly and happily take you, Ashling, to be my friend, my companion, my love, my dream, my future, my hopes, and my love — until my very last breath."*

*Ashling, without prepared vows, began by saying, "And that very last breath you speak of had better not happen until you are well past the age of one hundred."*

*Cornelius, standing next to Aidan, and proud as he'd ever been to be his youngest son's best man, whispered too loudly, "You had better listen to Ashling, Aidan. If you die too young, she'll never let you forget it!"*

*The church's acoustics were excellent, of course, and most of those gathered in the there could not avoid stifled laughs. Even the priest could not repress a grin.*

*In the late morning sun outside the church, where everyone had gathered after the ceremony to soak up the euphoria of the event and in anticipation of the reception to come and of the chatter that seemed to have a life of its own, Aidan and Ashling — Mr. and Mrs. McCann — posed as Margaret and others took photographs. Between requests for them to "smile," Aidan and Ashling shook hands and exchanged in small talk with each of the well wishers who were lingering only because the bride and groom had not yet left for the reception at Murtaugh's.*

*It took far less than an hour for some at the reception to become sufficiently inebriated to finally settle into some semblance of quiet enjoyment of the occasion. It was clearly an Irish event; the conversations were lively, the great wishes and often-repeated wishes for the couple flowing at least as freely as the Irish beer and Irish whiskey. Aidan and Ashling made sure to spend ample time at each of the tables their guests occupied, paying close attention to each individual, having something good to say about each guest, patting backs and rubbing shoulders and giving hugs and kisses when appropriate.*

*In a quiet moment, shortly before Murtaugh's waitresses began bringing out the food, Cornelius came up to where Aidan and Ashling were sitting. With him was Margaret, and Margaret had an envelope in her hand.*

*When she and Cornelius sat with Aidan and Ashling, Margaret put the envelope on the table and covered it with her left hand.*

*"Can you believe it?" Cornelius was saying as he sat. "I have been the best man for my own son! Have you ever heard of such a thing?"*

*"It was a great honor for you, dad," Margaret said, laying her hand on his. "I'm happy for you."*

*"Oh, yes, I'm happy," Cornelius said. In his never-lost Irish accent, the word came out "hah-ppy." But his smile said far more than his words.*

*"Did you see each of the people who came for the wedding?" Margaret asked her father.*

*"I believe I did," he said, still smiling and clearly on the verge of asking one of the waitresses to bring him another celebratory Jameson on*

*the rocks.*

*Margaret shook her head. "First," she said to him, "don't get another drink right now. And, second, I want you to turn in your seat and look at the table near the end of the bar."*

*"What is this you're asking me to do?" Cornelius said, looking uncertain.*

*"Just turn around and look," Margaret insisted.*

*Cornelius looked at Aidan. Aidan simply nodded. So Cornelius turned. The table near the end of the bar had six people around it. Four of them were friends of his from the neighborhood, one was a woman who'd often visit Ellen before Ellen took sick. The sixth was sitting with her back nearly toward him. Cornelius looked long and hard at her. Then, slowly and with great uncertainty, he said to Margaret: "I know them all — except that woman with the blue sweater. She's not from the parish. It's funny, though: she almost looks like my sister, Minnie. She does. But I've heard that she can no longer travel. Besides, I have no idea how she would know that Aidan and Ashling were being married today. I've written to no one there."*

*Margaret stood and put a hand on her father's shoulder. "It's Minnie, dad. Kenneth and I arranged for her to fly here for the wedding, but most importantly to see you again."*

*Cornelius stood. "Minnie?"*

*"Minnie," Margaret said."*

*"I haven't seen her in almost twenty years," he said. "She came here once with one of my brothers."*

*"Then you and she need to spend some time with each other," Margaret said. She held out her hand. "Let's go see your sister."*

*Cornelius stood and allowed Margaret to take his hand in hers. As she began to lead him from the table, she pushed the envelope toward Aidan and Ashling.*

*"Read it," she called out as Cornelius dragged her away. "It's from Anne."*

*Ashling opened the envelope. The folded sheet of paper she withdrew had a smaller piece of paper clipped to it. Ashling placed them on the table and unfolded them.*

*On the smaller sheet of paper, there was a note from Anne, just three sentences:*

*"When I spoke to you about Ian's wishes, I didn't know he had actually put anything on paper. I found this in his desk five days after the funeral, when I could barely begin to bear looking through his things. This is truly what he wanted, and I will honor all his wishes."*

*Ashling scanned the envelope's contents in silence, then passed Ian's note and Anne's comments to Aidan. She waited while he read them once, and then once again.*

*Aidan could not help laughing. "This is so damned much like Ian," he said to Ashling. "The quintessential negotiator. It must have been part of his DNA."*

*Aidan read his brother's writing again, and yet a third time.*

*"Did you read this whole thing?" Aidan asked Ashling. Without waiting for an answer, he continued: "If...if I will enroll as a freshman in any college and complete the year with grades that are no less than a 'B,' and if I work hard enough in my job to get a promotion within the next twelve months, Ian has set aside twenty-five thousand dollars so that you and I can have a head start in our new lives."*

*"That is wonderful," Ashling said.*

*"Now listen to this." Aidan began to read aloud. "'I have already set additional money aside, in good investments that will grow the total significantly over the next few years. If Aidan earns his bachelor's degree in whatever field he chooses, the money will be his. It will be at least fifty-thousand dollars, and could be as much seventy-thousand dollars.'"*

*All Ashling could manage to say was, "I can't believe it."*

*"Ian was always a carrot-and-stick kind of guy" Aidan said, not sure whether to smile or frown. "How am I going to do what he said?"*

*"It seems rather straightforward, luv," Ashling said. "After we get back from the honeymoon, we'll go to the university to see what courses they have that will help you in the future. You can begin with a class in the fall."*

*"But a bachelor's degree?"*

*"It doesn't have to be done in four years, Aidan. You could do two or three courses a year. If it takes you six or seven years, would it not be worth it?"*

*Aidan kept poring over the handwritten notes. "I'll have to think about it. I mean, work* and *school courses at the same time. I don't know if there are enough hours in the day."*

*"We'll find a way, luv. We will." Ashling reached for Aidan's hand. "But let's put that all aside for now. After all, we have a wedding to celebrate and guests to mingle with, and memories to make."*

*Wrapping his hand in hers, Ashling got Aidan up from the table and headed off to spend time with each of those who had come to share their joy.*

*A while later, they joined Cornelius and his sister Minnie, deeply wrapped in reminiscences and sharing wistful laughter. It was with delight that Cornelius introduced Aidan and Ashling to Minnie, and Minnie immediately took to the two of them.*

*"You are such a lovely couple," she said. "I've never seen such a beautifully simple wedding. I don't like those weddings where they have a flock of maids of honor and a herd of groomsmen and gowns and tuxedos and receptions the Queen would envy."*

*"Simple is best," Ashling told her, and quickly complemented Minnie on the simple and quite elegant dress she'd worn for the occasion.*

*"I've worn it for at least five weddings," Minnie said, proudly. "I'm not one to spend money for the sake of fashion."*

*"A wonderful attitude," Ashling said. "I intend to teach Aidan about frugality and simplicity."*

*Aidan gave Ashling a look tinged strongly in bewilderment. She simply winked at him.*

*Minnie caught the humor and smiled at the couple. Then she said to Aidan, "Your father has said you will be coming to Ireland for your honeymoon?"*

*"Yes, we will," Aidan said. "We were planning to postpone it until later — the wedding expenses and all that — but Ian's wife said she would give us the trip as a wedding gift. We'll be in Ireland in two weeks."*

*Minnie's expression turned serious and she shook her head. "Ah, your poor brother. Such a pity that he died so young, and so very unexpectedly. It has to be quite a loss for you. I know your dear father is still in shock about it."*

*"I miss him," Aidan said. "I really wish he could have been here today."*

*Then Minnie smiled, "Are you and Ashling planning to have children?"*

*Ashling answered: "We'll take whatever God brings our way. If it's meant to be..."*

*"...then it's meant to be," Minnie finished for her.*

*Ashling leaned down and kissed Minnie on the cheek. "I am so looking forward to spending more time with you in Ireland."*

*Minnie grinned brightly.*

*Minutes later, in response to a nod from Aidan, Cornelius picked up his glass of his glass of sparkling wine and tapped against it with a spoon. The light chime cut through the conversations that were woven together in a carpet of voices and the room slowly became silent.*

*Smiling broadly, he said, "Can you imagine that I am the best man for my son's wedding?"*

*The room broke out in cheer and applause. Cornelius seemed to be blushing.*

*"Aidan and Ashling have asked me to make a toast," he continued. "I've never given a toast before, at least not at a wedding. But I have written a few words that I hope will suit the occasion.*

*He pulled a folded piece of paper from his sport coat pocket. He unfolded it and again picked up his glass. Then, in a strong voice, he said, "Aidan and Ashling, the best wish I could have for you is that you have a life together that is as blessed and happy as the one Ellen and I had. To Aidan: you have not always been the best son I could imagine..."*

*The crowd erupted in laughter. Aidan had to look down at the floor. Ashling wrapped an arm around his waist and whispered something to him. When he looked up, he was laughing too.*

*"...but," Cornelius continued, "you have always been a good person and the kind of son your mother and I always cherished. To Ashling: from the first time we met you, Ellen considered you an extra daughter, and so did I. You have managed to make an honest man out of Aidan, and for that I thank you."*

*Again the room laughed.*

*As the room became quiet again, Cornelius said, "I didn't write down this other thing, but Aidan and Ashling are taking me to Ireland with them on their honeymoon!"*

*"Separate rooms, I hope," someone called out.*

*"If that was you shouting, Jimmy McParland," Cornelius said, scanning the faces surrounding him, "I'll be wanting a word with you outside as soon as we have a drink to the bride and groom." Then he laughed and shouted, "To Aidan and Ashling. May they have years and years of happiness!"*

*Glasses were raised, wishes shouted out to the couple, and glasses emptied.*

*It was done.*

## Epilogue

The writing was done and Jane decided to have everyone over for dinner. On the phone, Ted had told Sean, "She figures we should all celebrate the fact that you finally finished the book. I think she's happy that you won't be calling me away for periodic consultations."

Sean and Julie arrive just before seven.

In the living room, before dinner is on the table, Jane says to Sean, "When Ted told me that you were starting to a new book, I told him — and I have to be honest with you — that I wasn't sure you'd ever finish it."

Sean turns to Julie. "Jane has always assumed I have attention deficit disorder."

"You have to admit his attention span is not always the best," Jane says. "I think that's why he got into journalism: something new and different to deal with every day."

Julie gives Sean an appraising look. "You're probably right, Jane. But there have been a number of occasions where I've seen him focus for up to seven or eight minutes at a time."

"Cripes, the women are ganging up on me," Sean says, his voice dropping into mock despondency.

"We're doomed," Ted says, slumping in his seat. "These women won't be happy until they beat us down."

Jane turns to Julie. "That settles it. Only you and I will enjoy tonight's dinner. They have proven themselves unworthy."

"See what I mean?" Ted asks Sean.

Before Sean can come up with a witty response, Jane gets up and heads for the kitchen. "Come to the table, boys and girl. I'm about to serve dinner.

"See how it works?" Ted says to his friend. "First they dump on us, then they feed us. I guess they figure food heals all wounds."

"It does!" Jane calls from the kitchen. "Now sit!"

Dinner was filled with cross-table conversation that touched on virtually every topic except Sean's novel. In a way, it was a relief for Sean. For the past several days, he's been trying to control an undercurrent of uncertainty that has been chewing at him since he finished Aidan's story. He's never been able to know whether what he's written has been good or not. Even as a journalist, he's always depended on his editors to let him know if he's done a good job, just as he's depended on Ted and Julie to give him reliable feedback during the course of his writing.

After dinner — and before dessert — Ted says to Sean, "Can we see the last chapters now?"

Sean nods and rises from the table. Before heading to the living room to get the folder, he asks Jane, "Have you read what I wrote so far?"

"Pretty much."

"Good." Sean leaves the table and returns in a moment with a thick manila envelope. From it, he pulls three sheaves of paper, each held together with paper clips and, as if he were at an office staff meeting, passes them around to Jane, Ted, and Julie. Then he puts the empty envelope on the table and sits down, sipping from the wine Jane had served.

He's not sure how he will feel if, after reading the last chapter, their verdict on his choice of an ending is negative. He knows only that he has done his best. He wanted to avoid a trite ending, but an ending that left open possibilities for the characters. If he has succeeded in creating compelling characters, then — he reasons — the reader should fill in the kind of details they would like to see as the story ended. The readers will project their wishes for the story's outcome, regardless of what he's written. Giving a concrete, full-stop ending, Sean figures, is a cop-out and no more than a way of forcing an outcome on the readers. Let the reader imagine a bright or bleak future, if that's where he or she thinks is where the story might go. All Sean wants is that the reader finish the book with a feeling that it was worth the time spent to read it. And, maybe, that memories of Aidan and Ashling, and of Cornelius and Ian and Margaret, and all the others, would stick with the reader for a while.

That would make life good.

As Julie and his friends read the final pages, Sean leans back in his chair and waits for the verdict.

Then he begins to smile.

## About The Author

A New England native, and a descendant of Acadian immigrants to the United States, R.A Boudreau grew up in Lynn, Massachusetts ("Lynn, Lynn, city of sin, you never come out the way you went in…"). He attended St. John's Preparatory School in Danvers, Massachusetts, and Holy Cross College in Worcester, Massachusetts.

After working during a five-year period as a reporter for the Lynn, Mass., *Daily Item* and the Worcester, Mass., *Telegram*, he spent the rest of his career in communications and publications in both Massachusetts and Rhode Island.

Now retired and finally able to turn his time and efforts to writing fiction, he considers himself a pretty good endorsement of the "better late than never" philosophy.

He is currently working on a new novel, which – if his sweet wife doesn't burden him with too many household projects – should be completed by the end of 2012.

Stay tuned.

Made in the USA
Lexington, KY
28 February 2012